A Fist Full of Credits

The First Book in a New Apocalyptic LitRPG

By

Tao Wong & Craig Hamilton

License Notes

A Fist Full of Credits

Copyright © 2021 Tao Wong and Craig Hamilton. All rights reserved.
Copyright © 2021 Sarah Anderson Cover Designer

Published by Starlit Publishing
PO Box 30035
High Park PO
Toronto, ON
M6P 3K0
Canada

www.starlitpublishing.com

Ebook ISBN: 9781990491085
Print ISBN: 9781990491108
Hardcover ISBN: 9781990491092

Books in the

System Apocalypse Universe

Main Storyline

Life in the North

Redeemer of the Dead

The Cost of Survival

Cities in Chains

Coast on Fire

World Unbound

Stars Awoken

Rebel Star

Stars Asunder

Broken Council

Forbidden Zone

System Finale

System Apocalypse: Relentless

A Fist Full of Credits

System Apocalypse: Australia

Town Under

Flat Out

Anthologies and Short stories

System Apocalypse Short Story Anthology Volume 1

Valentines in an Apocalypse

A New Script

Daily Jobs, Coffee and an Awfully Big Adventure

Adventures in Clothing

Questing for Titles

Blue Screens of Death

My Grandmother's Tea Club

The Great Black Sea

A Game of Koopash (Newsletter exclusive)

Lana's story (Newsletter exclusive)

Debts and Dances (Newsletter exclusive)

Comic Series

The System Apocalypse Comics (7 Issues)

Contents

Prologue

I woke with a start, trapped in darkness.

A wave of agony swept through my body on the heels of awareness.

Heavy weights pressed down uncomfortably on my torso, pinning me in place, and I gasped in pain as recently broken ribs ground together with every labored breath. The tiny movements of my chest disturbed the dusty debris that covered me, and my wheezing devolved into short, racking coughs.

Exhausted by the time my hacking ceased, I lay unmoving and took stock of my injuries.

The fog that clouded my mind indicated a likely concussion. Heat radiated excruciatingly from blistered skin along my left arm and the side of my face. Blood trickled from numerous lacerations across my body.

Through the haze of pain, memories resurfaced.

I'd watched helplessly as explosions rippled down a hallway toward me and fire engulfed the rest of the squad in front of me. Tongues of flame lashed out and seared my skin, threatening to consume me as well, but the shockwave from the blasts channeled through the narrow hallway to catapult me backward beyond the fire's reach. My body crashed through a broken door and tumbled to a halt in a stairwell. More explosives detonated in the basement below, and the entire building lurched as the destroyed foundation collapsed.

The stairs fell away beneath me and I dropped, weightless for a moment, until the impact of the sudden stop drove the wind from my chest. The rest of the structure caved in around me, and the stairwell became both my shelter and my tomb.

In the darkness, the scorched and blistered faces of my squad mates swirled before me. The haunted visages stared at me accusingly, berating me for surviving when they had not and failing to bring justice to their killers.

Lost, alone, and buried.

Still gulping for air, and overwhelmed by pain, my mind spiraled until unconsciousness claimed me once again.

Chapter 1

I woke with a start at the slam of a nearby car door. The sound jolted me from the recurring nightmare of darkness and fire, and when my eyes cracked open, I found my vision obscured by a blue box filled with text. A momentary panic swept through me at the jarring transition back to wakefulness, and I instinctively reached for the rifle beside me.

My hand flailed until my brain woke up enough to recognize I was not in a military issue bunk and the rifle I reached for was nonexistent. Instead, I struggled to sit up in the reclined driver's seat of my Ford Explorer, and I swiped my arm through the floating blue box in front of me as I willed away the figment of my imagination.

Sleep deprivation had messed with me before, but never to the point of hallucination.

A few more of the blue boxes popped up after the first one disappeared, but I waved them away without reading them as I looked out my tinted windows for the source of the noise.

A few houses down the street from where I sat with my SUV backed into the driveway of an empty house with a "For Sale" sign out front, I saw exactly what I'd hoped for when I started this stakeout. A tall, lanky man with disheveled brown hair walked away from an ugly orange sedan parked at the house I'd been watching before I nodded off. The man wore a Hawaiian shirt, which looked particularly garish in the mid-morning light of cloudy western Pennsylvania. The sedan matched the vehicle registered to the subject I hunted, but just to be sure, I glanced at the mugshot lying on my passenger seat for confirmation.

The mugshot sat next to the official bail piece from the Criminal Division of the Court of Common Pleas of Allegheny County. My gaze drifted farther down the page to where the reward for $30,000 was listed for the man who had skipped a court appearance two days earlier. Below the reward, the bail piece noted the Allegheny County Jail as the drop-off location for the apprehended subject. That was standard for most of the bail jumpers out of Pittsburgh, and I had often turned in bounties there. Some of the guards even greeted me by name these days.

A fold-out map of the greater Pittsburgh area stuck out from beneath the assorted paperwork. A GPS was useful, but sometimes it paid to have a big picture view of the streets throughout my hunting grounds. More than once I had predicted where a bail jumper would flee after I knocked on the front door.

Along with the other papers that littered my passenger seat was a certified copy of the man's bail bond and a stack of printouts from his social media accounts. It amazed me how much information people, especially criminals who were trying to avoid the law, posted about themselves online. Most social media had geolocation tags embedded within each post, and if a person wasn't careful to lock it down, that information could be publicly accessed.

A few of those careless social media posts and several tagged photos of my target had led me here.

My attention was pulled from the paperwork of my profession as another pair of car doors slammed shut, and I cursed mentally. Two more men had gotten out of a beat-up pickup truck, now parked behind the orange sedan, and were walking up the driveway. The men greeted my target warmly, and the three exchanged handshakes before they all headed into the house.

With a sigh, I resigned myself to an even longer wait. I could confront the three together, but my experience had taught me to catch a subject alone whenever possible. You never knew when a person would feel the need to act tough in front of their friends, so waiting to take a bail jumper on their own increased the likelihood that I could bring the subject in quietly.

I rubbed my hands into my eyes, attempting to maximize my wakefulness, and felt the motion pull at the disfigured flesh that marred my left cheek. The burn scar tissue that ran down my neck and disappeared under my collar was far from the only reminder of my time in Afghanistan, but it was the most visible one.

In an attempt to distract myself from that line of thought, I picked up the cup in the center console holder and grimaced as I sipped from the styrofoam mug. The cheap gas station coffee was just as bad cold, but the bitter liquid brought with it an alertness that I had lacked.

As the sun peeked out from behind the clouds to glisten over the last of the late-morning dew, the two men left the house. Each of the men carried a plastic garbage bag, and the second man pulled the front door closed behind him. I saw no sign of my subject as the men loaded the bags into the bed of the pickup, then climbed into the cab. The truck pulled out of the driveway and headed down the street. I held still, barely even breathing, as the vehicle drove past where I sat parked, but neither man seemed to pay me any attention.

Once the truck had disappeared down the street, I slipped out of my Explorer and into the brisk, fresh air of the slightly chilly April morning. I had long ago disabled my automatic door light that could give away my presence at an inopportune time, so noise was my only concern as I eased the car door closed.

Stiff from sitting in my vehicle overnight and throughout the early morning, the old injuries across my body protested at my activity, and I attempted to stretch as I patted myself down to check that my gear remained securely in place.

From a drop-leg holster strapped to my thigh, I pulled my Beretta service pistol and confirmed that the M9A3 held a chambered round. After replacing the safed weapon in its holster, I ran my hand across the equipment on my belt as I twisted my waist from side to side to loosen the tight muscles in my lower back. The Kevlar plate carrier on my torso flopped from the motion, exposing slack in the harness, as my right hand found my extendable baton, handcuffs, and zip ties in their proper places. I tightened the offending strap, then tugged at the taser holster attached to the MOLLE straps on the front of the plate carrier.

My left hand fumbled over the other side of my belt, numbly feeling the spare magazines filled with 9mm ammunition and replacement cartridges for the taser. Alongside the spare ammo sat a small tactical flashlight and an emergency flare. Some might consider me paranoid, but I'd been trapped in utter darkness once before and never wanted to experience it again.

I flexed the fingers of my left hand, consciously ignoring the ever-present tingling sensation that remained after the limb had been burned and crushed during my service. The leftover nerve damage had resulted in my medical discharge from the Corps. I made sure that every piece of my gear could be reached with my right hand in a pinch, since I no longer trusted my left arm to function completely.

With my equipment secured, I left my vehicle and moved toward the house where the orange sedan remained parked. I glanced around the suburban neighborhood as I stalked across the intervening yards. Even this early in the spring, most of the lawns had a freshly mowed look. Mulch-filled flower beds lined many of the houses and driveways. The house of my target was a notable exception to the otherwise decent neighborhood. The grass was unkempt and out of place amongst the other well-tended residences.

Though it was late enough on a weekday morning that most people should have already left for work, I tried to keep my approach subtle. Best to avoid any nosy neighbors who might peek out from their blinds.

As I reached my destination and climbed the stairs to the front porch, the faint smell of ammonia tickled my nostrils and set off a warning bell in my mind. I'd given the place a thorough once-over during a drive-by the night before and noted the drawn blinds. That hadn't seemed particularly noteworthy at the time, but the added chemical aroma clearly indicated this bail retrieval might be more dangerous than I had anticipated.

Since the subject of a bail bond agreed to forfeit their normal constitutional protections in exchange for bail, state law allowed for a bail recovery agent to pursue a fugitive onto private property. The holder of a certified bond could legally enter the residence of the fugitive to perform an arrest.

A certified bond like the one which sat on the passenger seat of my Explorer.

My left hand slowly tested the handle of the front door and found it unlocked as my right pulled the taser from its holster. I turned the doorknob and eased the door open before I pushed my way inside.

Once through the door, the acrid chemical stench hit me like a physical impact and seared into the back of my throat. I instinctively held my breath as my eyes watered. On hooks beside the door hung several full-face industrial respirator masks, and I hurried to don one.

With the mask sealed over my face, I blinked to clear my vision. The mask smelled bad, but it was from body odor and not the noxious chemicals that filled this house. I was now positive that I'd stepped into a damned meth lab.

No longer half-blinded by the stinging fumes, I took in the layout. A set of stairs to my left turned sharply and ascended to the second floor as they climbed parallel to the hallway that extended straight ahead. To my right, the floor opened into a living room strewn with garbage and assorted debris.

"What did yinz guys forget now?"

The voice projected from down the hallway, and a figure stepped around the corner. The man took several steps toward me before realizing I was not one of the men who had just left. Despite the respirator the man wore, I recognized the shaggy hair and the gaudy shirt that peaked from under a white plastic chemical suit as he came to a halt.

"Freeze!" I commanded with the taser pointed at the man.

Under the clear mask, the man's eyes grew wide, and he instinctively stepped backward before stopping.

"I'm Harold Mason," I firmly introduced myself. "I'm a licensed bail recovery agent with a certified bond to take you in."

The man's surprised expression twisted into a sneer, and his foot slipped backward another step. I'd been in the business long enough to know he was about to run.

Fine. I'd given him the chance to come quietly.

I squeezed the trigger on the taser, which gave an audible pop as it deployed with a puff of carbon dioxide and fluttering confetti. The prongs flew out and embedded themselves into the man's torso as the wires uncoiled. I expected the rapid clicking of the taser pulse to follow, but it never began.

For a long moment, silence reigned and neither of us moved. He looked at the prongs lodged in his chest while I glanced at the taser in my hand and gave the trigger another squeeze.

Nothing.

"Ha!" The man exclaimed as he yanked the taser prongs free. Several expletives were muffled by the respirator. "-ing jagoff pig!"

The man reached around the corner and pulled a long cylindrical object from behind the wall. As the shotgun rose, I instinctively dropped the useless taser and reached for my holstered pistol. A flick of my finger released the strap holding the weapon in place, and I drew the pistol smoothly.

"Drop it," I commanded with my pistol pointed at the man's chest.

The shotgun thundered in response.

The impact to the left side of my chest twisted me partially to the side. Sharp pricks of fire stabbed into me, and agony ignited along my side and left arm where they were unprotected by the ceramic plates in my vest. The majority of the buckshot had been deflected by the armor over my torso.

Despite the pain, I squeezed the trigger of my pistol as soon as I steadied myself. The pistol barked, and the round caught my target in the shoulder, causing him to stumble backward.

I pushed myself upright and stalked down the hall. The man scrambled backward, clearly surprised that I was still on my feet. I was a little surprised myself, but my Kevlar had caught the worst of the blast, and pain was nothing new for me.

The man darted around the corner ahead of me, and I pursued. The sound of the shotgun slide being racked gave me a moment of warning, and I skidded to a halt before the end of the hall. I glanced around the corner and ducked back as the shotgun thundered again. The tight spread of the shot tore a plate-sized hole in the wall.

I stuck my pistol around the corner and blindly triggered two shots. A muffled yelp indicated a hit, so I stepped out with my pistol at the ready.

Only a flash of white caught my eye as my quarry disappeared again, this time into a room farther down the corridor. A splash of red low on the wall stood out as I followed. I'd wounded my target twice now, but he was still on the run, and the crash of glass breaking somewhere ahead spurred me to move faster.

The next room removed any doubt that this house was a meth lab. The combined kitchen and dining room was full of large glass bottles connected by a series of tubes. Cans of paint thinner and stacks of batteries lined one wall. Even through the filter of the mask, the stink of chemicals hung heavily in the air.

Along the far side of the dining room, the large picture window had been shattered, obviously the source of the breaking glass. Outside, I saw my target running toward the woods behind the house, having jumped through the window to make his escape. I vaguely recalled that wooded area being labeled Frick Park on the map when I researched where the bail jumper might be hiding.

As the man reached the treeline, I carefully snapped off another shot and was rewarded with a new spot of red blooming on the shoulder of the white chemical suit. The man stumbled from the hit and bounced off a tree before falling into the woods and out of view.

The pain from the buckshot in my left arm had faded to a distant throb as I hurdled the low wall of the busted kitchen window and jogged toward where the man had disappeared.

When I reached the treeline, a depression in the foliage was the only sign that remained where the man had fallen. A few scraps of the white chemical suit were caught on brambles, torn from the suit as he crawled farther into the forest. Fortunately, the early spring growth had sprouted enough to leave a clear trail, the vegetation parted and knocked aside where my quarry had fled.

I ducked under some low-hanging tree limbs and followed. I would not let him escape, not after taking shots at me.

As I ran, branches whipped across me, leaving scratches on the exposed skin of my hands and face. I ignored the stinging pain and kept up the pace.

Ahead, I heard my target crashing through the underbrush as I closed the distance between us.

I soon had the man in view, though there were plenty of trees to give him cover and he had not yet seen me catching up. I held my fire, figuring it was better to close more distance to give me a better shot.

He limped from the bullet wound in his leg, though oddly, the wound seemed to lack the significant blood trail that had been left inside the house.

I followed, gradually closing the distance as long minutes passed, but the man glanced back and finally noticed me trailing him. He turned sharply and fired the shotgun from his hip. The pellets from the shot blasted a chunk from a tree beside me, but this time, all of the shot missed.

I returned fire more accurately, a trio of shots aimed at his center of mass. A patch of bright crimson blossomed on the man's chest, the stain spreading across the white chemical suit. He staggered backward into a tree, then slowly slumped to the ground.

A blue box popped up in front of me, obscuring my vision, and pure agony spiked directly into my mind.

Chapter 2

The pain staggered me, and I stumbled to lean against a nearby tree. Eventually, the stabbing sensation in my head gradually faded, but I remained frozen in place as I read the text floating before me.

Congratulations! You are the 74th sentient to kill a member of the human race (and survive the encounter).

Rewards: +10,000 XP, +10,000 credits

Level Up!

You have reached the experience requirements for Level 2 without having taken the time to confirm your Class selection.

Since you were too focused on the pursuit and termination of a member of your own race, an appropriately bloody-minded Class has been added to the pool of options selected for you. Congratulations, killer!

Now pick your damn Class.

I stared at the blue box and slowly came to the undeniable realization that I was not hallucinating. I tentatively poked the box with my left index finger. A slight resistance met my touch, like sticking my finger into gelatin, but I could still see my finger going through the box. The window stuck to my finger for a moment as I moved it around, like dragging an app menu on my smartphone. When I pulled my hand away, the box hovered in place where I'd released it.

If the floating blue box was real and I wasn't having a complete mental break, then the first ones I'd seen back in my car were probably also real.

With some mental focus projected at the windows in front of me, I brought back up the previous notification boxes. They layered themselves on top of one another, with the first one at the top of the stack.

This time, I carefully read through each one of the windows.

Greetings citizen. As a peaceful and organised immersion into the Galactic Council has been declined (extensively and painfully we might add), your world has been declared a Dungeon World. Thank you. We were getting bored with the 12 that we had previously.

Several more paragraphs described how this powerful Galactic Council recommended that sentient inhabitants should leave the planet while the transformation into a Dungeon World occurred. Dungeons and monsters would be spawned randomly and increasingly all over the world for the next 373 days, so the likelihood of survival was low.

The next array of blue boxes cited a series of Galactic laws that made my eyes cross after the first sentence. Only my experiences with completing the court documents used in bounty hunting kept me on track. I eventually parsed out the legalese that indicated I had earned several Perks due to my location when the Galactic Council had activated Earth as a Dungeon World.

Additionally, the native inhabitants of Earth had been granted access to a user interface which provided the ability to acquire Classes and skills—and explained the blue notification boxes.

With all these notifications, things about Perks, and the need to select a Class, I felt stuck in an overwhelming video game come to life. I had never been much of a gamer, at least until I ended up hospitalized courtesy of the bombs that had killed my fireteam during a tour overseas. The handheld and console games in the hospital were ostensibly there to promote physical therapy and help wounded veterans recover their coordination. In reality, the games were just as useful in distracting myself and passing the time while I waited for my body to heal.

I hardly had considered myself good at any of those games, especially with my nerve-damaged left arm, but at least they'd given me an idea of what to expect now.

From what the notification messages implied, things on Earth would quickly grow more and more difficult, so I had to become more powerful if I wanted to survive. In video game terms, that meant I needed to gain levels by killing the monster spawns and clearing the dungeons mentioned in the introduction message. That meant if I wanted to live, I needed to pick a Class, just as the snarky welcome message had said, and start Leveling.

I prodded at the blue boxes for a bit until I pulled up the options for Class selection. A lengthy list appeared, but the top selections were highlighted as "System Recommendations." Most of the options listed were labeled as Basic Classes—Soldier, Scout, Ranger, Hunter, and Marine. However, a single Advanced Class sat at the top of the recommended list.

I pulled up the information on that class, and the interface expanded into a new window.

Advanced Class: Relentless Huntsman

Relentless Huntsmen are elite combatants skilled at tenaciously pursuing bounty targets for capture or elimination.

Class Abilities: +1 Per Level in Strength. +3 Per Level in Agility and Constitution. +2 Per Level in Intelligence and Charisma. +1 Per Level in Perception and Willpower. Additional 2 Free Attributes per Level.

+60% Mental Resistance. +20% Elemental Resistance

Warning! Minimum Attribute Requirements for the Relentless Huntsman Class not met. Class Skills Locked until minimum requirements met.

The class seemed like a good fit for me, focusing on endurance and speed. Unwilling to make a choice without at least looking at the other options, I also pulled up the statistics for the Basic Classes.

After I read through the other options, I was far from impressed with them. The Basic Classes only offered between 5 and 9 attribute points per level, while the Advanced Class option provided a much more substantial 15 points per level and added resistance bonuses.

On the other hand, if I chose the Advanced Class, my Class Skills would remain unavailable until I raised my attributes to certain ranks.

Despite the more immediate downside, it seemed like a straightforward choice if I planned for the future. I confirmed my selection of the Advanced Class. A warning window popped up in response.

Selection of this Advanced Class option will consume your Large Perk. Do you wish to continue with this option?

Y/N

I hadn't looked at any of the Perks yet, but the opportunity to earn two or three times as many attribute points per level was too good to pass up.

When I confirmed my selection and closed the Class information window, I got another new notification.

You have reached Level 2 as a Relentless Huntsman. Stat Points automatically distributed. You have 2 free attributes to distribute.
Class Skills Locked.

The Class Skill point normally awarded at Level 1 was unavailable to me, just as the description message had warned before I took the Class.

I decided to move on and closed the notification before I attempted to assign my remaining Small and Medium Perks. With a thought, first dozens and then hundreds of Perks scrolled through the window in front of me. I prodded at the window in the same way that I had managed to bring up the Class information, and I soon figured out how to sort through the menu.

I might not have been a gamer, but I was no idiot either.

I needed bonuses that would be as advantageous later as they might be now. I started off by looking for a Small Perk that would provide powerful long-term boosts to my Class abilities. After a few minutes of browsing through the options, I narrowed my selections before I settled on the one I thought would be most useful.

Gut Instinct

The hallmark of any seasoned investigator is knowing when to follow their intuition. You subtly absorb information from the System that leads to making the right decision. Whether in the heat of conflict or after considering all the facts, those around you will be amazed by your ability to always make the right call.

Effect: The user has an uncanny, System-assisted knack for making occasional connections others miss and discovering hidden information.

The Medium Perk took a bit more time to determine. While I had slightly fewer options available, they were all significantly more powerful than the abilities I had browsed through earlier. Finally, I found a Perk to help offset the fact that my Class Skills were currently unavailable.

Head Start

You're naturally gifted, starting off with advantages of which others can only dream.

Effect: Gain access to two additional Class Skill points that may be applied to any Tier I Class Skill, regardless of whether you currently meet the prerequisites of that Class Skill. These points do not count toward a Skill evolution but will not prevent the chosen Class Skill from evolving.

With my Perks now addressed, I closed those windows and found that a new notification waited for my review.

You have three unassigned Class Skill points. Would you like to assign them now? (Y/N)

Interesting. It seemed as though I could use the Class Skill point from Level 1 now, even if it was not normally available. A bug in the System, one I'd be happy to exploit.

I selected the yes option, and a new screen appeared that showed my Class Skill tree. The tree had three main branches labeled "Utility," "Pursuit," and "Combat." Each of the main branches had four tiers of abilities. Between the three main branches were two smaller columns that seemed to grow out of the primary paths. Only the first row was highlighted as available now, with everything in the levels above grayed out and unable to be selected.

Reading through the available options took a minute, but I felt pretty comfortable with my plans for the three Class Skill points provided by the perk.

I selected the first skill in the Combat tree and applied my first point to the Tier 1 ability. A new notification popped to the fore over the other visible boxes.

Class Skill Acquired

Hinder (Level 1)

Effect: All physical movement by a designated target within 10 feet is Significantly Impaired for 1 minute. Cost: 40 Stamina + 20 Mana.

I closed that Skill window, then applied a point toward the first skill in the Pursuit tree, which resulted in another pop-up.

Class Skill Acquired

Keen Senses (Level 1)

The user is more in tune with their body and more accurately interprets information gained from their surroundings. This manifests in the user as increases to vision, audition, gustation, olfaction, tactition, and proprioception. Mana regeneration reduced by 5 Mana per minute permanently.

Once I closed that latest notification, I made my final selection from the first tier of abilities, with the Class Skill that lay in the column between the Pursuit and Utility trees. As I spent my last free point, another box appeared to display the results of my final selection.

Class Skill Acquired

On the Hunt (Level 1)

The Relentless Huntsman has the ability to disguise their visible titles, class, level, and stats. Effectiveness is based on the user's Skill level and Charisma. Mana regeneration reduced by 5 Mana per minute permanently.

The ability to hide information about myself seemed wise, especially considering how my Class had been acquired. Even if the world was massively changed as a result of whatever was going on, I couldn't imagine polite society being comfortable with an individual who advertised his presence as a killer.

With all Skill points applied, the window closed itself, and I finally found that no more blue boxes waited for my attention. Without the distraction of the windows, I immediately noticed the increases to my perception granted by the Keen Senses ability. The colors of the forest seemed brighter and more intense. I heard the gentle straining of trees in the morning breeze and smelled the coppery tang of blood from the body a few paces away. It took me a minute to adjust to the new sensations before I could focus back on my current situation.

According to the notifications that granted me Perks, the Greater Pittsburgh Area had been designated as a Level 80 Zone. At only Level 2, I needed to get the hell out of here.

No longer able to distract myself otherwise, I finally regarded the corpse a few yards in front of me. The earlier notifications had told me that I'd killed him, but I felt uncomfortable trusting the blue boxes completely.

I walked over to the body and kicked the shotgun out of his limp grasp. When he didn't react, I leaned over and picked up the weapon. I looked over the gun, checking it for any damage that might have happened during the gunfight, but I found nothing wrong.

A thought popped into my head. If things worked like a video game now, then maybe I had an inventory system like a video game too.

As I had that thought, a five-by-five grid appeared in front of me. I tried to push the shotgun into the grid, but a red border flashed around the outline of the grid and I felt the sensation of the gun being pushed back. I tried with a few other items that I carried, but each of them also received the red flash and the pulse of rejection. I frowned. I had an Inventory, but I couldn't put anything into it for some reason.

Again, I sensed that I should be moving on soon. Maybe the feeling was part of my new Gut Instinct Perk.

I looked at the body by my feet, uncomfortable with leaving it behind. Pulling my smart phone from my pocket, I tried to activate it, but the screen was black. I held down the power button for several seconds, yet the screen remained dark.

My newly sensitive hearing picked up a faint rustle in the undergrowth, just before a growl from that direction interrupted my attempts to get my cell phone turned on. I jammed the nonfunctional phone back into my pocket and racked the slide on the shotgun. With a shell in the chamber, I flipped the ready weapon up onto my left shoulder as I pulled my pistol and slowly stepped back the way I had come—away from the body and farther from the approaching noises.

Occasional snuffles interspersed with the growls grew louder as a shadow emerged from the foliage and revealed the shuffling form of a black bear. I continued backing away as it sniffed around like a dog until its nose twitched as it reached the corpse.

The sharp snap of a branch breaking shattered the quiet as my foot crunched down on an unseen tree limb. The bear's head jerked around with a snarl, and it locked eyes with me. When it noticed me continuing to back up, the creature's whole body swung around to face me, and it pawed at the ground with a roar. The bear's eyes flashed red, and it lumbered toward me in a run.

I squeezed the trigger on my pistol, the recoil raising the barrel, and I lowered it to fire again as soon as the weapon dropped back on target. I emptied the magazine into the charging bear, which seemed largely unaffected by my shots. I dropped the empty pistol and leveled the shotgun as I stepped around a tree, putting the trunk between the bear and me.

The bear rammed its shoulder into the tree, roaring and swiping at me as it tried to reach me around the trunk. Desperately, I mentally reached for my new Class Skill in the same way that I had controlled the translucent blue windows. In response to my will, an invisible rush of energy flowed through me and out to cover the bear. The force of Hinder pressed down on the bear, and its movements grew sluggish, as if suddenly burdened with heavy weights across its body or moving through a viscous liquid.

The now-lethargic bear moved as if it was in a slow-motion video, and I took a second to aim before I fired the shotgun. The buckshot blasted into the bear's face, and its right eye exploded in a splash of gooey pulp.

The bear snarled and shuffled around the tree before it lunged at me again. I dodged the slow-moving attack and pumped the slide on the shotgun as I retreated. I fired, then stepped behind another tree as the bear chased me. I'd hit it twice in the face, and blood streamed down the bear's snout to splatter across the forest floor with each of its angry roars.

Suddenly, the bear sped up, and it pounced forward with renewed momentum. I dove to the side, but claws raked through the back of my left hamstring. I screamed in pain as I tumbled across the ground with the realization that Hinder had already worn off from the bear. I rolled behind the trunk of a tree and activated Hinder once again as the beast circled me.

When the bear lunged at me, I jammed the barrel of the shotgun into the beast's snarling mouth and yanked the trigger. The blast exploded out of the back of the bear's skull, and the beast dropped like a puppet with the strings cut as the slow-motion effect ended. Stuck in the shotgun's trigger guard, my right index finger snapped as the shotgun was jerked from my grip when the bear collapsed.

I cursed as I cradled my broken finger, relieved to still be alive. Pain from the back of my leg burned, and I tugged at the shotgun with my left hand. It took some work with only one decent hand, but I eventually pulled the shotgun from the bear's mouth. Then I snarled disgustedly when I noticed the weapon's barrel was crumpled and bent from the impact of the bear's jaw closing down upon it.

I dropped the now useless shotgun as I sarcastically asked the deceased bear, "I don't suppose you at least have any loot?"

When a window popped up over the bear, I was only half surprised.

Welcome to video game world.

The window contained a stack of bear meat and a juvenile bear pelt. With a thought, my Inventory window opened, and I tried to shove the loot from the window over the bear into my Inventory with a dragging motion. Only the bear meat moved into my Inventory window, so I tried again.

This time the loot window flashed red, and a new notification popped up.

Juvenile Bear Pelt corrupted due to incomplete System integration. This item is not available to be looted.

I sighed. That figured.

Painfully, I pushed myself to my feet with the ruined shotgun. My right index finger was a swollen mass of dark blue and purple flesh, but I could still move the rest of my hand without too much pain. I'd have to splint it with the first aid kit I kept in my car with all of my extra gear.

Then I paused, looking at the title of the loot window that still hovered over the bear.

Black Bear Cub.

Cub.

About the time I pieced together that this was bad news, an earthshaking roar echoed distantly through the forest. The rumbling sound vibrated in the hollow of my chest, and I heard the pain and anger that filled the bellow.

This time, I didn't even try to locate the source.

I turned and limped into an agonizing run.

Chapter 3

My heartbeat thundered in my ears as I stumbled through the woods on one good leg, all too slowly navigating the path back the way I'd come. The enraged roars grew closer as their source crashed through the forest behind me. I could only imagine how large the creature pursuing me must be as I heard trees shattering and the lumbering footfalls of the massive creature. I dared not look back and pushed myself to move faster.

I reached the edge of the forest and staggered across the unkempt lawn. When I got to the broken window, I placed both hands on the windowsill, and my broken finger screamed at me as I vaulted up into the house. A few pieces of glass dug into my hands, but I was far more worried about the roaring monster chasing me than the pain in my hands.

I turned to look back at the forest just in time to see an even more massive bear burst out of the treeline. If the juvenile bear had been the size of a small pony, this bear was sized more like a truck. A lifted, extended cab, heavy duty truck with dual rear wheels.

Just like the younger bear, the enraged mother was completely fixated on me, and the beast's eyes blazed red as the creature charged forward.

The house shuddered as the beast impacted, and I stumbled backward as cracks appeared around the window through which the bear's head jutted into the house. The massive jaw snapped shut a foot shy of where I stood. I smelled the nauseating carrion scent of the bear's breath, even over the chemical smell that still permeated the house.

With my pistol lying discarded somewhere back in the forest, I lacked a ranged weapon to fight the massive creature. I sure as hell wasn't going to try to hit the thing with my extendable baton or a folding pocket knife. Instead, I grabbed one of the cans of paint thinner from where they were stacked along the dining room wall. As hard as I could, I flung the can at the bear. The can crumpled as it collided with the bear's snout, and the liquid inside splashed out over the creature. The bear snarled and pulled back slightly.

I scooped up another can and launched it at the bear, followed quickly by two more. Each impact drenched the bear further, and it flinched with each impact, the harsh chemical smell clearly leaving it unsettled but not actually causing damage.

The bear rallied and launched itself at the window again. The house rumbled dangerously, and the corner of the window gave way as the bear pushed to get farther inside. I backed up toward the kitchen, away from the bear's snapping jaws.

I continued to throw cans of paint thinner at the bear, which only enraged the beast further. All signs of intelligence had fled from the bear's eyes. It was consumed by the desire to tear me apart. The maddened creature had pushed its shoulders completely through the wall, wedging itself inside the building as it strained to reach me.

As sickening as the bear's breath had smelled, the eye-searing fumes of meth lab chemicals were building up again now that the window was plugged by a bear with its fur matted down by paint thinner. Then I paused, struck by inspiration despite the thrashing beast that continued to force itself through the side of the house.

"This is a bad idea," I muttered as I pulled the emergency flare from my belt.

I removed the end cap and flicked open the striking surface on it. I gripped the flare tightly with my right hand pointing away from my body, then I ground the striker against the end with a flick of my wrist, just like lighting a giant match. The flare ignited with a hiss and filled the room with an infernal glow. Flame streamed from the end of the flare, and the bear jerked its head away as it recoiled from the sudden bright light.

I stepped forward as the bear struggled to retreat from the flare in my hand, but it had pushed too far into the house and was stuck in the window frame. Finding that retreat was not possible, the bear lunged forward once more. I activated Hinder, now that the bear was so close, and the beast slowed just enough that I dodged as its massive jaws snapped shut right in front of me. Then I lunged forward and stabbed the lit flare into the bear's snout.

Flames burst up from the point of impact and raced to cover the bear in a living blanket of fire. I stumbled backward, repelled by the heat, and the bear howled as it reared up. The creature shook its head up and down, first off the ceiling then the floor, in an attempt to extinguish the searing flame. The only thing the flailing beast accomplished was spreading the conflagration around the chemically infused room.

I coughed and struggled to breathe through the smoke as I crawled through the kitchen and out into the hallway. Behind me, the blaze caught on the floor and climbed the walls. The bear wheezed and whined from the midst of the inferno, the broiling air searing it from the inside as it breathed.

I dragged myself around the corner of the hallway and pushed myself back onto my feet as I neared the front door. I turned the door handle, but before I could pull the door open, the house shook as the chemical stockpile in the kitchen exploded. I glanced back down the hallway, then barely squeezed my eyes shut before a wave of flame washed over me.

The searing force bashed me face-first into the door, and I felt my nose shatter an instant before the door gave way from the force of the explosion. I was flung from the house, airborne momentarily before skipping off the roof of the orange sedan and crashing onto the cement driveway with an impact that drove the air from my lungs. My momentum scraped me along

25

the concrete before I slowed to a halt a few inches from the street at the end of the driveway.

I gasped and rolled onto my side as blood from my broken nose streamed down my face. On my status in the corner of my vision, my health pool blinked red for long moments before it slowly ticked upward. I lay there gulping air for several minutes until I finally caught my breath and my health no longer sat in the red.

An experience notification blinked in the corner of my vision. The angry mama bear must have died in the explosion, just before I was thrown from the building. I was only still alive because of the increased Constitution from leveling up earlier.

I sat up and looked at the house. The building blazed merrily, and smoke billowed into the overcast sky. Other smoke trails, some near and some far, reached skyward. Gunshots echoed in the distance as the apocalypse spread its misery liberally, and I had the feeling that many would not live to see tomorrow.

Chapter 4

I opened the driver's door on my Explorer and leaned inside, having finally made it back to my car after looting what was left of mama bear. Most of the body had been consumed by flames from the still burning meth lab, but I'd added a few more chunks of bear meat and strips of bear pelt to my Inventory, in addition to some sharpened claws and a handful of giant bear bones.

I had a hunch about what would happen, but I slipped my key into the ignition and turned it anyways.

Nothing. Not even a click.

I sighed, disappointed but not surprised. One of the drill instructors during Marine Corps Recruit Training had often spouted a platitude that applied here. I could almost hear his voice shouting in my head, "Once is coincidence, twice happenstance, but three times is enemy action."

After the taser failed to taze and I found my smartphone dead, I'd suspected that anything electronic would be fried. With no phones, there would be no calling for help. Everyone in the world was now on their own with only the resources and people they could reach quickly.

Things clearly worked differently now.

It might have been about a half hour since I had blown up the house, and in that time, my broken finger had set itself and my shredded hamstring had knit itself back together.

I grabbed a granola bar and a water bottle from my center console, then I closed the driver's door and walked around to open the back of my Explorer as I snacked. My vehicle was a used police interceptor model and the rear bed contained a low-profile vault system. I twisted the combination dial on the vault and the lock clicked open, which allowed me to pull out a padded drawer filled with weapons and ammunition.

A sudden chill ran down my spine and the hair on the back of my neck stood up. I felt the odd sensation of being watched.

I grabbed a Colt 1911 pistol from my armory drawer and slipped in a loaded magazine, then I spun around with the pistol at the ready as I looked for whoever was watching me. My eyes carefully traced over the houses in the neighborhood, but nothing stood out. I waited for several minutes before the sensation finally faded. Whatever had been watching me was gone, but I had seen no sign of it.

Without being able to do anything about the mysterious watcher, I slipped the pistol into my empty thigh holster before I replaced the 9mm filled magazines on my utility belt with .45 caliber ones. Once finished with the ammo, I looked over the rest of the drawer. I doubted that most of the less-than-lethal options I had would be of much use in this new world. I still had a few decent choices though.

A sheathed combat knife replaced the empty taser holster on the chest of my plate carrier, and I pulled the pouch with the zip-tie restraints off my belt, leaving it on top of the weapons vault. The dead flashlight, useless taser cartridges, and empty flare holder joined the pile of discarded gear.

I dug through the accumulated junk on top of the vault and pulled free a small backpack. The khaki-colored pack was my bug-out bag and was filled with a first aid kit, a change of clothes, a few military surplus Meals-Ready-to-Eat, and a stainless-steel water bottle. I strapped a tactical axe to the side of the pack before I swung the bag onto my back and tightened the shoulder straps.

Next, I lifted a Remington 870 breaching shotgun from the vault and settled the sling over my head. If I ended up in a situation where I needed to drop the weapon, the sling was designed to pull it out of the way so that I could still use my hands without losing the gun.

Finally, I grabbed a pouch of 12-gauge shotgun shells and looped it onto my belt where the zip ties had been. I gave the back of my vehicle one last look before I slid the vault drawer shut then closed up the back of my Explorer.

With my mundane needs addressed, I brought up my new character sheet. The first thing I noticed was that next to each of my attribute scores was a second value within parentheses. The second number was significantly larger than the first and, after staring at the screen for a minute, I realized that they were the target values I needed to reach to meet the minimums for the Class. Only when I'd raised all of the stats to the noted value would I gain access to my Class Skills.

For now, I had two attribute points to spend. After the automatic points had been assigned from the levels I'd gained so far, my stats were currently almost evenly distributed. Since my gear strongly favored ranged combat, I decided I needed to maximize my dexterity and accuracy. I dropped a point each into Agility and Perception, then confirmed the selection.

Before I closed out of the character screen, I decided to experiment with one of my new Class Skills.

I activated On the Hunt, the Class Skill which allowed me to disguise various aspects of my status, and I changed my first name from Harold to Hal. The screen updated, but an asterisk appeared after my name.

I focused on the asterisk, and a notification informed me that only a penetrating Skill of a higher tier would reveal the information I had hidden.

Satisfied with my first experiment, I modified my visible class from Relentless Huntsman to Hunter.

I felt an almost inexplicable compulsion to hide my actual Class, and I figured that a hunter would seem less threatening to most people since it would also disguise my military background. A hunter should also be much more common since the first day of deer season was practically an official holiday in western Pennsylvania.

Finally, I modified my Status to disguise the fact that On the Hunt was activated and affecting me.

Status Screen			
Name:	Hal Mason*	Class:	Hunter*
Race:	Human (Male)	Level:	2
Titles			
None			
Health:	120	Stamina:	120
Mana:	150		
Status			
Normal*			
Attributes			
Strength	15 (30)	Agility	13 (60)
Constitution	12 (50)	Perception	18 (40)
Intelligence	15 (40)	Willpower	16 (30)
Charisma	14 (40)	Luck	16

Class Skills			
Hinder	1	Keen Senses	1
On the Hunt	1		
Perks			
Gut Instinct			
Combat Spells			
None			

Finished with my changes, I saw that my health points had climbed back to nearly full, and my Mana points were maxed out. Satisfied with my changes and what I saw with my recovered health, I exited the status screen.

I twisted my shoulders from side to side, then bounced a few times on my toes as I ensured all of my gear remained secure. I froze in place with a sudden realization, then I looked at my left hand in wonder. Only now did I recognize that my nerve damage had disappeared when this game-like system started up. I'd been too distracted by fighting for my life and the novelty of the windows to notice that I had actually felt them with my left hand.

I was moving freely, without pain, and the numbness that had plagued my left side for years was gone! I flexed the fingers of my left hand tentatively as I rubbed the fingers over each other and reveled in the sensation. Then I ran my left hand over my face and tempered some of my enthusiasm. Though sensation had returned, the scars from the bomb blast still marred the skin of my face.

I looked myself over in the reflection of my car's tinted windows.

Blood remained smeared across my face and had caked up on my shirt and vest. The left leg of my pants was shredded in a ragged tear from my butt to my knee, and my left cheek felt a bit breezy. The rest of my clothes were singed and had a few holes from where sparks from the flaming house had burned through. I reeked of smoke and charred flesh.

Despite my disheveled state, I felt better than I had in years. Something about this changed world certainly agreed with me, and part of me wondered if I would keep feeling stronger as I gained more experience.

The competitive side of myself that had once pushed me into becoming a Marine and through Recruit Training was coming alive again.

I needed more Levels.

Chapter 5

I left my keys on the driver's seat of the unlocked Explorer before I walked down the driveway and onto the street. Maybe someone would find something useful inside someday. I probably could have taken more, but I had every reason to expect trouble, and I strongly believed in moving light when expecting a fight.

I followed the winding streets as I worked my way north through the neighborhood and onto Beechwood Boulevard. Pittsburgh was an oddly unique city. Sometimes the roads were laid out in an organized grid, then at other points, they twisted randomly. Often the turns were to accommodate the uneven or hilly terrain, but just as often, roads contorted for no reason.

I was surprised by how quiet the neighborhood seemed. Most people would have already left for work before things got weird, or they were still huddled inside their homes in the hope that this was all a nightmare.

Or they were already dead.

The sensation of being watched struck me again, and I looked around. This time the feeling lacked the hair-raising chill, seeming both less foreboding and more immediate somehow.

I glanced at one house and saw the large picture window that looked over the front porch was streaked with blood. An abnormally large Chihuahua stared at me from inside the window, its muzzle matted with blood that dripped out of sight below the windowsill.

When the dog locked eyes with me, it went ballistic. The Chihuahua yipped and spun in a circle before it lunged at the window, cracking the glass slightly and adding another bloody streak to it. Emboldened by the fracture, the dog rammed itself into the window again. This time, the glass shattered, and the huge dog leapt onto the porch.

The rain of broken glass still fell onto the patio as the dog charged me. As it grew closer, I saw exactly how mutated the dog had become. Instead of being about the size of a boot, the growling dog had a head nearly the size of a basketball and would have stood up almost to my waist.

As it closed, I hit it with Hinder and drew my combat knife with the desire to save my limited ammunition. I stepped toward the Chihuahua and stabbed up into the dog's jaw. My knife sank deeply into the dog's head, but the damage failed to kill the creature. It yipped annoyingly as I kept my grip on the knife and pulled it free.

The beast scrambled to turn toward me with its jaws snapping. With Hinder still active, I easily avoided its attacks and jabbed my knife horizontally into the dog's ear. This time, the blade reached the creature's brain, and it tripped over its own feet as it lost control of its limbs and tumbled to the ground.

The legs still twitched as I knelt beside the animal and wiped the blade clean on its fur before I returned the knife to its sheath. The dog's blood flowed from its wounds to join the gore around its maw. If I had to guess from the available evidence, the creature had disposed of its former owner not long before it had attacked me.

I looted the not-so-little monster, receiving a small pelt and more hunks of meat. The inventory created a pile for each unique item, so even though I had both dog and bear meat, the multiple pieces of animal flesh only took up a single square in the five-by-five grid.

I contemplated the two stacks of meat in my Inventory. Some cultures consider dog a delicacy, but I would rather eat the bear meat if given a choice. While I'd eaten worse things on deployment, most of those had been on a dare. I felt the start of a grin as I recalled the hundred bucks I'd made from my squad mates for finishing a serving of khash. The disgusted expressions on their faces had been worth the nauseated roiling the cow hoof dish had left in my stomach.

As always, the thoughts of my time in the service and the recollection of my fireteam quickly dampened my mood. To banish the negative emotions, I pushed myself back to my feet and continued down the road.

Since vehicles were no longer working, I didn't have to worry about being hit by a car, so I kept to the middle of the road in the hopes that I'd have more time to respond to a threat—like mutated dogs jumping through windows. Equipped with my guns, I hoped I would have the time to respond to any danger from range first.

The neighborhood was strangely quiet, and it felt a little unsettling. Despite the occasional crash or distant scream, I stuck to the road. I wasn't going into any houses unless forced. Close-quarters battle against mutated monsters sounded like a good way to get dead fast. At only Level 2, I had no way of knowing how strong the creatures around here might end up.

The main road began curving back toward the park. Since I had no desire to repeat my close encounter of the bear-kind, I opted to cut over several smaller side streets instead. After a short stretch, the side street turned away from the park, and I followed the pavement around the corner. Along the edge of the road sat a number of wooden planters filled with early spring growth.

The plants looked odd from a distance, and my unease increased as I grew closer. They resembled tomato plants, especially the leaves, but tomato plants generally didn't move. The waving tentacles that reached toward me as I approached were clearly something else. An empty shoe lay ominously next to one of the planters closest to the road.

Curious, I prodded the nearest plant with my shotgun. The tentacles shot upward and wrapped around the muzzle of the gun before they tried pulling me toward it. I yanked on the shotgun's pistol grip as I stepped away and onto the street. The plant refused to release my weapon and kept a tentacle wrapped around the barrel of the gun.

Tension grew before the plant came uprooted and flew toward me in a cloud of earth. Since the plant still held onto the shotgun, I jammed the weapon forward and down, pressing the plant into the ground. The jagged end of the shotgun's breaching barrel dug into the fibers of the plant's small body and held it in place as I smashed my foot on it and ground the plant into the street. The plant fibers ripped apart and sap smeared the asphalt.

A moment later, an experience notification popped up to inform me of the death of a *Young Carnivorous Killer Tomato*.

I considered the green-smeared sap on the pavement for a moment before I looked back at the other plants. If the plant-thing had been a little stronger, or if I had been a little weaker, it might have pulled me down and wrapped me up within the tentacles. I wasn't going to leave these other plants to get strong enough to take down someone else. Especially when they gave me experience in the process.

Decision made, I repeated the process with each of the dozen killer tomato plants that filled the wooden planters. Several sweaty minutes later, the street had become a goopy mess of plant sap and shredded plant fibers. A glance at my status showed that the experience gained had almost pushed me up to the next Level. Not bad for a few minutes of work.

I left the uprooted planters behind as I cut off-road between the garden and the house next to it. I dropped downhill slightly as I passed through another backyard. I soon rejoined the road at a point just east of where Beachwood came down the hill and curved to run alongside Forbes Avenue.

Here I saw the first signs of other people. Traffic was jammed up on Forbes, the main thoroughfare for the city district that headed toward downtown and the Cultural District in the distance. The cars here were unmoving and most had their doors left open while pedestrians ran in all directions. Several people shrieked as they passed me, clearly fleeing from something, with their eyes widened in panic.

I headed the way they had come and pulled the shotgun snugly up to my shoulder, keeping the muzzle angled down as I searched for the source of the terror affecting the people running away.

A series of cracks echoed nearby when I stepped onto Forbes and drew my attention to the nearby intersection. A Pittsburgh police officer stood on the hood of a police cruiser parked alongside the road and fired his weapon toward the ground. From my position, I couldn't see the officer's target, and I cautiously worked my way to the far side of the road as I approached.

Beyond the police cruiser, a pair of municipal maintenance trucks sat parked alongside the road. It looked like a typical spring pothole repair crew, except that the half dozen road crew members also stood on top of vehicles throughout the street as they swung shovels, rakes, and even sledgehammers down toward the ground. As I approached, I saw that the street seemed to writhe beneath the vehicles. The stench of sewage filled the air.

Then I realized that the gray tide wasn't the street, and my skin crawled in revulsion.

Out of the storm drains along both sides of the road poured a flood of sewer rats the size of small dogs. The rats' matted gray fur blended with the asphalt and the other rats as they swarmed, making it nearly impossible to pick out individual creatures.

At some of the vehicles, the rats climbed up over each other, creating a mounded pile in their attempt to reach the people who stood above them. I headed toward the closest mound that grew near the back of the police cruiser. At the front of the vehicle, the cop fired into the writhing mass. The officer's shots were steady and disciplined, despite the rising tide of rats that climbed higher and higher toward him.

I pulled the trigger on the shotgun, and the rear pile of rats disintegrated in a splash of gore. I racked the shotgun to chamber a new round and strode toward the front of the vehicle. I stepped, then fired into the swarming rats again. The blast pushed back the advancing tide, and I pumped the slide again.

At the front of the cruiser, the tide crested over the hood and the officer kicked at the top of the pile that rushed toward him. His kick flung the first several rats airborne, but the rest swarmed up his legs, and he fell with a hideous scream as the rats flowed over him. His horrific screams continued even after he disappeared under the throng, and I leveled the shotgun at the swarm.

I fired, and the officer's screams grew mercifully silent. I chambered another shell and fired again at the swarm. The flood of rats seemed to hesitate and recoiled from my continued fire, so I took advantage of the opportunity and thumbed several shells into the shotgun from the pouch on my belt before I continued.

In the middle of the road, a towering black man in a neon safety vest stood on an empty blue sedan and slammed a wide-headed steel shovel onto another pile of the rats. The forceful impact pulped the majority of the mound, and the man moved to counter another growing pile as the sedan sagged precipitously under the muscular man's weight.

I moved toward the bulky road worker and fired each time I saw a large cluster of rats. Only a few of the rats darted toward me individually, and I easily smashed or kicked the lone rodents that reached me.

I attempted to slow some of the nearer rats and found that Hinder only worked on individual monsters, making the Class Skill almost completely ineffective against a larger group. The fragile creatures died easily on their own, but their danger lay in their large numbers.

A few more blasts from my shotgun cleared the area around the sedan, and the big man jumped down beside me. Up close, he looked like a middle-aged bodybuilder. He loomed over me, taller by several inches. I didn't take much more time than that quick appraisal before I got back to rodent killing. The two of us worked our way up the street, my shotgun clearing the largest congregations of rodents as the man's steel shovel took care of any smaller groups that tried to get around us.

Several more of the maintenance workers were swarmed by rats before we could reach them, but as soon as we cleared the massed rats away from the few surviving members of the road crew, the tide of rodents ebbed away into the storm drains alongside the road. Whether the creatures had retreated temporarily or just gone in search of easier prey, it was impossible to tell.

Left in the street, between and around stopped cars, piles of bloody meat and gore-stained clothing marked the spots where the people had been too slow to flee or fight back.

My belt pouch of shotgun shells was nearly empty by the time I finished reloading the weapon, then it took several minutes to loot the area. I tried looting from what was left of the other fallen people, but no loot window popped up in response to my attempts. Maybe only the killer could obtain the loot, which meant that only things physically on their person would be left behind and anything in their Inventory would be lost.

My Inventory accumulated a number of greasy rat pelts and a small number of Credits. That last item came from the slain officer, as I had been responsible for the man's death. A sickened feeling twisted my stomach before my brain justified the killing with the rationale that the man would have died anyways under the swarm of rats.

When I brought up my Inventory window for a closer look, I found that the Galactic Credits appeared in a tracker attached to the bottom of the window. From the format of the counter, it looked more like currency than anything, though without any idea of what Credits might be used for, I just felt fortunate that they didn't take up any of my precious few Inventory slots.

I pushed the doubts from my mind as I walked up to where the surviving road crew had gathered by their trucks. The muscular man I'd fought beside drank water from an orange cooler jug mounted on the back of the truck, and a shaky younger guy puked onto the curb behind him. A stocky brunette was the only other survivor, and her curly hair peeked out from under her white hardhat as she chatted with the bodybuilder. The broad-shouldered man pulled off his hardhat and wiped the sweat from his brow, revealing a smoothly shaved pate.

As I reached them, the two halted their conversation and looked at me.

I nodded in greeting. "You should loot anything you can."

"Loot?" the woman questioned.

"Yes," I replied. "Life is like a video game now. Touch something that you've killed and think about looting it. You should be able to put whatever you get in your Inventory."

The big man frowned for a moment without saying anything, then he moved over to a pulped pile of rats and knelt. He looked surprised a moment later.

"It worked!" The man's gravelly exclamation rumbled with the intensity I expected from someone that intimidating in size. He wiped his hand off on asphalt-stained jeans as he stood and walked back over to where I waited. Then he offered me his hand. "I go by Zeke. The lady is Paula, and the kid is Adam."

"Hal," I replied as I gave his hand a firm shake and looked over the three.

Zeke seemed like the steadiest of them. Paula's eyes darted all around as her head twitched from side to side at the slightest sound. Adam had finished throwing up and returned to join us at the back of the truck, but his gaze remained distant and unfocused.

I'd seen that thousand-yard stare before and, combined with his pale skin and rapid breathing, mentally diagnosed him with shock. Not much we could do for him now though. Until we found someplace safe, the only hope was that he would snap out of it.

"You seem pretty geared up for this," commented Zeke.

I shrugged. "I was trying to bring in a wanted bail jumper when this all started. I've been lucky so far."

"You're a cop?" Paula questioned, hope in her voice.

I shook my head. "Bounty hunter."

"Oh." Disappointment filled her single syllable response.

I understood the dismay. It was only natural that in times of chaos, people craved order. I wasn't one of them. Instead, I was becoming someone who reveled in the chaos.

I couldn't help but smile to myself as I saw my latest notifications.

Level Up!

You have reached Level 3 as a Relentless Huntsman. Stat Points automatically distributed. You have 2 free attributes to distribute.
Class Skills Locked.

"What Class did you all get?" I asked as I closed the notification.

"Demolitionist," replied Zeke. "It's a hybrid Class that has combat and non-combat Class Skills from a race called the Gimsar, and it specializes on attacks to armor or structures. Right now, I've got a Shatter ability that can permanently damage a target's armor to expose them to follow-on attacks."

"That sounds useful," I said.

Paula sighed. "More useful than my Class."

"What makes you say that?" I asked.

"Surveyor is a non-combat class," the woman replied. "So unless you care about the distances between designated points or laying out a city grid, I'm not much use."

"Oh, that could be useful if we survive this," I said. I hoped we survived to the point where civilians would be able to use a Class that wasn't focused on killing anything that moved.

Paula rolled her eyes and gestured to the carnage around us, the corpses proving her point.

"What about Adam?" I asked.

Upon hearing his name, the young man blinked and seemed to notice me for the first time. His expression remained blank, and I shared a look with Zeke, who only shrugged.

"What is your Class?" I asked him.

"Class?" Adam asked. "Uh, Operator?"

"What exactly does that do?" Zeke asked.

Adam's gaze grew distant as if looking at something we couldn't see, likely his status menus. "I can run equipment, and it uses less Mana."

I looked at the cars that filled the streets in either direction. "Vehicles?"

"Maybe?" Adam said, being less than helpful. "My current skill only allows for passive efficiency for Mana batteries. So, I guess if a vehicle has a Mana battery?"

I doubted we would find a working vehicle if all electronics were fried, like my phone. Or my own car. This whole video game thing felt like it was rigged.

"My kids," Zeke cried out. His sudden, wide-eyed realization grabbed my attention as he unconsciously twisted a gold band on his ring finger. "I've got to get to my kids."

"Where are your kids again?" Paula asked.

"Montour High School," replied Zeke. "Over in McKees Rocks, just this side of Robinson."

I had a pretty good understanding of the local geography from the bounty hunting I'd done through the area. The suburb Zeke had named was located outside the west of the city limits, completely the opposite side of Pittsburgh from where we were. However, with no immediate family of my own, I wasn't driven toward anything besides surviving, and I had the sense that staying put was a bad idea. Still, I was reluctant to volunteer. I wasn't the hero type.

"My Jake can take care of himself," said Paula with a firm nod. "I'll come along."

Her statement was the first bit of confidence I'd seen from her.

"Adam?" Zeke questioned.

The young man blinked and seemed to come to himself again. "Uh, yeah?"

From the way he looked around as if seeing his surroundings for the first time, I sensed that Adam had no clue what he'd just agreed to help with. Zeke must have seen the look too.

"We're going west, Adam," the big man said before he took another drink from the truck's water jug.

Then Zeke looked at me, and I raised an eyebrow.

"Look, man," said Zeke, "I don't have much, but if you'll help out, then you can keep whatever I can scrounge up on the way. Money, loot, you name it."

I considered the offer. It wasn't like I had anywhere else to be, and I liked my odds of surviving with a group better than being on my own. One of the many lessons of the Rockpile was that everyone needed someone to watch their back.

"Okay," I finally said. "I'll take the loot."

Zeke sighed in relief at my acceptance. He'd clearly been worried that I would refuse. He gestured to the jug, offering a drink, and I accepted with a nod. Paula just clutched her steel shovel and shook her head, unwilling to release her grip on the makeshift weapon. I stepped up to the back of the truck, then stuck my head under the jug's spout and drank deeply. When I pulled my head back up, I found Zeke digging into the back of the other truck. After he rooted around briefly, he grunted and pulled out a massive sledgehammer with a solid hickory shaft. He spun the heavy tool easily and smacked the haft into his palm as he held it in front of him, then nodded confidently.

Meanwhile, Adam had wandered to the police cruiser and opened the trunk. By the time I finished drinking water from the jug, the scrawny youth had returned carrying the officer's AR-15. Several magazines were stuffed into the front pockets of his reflective neon safety vest.

I suspected that the young man may not be the most steady person to trust at my back with a firearm, but with the white-knuckled grip he had on the gun, I wasn't going to voice my opinion now.

"West then," said Paula nervously.

I nodded, leading the way west down the straight but cluttered stretch of Forbes Avenue, leaving behind the splattered flesh and blood of both monsters and those who had fallen to them.

Chapter 6

We had nearly reached the heart of the Squirrel Hill neighborhood before we were attacked again.

Residential homes had given way to commercial storefronts, and we had just passed a local bank branch. Ahead, the second-floor windows of the Squirrel Hill branch of the Carnegie Library of Pittsburgh gleamed in the mid-morning light over the intersection of Forbes and Murray Avenues.

Even with the heightened awareness provided by my Keen Senses, the first warning I had from the next danger was the sound of panicked firing behind me as Adam opened up with the police issue AR. I turned back toward the sound and instinctively raised my shotgun to point at a potential threat.

Far behind us, a small herd of deer were running down the street in our direction. The half-dozen animals bounded up, over, and around the vehicles in the street. Unlike most of the animals I had encountered so far this morning, these seemed to be normally sized. The deer moved quickly though, and none of them seemed to be taking damage from the rapidly firing rifle.

Adam was a poor marksman.

"Stop shooting," I commanded. "Wait until they get closer or you're just wasting ammo."

Adam looked chagrined, but he complied with my instruction and ceased his ineffectual fire.

The herd rushed closer, and I watched as several pedestrians hurried out of the animals' path. One individual, too far away for me to determine whether it was a man or woman, moved too slowly, and a deer on the outer edge of the throng casually swung closer to the fleeing figure. Still moving at speed, the deer flicked its head sideways to catch the individual on its multi-tined antlers. The antlers seemed to pass through the fleeing figure with no resistance, and a cloud of viscera erupted from the person as their torso was shredded, and the body was thrown away to impact limply against the nearest building.

Zeke and Paula traded nervous glances.

I looked at the bank and had an idea.

"Get behind the columns," I shouted as I pointed at the bank beside us. "Adam, give them cover. Zeke and Paula, smash any of them that get close."

My instructions shook the group into action, and they moved to follow my hasty plan. Instead of joining them, I moved to the opposite side of the street and crawled into the bed of a full-sized pickup truck that sat empty with the cab doors open.

"What are you doing?" I heard the concern in Zeke's deep voice.

"Splitting them up." I looked at the approaching deer that were almost within range now. "Hopefully," I muttered to myself.

The much closer herd of deer had spread out slightly by the time they reached us, dodging around the abandoned vehicles in the street. The first couple deer seemed fixated on me, so I prepared myself to meet them.

As the first deer reached my truck, it jumped and lowered its head to impale me with its antlers. I activated Hinder, and the deer seemed to hang in the air as it was slowed by the Class Skill. I fired at the airborne creature, then I jumped backward onto the cab of the truck as I pumped the shotgun slide to chamber a new shell. The second deer ran around the side of the truck, keeping its head turned toward me as it passed.

The use of Hinder and the impact of my close-range shot had killed some of the first deer's momentum, which kept it from landing completely in the truck bed, but the shot hadn't done as much damage as I hoped. The deer scrambled to pull itself up, and I fired again. This time the impact seemed to stun the deer, and I jumped off the cab to fire again at a much closer range.

The third shot ripped away most of the flesh from the creature's skull, leaving bone and ragged muscle exposed.

The deer swiped its antlers at me and the tines glittered with metallic sharpness, but I easily avoided the weakened movement and pumped the shotgun as I stepped forward again. I placed the barrel against the exposed bone of the deer's head and pulled the trigger. The fourth shot shattered the creature's skull, and the beast dropped to hang halfway over the side of the truck bed.

Somehow the deer still attempted to scramble to its feet, so I pulled my combat knife and dropped the shotgun to hang from its sling. I grabbed the deer by the base of its antlers and held the beast still as I repeatedly stabbed my knife into the head wound.

When the deer finally stopped moving, I sheathed my knife and pulled the last handful of spare shells from the pouch on my belt. I pushed them one at a time into the Remington's mag tube.

A clattering from behind me pulled my attention away from my kill as the truck shook under my feet. The second deer had circled the vehicle and leaped onto the hood while I fought the first creature. It clambered awkwardly over the cab as it rushed toward me.

A quick pump of the shotgun's slide chambered a new shell, and I activated Hinder on my new target as I fired. The deer took the damage in stride and jumped down into the bed, lunging toward me with its antlers flashing. I dodged and found that I moved faster than the nimble deer with my ability active on it.

Now alongside the deer's flank in the narrow truck bed, I jammed my shoulder into the deer. I pushed off the side of the truck bed for leverage as the creature attempted to spin, but my actions threw the deer off balance and caused it to stumble sideways. If it had more room, it may have recovered, but its lower legs caught on the far side of the truck bed, and it tilted precariously without the space to balance itself.

With no more room to sidestep, I heaved harder and the deer tripped over the side of the truck bed, falling to land twisted on the street below. On its back, the deer flailed its legs to right itself as I racked the shotgun slide and fired into the underside of the prone beast. It took several shots that each tore deeper into the creature's vulnerable underbelly before the beast's flailing legs flopped over to lay still.

Too intently focused on finishing off the second deer, I missed the approach of the third.

It lunged at me from behind the truck, and I reacted too late to completely avoid injury. Even as I twisted away, I found out how razor-sharp the antlers were. The tines ripped easily through the flesh of my left forearm and sliced down to the bone. The attack severed the tendons that held my grip on the shotgun slide. Agony raced up my left arm as my hand flopped open, and the weapon slipped free from my lifeless hand as blood spurted freely from the deep gashes.

With my teeth gritted in pain and unable to chamber a new round quickly with only one arm, I released the shotgun and let the sling pull it out of the way. I clutched my wounded arm tightly to my chest as I drew my Colt pistol with my uninjured right hand.

The deer that had wounded me had spun around after running past the truck and now leaped up as it slashed its antlers at me again over the edge of the truck bed. I saw it coming and activated Hinder in time to easily dodge the slowed creature.

I absently noted that my Stamina bar was nearly empty now, and though it gradually recovered, it was far too depleted to activate the ability anymore.

I hoped I wouldn't need it again and resolved to better manage my abilities in future fights.

Though my stamina was low, Hinder remained in effect even as the deer landed. I had the Colt leveled and opened fire. The semi-automatic pistol thundered with each trigger pull, and the deer staggered as each round impacted it just behind the shoulder. Each shot hammered into the same spot, punching deeper into the animal's chest cavity as I aimed for the deer's heart and lungs.

After my third shot, the deer stumbled and fell to the ground with blood spraying out of its mouth with every breath. I fired yet again into the same spot and the wounded animal shuddered and went still.

I looked around for more threats and saw none close to me.

Two deer were still up though, and they menaced the other members of my group where they huddled between the marble columns of the bank entrance. A third deer had fallen some distance down the street. It looked as though Adam had gotten some lucky shots into it.

Behind the columns, Paula was seated with her back up against the bank wall and a pool of blood beneath her. Zeke swung his sledgehammer back and forth, the long handle of the weapon keeping the last two deer at bay. Adam appeared to have run out of ammo though, and he knelt between Paula and Zeke, pulling a magazine from the front of his vest and fumbling as he tried to reload the rifle.

My left arm still hurt and trickled blood, but it no longer spurted as it had when the wound first occurred. I still couldn't move my left hand though.

I jumped down from the truck and moved toward where the others fought. Adam still struggled to seat the magazine into the AR's receiver, so I kept moving sideways as I shifted my position to ensure that any shots I fired wouldn't hit the group. Once I was sure that I wouldn't hit the others, I fired into the side of the closest deer.

My attack surprised the creatures, and Zeke took advantage of their hesitation. While my shots injured the deer nearest to me, he took a wild overhead swing at the one on the far side. The heavy head of the sledgehammer crushed the deer's skull, and it dropped instantly.

I kept shooting at my target until the slide locked back. I holstered the empty pistol, unwilling to risk a reload with my wounded arm and unmoving hand. Instead, I reached behind me and ripped the survival axe free from the straps on the side of my pack.

My shots had injured the deer but hadn't done enough damage to kill it. It limped backward on three legs as I moved closer, swinging its razor-sharp antlers toward me. I targeted the deer with Hinder as I reached it, only for nothing to happen as my depleted Stamina blinked in warning.

Without the help of my Class Skill, I had to rely on more conventional means.

I circled the deer, forcing it to spin on its wounded front leg as it tried to keep those sharpened antlers pointed at me. Since it had one injured leg, I moved faster than it could turn and I lunged forward, hacking my axe into the back of the deer's neck. I pulled the axe free and jumped back as the deer swung its head, slashing antlers through the space I had vacated. I continued circling and waiting for the opportunity to strike once again.

Hooves scraped across the asphalt as the wounded animal spun in an attempt to keep me in front of it. Blood trickled from the torn flesh on the back of the deer's neck, the rivulets dripping down around the neck and onto the animal's chest. With each panicked motion, crimson drops arced away from the creature to splash onto the pavement beneath it and the tang of blood filled the air.

My nostrils flared at the scent and saliva flooded my mouth. I swallowed and breathed deeply, pushing down the bloodlust as I circled my prey. The tempo of the fight now firmly in my control, I kept the animal off balance with feints and an ever-increasing pace. Each time the deer failed to turn fast enough, I darted in for another chop.

Wounded and bleeding heavily, the deer faltered and turned even slower after every successful assault. Finally, when the creature had nearly exhausted itself, I sprang in for the kill shot. The powerful blow to the back of the deer's spine severed it with a sharp snap, and the beast crumpled to the ground. I stepped up to the dying beast and finished it with another heavy stroke of my axe that dug deeply into the back of its head.

With all the creatures now dealt with, I turned back to the group. Zeke and Adam were helping Paula to her feet. The woman's right thigh was a shredded mass of flesh where it had been gashed by one of the deer. Below that point, her jeans were soaked red with blood. The worst of the bleeding seemed to have stopped though, just as the bleeding had now stopped from my own gravely injured arm.

Apparently, we all healed far more quickly in this new world, and anything that didn't kill you right away left the chance for survival.

Seeing my compatriots out of immediate danger, I cleaned the blade of the axe on the deer's fur and strapped it back onto my pack. Then I looted the deer I had killed while I acknowledged the experience notifications that blinked at the edge of my vision.

Deer pelts, raw venison, and razorhorn antlers made up the majority of the items I pulled into my Inventory, and I wished yet again that I had a way of knowing the value of the items I carried. I also looted a few razorhorn hooves, razorhorn bones, and some random organs.

When I looked at my inventory, I noticed that the grid was filling up with animal parts. I hoped that at some point in the near future, the space available to me would increase. Otherwise, I would soon be forced into leaving loot behind.

After my looting spree, I met back up with the others in the middle of the road.

"You okay?" I asked Paula.

The woman had one arm over the shoulders of Adam and Zeke, though the taller Zeke was hunched over slightly to keep level with Adam. Paula looked at her leg, then up again for a second before her gaze drew distant.

"I think so," she said hesitantly. "My health points are climbing back up slowly."

A voice from down the road interrupted our conversation. "Yinz all right?"

I looked up to see a young man dressed in business casual holding the library door open and leaning out slightly to look at us, as if unwilling to actually step outside of the building. Without waiting for us to answer, the young man jerked his head from side to side as he looked around before he beckoned us over with a gesture.

"You should get over here, this is a Safe Zone," the man said.

I heard the capitalization in his words and looked at the others. They all looked back at me, clearly waiting for my opinion. I turned toward the man in the door.

"Okay, we'll be right there," I said, matching action to words as I headed in that direction.

Chapter 7

As we passed from the sidewalk through the doorway into the library, a new message popped up over my vision.

You Have Entered a Safe Zone (Carnegie Public Library of Pittsburgh, Squirrel Hill Branch)

Mana flows in this area are stabilized. No monster spawning will happen.

This Safe Space includes:

A Library (+10% Research Progression)

"A Safe Zone?" asked Zeke, clearly having received the same notification.

"Yes," the young man replied. "It's a Safe Zone because of the children in the daycare program."

He nodded toward the center of the library. I looked in the direction he indicated and saw an older, gray-haired woman seated in a red plastic chair and reading aloud from a brightly colored book to a group of young children who sat circled around her. Somehow, the old woman seemed imperceptibly more frail than everyone around her.

I considered a moment before realization sank in.

"She did something, didn't she?" I said softly.

The young man nodded sadly. "The System offered Mrs. Lynne a unique Basic class. She turned it down in order to make this place safe and used her Perks too. Now she's only got something very Basic." Then the young man's eyes grew hard as he looked at us. "You're not going to give us any trouble, are you?"

I shook my head. "I wasn't planning on it."

I looked at the others, who were also shaking their heads.

"GOOD," stated a robotic voice from the shadows.

The whine of machinery echoed through the library entrance as a large mecha stepped forward. The mechanized contraption had two arms and two legs. Seated in an elevated control chair that looked very much as if it had once been a motorized wheelchair was a spindly young man with a goggled hood completely covering his head. A mass of wires and tubes ran back from the hood to the machinery behind him. The legs of the mecha extended from hips that were placed just outside the wheels of the motorized chair. The long arms each ended in a rotor saw and had a nozzle just outside the blade that looked like a flamethrower. The whole thing gave the impression of a cross between something a cosplay group would do for charity to decorate a child's wheelchair for a parade and a lethal war machine from the grim darkness of the far future.

"Woah," said Adam as the mecha took a thundering stride toward us that vibrated the floor beneath our feet.

"I WOULD HATE TO BE FORCED TO DISASSEMBLE YOU IF YOU BECAME A PROBLEM," stated the robotic voice, coming from a grille on the hooded head. The saw blades whirled for a single rotation to emphasize the threat.

"I would hate that too," Paula said, wide-eyed.

"We weren't planning on staying long," I added.

"We're headed west," said Zeke. "I need to get to my kids."

"WEST," the mecha stated. "THERE IS A SHOP TO THE WEST. YOU SHOULD HEAD THERE FIRST AND PURCHASE SYSTEM WEAPONS AND UPGRADES. YOU WILL NEED THEM."

"A shop?" I asked.

"A SYSTEM SHOP IS LOCATED IN THE CATHEDRAL OF LEARNING."

"Thank you," I said politely, unsure of what exactly a shop meant. I liked the sound of upgrades though.

With its greeting and threat completed, the mecha stomped backward into the shadows.

"You get used to him pretty quick," said the first young man apologetically. "It was pretty weird at first, but he's definitely stopped some strange creatures from following people through the door."

"That seems like an interesting Perk," I replied, then offered my hand. "I'm Hal."

Introductions all around followed. The young man who had called us to the library was Jeremy and the mechanical guardian was Evan.

I got the sense that Jeremy was the overly friendly talkative type, and he proved to be a font for information. Before today, their roles had been reversed. Jeremy had volunteered as a caretaker for the wheelchair-bound Evan, who often spent his free time in the library where his mind could explore the world through the books he read. This morning, Evan had selected a Perk to become the mechanized guardian for the library, as well as a lesser Perk that provided a database filled with information about this new world.

Jeremy went on to fill us in about the Safe Zone and Shop that Evan had mentioned, including that the Shop could even impart magical abilities if you could afford the price.

While the conversation ran on, full feeling and movement gradually returned to my left arm as it healed. After about ten minutes, I cautiously exercised it a little more vigorously to ensure that it was back to normal.

With full mobility restored, I unloaded my weapons and took stock of my inventory before I reloaded the guns on the library counter. I only had three shells left for the shotgun, so I would have to make them count. Fortunately, I still had three full magazines for the Colt.

"How are you doing for ammo?" I asked Adam during a break in the conversation.

"Just one full mag," he replied. "I've got a few extra rounds on top of that."

"You'll have to be careful with your shots," I said. "Especially since it seems to me like firearms aren't doing the kind of damage they should."

"That's right," Jeremy said. "Your weapons aren't System weapons, so they will be less and less effective against higher leveled creatures."

"Great. Even these?" Zeke hefted his massive sledgehammer.

Jeremy nodded. "Yep. It'll still do damage, but System creatures will have resistances to being hurt by it. You'll need to purchase weapons integrated with the System from the Shop to do full damage."

"You keep saying System as if it's a title," I said.

"It is," replied Jeremy. "The System is what all of this is called. The blue windows, the Levels, the experience points. All of it."

I nodded in understanding. The System was the video game world we lived in now.

We definitely needed to get to this Shop. Without System weapons, we wouldn't have a chance once the mutations climbed higher and got closer to the actual level of the zone.

I opened up my status sheet and looked it over. Moving fast and shooting accurately were still my best bets to stay alive, so I dropped my free Attributes into Agility and Perception yet again.

That last fight had pushed my experience up quite a bit, especially since I had performed the majority of the kills, and I was already a good portion of the way to my next level.

Unfortunately, my attributes were still far below the minimums needed to unlock my Class Skills. Some quick mental math showed me that I would have to get through Level 15 or so before I could fully unlock my Class.

Status Screen			
Name:	Hal Mason*	Class:	Hunter*
Race:	Human (Male)	Level:	3
Titles			
None			
Health:	150	Stamina:	150
Mana:	170		
Status			
Normal*			
Attributes			
Strength	16 (30)	Agility	17 (60)
Constitutio n	15 (50)	Perception	20 (40)
Intelligence	17 (40)	Willpower	17 (30)
Charisma	16 (40)	Luck	16

Class Skills			
Hinder	1	Keen Senses	1
On the Hunt	1		
Perks			
Gut Instinct			
Combat Spells			
None			

I closed the status window and looked around.

Paula poked at the restored flesh of her leg, visible through the gaps in her slashed and blood-stained jeans.

Zeke fidgeted with his hammer, clearly preoccupied as he worried about his kids and impatient to get moving again.

Adam stared at the door as if dreading what was outside.

I stretched to loosen up before we headed back out, and my movements drew the attention of the others.

"Well, Jeremy, thanks for all the info. It's definitely been educational, but I think we need to get moving," I said then nodded toward the door. "Shall we?"

Zeke nodded solemnly and threw his hammer onto his shoulder before walking to the door and pushing it open. I followed along, with Paula just behind.

Adam stood still. "I can't." He shook his head over and over. "I can't go back out there."

The rest of us looked back at him. He hadn't moved from the front desk and clutched at the rifle with a white-knuckled grip.

"I'm not going to make him go anywhere." I shrugged.

"I understand, man," Zeke said as he looked toward Adam. "But I gotta get to my kids."

Paula walked back over to Adam and placed a hand on his shoulder.

"You can stay here," she said, then looked at Jeremy. "He can stay here, right?"

"I don't think there will be any problem with that," replied the young man. "As long as he's willing to help out around the place."

"I can help here," Adam said frantically. "Just don't make me go back outside."

Zeke walked back over to the young man and patted him on the back before giving him a handshake to say goodbye. The interaction calmed Adam a bit.

"Good luck, kid," said Zeke.

The big man turned back to the door and pushed his way out. I nodded at Adam and followed, Paula bringing up the rear.

Chapter 8

The sun was nearly overhead, occasionally peeking through the clouds, when the three of us walked back outside. More pedestrians were out on the street now as people came to terms with the world that had changed. Most people were armed or tightly clutched improvised weapons, everything from baseball bats to hockey sticks. Everyone seemed hurried as they scampered from building to building. Nervous glances were exchanged, though most refused eye contact.

An atmosphere of anxious anticipation filled the air, as if danger could explode at any moment. It felt like being back on patrol through a warzone, something I'd hoped to never experience again.

Things were different now though. I was stronger, faster, and had superhuman abilities.

Here I could fight the dangers.

The farther we got from Murray Avenue as we walked west down Forbes, the more the foot traffic died off, and within a block, the busy storefronts gave way to a more sedated residential area. The houses were generously spaced apart and well kept, with neatly manicured lawns and shrubbery.

The three of us talked as we traveled. Zeke revealed that his wife had passed on from cancer almost a decade ago. That left him alone to care for their two children who were now in high school, two years apart.

Paula and her husband, Jake, were childless and spent most of their free time volunteering at animal shelters.

Under normal conditions, getting to the Cathedral of Learning would have been a brisk forty-minute walk, at most. The need to stay alert and deal with the occasional monster spawn forced us to move more slowly. None of the single monsters were particularly threatening, not with three of us, and I held back whenever possible to conserve my ammo. I still led the way, scouting ahead as Paula and Zeke hung back slightly to either side of me as we walked down the street.

This stretch of Forbes Avenue ran straight and mostly level through the neighborhood. After several blocks, we reached a Y-intersection. Here Forbes Avenue turned north to curve gently downhill toward the campus of Carnegie Mellon University. The offshoot straight ahead climbed a slight rise as it headed through a golf course and into Schenley Park.

I looked back at the group behind me. "Straight ahead through the park or down around by Carnegie Mellon?"

"Distance-wise, it's about the same, isn't it?" said Paula.

"Just about," Zeke replied. "I don't want to deal with the CMU students though. Let's go straight."

"Through the park it is," I stated.

Wide fields with gently rolling hills bordered either side of the road ahead, the open ground dotted with putting greens. Occasional rows of trees were spaced out along the road, but since they were cultivated as part of the golf course, there was no ground clutter that could give cover to any hidden monsters.

The frequency of the trees increased from managed landscaping to naturally forested as we reached the end of the golf course and entered the main part of Schenley Park.

The road twisted north then south again as it continued west. The street widened slightly and added rows of parking on either side as it curved toward the Phipps Conservatory. But before the Conservatory came into view, the trees above us rustled ominously and a pungent odor assaulted my nose.

Paula gagged at the sudden stench, and I looked up as a half-dozen giant stink bugs dropped to the ground from the trees on either side of the road. The massive insects had each grown to the size of a sofa, and their spindly legs dented and ripped through the cars parked along the street as they crawled over the vehicles. Noxious clouds emanated from the bugs as they closed around us.

As the clouds of fumes rolled over me, a notification popped up.

Poison Effect Resisted

I stepped toward the closest insect and fired my shotgun. Most of the pellets deflected off the hardened carapace, but a few sank into softer flesh around the eyes and proboscis. I dropped the ineffective shotgun on its sling and drew my pistol.

Behind me, Zeke coughed lightly as if only slightly affected by the gases, but Paula retched violently. I could spare no time for them as the two nearest insects charged at me.

I fired my Colt, each carefully aimed shot targeting the eyes of the first bug. Goo splashed out of the wounds, and the bug toppled as its momentum carried it forward. The second bug had almost reached me, and I jumped sideways onto the corpse of the first bug as it skidded to a lifeless halt.

My movement confused the still living bug, and it paused with antenna waving as it tried to locate me. I took advantage of the unmoving target and double-tapped it in the same head location as the first.

I turned to look at my companions. Zeke had dealt with one bug, which lay in a crumpled heap behind him. Even as I watched, he smashed aside a probing leg with his sledgehammer, then brought the weapon up overhead. The hammer never stopped swinging as he brought it down to crush the insect's head.

A scream jerked my attention over to Paula. The last two stink bugs had her pinned to the ground beneath them. Each insect had proboscises jammed into her torso, and the woman shook violently as her muscles seized from the poison effects. She batted at the tubelike appendages pumping toxins into her body as her screams grew weaker and her movements slowed.

Zeke was closer than me, but we both charged to her aid and reached the last two bugs at the same time. The big man hit one with another overhead strike that crumpled in a section of its carapace, and the wounded bug released Paula as it stumbled back.

I slid under the other bug, knife in hand, and activated Hinder. I sliced deeply into the insect's soft underbelly as I passed under it. Guts and goo squirted from the cut, mostly missing me as I rolled out from under the giant insect.

More noxious gases roiled forth from the injured bugs, but I still resisted their effects. Zeke coughed again, affected but not disabled. He powered through the poison and whaled away at the bug until it was a lifeless, crumpled husk.

My target, wounded by the gaping hole in its underside and slowed by my Class Skill, couldn't keep up with me. I circled and slashed at exposed joints as it failed to turn fast enough. After only a few more hits, I finished it by stabbing it through the eye. I confirmed it was dead with a glance at my experience notifications and turned to find Zeke already kneeling beside Paula.

I walked over to them. When I got closer, I saw that all of Paula's exposed flesh had turned a pale, translucent white. Where the insects had injected her torso, it had withered as her insides liquefied. Zeke shook his head and looked at me.

"She's gone," he said sadly, then coughed violently. He wheezed. "It's my fault."

I grabbed him under his shoulders and lifted him to his feet, pulling him away to fresher air. "Let's get out of this cloud."

Once free of the fumes, Zeke sank to his knees again and stared back at Paula's body. "If she hadn't come with me, she'd still be alive."

"You can't know that," I said softly. "You have no idea what people might be running into out there. The world has gone crazy."

"She chose to come with me," Zeke argued.

"That's right," I replied and placed a hand on his shoulder. "She thought that you getting to your kids was something important, and that was her choice. Honor her for that."

My words quieted Zeke, but he still sat unmoving with his gaze fixed back on Paula. I gave a firm pat to Zeke's back, then went to loot the giant bugs as the stinking cloud dissipated.

After nearly filling my Inventory with bug guts and carapace pieces, I really hoped that we would get to this Shop before my Inventory got completely full. I hated the thought of leaving potentially valuable loot behind.

I went back to Zeke and offered him my hand. "You gonna be okay, big guy?"

After a moment, he grasped my hand and allowed me to easily pull him back to his feet. Both of us were slightly surprised by how effortlessly I'd pulled him up. Strength was my lowest physical attribute, but even that had increased to the peak of human conditioning. My agility was over triple what it had been, and I could only imagine how much faster I had become. My shooting accuracy had certainly benefited from my increases to Perception and Agility.

"How are you handling all of this so well?" Zeke countered.

I met his eyes. "It's not the first time people around me have died badly." I rubbed a finger over a couple of the holes in my Kevlar plate carrier. "I've been shot, burned, and blown up. Somehow, you get used to the horror of war or it overwhelms and drowns you."

Something in my voice caused Zeke to look at me intently, and the big fellow searched my face. His eyes widened as though noticing the burn scars on my cheek for the first time. His gaze traced the ripples of the scar tissue down my neck where they disappeared under my T-shirt and plate carrier. Then he looked back up at me.

"You're not just a bounty hunter," Zeke said. "You were military."

I shook my head and forced myself to turn away—from Zeke, from Paula, and from the carnage that lay behind in the wake of our latest fight. I didn't want to think about the reminders of my past or fallen comrades.

"Let's get going," I said.

It took a few steps before my strides regained confidence. By then, Zeke let out a heartfelt sigh before his ponderous footsteps followed along behind me.

Chapter 9

We continued following the road. It curved in a gentle bend in front of Phipps Conservatory, but I halted as soon as I caught sight of the Conservatory's greenhouse windows. Or what was left of them.

Almost all of the massive panes had been shattered, and from the scattered glass, it was obvious they had been smashed from inside. From within, masses of vines and brilliantly colored flowers stretched out. Some of the plants climbed upward along the outside of the buildings, while others ran out along the ground and reached almost to the road.

"Oh, hell no," exclaimed Zeke as he caught up to me.

"Agreed," I said. "I've had my fill of killer plants for the day already."

We edged toward the far side of the street as we worked our way past. In several places, thorny vines had wrapped themselves around cars on the side of the street nearest the Conservatory. We gave those spots extra distance as we went by.

Occasionally, a pained scream echoed from inside the building. Each time it happened, I shuddered before continuing on.

Zeke just shook his head and said, "Nope. Nope. Nope."

Once we were halfway through the parking lot, the vines no longer expanded out onto the road and we were well beyond their reach.

I sighed in relief. "That was like 'Little Shop of Horrors' on steroids. That movie gave me nightmares as a kid."

"Never saw it," replied Zeke. "Don't think I'd want to now either."

"Well, good news," I said as I pointed at a towering rectangular building that rose above the cityscape in front of us. "That's where the System Shop is supposed to be."

We both instinctively picked up our pace as we crossed the Schenley Bridge. The main branch of the Carnegie Library of Pittsburgh was on our right, sharing a massive beige stone building with the Carnegie Museum of Natural History.

We made it by the library and bypassed Schenley Plaza without incident. That brought us up to intersect with Forbes Avenue once again as the road passed between us and the Cathedral of Learning.

Zeke and I crossed the street, easily moving around stalled and abandoned cars.

Once across, we found ourselves facing several blue-armored figures that moved to block our path. The suits had massive shoulder pauldrons and greaves that thundered with every step on the paved ground. Each of them also carried a blocky looking rifle with a short barrel several inches in diameter.

"Halt and be recognized," stated the closest figure in a deep, synthesized voice.

I stopped and held my hands away from my body. "We're not looking for trouble. We heard that there's a Shop at the Cathedral of Learning."

I really didn't want to fight any of these guys. Their heavy armor looked like powerful, high-level gear.

The first figure looked us over for a moment, then removed its helmet to reveal a scrawny teenager who appeared all too pleased with himself.

"Relax," the kid said as he waved an armored thumb back over his shoulder to point at the towering limestone building. "The Shop is just inside."

"Is that where you got the armor?" I asked.

"Yep!" the teenager exclaimed. "It's just like the marine armor from a tabletop game we all play."

"Oh, okay," I replied, surprised by the teen's enthusiasm. I'd take his word for it.

One of the figures at the back leaned forward. "Knowledge is power, guard it well."

The solemn effect was ruined when he high-fived one of the others.

The helmetless teen waved Zeke and me past, so we left the group and headed up to the Cathedral itself. Zeke glanced at me, rolling his eyes at the kids and their antics. As we reached the rear entrance of the gothic-style building Zeke pulled open one of the heavy wooden doors.

The chaotic babble of a large gathering boiled out of the door the instant it opened, and we found a tightly packed crowd of people that nearly blocked the entryway. Those nearest to us recoiled as the door swung open, and fear filled their expressions, even after they saw it was just the two of us.

Zeke looked at me for direction as the people stared at us apprehensively. I shrugged at Zeke, so the big man pressed his way into the crowd, and I followed him inside. As I stepped through the doorway and into the stale air of the densely packed room, a notification displayed in my vision.

You Have Entered a Safe Zone (Cathedral of Learning, University of Pittsburgh)

Mana flows in this area are stabilized. No monster spawning will happen.
This Safe Space includes:
Village of Oakland, Pittsburgh City Centre
A School (+10% Skill Progression)
The Shop

I dismissed the blue box as the smells of massed humanity filled my nostrils. Despite the fact that the Commons Room was nearly an acre of green slate floor under a four-story vaulted ceiling, the room was filled with warm air generated by the presence of so many people packed tightly together, and I picked out the scents of unwashed bodies, sweat, and fear.

I was focused on sticking tight to Zeke as he pushed our way through the masses. I barely had any attention to marvel at the solid construction of the towering building, the blocks of limestone and massive arches holding the gothic ceiling aloft.

It took several minutes for Zeke and me to push our way to the far end of the hall. It was painfully obvious that the people hiding here had not made any efforts to increase their experience.

At the back of the room, wrought-iron grates led to a bank of elevators. On the wall above the heavy and decorative grating were inscribed the lines of an oddly appropriate poem.

"Here is eternal spring; for you the very stars of heaven are new."

Beneath the inscription at the base of the iron wall sat a silver pedestal with an emerald crystal ball floating above it. Despite the crowd that filled the hall, the area around the pedestal remained clear. Zeke plowed his way to the open area, and I stepped up beside him as we considered the floating crystal.

As I watched, a young blond woman strode up to the crystal and placed her hand on it. Then she abruptly disappeared.

One second, she was there, and the next, the woman had completely vanished.

Zeke and I shared a look, but no one else nearby reacted to the event. A few minutes later, a woman materialized in the space next to the crystal. Only the blond hair clued me in that this was the same woman who had vanished earlier. In place of ripped jeans and a hooded sweatshirt, the young woman wore a skintight jumpsuit that highlighted her athletic figure.

"Is that the Shop?" I asked as I stepped over to the woman.

"Yeah," the blonde replied. "Just put your hand on it, and it'll teleport you."

"Thanks," I replied.

The woman nodded and slipped off through the crowd. Somehow, I doubted the blonde would be one of the people who stayed inside, playing it safe.

I stepped up to the floating crystal and eyed it with suspicion before I slowly placed my left palm on it. I barely felt the cool, glassy surface before I found myself transported elsewhere.

The murmur of the crowded cathedral was silenced instantly, and the stifling warmth of the packed room dropped to a refreshingly cool temperature. The cleanliness of the fresh air was a noticeable change from the packed interior of the Cathedral of Learning.

I found myself in the entrance of a lengthy hall filled with display cases and oddly shaped mannequins. As far as I could tell, each mannequin was unique in shape. While some were humanoid, many others had multiple arms or legs. They were clad in everything from woven grass and cloth to futuristic-looking power armor. The more primitive figures were armed with wooden or metal melee weapons, while the more advanced figures carried glowing energy blades or sleek and deadly looking rifles. Behind the display cases, more weapons and armor hung on the walls in orderly arrangements. The place felt like a charming mix between a museum and a convention dealer hall filled with merchandise.

The atmosphere of the location relaxed me, despite my intentions to keep my guard up as I looked around.

"Ah, a Hunter from the new Dungeon World," said a cultured voice. "Greetings, Adventurer."

I turned and found myself standing only a few paces from a quadrupedal figure. At first glance, I took the creature to be a centaur, but the anatomy wasn't quite right. The figure stood as tall as I did and had a thickly muscular humanoid torso clad in a tuxedo-like ensemble, complete with white ruffled shirt and a golden cummerbund. Below the cummerbund, thick chestnut fur covered the lower half of the creature, down to just above the knees of the four cloven-hoofed legs. The fur reminded me of sheep's wool, despite the difference in color. Adding to the sheep parallel, the creature's forehead sprouted curving, silvery ram's horns that spiraled out to sharpened points. Despite the horns, the creature's face looked remarkably human.

I'd just come face to face with my first actual alien.

"Greetings, shopkeeper," I stammered. "I'm afraid I don't know the etiquette for this place."

"That is no difficulty here, my friend," exclaimed the ram man. "I am Ryk of the Silverhorn Clan, and this Shop is one of many operated by the clan. Here you may use Galactic Credits to buy almost any item your mind can imagine, as well as purchase information or Class Skills directly from the System."

"What if I have materials to sell?" I asked, conscious that my inventory was currently full of monster parts and that I was otherwise somewhat light on funds.

Ryk perked up. "We will buy. Crafting materials from a Dungeon World will sell very well." The ram man gestured and directed me over to a large metallic table. "This table has a built-in stasis field that will preserve your items while we perform an appraisal and agree on a suitable price."

I pulled monster bits from my inventory and placed them on the table. Ryk hadn't lied about the stasis field—none of the monster meats or organs leaked anywhere on the table despite how bloody and gooey some of them appeared. All of the parts appeared freshly harvested, preserved by the System within my Inventory.

Except for one of the last items I pulled free.

When I drew out the bones of the mother bear, the femur looked as if it had been gnawed on by something with tiny, but very sharp, teeth. It reminded me of a chewed up doggy bone.

The marred femur also grabbed Ryk's attention, and his brow furled in confusion as he leaned over the table to closely examine it. "Did some wild animals get to this beast before you looted it?"

"No," I said as I shook my head. "I killed it with an explosion and got to it only a few minutes later."

"Hmm," muttered the ram man as he peered at the bone. "No aura on the bone. That should be impossible." He looked back at me with his eyes narrowed. "You may have attracted the attention of someone or something very powerful, my friend. You should be careful that your actions do not offend."

"How can you know that?" I asked.

"Shopkeepers typically have very high appraisal and analysis skills," he replied. "If I am unable to determine a source, then significant power has obscured it."

I thought back to the chilling sensation of being watched when I had been rearming myself. It had happened right after I looted the bear, so I strongly suspected the events were linked.

"Well," I said with a slight shrug, "I doubt there's much I can do about it. Not now, anyway." I gestured to the table. "How much is this all worth?"

Ryk looked over the piled meat, bones, organs, and other assorted bits of monsters for a moment before he looked back at me. "I can give you seven thousand Credits for all of it."

I looked at the shopkeeper, who clearly expected me to respond. It reminded me of my experiences browsing some of the open-air markets when I had been deployed overseas. It was an insult to most of those shopkeepers if you didn't take their haggling seriously.

"Seven thousand seems pretty low," I said cautiously. "I was thinking more like twelve."

The ram man's eyes grew wide, and he exaggeratedly clutched at his chest. "Twelve thousand! I would go broke to pay out that much. Nine thousand Credits is a much more reasonable price."

"That still seems low, how about ten thousand?" I countered.

Ryk shook his head reluctantly, having dispensed with the previous theatrics. "I can't do more than nine."

"I'll go for nine thousand Credits." I nodded.

"It's a deal then," said Ryk.

A notification appeared in front of me. When I accepted the prompt, the materials on the table in front of me glowed before they disappeared as the goods were teleported away by the Shop.

As the table cleared, the Credit balance in my Inventory scrolled upward. Between the items that I had just sold, my bonus for the world first kill, and the various small amounts I had looted, I now had just under twenty thousand Credits total. I hoped that was enough to get System-registered weapons and some armor.

I closed my Inventory screen and looked at Ryk, who waited patiently for my attention. When he saw that I was no longer absorbed by my status screens, he motioned for me to join him beside one of the glass cases that lined the room.

"I presume you are now looking to spend some of your newfound Credits?" Ryk asked.

"Yes." I nodded. "I'm looking for weapons and armor."

"Well, please take a look through the displays," said Ryk. "Each case will display the item's statistics next to it, along with graphics showing the item in use and recommendations from experienced Adventurers."

"Thank you," I replied.

"And if I might offer a suggestion," continued Ryk. "I would recommend that you not neglect magical abilities or Class Skills."

I thanked him and browsed through the massive collection on display. Weapons were the first thing on my mind, and there were so many that I was almost overwhelmed. If I could think of it, the Shop had a display for it.

There were all types of melee weapons, from knives to swords to polearms and everything in between. There were firearms of all classifications, from pistol to carbine to rifle and matching sections for energy weapons. Then there were more esoteric weapons that shot out nets or chemicals or spat balls of toxic sludge. I even found one odd melee weapon that looked like a large tentacle on the end of a handle.

Within each category, the weapons were divided into Tiers V through I, with V being the lowest. The weapons in Tier V were mass produced and tended to be cheaply made. On the other hand, those Tier V weapons were also the lowest priced. The quality of weapons increased with each tier as they became more unique and powerful. They also became significantly more expensive. Above Tier I, there were only individual unique items. These items were exclusively hand-crafted and were the most expensive of all. Nothing in that tier fell within my current purchasing power.

The Shop had a shopping cart type menu to track desired purchases, so I added a weapon from the energy weapons category. These weapons had a natural recharge rate, so even if I used up the stored rounds completely, the weapon regenerated charges over time. I really liked the idea of never running permanently out of ammo. All of the weapons in this category looked sleek and futuristic. It would be interesting to see how the weapons fired and not have to deal with any recoil. I eventually added a pair of beam pistols from the energy pistol category to my cart.

Silversmith Mark II Beam Pistol (Upgradeable)

Base Damage: 18
Battery Capacity: 24/24
Recharge Rate: 2 per hour per GMU
Cost: 1,400 Credits

Next, I browsed through the projectile weapons. The selection was as varied as the energy weapons, but I had a much better understanding of how firearms worked, given my life experiences and military training. It took some time, but I eventually found a System weapon that resembled my Colt and added it to my cart too.

Luxor Series III Projectile Pistol

Base Damage: N/A (Dependent Upon Ammunition)
Ammo Capacity: 12/12
Ammunition Types: Standard, Armor Piercing, High Explosive, Tracer, Hollow Point
Cost: 1,200 Credits

Of course, the projectile ammunition was all sold separately, so I bought two hundred rounds of Standard ammunition for the Luxor. I really wanted some of the more exotic ammo types, like armor-piercing or high explosive, but those variants were even more expensive.

Satisfied with my initial ranged weapon options for now, I decided to pick up a couple melee weapons too. I strongly believed in the principle of Rule #9 from a popular television show—never go anywhere without a knife. My axe had come in useful a number of times so far, so I took the time to pick out one of each.

Tier V Knife

Base Damage: 11
Durability: 140/140
Special Abilities: None
Cost: 600 Credits

Tier IV Hand-axe

Base Damage: 25
Durability: 200/200
Special Abilities: None
Cost: 1,500 Credits

Now that I had picked out an assortment of weapons, I needed to look at my options for armor.

The armor selections were also diverse. The options ranged from reinforced clothing and sets of powered armor, to energy shields that could be worn or deployed to protect an area.

I mentally checked off another forty-five hundred Credits when I added a mid-grade Adventurer's jumpsuit to my cart. The dark gray set of overalls fit snugly and featured built-in armor plates over the torso, shoulders, and thighs. The plates were segmented and designed to allow freedom of movement. The suit came with a heavy-duty pair of boots that were also armored all the way up to the knee.

I picked up a shield generator belt and a couple of the deployable shields. I hadn't encountered any ranged attackers yet, but I figured spending another three thousand Credits now would save me trouble later.

I also found a gear pack that seemed practical for the wandering type of adventuring I seemed to have fallen into. I added it to the list of potential purchases that waited for my confirmation.

Adventurer's Gear Pack (Human)

Designed to be compacted down to fit within a single System inventory space, this kit contains commonly used items like high tensile strength cable, a grappling hook, a camouflaged tarp, a sleeping bag, fire starter, water purifier, and five days' worth of human compatible rations.

Cost: 1,000 Credits

When I sorted the Adventurer's kit for the human variant, I stumbled upon another interesting human-centric Shop item and I pulled it up for a closer examination.

Human Genome Treatments

Genome Treatments are individually tailored for each client. Each treatment's goal is to fix and optimize the client's base genetic code, removing errors due to aging and radiation. Optional improvements include the removal of less-than-optimal genetic code and the addition of best practice genes.

Base Cost: 10,000 Credits

Removal of Genes: 2,500 Credits

Insertion of Genes: 2,500 Credits

Whew. That was pricey and out of my range for now with everything I was already looking to purchase. Maybe someday.

Before I forgot, I decided to follow the shopkeeper's recommendation and looked up magical abilities.

I quickly found a Minor Healing spell for ten thousand Credits, and I blinked in surprise at the cost. No, the cost wasn't a typo. Related spells at the same level also cost in the tens of thousands of Credits. Unfortunately, on top of the high cost, the spell also carried a prerequisite that had to be met before the spell could be learned. The requirement listed that the user must also possess "Base Mana Manipulation."

Another search of the Shop for Mana Manipulation returned multiple results at a variety of prices. Some results seemed tailored for specific races, but I didn't like spending more than I absolutely needed. I already wouldn't be able to afford the Genome Treatment if I went with my current purchase selection for weapons and armor. That there were different options for what appeared to be the same things still bugged me.

I glanced at Ryk, who followed patiently as I browsed from case to case. I gestured to the floating screen in front of me and asked, "Is there a difference between the human specialty Mana Manipulation skill and the generic one?"

"I should tell you that the human-focused one will guarantee better results," replied Ryk. "But in all actuality, you'll be fine with the generic one unless you have some kind of rare penalty to your learning comprehension or an anti-magic affinity."

"Why are you being so selflessly helpful?" I asked warily. "You'd make more Credits by convincing me to go for the more expensive option."

"The Silverhorn clan believes that satisfied customers will be repeat customers and that long-term customers will benefit us far more over time than making a few extra Credits now," Ryk replied. "There are certainly Shops that are trying to take advantage of human naivety and inexperience."

"Oh," I said. "I appreciate your honesty."

"And I would appreciate your continued patronage," said Ryk. "The System selected this Shop as your default, but you have the option to change it upon future visits."

I went back to the magic menu and added "The Basics of Mana Manipulation" to my purchase queue. I would have to earn more Credits before I could afford any actual spells.

I brought up the cart to review my selections and winced at the total, sitting at just over fourteen thousand Credits.

Before I finalized my purchases, I took one last look through the weapons section of the hall. As I walked past one display case, an oddly shaped weapon I had overlooked earlier caught my attention, and my eyes grew wide as I read the weapon description.

Hybrid weapons used energy like the beam weapons did. However, instead of firing that energy to cause damage directly, hybrid weapons used that energy to accelerate solid projectiles to incredible speeds. Not only did the weapon projectile cause damage based on the payload, the added energy gave a damage bonus.

Railguns. I could buy a handheld railgun!

Where the beam weapons had looked futuristically sleek and slim, the hybrid weapons were blocky and bulky. A cylindrical bank of capacitors hung under the barrel, giving the weapon a rectangular profile when viewed from the side, but almost resembling something similar to the dual cylinders of an over-under shotgun from the front. The rifle had a bullpup design with the magazine for the projectiles inserted at the base of the stock, toward the rear of the weapon.

I added a hybrid rifle to my desired purchases, along with a hundred rounds of Standard ammo for it.

Banshce III Hybrid Gauss Rifle

Base Damage: N/A (Dependent Upon Ammunition)
Ammo Capacity: 15/15
Battery Capacity: 30/30
Recharge Rate: 4 per hour per GMU
Cost: 5,400 Credits

A red case, marked with a symbol in the shape of an odd white skull, sat at the bottom of the weapon case below the hybrid weapon display.

"What's that red box?" I asked Ryk.

Ryk frowned with a confused expression and stepped up to look over my shoulder. "Hmm, I don't remember stocking that into inventory, but it looks like a sample case of special rounds for the hybrid rifles. You know, the kind of thing manufacturer's give out as promos? I just don't have anything in my records for it."

The ram man focused on the red box, then glanced at me from the corner of his eye, his gaze filled with speculative intensity.

"Tell you what," Ryk said. "If you buy that Banshee rifle, I'll throw in the sample rounds for free."

"That sounds like a deal to me," I replied. "I definitely want that weapon. It looks awesome."

"It has far more than looks going for it," said Ryk confidently. "You'll find it effective against the most deadly of foes."

I nodded in agreement and continued on through the Shop.

Finally, I found myself browsing a display tablet that listed the information available to purchase from the System. There were books about hidden quests and ways to obtain rare Perks, but the costs for these were astronomical. Information on Classes and Class Skills were also up for purchase and much more varied in price. Maps of the zone's classifications with likely levels and Shop locations on Earth were within my reach, so I added some of those basics to my cart. One of the items was a manual supposedly designed just for the humans newly introduced to the System, so I added it to my cart.

Thrasher's Guide to Surviving the Apocalypse on Earth

This guide imparts basic information about the System, the current apocalypse, and future plans. Included are explanations of common skills, magic, technology, Safe Points, the Shop, and more.
Cost: 50 Credits.

I confirmed my shopping cart selections and watched as my Credits dwindled from thousands down to just 318. As the Credits were drained, my new items appeared in my Inventory and a notification appeared.

The System Quest Update

The journey to understanding the origins of the System and Mana has many beginnings, but all roads lead to the understanding of Mana. You have taken your first step in understanding the System.
Requirement: Learn Mana Manipulation.
Reward: 500 XP

Well, that was interesting. I pulled up my status menus and found that I did indeed have a new quest that matched the update I had received.

The System Quest
Find out what the System is.
Rewards: Knowledge is power.

A chill crawled down my spine as I read the quest reward. It was the second time I had heard that particular phrase, even if the teenagers outside of the Cathedral had been screwing around by chanting something from a video game. I didn't believe in coincidences.

With my Credits depleted and feeling a little unsettled, I closed the Inventory windows and looked at Ryk. "I don't suppose you have a place I could change into my new armor, would you?"

"Of course," replied Ryk.

The ram man beckoned me to follow and clopped off between several display cases. He stopped a few feet later beside one of the larger mannequins and pointed at the wall behind it. Within the wall was the rectangular outline of a door with a slight indent about where a doorknob would appear. I placed my hand within the indentation, and the door responded by sliding back into the wall.

Behind the door was a small room with a table, chair, and a wall-mounted mirror.

"I'll be waiting for you whenever you are finished with changing out your equipment," said Ryk as I walked into the room.

As soon as I was completely within the room, the door slid shut behind me and left me alone for the first time since I had encountered the road crew all those long hours ago. I sank down into the padded chair and closed my eyes as I leaned back against the wall and breathed deeply.

In one sense, the excitement and danger invigorated me in ways I couldn't fully explain. Still, combat stressors were multiplicative in effect on the body. The need for constant alertness added up and contributed to fatigue. My improved constitution and other attributes gained from leveling up seemed to be improving my health beyond the human norm, but it still felt good to relax and not feel the pressure of reacting at a moment's notice to a life-or-death situation.

I only sat for a minute before standing and stripping off my bloodstained clothes. The new armored jumpsuit slid on easily, and I snapped the various armored plates into place before buckling the armored greaves that locked my boots in place. The suit fit snugly but was surprisingly comfortable for as tight as it appeared when I looked over myself in the mirror.

Once I was dressed, I took a moment to fold my old clothing and neatly arrange all of my old weapons and equipment on the table.

I twisted my torso from side to side, bent forward and backward, then jumped up and down a couple times as I worked through testing my mobility in this new outfit. Surprisingly, my mobility wasn't decreased in the slightest. Instead, my range of motion was actually increased over the gear I had worn previously.

A customizable weapon harness had been included with the armored suit, so I spent several minutes arranging the holsters and pouches to my liking. A holster that could carry any of my pistols sat on each hip. The axe was sheathed in the small of my back, able to be drawn easily with my right hand, but I could still reach it with my left. An inverted scabbard on my chest held the combat knife over my heart where I could reach it with either hand. I decided to keep the railgun and other spare weapons in my Inventory. It might take time to pull them out, but having spares seemed smart, and I thought the railgun would be too bulky to carry comfortably.

Finished with equipping myself and satisfied with everything I had bought, I opened the door. True to his word, Ryk waited outside.

I gestured to the table where my damaged clothes and weapons sat. "What can I do with all of my old stuff?"

"Actually," said Ryk, "I have a proposal for you about that."

"Go on," I replied.

"I'll give you five hundred Credits for all of your pre-System weapons and the clothing you arrived here in," Ryk offered. "It would be an honor to add your likeness to the exhibits we have on display."

I really couldn't turn down the offer, as low on funds as I was at the moment. The weapons weren't going to do me any good, since they had been doing less and less damage as the day wore on. Some of the other gear held sentimental value, but it was nothing I couldn't live without.

After only a moment of hesitation, I said, "Sure."

The Credits poured into my inventory as Ryk closed the door behind me. He turned to me and offered me his hand.

"I believe in your culture, a handshake is appropriate for concluding business," said Ryk.

I shook his hand firmly.

"Thank you for your business, and good luck," said Ryk. "I certainly hope to see you again."

"Thank you for the gear and advice," I replied before releasing the handshake.

As our hands parted, the world around me fell away and I found myself back in the Cathedral of Learning with my hand hovering just above the emerald crystal.

I looked around as I stepped away from the crystal. I saw no sign of Zeke in the crowd nearby and figured he must still be in the Shop. I leaned against a nearby wall as I pulled up my digital copy of *Thrasher's Guide* in one of my System windows.

I only made it through a half dozen pages before Zeke popped into existence beside the crystal. The big man was now also clad in an armored jumpsuit, though the hardened plates that covered his armor were much thicker than the ones on my suit. His sledgehammer had been exchanged for a massive two-handed Warhammer. The front face of the hammer was serrated, and the backside of the head narrowed down into a single spike.

Zeke easily swung the heavy weapon up onto one shoulder as he turned around and caught sight of me. I closed the System window with the guidebook and pushed off the wall to stride over to him.

The crowd murmured around us and made it difficult to speak over the noise. I jerked my head toward the front doors, and Zeke nodded before pushing his way through the throng. I followed in his wake.

It only took a couple minutes to work our way back out of the packed building. Most of the conversations I overheard as we passed by were people who couldn't believe what was happening or were too terrified by the things they had seen to go back outside.

When we reached the door, the people nearby gave us a wide berth as they took in our heavily armed appearances and it became obvious that we were going out. Zeke shook his head sadly as he opened the door, but I could barely hold in a frown.

I knew that if these people just waited inside, things would only get worse. The levels around here were no starter zones. The map I'd purchased showed that the majority of the state consisted of zones in the mid-forties with a variety of areas that both climbed higher and dropped lower. There was a solitary newbie zone around level 10 that stretched from Hershey to Elysburg, but that zone was practically on the opposite end of the state.

From the first few pages of the guide I'd managed to get through, it was obvious that the more time passed and the more Mana in the area stabilized, the higher the level the monsters would become.

All of humanity had been unwillingly entered into a race for life or death. We had to level up before the zone out-leveled us, and it was obvious that most people were going to fall far behind the pace needed to survive.

Chapter 10

The wooden doors to the Cathedral of Learning thudded shut behind Zeke and me, cutting off the concerned chatter from the crowd inside. I sighed and pushed aside my concern for those who remained behind. If they weren't willing to fight for themselves, there was nothing I could do for them. I could only do my best to survive now.

"How did you make out in the Shop?" I asked. Despite our agreement that I would receive Zeke's share of the loot, I recognized that we both stood a better chance of surviving if we each had decent equipment. He tried to insist at first, but ultimately gave in and kept his loot. Thankfully, his desire to reach his kids outweighed his need to stand around arguing about who got more bug guts and deer antlers.

Zeke shrugged. "Got a new hammer and some armor but couldn't afford much else."

"I mostly focused on gear too," I said. "I did get a map though."

"Oh?"

"There's another Shop downtown on the north side of the rivers and one up on Mount Washington, so depending on how we head toward your kids, we should pass one of them."

"Would it be better to go through the North Shore or up over Mount Washington?" Zeke asked.

"I'm not sure," I replied. "I couldn't afford any more information, but the map shows that Fort Duquesne is an actual fort now, so maybe we just wait to make the decision about our route there?"

"That works," replied Zeke.

Since Zeke and I had exited the building on the opposite side from where we entered, we now faced Fifth Avenue. I turned left and led us southwest down the street.

A block and a half later, we reached the sprawling complex of the University of Pittsburgh Medical Center. On our right, UPMC Presbyterian sat back from the road, with a few administrative buildings between the main hospital and us, but the silence that seemed to emanate from the darkened building creeped me out a bit. I thought hospitals were eerie at the best of times, and the end of the world only seemed to magnify that feeling.

We passed UPMC Montefiore next, also without incident. Even though the building loomed above us on our right, I didn't see any movement within. After some of the things I had already encountered today, I was fine with not being ambushed by yet another mutated monster.

A block later, we followed Fifth Avenue as it curved past a towering apartment building, and I found that mutated monsters were far from done with us yet.

Racoons the size of large dogs snarled at Zeke and me from a pile of smashed recycling bins. There was nothing cute about the rabid trash pandas when the pack of beasts charged at us, but with our new and upgraded equipment, the monsters proved to be little challenge.

The first of my new beam pistols eliminated two of the racoons before they reached us, then I switched to my knife and axe to assist Zeke with finishing off the last several. Neither of us suffered a scratch before the beasts were all dead. The usual bits of bone and fur went into my Inventory when the fight was over.

"That was way easier," Zeke commented as we finished looting.

"No kidding. Having System weapons makes a huge difference."

Zeke nodded.

We continued down Fifth Avenue, below a forested hill that rose on the right as we slowly descended toward downtown. Several times, enraged animals rushed from the trees or brush to attack us, but Zeke and I easily fought our way through the mutated wildlife. Streaks of blood on the street and chunks of gore remained in a number of places to attest that others had been less successful.

Occasionally we encountered another survivor or two.

Sometimes it was an armed guardian sitting on their front porch and regarding us with suspicion. Often it would be the twitch of a window curtain pulled aside just enough to let us know we were being watched. Zeke would stop and wave at the observer. If they came out of their house to talk, then we would give them some info and fill them in on the location of the Shop before we moved on.

We never stayed for long as Zeke's concern for his kids kept us pressing onward.

These regular encounters slowed us. Even though a brisk walk should have gotten us downtown within an hour, it was late in the afternoon before we reached the edges of the district.

I'd gained another Level, without the chance to review any notifications along the way, but had completely depleted the charges from one beam pistol and was halfway through the second. I had turned to fighting with melee weapons to preserve the remaining charges, letting Zeke draw the monsters' attention while I struck from behind.

It took another hour of constant skirmishing to push our way past PPG Paints Arena, the home of the Pittsburgh Penguins hockey team, and into the heart of downtown.

It was like entering a war zone.

A smoky haze filled the air with the scent of fire, gun smoke, and blood. Corpses were lying on the streets and sidewalks or slumped in doorways, and several ominous blood trails hinted where bodies of the dead or wounded had been dragged inside.

We passed a pizza shop I had visited on a date only a month or two ago. The front windows were already smashed out and the take-out cooler just inside the front door emptied of six-packs.

I thought back to that evening and frowned. It had turned out that appreciation of a decent pie was about the only thing we had in common, and the rest of the night had gone poorly. She'd pressured me on my war experiences, even after I'd expressed hesitation about opening up that quickly to someone I had just met. The woman had stormed out not long after, leaving me to pay the entire check.

At least I had gotten the leftover slices.

I wondered what had happened to Jessie. Or was it Julia? Jamie?

I gave up trying to remember the J-name and focused on the dangers around us. Errant thoughts could be deadly in a combat zone and the present demanded my focus.

Small groups of people nervously gathered on corners and watched Zeke and me warily as we passed. Almost everyone was armed in some manner, mostly with baseball bats, knives, or guns, but makeshift weapons—like clubs made from the leg of a table—were also prevalent.

I saw hockey and football pads being worn as protective armor, though I wasn't sure that the plastics would really defend against the teeth and claws of the many mutated creatures that seemed to be popping up everywhere.

I didn't see many System weapons, and the simmering hostility radiating from the groups encouraged Zeke and me to keep our distance from everyone. I probably could have done more to pass on some useful information, but tensions were high as everyone looked around for monsters that could attack at any moment.

The sound of gunfire rattled both near and distant, the occasional stray shot whining through the air overhead or ricocheting off a nearby building.

Twice as we traveled cautiously block by block, the corner groups devolved into skirmishes that blocked our progress. The first time, we made it past after the roiling melee worked its way to the far side of the street.

The second time, we weren't so lucky.

Two men in black and gold Pittsburgh Steelers jerseys broke off from the scuffle and homed in on where we stood on the sidewalk. As they approached, I saw the jerseys were in poor shape, along with the rest of their attire. The fabrics were shredded and torn, filled with unpatched holes. Despite the appearance of their clothes, there was nothing shoddy about the length of broken metal pipe carried by the first man or the massive pipe wrench carried by his friend. Both weapons were gore-spattered from previous fights.

"Youz got some nice gear, boys," said the first yinzer.

"Just put them fancy toys on the ground, and no one has to get hurt." The second chuckled as he patted the head of the wrench in an attempt to look menacing.

I rolled my eyes. "How 'bout you get out of our way, and no one has to get hurt?"

"You had your chance," the man with the pipe sneered as he lunged forward, the length of metal spearing toward my face.

I sighed and held up my left hand, catching the end of the pipe with my palm. The jagged end of the pipe dug into my flesh, but my greater strength brough the man to a sudden halt.

The man's eyes grew wide in surprise, but I stepped forward and decked him with a sharp right hook before he could react further. The man staggered backward, and I stepped closer as I followed up with a one-two combination that dropped him hard. The man's head thumped as it bounced off the concrete sidewalk, and he flopped backward, stunned from the impact with the ground.

I turned my head to look at the second man, who had only managed to take a single step forward before I'd floored his partner. He froze as I grinned, daring him to make a move. He didn't, raising one hand defensively as he lowered the wrench.

"Let's go, Zeke," I said.

The big man stepped past me, and the limp man on the ground let out a painful moan as we left the two would-be muggers.

The street fight had moved on during our confrontation, leaving our path ahead clear, so we kept heading down Fifth Avenue toward the park.

Two empty blocks later, the faintest whisper of a footstep from just behind me alerted me to a new threat. I dove to my right, rolling between a pair of stopped cars and popping back to my feet as my attacker recovered from a wild swing that had whiffed over my head.

It was the man I'd knocked senseless just minutes before, the blood on his head still fresh from where it had bounced off the sidewalk.

"I'm gonna kill you," the man said.

Some people just never learned their lessons.

The man rushed toward me with another reckless swing of the pipe. I leaned away, taking a half-step backward out of range of the attack as I drew the axe from the sheath in the small of my back.

I met the return swing of the pipe with the haft of my axe, blocking the blow just above my hand. I yanked my weapon down and hooked the pipe between the shaft and the backside of the axe head. I continued pulling down, dragging the man off balance, and he stumbled forward. Jerking my axe free of his weapon, I swung it into the back of the man's thigh just above the knee. The blade sank deep into the flesh and bit into the bone.

I pulled my weapon from the wound as the man screamed and tumbled to the ground. I kicked him onto his back and rested an armored boot on his throat. The man gagged and clutched at my boot.

"You had your chance," I said while drawing my beam pistol with my left hand.

The man's eyes grew wide as I threw his earlier comment back at him. I fired directly into the man's face, and he screamed as the energy blast burned away at him. Flesh charred and crackled, but the screaming didn't stop.

Deciding against using another charge for the pistol, I stomped my armored boot down onto the man's head. With an ugly crunch, the screaming cut off sharply, and the man's body grew still.

Taking no chances this time, I stomped twice more. Flesh and bone ground into the street beneath my boot, and I looked up to see Zeke and the second goon staring at me. They were locked together in midswing, Zeke pushing his hammer against the second guy's massive wrench.

When the second guy saw me looking his way, he pushed off from Zeke and turned to run. I raised the beam pistol and shot him in the back as he fled. The shot staggered him, but he continued to run, and I lowered my aim before I fired again. My second shot clipped the back of his leg and dropped him to the ground, but he kept crawling in a desperate attempt to get away.

I stalked after the wounded man, holstering the beam pistol to let it recharge. When I reached him, I stepped onto his back and pinned him in place as he cried.

Ignoring the man's sobs, I knelt and slammed the axe into the back of his skull. The blade gave a solid *thunk*, as if chopping into a melon. I levered the axe head free and hacked down again as blood splashed everywhere. I repeated the attack until there was no doubt the man was dead.

I pushed myself back to my feet, covered in blood. I hesitated then leaned down, tore free the dead man's jersey, and used it to wipe the worst of the gore from myself and the blade of my axe.

"Was that really necessary?" Zeke asked softly.

"Yes." I sighed. "They attacked us twice, and the second time was almost a surprise. Imagine if we'd been distracted by something or caught up in another fight."

I looted the two corpses, finding nothing of value, before we continued on.

We angled onto Liberty Avenue and followed the wider street west to the edge of Point State Park as the sun touched the horizon, casting the sky in shades of yellow, pink, and ever-deepening red.

Stepping out from the shadows of the towering buildings of downtown almost felt like entering a different world. Tired from the long day, but unwilling to take chances this close to where we hoped to rest, I scanned the peninsula.

The Interstate 279 overpasses and ramps crossed above the near end of the park, but beyond them I saw the granite walls of what had to be Fort Duquesne. Before today, the pre-colonial fort had been marked in the ground with the granite outline of a four-pointed star. Now that outline had risen from the ground in uneven walls that topped out about four feet high and expanded to stretch across the entire peninsula that jutted out into the intersection of the Ohio, Allegheny, and Monongahela rivers.

At the closest corner of the fort, an automated turret sat waiting for a threat to appear. Along the straight stretch of the northeast wall, between the pointed corners, sat a gap in the wall where it overlooked the open field that surrounded the fort and separated it from the city proper. In front of the gap stood several figures guarding the opening. Oddly enough, most of the trees that had decorated the park were now down, affording clear lines of fire for the turret across the entire peninsula.

The vibrant grass of the green field was cratered in places, singes surrounding the divots, whose centers smoked faintly. A few charred bodies, both human and otherwise, littered the field. A faint breeze wafted across my face, carrying with it the scents of smoke and death.

As Zeke and I approached, the figures by the fort watched us warily but without the open hostility and resentment displayed by the people downtown. Two, a man and a woman, were clad in dark green pants and tan shirts, the uniform of park rangers from the Pennsylvania Department of Conservation and Natural Resources. A third man, shorter and stockier than the rangers, wore dress pants and a collared shirt with a loosened tie. The shirt had the top buttons open, with the tie's knot hanging just past them. The group's final figure was another woman, clad in a sky-blue dress and leaning tiredly against the wall beside the gate as she panted in an apparent attempt to catch her breath. One foot was missing a shoe, her foot swollen and dripping blood.

The stocky man turned away from us and placed both of his hands on the wall. A glow surrounded the section of the wall near him, and it slowly shifted upward, growing out of the ground. The granite section rose until it was even with the part of the wall next to the gap, where I would imagine a gate would be if the walls were tall enough. When the wall stopped rising, the man's hands dropped from the wall, and he sank to his knees, his body shaking with exhaustion.

The rest of the group watched Zeke and me as we walked toward the gate, and the turret tracked our movements. I held my hands out to my sides, showing them empty and well away from my holstered weapons as I continued walking closer.

"That's close enough," said the male ranger, his face strained with tension and hand resting on his holstered sidearm.

The female ranger looked just as stressed, but she was unarmed, which meant she was likely one of the rangers on the educational or environmental side of the department, rather than the law enforcement branch like her counterpart.

"Easy," I placatingly replied with my hands still held out open. "We're not looking for trouble. We're just looking for a place to hole up before it gets dark, and the System has this place flagged as a fort."

"The System?" asked the armed ranger.

I nodded, gesturing around us. "It's what's responsible for this. The Mana, the levels, and the mutated monsters."

From there, I spent several minutes explaining everything I'd learned about the System and the Shops.

By the time I'd finished covering everything I knew, the stocky man had recovered and joined in on the conversation. Carl Jenkins introduced himself as a Civil Engineer class, with abilities allowing him to spend Mana on buildings to upgrade and reinforce them. That ability was how they had upgraded the fort walls.

It was slow work. Carl could only affect one section at a time. And they'd had to fight off several waves of mutated creatures as Carl worked. They had also encountered several groups of people who had attempted to take over the fort. The fights had been short, thanks to the turret that defended the approach, but the group didn't have the Credits to purchase any further upgrades to the fort defenses.

According to the System, the fort belonged to the two rangers, Jared Smith and Chrystal Branton. They'd been conducting an early morning maintenance inspection of the park when the System came online and granted them ownership. Carl had been in one of the first groups of civilians that had arrived at the fort, fleeing a monster group that had spawned in a nearby office building. The injured woman in the blue dress was Erica Davis, a Secretary and the only survivor of the latest group to reach the fort before Zeke and me.

It turned out that most people had ended up with non-combat Classes, and that left them at a significant disadvantage when faced with the life-threatening reality of a Dungeon World.

After some further discussion, Zeke and I agreed to help defend the fort for the rest of the night in exchange for being allowed inside. The obvious relief on the strained faces of the two rangers was palpable.

Zeke headed inside with everyone to take a break, except for Carl, who remained outside with me to continue working on the walls.

By the time night fell completely, the two of us had made three full laps around the perimeter walls, which now stood nearly six feet tall. The effort had netted Carl two levels in his Class, and he spent a Skill Point on his Reinforce Structure Skill, increasing both the efficiency and effect of the ability.

I'd handily fended off several monster waves while Carl worked, only one of which had been remotely threatening. The mutated catfish walking out of the river on their whiskers had given me a start, but I'd burned enough of the swarming fish down with my energy pistols, so the remaining few were unable to overwhelm me before I hacked them apart with my axe.

That attack had drawn the attention of several others within the fort, who ended up coming outside the walls once the fighting had ended. The more salvageable fish were carved up into catfish fillets and grilled over an open flame started by one of the rangers. The number of monsters, and the unusual size of the fish, meant that there was plenty to go around. I snagged a second catfish steak before I returned to guarding the Civil Engineer.

At the end of the third lap, Carl was dead on his feet. I ended up half-carrying the stocky man into the fort with his arm over my shoulder. Once inside, the man slumped to the ground with his back up against the inner wall and was snoring almost immediately.

Despite the sun having set hours ago, the full moon gave enough light to easily see, and I looked around the inside of the fort for the first time. I found that there really wasn't much to it beyond the walls. Several groups of people huddled together throughout, almost everyone laid out and asleep. In the center of the fort, a faintly glowing crystal hovered at about waist height. That crystal gave the rangers control of the fort, and I saw the two of them passed out beneath it.

I stepped back to the gap in the wall, still not high enough to really warrant a gate, and I realized that I was exhausted too. It was a strange sensation, since I wasn't physically tired. My Constitution had more than doubled over the course of the day, and by now I was probably approaching the sort of conditioning that would have previously been reserved for Olympic Triathletes.

My mind just felt sluggish in a way that the numbers in my status couldn't define, the weariness born of constant threat and staying at the ready for any danger that might appear.

I lowered myself to the ground in the entrance to the fort. Resting my back against the side wall, I stretched my legs across the opening. Anyone entering would have to quite literally trip over me to get inside.

I glanced over the people gathered inside the walls again and wondered what I was doing here. Despite my aversion to heroics, I had somehow ended up as a guardian. Would they still trust me with their safety if they knew everything I had done?

Zeke, stretched out on the ground on the far side of the fort, knew I held few qualms about killing after my actions with the would-be muggers. But even he still trusted that I would keep my word in helping him reach his kids.

I shook off my doubts and returned my attention to the area outside the fort.

With things quiet for the time being, I pulled up my notifications and worked through them.

Level Up! *3

You have reached Level 6 as a Relentless Huntsman. Stat Points automatically distributed. You have 6 free attributes to distribute.
Class Skills Locked.

I hadn't assigned any points since the library back in Squirrel Hill, so my levels had been creeping up since then. I looked through the accumulated experience updates, skimming over the numbers, and raised an eyebrow in surprise.

My largest single-kill experience amounts had been from the two men who had attacked as we passed through downtown. Apparently killing people garnered far more experience than slaying monsters.

I pondered the implications of what that might mean in the long term as I split my free attributes between Perception and Agility again. I still had quite a ways to go before I hit the minimum attributes to unlock the rest of my Class Skills. With the attribute selection confirmed, I looked over my updated status screen.

Status Screen			
Name:	Hal Mason*	Class:	Hunter*
Race:	Human (Male)	Level:	6
Titles			
None			
Health:	240	Stamina:	240
Mana:	230		
Status			
Normal*			
Attributes			
Strength	19 (30)	Agility	29 (60)
Constitution	24 (50)	Perception	26 (40)
Intelligence	23 (40)	Willpower	20 (30)
Charisma	22 (40)	Luck	16

Class Skills			
Hinder	1	Keen Senses	1
On the Hunt	1		
Perks			
Gut Instinct			
Combat Spells			
None			

I swiped away the general status menu and took another look over my Class Skills screen despite all the abilities being grayed out. After a few moments, I closed the window before I could get too frustrated over how helpful those Class Skills might have been throughout the day. At least I had higher than normal attributes to make up for the lack of additional abilities. I'd picked up enough from talking with Zeke and the rangers to understand that everyone with Basic Classes received far fewer attributes per level. I felt fortunate that no one seemed keen to discuss specific attributes.

With no more notifications or windows demanding my attention, I stretched out my awareness with Keen Senses and listened to the night.

Crickets chirped and frogs croaked while other unidentified creatures bubbled and splashed in the surrounding rivers. It sounded like the fullness of nature that might be found in the depths of the wilderness and not at all the usual nighttime sounds for the heart of a city with three hundred thousand residents—though I imagined that population would be significantly reduced after today.

I leaned back and looked up, surprised to find the night sky remarkably clear. The advent of the System had killed anything with electricity, so the light pollution from the city was a thing of the past. I enjoyed the view as a shooting star streaked overhead—probably a satellite unable to maintain orbit without electrical systems to sustain it. Idly, I wondered what had happened to the astronauts on the International Space Station. I imagined if they were able to survive somehow, they would have quite the story to tell.

I closed my eyes and rested, still alert but allowing the stress of the day to fade. Tomorrow would bring new challenges soon enough.

Chapter 11

A warbling voice from within the walls of the fort jerked me back to the present from my relaxed state, and I leapt to my feet with the concern that I had somehow allowed a threat to slip past. The moon still sat high in the sky, though its light was shuttered by thick clouds. I felt as though I hadn't rested long at all.

I quickly located the source of the noise and headed toward two young women who were sitting alone, as far from any other groups as they could get. I kicked Zeke's foot as I jogged by where he slept next to the two rangers.

"Trouble," I said in response to his grumbling question.

As I grew closer to the girls, I heard that the murmuring voice was coming from a girl who sat with her back to me, clutching her knees to her chest while she rocked back and forth in time with her strange incantation. Her companion was facing me, pressing herself back against the wall, and terror was etched across her face as she stared at the chanting woman.

I knelt next to the rocking woman and looked at her friend. "What's going on?"

The terrified friend shook herself at my question, then seemed to see me for the first time. "She does this, this"—she visibly struggled to find an explanation—"thing."

"What does this thing do?"

"I don't know," the woman said, sounding frustrated. "But bad things always happen right after." She grabbed my arm. "Always!"

The chanting woman continued, the words twisting through my ears in a language not of this world. The tones were discordant and listening was almost painful.

Then her tone shifted, and I could almost understand the words pouring from her mouth.

"Twas brillig, and the slithy toves," she murmured.

"Did gyre and gimble in the wabe:

"All mimsy were the borogoves,

"And the mome raths outgrabe."

The rocking girl suddenly stilled, and her voice stopped as she turned her head toward me. Her clenched eyelids opened, but I could only see the whites of her eyes, glowing faintly and bathing the area with ethereal light. A chill ran down my spine as the woman focused her attention on me.

"And, as in uffish thought he stood," the woman chanted in a singsong voice.

"The Jabberwock, with eyes of flame,

"Came wiffling through the tulgey wood,

"And burbled as it came!"

Her arm flashed out and clutched at my shoulder. Her face twisted, desperately imploring me to understand her words.

"Beware the Jabberwock, my son!

"The jaws that bite, the claws that catch!

"Naught vorpal forged, lays under this sun,

"Solely rouged, the manxome foe dispatch!"

With the final word, the ghostly radiance surrounding the girl faded, and she went limp. I lunged forward, catching her before she collapsed completely, and lowered her gently to the ground.

"What the hell was that?" Zeke asked, having caught up to me while everything was going on.

"I have no idea." I nodded toward the other woman. "But her friend says that bad things tend to happen afterward."

The woman nodded, her eyes wide. "She's an Oracle. One of her Class Skills lets her see the outcomes of potential futures."

"And how long do we have before these potential futures come into being?" I asked.

"Not long," said the woman, looking around nervously.

A soft blue light suddenly bathed us in illumination from above. The fort was lit up, and I saw that several people around us had been disturbed by the Oracle's rambling proclamation.

I looked up then over toward the city, searching for the origin of the light. To the east, far above the tallest buildings of downtown Pittsburgh, I found the source. A rectangular glowing field shimmered in the sky, parallel to the ground. From here, I could only tell that it was massive, hundreds of feet in length and width.

The field rippled violently and a long, dark shape snaked through the center of the disturbance, curling and twisting back around its own body. The thing hovered in the air below the portal as if unbound by gravity. The portal's blue light glinted metallically off the sinuous shape as if reflecting from scales that covered the worm-like creature, but it was too dark and distant to make out any more details.

The shadowy shape drifted lower and continued circling until it finally finished emerging from the portal. An instant later, the portal snapped closed, returning the world to darkness.

I sat stunned for a moment and looked at the others around me. The rangers had joined Zeke, and we all shared wide-eyed glances.

"I'm going out on a limb here," I said slowly, "but I'm guessing that was our jabberwock."

Zeke shook his head. "Shit."

The rangers remained mute.

"How do we fight that?" Zeke asked.

I snorted. "I don't think we do. That seems like a whole lot of nasty best avoided."

The big man blinked at me, then pointedly glanced at the unconscious Oracle before looking back at me. "I get the feeling we're not going to get much of a choice."

A loud crash from the distance interrupted our conversation, and I turned back toward downtown. At first I couldn't see anything besides the usual city skyline, but after a moment, the moon finally emerged from behind the clouds, and I froze. With my enhanced perception, I could finally see the buildings of downtown clearly, and I saw a massive creature of nightmare perched on the top of the U.S. Steel Tower.

The creature had an ungainly large head with red glowing eyes. Just below the eyes were a pair of tentacles that hung down like whiskers along either side of a short, stubby nose and a tall, fang-filled maw that slowly gnashed open and closed. A line of spiked scales stuck up along a ridge running down the back of the creature's slender neck, a neck that took up nearly a third of the creature's overall length. The spiked ridge continued onto a thicker, four-limbed torso, then continued along a narrow tail that made up the final third of the lengthy creature. Each of the creature's lanky arms ended in spidery, three-fingered claws. Atop the shoulders for the first set of spindly limbs were a pair of bat-like wings that fluttered sedately as it perched at the edge of the tallest building in Pittsburgh, just above the giant UPMC sign at the top of the building.

The jabberwock threw back its head and let out a warbling screech. The noise pierced my ears, and I dropped to my knees in agony, cupping my hands over my ears in a futile attempt to block the sound. Around me, the others had also fallen to the ground, writhing in pain as the deafening shriek reverberated around us.

Fear Effect Resisted

The notification popped into the corner of my vision as I forced myself back to my feet, and the pain seemed to lessen significantly. I felt moisture trickle from my ears and wiped it away, finding my hands slick with blood. Finally, the horrific noise trailed off, and I watched the jabberwock crawl forward over the building's edge, knocking away the giant M from the UPMC sign. The white letter tumbled out of sight behind the other tall buildings as the creature climbed down the face of the tower. The creature's claws crumbled the structure's surface to dust as they tore gaping rents into the building before it disappeared from view.

The others around me slowly recovered, but it still took several minutes before everyone regained their feet.

"Where did it go?"

"Into the city," I replied.

Distant gunshots echoed rapidly, then a faint scream that suddenly cut off.

Our group moved to the gap in the fort walls and looked out toward downtown. The damage and the fear effect had awakened all of the refugees. I stepped outside the fort to keep watch and avoid their panicked clamoring, but the rangers were eventually able to calm everyone and put people to work strengthening the fort's defenses. That included Carl, who looked haggard but channeled his Mana into the walls again anyways.

Over the next several hours, more gunshots, massive crashes, flashes of red light, and periodic screams broke through the formerly still night as the jabberwock rampaged through the city. In the meantime, the fort's walls rose another two feet and had gained crenellations at regular intervals where there were firing positions from within the walls.

As the sun peeked over the horizon, our respite ended.

A group of a half dozen people broke free from the buildings of the heart of the city, running in our direction. The emerald-scaled jabberwock pursued almost casually out from behind the downtown Wyndham hotel. Bounding forward while standing on its hind legs to glide with its undersized bat wings, the monster stood nearly to the height of the hotel's three-story conference center as it batted the last runner in the group into the air and devoured them with a single chomping bite.

The people screamed, sprinting faster. The creature only chuffed and wiffled, seemingly laughing at the terror it inspired before lunging forward to consume another victim.

An energy beam lanced out from the fort's automated turret and smacked the jabberwork at the base of its neck. The creature drew up short in surprise, forgetting about its victims as it looked around for its attacker. Spotting the turret, the beast's crimson eyes glowed brighter for a second before rays of fire shot from each eye. The beams swept across the corner of the fort and the turret exploded in a massive blast as the walls evaporated under the energy of the attack.

Though I was half a length of the walls away, the explosion picked me up and flung me twenty feet. Even while airborne, my amped perception noted that the jabberwock's attack had a two-part effect. The fiery beams seared through the turret, wall, and the ground as they swept across the area. Then the explosive eruption from wherever the rays touched was a secondary effect that fired in the wake of the primary attack.

Mental note, don't get touched by the rays.

I rolled as my body tumbled into the ground. The movement spread the force of the impact as my body flipped up over my shoulders, and I pushed off, flinging my torso upright as I landed on my feet.

I wiped my dew-slicked hands on my pants before pulling the pistols from the holsters at my hips, then I ran to the northeast. I hoped to get some distance between myself and the fort before making an attempt to lure the beast away. I looked over and saw that the monster was charging after the people again, the runners continuing to flee toward the fort.

The jabberwock hopped onto the Fort Pitt blockhouse with one leg, preparing to use the building's height to push itself up into another gliding bound. Instead, the last remaining structure of the colonial era fort collapsed under the monster's weight, and its leg plunged through the roof of the old building. The creature's momentum instantly stalled as it fell.

Taking advantage of the opportunity, with the jabberwock caught in place, I stopped running and carefully aimed at the beast. Most of the creature's body was protected by dark green scales, but there was one obvious place where I could hurt it. I fired the projectile pistol first, then squeezed the trigger on the beam pistol.

Both attacks landed on target simultaneously, and the jabberwock howled as its right eye exploded from the combined damage. I almost celebrated the creature's cry of pain, but the green health bar above the monster only dropped the barest amount from the attacks.

At least with it half-blinded, maybe we had a chance.

I fired again. This time, my shots glanced off the scales around the hole that had been its eye, failing to cause real damage, though the shots grabbed the beast's attention.

Its ugly head turned toward me as it regarded me with a baleful gaze. Then the sole eye grew bright, and I sprinted as fast as I could. Heat flashed behind me, and I desperately dove forward, expecting the fiery beam to sweep across me any moment.

Instead, the burning sensation at my back cut off suddenly as the jabberwock gave another cry, and I looked back to find that others had taken advantage of my distraction.

The ranger Jared fired his pistol up at the creature from close range, his shots impacting around its face as he aimed for the monster's remaining eye. The jabberwock twisted its head up and away from the attack, protecting the eye but exposing the underside of its neck, where the scales were smaller and more yellow than the larger emerald scales that protected most of the creature.

Zeke had ascended the rubble of the blockhouse, and his giant hammer smacked into the finer scales at the base of the creature's neck, just above where the torso flared out into the wider shoulders that supported the wings and the forward set of arms. The big man drummed his weapon into the same spot several times without seeming to have much effect; then he hesitated, and the head of his hammer glowed.

He spun the glowing weapon in a complete circle overhead before slamming the strike home. Several scales shattered beneath the blow, and shards of shattered scale sprayed out from the impact. The jabberwock howled again, flinching as the two men continued their attacks.

Then Jared's weapon ran out of ammo.

When the pistol stopped firing, the jabberwock cautiously canted its head to the side. Finding the ranger fumbling the reload, the creature looked down and batted Zeke away with a casual swipe of its claws. Blood sprayed in a crimson arc as the giant man was flung several hundred feet by the power of the blow. He impacted with the granite wall of Fort Duquesne before crumpling limply to the ground.

Before Zeke had even landed, the jabberwock bent its long neck and chomped down on the ranger so quickly that the man never got the chance to scream. The jabberwock swallowed then threw back its ungainly head, launching into the piercing screech that had been so debilitating when it first arrived.

Fear Effect Resisted

I resisted the effect again, but I saw those left at the fort were once again prone on the ground as the jabberwock finally managed to free its leg from the wreckage of the blockhouse.

I fired at the creature, emptying both pistols as quickly as I could shoot. The jabberwock turned and advanced toward me with a limp. Far slower than its earlier rush toward the fort, the monster clearly favored the limb that had been caught in the blockhouse.

Taking advantage of the extra time, I stowed both pistols in my Inventory and retrieved my fully loaded and charged backups. Instead of firing right away, I holstered the weapons and pulled out the hybrid rifle. I braced myself into a steady shooting position and pulled the stock of the weapon tight to my shoulder. As I lined up the weapon with the damaged area on the jabberwock's neck, I gently squeezed the trigger.

Nothing happened for a split second, and I almost lowered the weapon to figure out what was wrong.

Before I could react, the weapon whined loudly. Power built over the span of a second, as the coils around the length of the rifled barrel were flooded with Mana. Each ring lit up brightly as it accumulated a full charge. When all the coils were lit, the weapon vibrated in my hands.

115

The stock kicked firmly back into my shoulder as a brilliant column of silver light streaked from the end of the weapon's barrel to split the air. Within the column of white light swirled a bolt of lightning that carried the hybrid weapon's projectile. The lightning and projectile slammed into the base of the monster's neck, at the center of the section where Zeke's ability had shattered the scales. The creature staggered and whined in pain.

I blinked from the afterimage of the weapon's radiant light and looked up at the jabberwock. The damaged area of shattered scales looked larger than it had been. The impact site smoked faintly, and some green ichor dripped from the wound. Hopefully, I glanced above the monster to look at its status.

The green health bar above the creature had only dropped by a finger.

Snarling, I raised the weapon back to my shoulder. Over and over, the hybrid weapon whined and flashed, until the magazine finally ran dry and the rifle clicked on an empty chamber.

I ejected the depleted magazine and stuffed it into my Inventory. I summoned a fully loaded magazine into my open palm and jammed it into the open mag well. Then I cocked the rifle to chamber a new round.

The jabberwock shook itself while I reloaded, and it took advantage of the slack in my attacks to crawl forward once again. It was definitely hurt. The health bar had dropped by about a quarter.

But as I watched, the green health bar floating above the monster ticked back upward as the creature's natural regeneration kicked in.

I glanced at the counter below the hybrid rifle's sights. Only fifteen energy charges remained. I might have nearly a hundred rounds of ammunition, but without energy charges, the weapon wouldn't fire.

I shifted the heavy rifle to my left shoulder and pulled my beam pistol. A shot from the beam pistol into the wounded jabberwock only flickered its health bar, but the climbing health bar halted. I stepped back and counted until the monster's health bar ticked up again.

Counting, I stepped back again as I switched pistols, then I fired the projectile pistol just before the creature's health could go up.

I cycled through all of my weapons as I counted and stepped. Leading the jabberwock away from the park, I continued to wage war on its regeneration. I took one shot with each pistol before I fired a round from the hybrid railgun.

In between shots, I reloaded empty magazines for my Luxor projectile pistol. I frantically pulled ammunition from my inventory, reloaded individual rounds into spare magazines, then stowed everything so I could take another shot.

The jabberwock remained laser-focused on me as I kept up the constant attacks, and it pursued me away from the fort. My constant harassment drew the beast north until I reached Fort Duquesne Boulevard, the street which bordered the northern edges of downtown. I still spaced my shots at regular intervals as I backed up the street, but energy charges on both pistols and the hybrid rifle were getting low.

Then the jabberwock wiffled, that twisted sound I had associated with merciless laughter. It looked down at the leg that it had been limping on and flexed it tentatively before wiffling again.

I realized that I'd been so focused on keeping the chest wound and the creature's overall health from regenerating, the wounded leg had healed itself.

Shit.

I glanced around quickly, knowing I was dead if I stayed in the open. There was nothing to my right. The north side of the street dropped off toward the Allegheny River. On my left, a towering condominium building rose high overhead.

I bolted left. But the building's glass doors seemed impossibly far away. The jabberwock leapt into the air and glided forward, its gruesome head reaching toward me. There was no point trying to open the door. I crashed through the glass as the jabberwock's maw snapped at my heels. Shattered glass cascaded around me, and I struggled to keep moving. Behind me, I heard the jabberwock gnashing. The creature sounded seriously annoyed.

I retreated through the devastated lobby and found the stairs. I ran up several flights and silently thanked the System that the lack of electricity had disabled the building security system.

I exited the stairs on the fourth floor and found a small lounge. Ignoring the clamoring of the jabberwock as it tore into the building after me, I slumped onto a long couch to take stock of my situation and reload my weapons.

One beam pistol was completely out of charges, and the other only had two left. I also only had three charges remaining for the hybrid rifle, so I didn't bother reloading that. I filled the magazines for the Luxor projectile pistols, then slouched as I attempted to relax for what might be the last time.

I chuckled. I'd really managed to piss that thing off from the commotion it continued to make as it ripped through the building. I leaned my head back and winced at something digging into my side. Without looking, I pulled the hybrid weapon ammo case from my belt and almost tossed it aside.

My hand froze, and I sat up sharply, bringing the case up in front of me.

The red case!

Red. Rouge.

My hands shook as I opened the case and looked inside. Six wicked-looking hybrid projectile rounds sat nestled in a clear lattice framework. Each round had a different colored band around the middle, and my eyes were drawn to the one banded in red.

I grabbed the hybrid rifle from my Inventory, ejected the magazine, and cleared the round from the chamber. I stuck the cleared round back into the mag, then put the red specialty round in on top of it.

I still had enough energy for three shots though. At random, I picked the green and orange banded rounds and added them to the magazine before pushing it back into the hybrid rifle and charging it. I closed the red case and returned it to my belt before I got back to my feet.

The building shook as the jabberwock tore through it, growing very close now. I went back into the main hallway and faced the sounds of destruction. A moment later, the jabberwock smashed up through the floor, and it caught sight of me with its good eye. The other eye remained cloudy and unfocused, though clearly healing from my initial attack upon the creature.

I tried hitting it with Hinder, but the creature seemed unaffected by the Class Skill. The massive power difference between us, and the monster's innate resistances, was apparently too great for my ability to overcome.

Without further hesitation, I fired the hybrid rifle. Unlike the previous firings of the weapon, this time the beam of light that struck the jabberwock was a pale green. When the projectile within the beam impacted the monster's snout, a cloud blossomed around the beast's face, and it coughed.

I backed down the hall, away from the jabberwock and the spreading gas cloud that now surrounded it. My movements focused the monster back onto me, and it once again tore through the building toward me.

The hallway walls crumbled around the jabberwock as it clawed its way forward, and the entire building shook as I fired the hybrid rifle again.

The orange beam raised the temperature in the hallway and singed the beige walls into a darkening brown. The projectile flared into a raging inferno that charred the entire forward half of the monster. When the billowing flames reached the gas cloud, the gas flashed into a detonation that slammed the jabberwock's head down through the floor of the hallway. The explosion staggered me, and I stumbled back against the tall window at the end of the hallway.

Then the jabberwock's head tore up through the floor, almost at my feet, and there was nowhere left to run.

It had used so much force to push through the floor that its head bounced off the ceiling before the fanged maw snapped toward me. Ceiling tiles rained down as it lunged. I threw myself backward through the window and leveled the hybrid rifle.

In the instant before I fell, everything seemed to slow. I felt glass slice into the back of my neck as the window shattered around me. The jabberwock's fangs reached closer. And I focused on a singular point as I squeezed the trigger.

But not at the monster's face.

Just below the monster's lunging maw and waving tentacles, I saw charred flesh peeking from the shattered hole in the scales at the base of the jabberwock's neck. The spot where Zeke's Class Skill had left the monster vulnerable. That was where I aimed.

The rifle whined, and a crimson beam shot directly into the spot at the center of where the wound gaped. The projectile punched through the hole left by Zeke's destructive ability, and a ring of red energy lit up the monster's neck from the inside. The brilliant energy glowed beneath the monster's scales as the energy disk sliced cleanly through the cracked and broken scales that protected the monster's neck, leaving intact only the undamaged scales unaffected by Zeke's final attack.

The round had severed the jabberwock's spine from the inside. An internal decapitation.

That was all I saw before my fall cut off the view.

A sense of weightlessness filled me briefly, wind rushing over the back of my head, as I fell forty feet to the ground. Then my body crashed into the paved plaza, driving the breath from my lungs with an audible crack that was equal parts the cobblestones and my spine.

Above me, the lunging of the jabberwock had imparted enough momentum to the monster's head that its own force completed the work all of our attacks had been unable to accomplish. The intact scales were torn free as the severed head catapulted clear of the building and tumbled through the air, falling towards me.

Terror gripped me as it looked like I had survived the monster only to be crushed by the fall of its severed head. The massive skulled crashed down next to me, showering me with shattered paver bits and gore.

I gasped, forcing air into my lungs, as I attempted to breathe normally and eyed my status. A helpful notification informed me that I suffered from a concussion, but the pain that pulsed through my skull made that obvious. Besides that, my status was a mess of broken bones and internal damage, but the timers for each detrimental effect slowly ticked down. I felt the System heal my broken body now that combat had ended.

Several minutes passed before I was able to pull myself from the cratered courtyard. I stowed the depleted hybrid rifle in my Inventory, then sat up and cradled my pounding head in my hands. When the throbbing in my brain subsided, I crawled tentatively to my feet.

I kicked the head of the jabberwock, which did nothing except bruise my toe, but it made me feel better. Then I attempted to loot the monster.

I received a stack of Jabberwock Fangs that were the length of my arm, a half dozen Jabberwock Claws that stood nearly as tall as my six-foot height, and a pile of Jabberwock Scales that looked as though they would make great armor plates. The final loot items I received were a pair of Ruby Jabberwock Eyes that glowed orange and red like the dying embers of a campfire.

After I pulled everything into my Inventory, I looked at the building above me where I could see the torso of the beast hanging slightly out of the fourth floor. I was thankful I hadn't needed to climb up there to loot the beast.

When I looked at my inventory, I noticed that it had gained capacity. Instead of the initial five-by-five grid, my holding space was now six-by-six. That was a welcome discovery, especially now that I had looted the jabberwock bits.

I left the corpse and headed back toward the park and what was left of the fort.

Even at my slow pace, I soon caught sight of the damaged structure. Smoke wafted up from the corner of the fort where the turret had been, but all that remained of the walls there was a pile of debris. Just beyond the rubble, along the southeast section of the wall, several people stood together in a small clump.

I pushed my way through them and found Chrystal on her knees, attempting to hold together the ruin of Zeke's torso. The big man was in a bad way. The jabberwock's claws had torn deep into his chest and stomach. Exposed bits of broken ribs stuck up from the gaping slashes that leaked blood and other fluids to pool on the ground beneath him.

I glanced at the health bar above Zeke's head and found it nearly depleted. Even as I crouched beside him, the bar ticked downward from the continued bleeding and internal damage.

"Nobody has any healing spells or Class Skills," said a distraught Chrystal. "We can't stop the Bleed effect."

"Shit." I didn't have any words for the situation.

Zeke gasped with each breath, teeth gritted against the pain. Sweat glistened on the dark skin of his shaved head. He looked at me, and I saw the knowledge in his eyes that he wouldn't make it. With one hand, he clutched my arm weakly.

"My kids, Hal," Zeke said, his voice faint and raspy. "Please make sure my kids are safe."

"I'll do what I can," I said. "I promise."

Quest Accepted: Reach Montour High School and discover the fate of the Thomas children.

Zeke nodded at me appreciatively, and I knew he'd seen the prompt too. Words had power in this changed world.

Then Zeke glanced to the side, and his eyes grew distant as he watched his health count down with each tick of the Bleed effect. The bar above his head bottomed out, and Zeke's arm fell limply to the ground.

I stood and pushed my way out of the gathered crowd. I strode several paces away, filled with the need to put some distance between other people and myself. I stared at the Pittsburgh skyline without really seeing it as the sun finally crested above the horizon.

I had watched people die before. I had even seen the deaths of people I'd fought beside, some of them going out far more violently than Zeke.

That thought reminded me of the explosions that had torn through a building on the other side of the world. The blast that had wiped out my squad and left me half crippled. I had never really come to terms with that.

The VA docs labeled it survivor's guilt.

They were wrong. I didn't feel guilty that my life had continued. My conflicted emotions were the result of my inability to fight back. My injuries had merited a medical discharge, so I'd never returned to the battlefield and never found out which group or warlord had set us up to die.

This time it would be different, I promised myself.

I looked at the typically overcast western Pennsylvania sky. No sign of the midnight portal remained where the jabberwock had emerged into our world. The monster had never used a portal ability throughout the rest of the time it had been here, so someone, or something, else had brought it here. Probably the same aliens that had turned our planet into this Dungeon World.

Someday I would find out. And then make them pay.

Chapter 12

We buried Zeke and the remains of the others under the corner of the fort, in the trench left behind by the jabberwock's beam attack. I slipped Zeke's gear into my Inventory as we moved the bodies, and no one either noticed or cared enough to say anything. When the dead had been placed, Carl applied his skills to reform the walls over top them.

It took some time for the walls to completely cover the area, and I pulled up my notifications while I waited.

Congratulations. You survived an entire day! You humans really are an excellent bunch. Only 60% of you died yesterday. We are impressed. Have a cookie. And some experience. Remember, monster spawning will increase over the next week.

The message popped up first when I reviewed my accumulated notifications for the morning, though I wasn't particularly surprised by the contents of the message. If things like the jabberwock had portaled in across the world on top of the increasing monster spawns, then the stated death toll was certainly conceivable.

Congratulations!
You have helped kill a Young Jabberwock (Level 52).
+24,840 XP (XP apportioned according to damage done)

If that was a youth version, I would hate to see it all grown up.

Title Gained
For your continuous actions in dispatching higher leveled foes by exploiting vulnerable portions of their defenses, you have been awarded the title "Sharp Eyed." Critical hit chance increased by 10% and all critical damage dealt is increased by a further +10%.

Congratulations!

For achieving your first title, you receive a bonus +5,000 XP.

Level Up! * 2

You have reached Level 8 as a Relentless Huntsman. Stat Points automatically distributed. You have 4 free attributes to distribute.
Class Skills Locked.

The Level gains were definitely slowing down, and I was still blocked from accessing my Class Skills. If I hadn't picked the Head Start perk off the bat, I would probably have been in real trouble. I might never have even made it to the Shop to get geared up.

Then without the hybrid rifle and the specialty ammo, I would certainly be dead.

I pulled up my status sheet and did mental math with the attribute requirements. I had a ways to go before I needed to spread out my Attributes beyond Agility and Perception, so I dropped two points into each of my primary attributes.

Then I looked at the Title section and considered the honorific within. I really didn't want anyone digging into my status to consider how I might have obtained it. With a thought, the Title noted itself as hidden.

Status Screen			
Name:	Hal Mason*	Class:	Hunter*
Race:	Human (Male)	Level:	8

Titles			
Sharp Eyed (Title hidden)*			
Health:	300	Stamina:	300
Mana:	270		
Status			
Normal*			
Attributes			
Strength	21 (30)	Agility	37 (60)
Constitution	30 (50)	Perception	30 (40)
Intelligence	27 (40)	Willpower	22 (30)
Charisma	26 (40)	Luck	16
Class Skills			
Hinder	1	Keen Senses	1
On the Hunt	1		
Perks			
Gut Instinct			

Spells
None

By the time Carl had finished with his fixes to the walls, the sun had climbed the sky and my status updates were long completed.

Satisfied that the defenses were rebuilt, I walked over to the plaza that held the concentric circles of the now-empty basin for a large fountain. Located at the tip of the peninsula that jutted out into the conjunction of the three rivers of Pittsburgh, the point would normally be packed with couples and families on a sunny spring morning like today. Yet I stood alone as I debated my next moves. I needed to plan which Shop would be most in line with the route I needed to follow in order to reach Zeke's kids.

My first option was to head west and cross the Allegheny River, then make a stop at the Shop that my map marked as inhabiting the former River's Casino. I saw two problems with that option. The first problem was that I would need to cross the Ohio River afterward, and the closest route, across the West End Bridge, looked like a poor choice. The bridge was a twisted wreck that sloped down into the river on either side of a large gap in the middle of the bridge.

The second problem was highlighted by the unusual fireworks that exploded intermittently above the Casino after the jabberwock's death. Whoever launched them likely hadn't wanted to attract the monster's attention, but the explosives had to be System tech. I'd never heard of fireworks that spelled out "Shop here" in hovering, glittering lights before they burned out. To me, that said someone from off-world probably held the Shop there now.

My desire to avoid alien complications only left my other option—head south and work my way up to the top of Mount Washington, where Pittsburgh's third Shop was located in Saint Mary of the Mount Church. With the bridge to the west out, that was my best option even though I wasn't looking forward to the climb.

I hoped my accumulated loot would net me enough Credits that I could afford some spells. If either Zeke or I had been able to afford even a simple healing spell, the big man would still be alive.

On top of the spells, I needed more efficient transportation. I'd spent plenty of miles hoofing it back in my military days and wanted something that could get me around a bit more quickly.

I left the fountain and walked past the fort as I headed east to the nearest still-standing bridges.

"You're leaving us?" Chrystal asked as she hurried after me.

I stopped and looked back at the ranger with a shrug. "Zeke gave me a quest."

"Where are you going?"

I pointed vaguely to the west. "Gotta check where his kids went to school and find out what happened to them."

"Oh. We really hoped you'd stay."

"Sorry," I said unapologetically. "There's really nothing for me here, and I owe Zeke at least that much."

"I understand," Chrystal replied. "I guess this is goodbye then."

I nodded. "Goodbye, Chrystal."

I headed south and east from the fort until I left the park and found my way back to the city streets. Cars still littered the streets, but surprisingly few people were out and about. Likely the whole jabberwock incident had encouraged people to leave the area if they could. I walked along Fort Pitt Boulevard and continued east until I reached the Smithfield Street Bridge.

I turned south onto the wide pedestrian walkway that ran along either side of the bridge over the Monongahela River. I crossed the wide river without incident, thankful that the catfish monsters from the previous day remained out of sight.

They'd smelled terrible.

Once across the bridge, I turned left on West Carson Street and followed it until I found a side street that wound up the side of Mount Washington. In typical Pittsburgh fashion for excess, Mount Washington wasn't an actual mountain but a very large hill. Of course, the hill was both steep enough and tall enough that multiple tunnels ran through it, so maybe it wasn't a complete exaggeration.

I grumbled to myself again about the lack of vehicular transportation as I climbed the steep incline. Even with my increased Constitution, the hill was a hike.

I took a chance by going off road halfway up the hill. A narrow footpath traveled more straight uphill than the winding road, so I followed it instead. Other than the half dozen easily dispatched rabbits with razor-sharp teeth that swarmed at me from some bushes alongside the trail, the shortcut proved worth it.

After a few more twists and a turn up another side street, I reached the road regarded as the most scenic view of the city. The length of Grandview Avenue ran along the crest of Mount Washington and several cement platforms made up overlooks that jutted out from the hillside to provide commanding views of the city below. I stepped out onto the Upper Incline Scenic Overlook and gazed down at the city.

Far below, on the far side of the river, I saw the raised walls of Fort Duquesne and the tiny people who moved through the park. I wondered if anyone up here had watched the jabberwock's rampage through the city and the fight that ensued.

In the daylight, I could clearly make out the damage left on the U.S. Steel Tower by the jabberwock. The top of the building had crumbled in where the creature had crawled across it, and the remaining letters of U, P, and C hung unevenly, as if about to follow the M in tumbling to the ground.

A haze of smoke drifted around the tall buildings of downtown, the result of several smoldering buildings throughout the city. Gunshots still echoed intermittently as people fought for their lives against the monster spawns and each other.

I pushed away from the railing and left the overlook. The longer it took to reach the Shop and get transportation, the higher the likelihood of failing my quest.

The hill rose slightly as I followed the wide sidewalk that ran alongside Grandview Avenue. It wasn't long before I found the street blocked off by a line of cars tipped onto their sides at an intersection near the crest of the hill, just before I reached the location of the Shop. Placed bumper to bumper, the vehicles formed an effective makeshift barricade that ran from the edge of the sharp-off at the edge of the hill toward the community center building on the corner, then on out of sight as the wall continued around the block.

Over the top of the barricade, several nervous individuals watched my approach. As I got closer, I saw that they were all armed. I had a brief flashback to my arrival at the fort the previous evening as I kept my empty hands away from my holstered weapons.

"Hello, the wall," I said loudly in greeting.

Several of the people looked at each other nervously, all of them glancing at a middle-aged man toward the center of the wall.

"What do you want?" The man's voice was weary and filled with distrust.

"I just want to use the Shop and continue on my way," I said. "I'm not here to cause any trouble."

"How do you know about the Shop?" If anything, the suspicion in the voice had grown sharply.

"It's marked on a map I got from another Shop." I pointed toward the northeast, in the general direction of the Cathedral of Learning.

"There are other Shops?"

"Yes," I replied. "Three throughout the city, and others spread around in larger towns."

"Oh," said the man, who regarded me intently for a moment then waved me forward. "Fine, come on up."

I was directed to a section of the makeshift wall where the vehicles weren't as close together as they initially appeared. Instead of being in a straight line, two of the cars had been angled to create a slight gap that wasn't visible from a straight-on view. The gap was only large enough for me to squeeze through when I turned sideways.

Once inside the walls, I saw that several pickup trucks had been backed up against the inside of the vehicular walls. The truck beds gave a raised fighting platform, high enough for the guards inside the walls to peer out over them. The height advantage would allow them to have clear fields of fire for the futuristic rifles they carried.

More armed individuals were waiting for me inside, previously hidden from view by the walls. Several teens were detailed to escort me to the nearby church, and I caught sight of another one running ahead, presumably to let whoever was in charge know about my arrival. By the time I was escorted to the church itself, several people had gathered outside the corner of the gothic brick building. Their leader was clearly the black-robed priest in their center. The priest was an older man with graying hair and a deeply lined face.

"Greetings, Adventurer," said the priest. "I am Father McCulley."

"Hal Mason. What do you mean by Adventurer?" I asked with my brow furrowed. That was the second time I had been called by that term. The Shopkeeper had first addressed me with that moniker.

The priest nodded warmly. "That is the socially acceptable term under this new System for those who brave the dangers outside of the Safe Zones."

"I didn't know that," I replied.

The priest sighed. "There is much we are all learning about this new world."

"I haven't had a chance to read the guidebook as much as I would like," I said.

"*Thrasher's Guide*?" At my nod, Father McCulley continued. "It does have quite a bit of helpful information. I would recommend making the time to study it thoroughly."

The priest asked about my experiences so far under the System, and I answered his questions honestly. Though I tried to gloss over actually killing the jabberwock, the perceptive priest still figured it out.

"So that was you?" Father McCulley eyed me with speculation. "What was that thing?"

"A jabberwock," I admitted. "Several who fought beside me did not survive, but their sacrifices led to the creature's death."

"We saw part of the battle from here." Father McCulley gestured to the overlook across the street from where we stood. "It is fortunate that you killed the monster, otherwise it may have continued to grow even stronger."

I hadn't thought of that aspect, but the priest was right. The more people the creature killed, the stronger it would have become as it accumulated experience, just like us. And that was true for every monster in this System.

"Well," I finally said, "I'll do what I can to keep the monsters I find from getting any stronger."

"What do you seek here?" Father McCulley asked.

"I need to use the Shop to purchase some working transportation. I have a quest that requires something more effective than my own two feet."

"That's fair." The priest nodded and looked at the others who had gathered around us and had listened intently as we talked. "I'm satisfied with this young man. I have no issues with him being admitted to the church for use of the Shop."

The others seemed to agree, and I was quickly directed through the double-wide arch-over front doors and into the church.

You Have Entered a Safe Zone (Saint Mary of the Mount Church)
Mana flows in this area are stabilized. No monster spawning will happen.
This Safe Space includes:
Village of Mount Washington, Pittsburgh City Center
A Hospice (+10% Negative Effect Recovery)
The Shop

The interior of the church was beautiful. The morning sunlight streamed into the sanctuary through massive stained-glass windows all around the long hall. At the front of the sanctuary, a deacon chanted in Latin as he guided a small crowd through Mass.

The glowing multifaceted silver crystal hovered in the aisle between the final row of pews at the rear of the sanctuary. The brilliant colors of the stained glass windows reflected from the crystal's shimmering surface in a kaleidoscopic effect that lit up the back of the large room.

I stepped up to the crystal and placed my hand on its cool surface. Instantly, I found myself at the entrance of the same Shop I had visited previously.

Ryk waited beside the threshold and nodded respectfully to me. "Welcome back, Adventurer Mason."

"Thank you, Ryk," I said. "I have some stuff to unload if you want to get to haggling."

"Of course, sir," replied Ryk as he directed me toward the stasis table with a gesture.

I emptied my Inventory onto the table. I hesitated as Zeke's gear drew a sharp glance from Ryk, but he was quickly distracted by the loot from the jabberwock. With the shopkeeper focused on the monster loot, I had second thoughts and put Zeke's hammer back into my Inventory on impulse.

"You have had an interesting time, haven't you?" Ryk asked rhetorically as he picked up one of the shimmering gemstone-like eyes of the jabberwock and peered at it through an eyepiece that looked similar to a jeweler's loupe.

"I'll offer you fifty-two thousand Credits," said Ryk as he stored the eyepiece and returned the eye to the table.

"Sixty thousand," I countered automatically.

"Fifty-five," said Ryk.

"Fifty-seven," I replied. "And you'll tell me who might create a portal for a jabberwock raid boss to show up on the first day of System integration."

Ryk's eyes narrowed, and he looked at me intently. "Fine."

The Credits appeared in my account notifications as the items spread over the table disappeared. I felt a slight twinge of guilt as Zeke's remaining equipment vanished, but even I hadn't met the strength requirements for the armor. No one at the fort could have used the gear either, and this way it would do me some good.

"The information wouldn't have cost much in any case," said Ryk. "It's standard practice for the Galactic Council to move additional monsters to a new Dungeon World in order to increase the variety of creatures spawning there." Despite the shopkeeper's casual tone, his demeanor displayed an unusual tension.

"I see," I said carefully.

The Shopkeeper nodded once, clearly relieved that I understood the gravity of the information.

I certainly understood. The beings responsible for the jabberwock were the same ones who controlled the System and the blue message boxes that had appeared each morning so far. The beings who had made my planet a Dungeon World. Those entities may as well be deities with how many orders of magnitude their power exceeded mine. I understood that.

But now I knew. Now, I had a target.

"Thanks," I said as I forced myself into a cheerful expression. "How about we look at some transportation options next?"

"That sounds like an excellent suggestion," replied Ryk.

The quadruped shopkeeper beckoned me to follow as he led the way down a hallway and into a spacious room with a complex array of machinery hanging from the ceiling far above. The air smelled faintly of ozone, oil, and metal. Ryk stopped just inside the door, beside a console that stuck out from the wall.

"This is what we call 'The Garage,'" explained the shopkeeper proudly. "The hard-light projectors in the ceiling will allow you to simulate any vehicle in our inventory smaller than a frigate-class starship."

"I doubt I can afford anything that large," I said.

Ryk shrugged and smiled. "Maybe not today, but there's always the future."

I stepped up to the console and looked at the available options. There were many.

Monster trucks with tires taller than me. Hovering jetcycles. Land skimmers that could reach a respectable altitude. Personal jetpacks. Armored dune buggies. Motorcycles that could turn into armored mecha.

I spent far too much time cycling through the possibilities and test drove several vehicles until I found a few comfortable options within my price range. I eventually settled on a heavily armored off-road motorcycle that was popular with lower ranked Hakarta mercenary companies for their rugged performance in hostile terrain at a reasonable cost. The low-slung bike had wide, thickly ridged tires that were only slightly more narrow than the body of the bike itself. The rider sat just ahead and only slightly above the rear tire, behind a blocky engine housing covered in thick armor plates. The front tire extended out from the front armor plates enough to make turning and climbing steep inclines possible.

The sole upgrade I took to the rugged vehicle was the ability to fit it into my Inventory. The upgrade used up one of the bike's hard points that would normally be used to link weapons or specialized equipment, but I couldn't afford anything flashy now, and the ability to pull the bike in my System storage outweighed the cost of the Nano Garage Module. While the stored bike would take up two spaces in my Inventory, I thought that was better than having someone try to run off with the thing.

The bike also had an optional, but strongly recommended, connection for a Neural Link that would allow me to remotely control the bike from a short distance away. I added the bike and a relatively inexpensive Neural

Link to my virtual shopping cart before I asked Ryk to guide me back to the main floor of the shop.

I restocked my munitions and added the full Human Genome Treatment to my purchases, both scrubbing defective genes from my DNA and optimizing my current genetic code. The ammunition included a full set of the specialty rounds for the hybrid rifle, each in their own color-coded magazine for easy identification. The ammo was significantly more expensive than the standard rounds, but I wanted to be prepared if I ran into any more creatures that would normally have been far out of my league.

Then I rectified my lack of healing options by adding the most basic healing spell I could find to my shopping list.

Minor Healing (I)

Effect: Heals 20 Health per casting.

Target must be in contact during healing. Cooldown 60 seconds.

Cost: 20 Mana.

Once I had some capacity for healing myself and others, I spent time browsing through offensive spells that I could afford. I needed a spell that dealt damage at a distance and played to my strengths. While I had Hinder for enemies who managed to reach close range, I wanted something that could help keep space between those enemies and me while I whittled them down with my accurate weapons attacks. Finally, I found something that met those needs.

Frostbolt (I)

Effect: Creates a Frost bolt from the user's Mana, which can be directed to damage a target. The dart does 10 Ice damage and slows the target by 2%. Slow effect stacks up to three times (6%). Cooldown 10 seconds.
Cost: 25 Mana.

Finally, I added a pair of significantly cheaper utility spells to my repertoire. *Cleanse* and *Create Water* seemed inherently useful and were listed as "strongly recommended" for those new to the adventuring profession.

I reviewed my list, sighed at the total amount, then looked at Ryk before I confirmed my selections.

"I think the only reason you cut me such a good deal when we haggle is that you know I'm just going to turn around and spend it all here anyways," I said wryly.

Ryk shrugged innocently, but the hint of a smirk tugged at the corner of his mouth.

I sighed dramatically and locked in my purchases, then watched as the Credits drained from my account. The shopkeeper looked at me with a wordless question, and I nodded to show I was prepared for the changes to come. Darkness crept in at the edges of my vision, and I blacked out for a moment.

An instant later, or so it seemed, I opened my eyes to find myself seated near the entrance of Ryk's Shop.

"Good, you're awake," said Ryk. "How does the Genome Treatment and Neural Link feel?"

My vision was slightly sharper, noticeable even on top of the improvements already granted by my Keen Senses Class Skill. The treatment had resolved any minor genetic flaws throughout my body, but it seemed most notable in my vision, even though my eyes had been close to perfect before. I stood and felt as if my point of view had shifted slightly upward. I looked at myself in the reflection of the display cases and found a more ruggedly handsome version of myself staring back at me.

The process had even removed the scars from my face, and I ran a hand over the unblemished skin of my jaw in wonder!

I was still me, just better looking and a little taller.

I could also feel the connection that linked me to my new bike in the back of my mind. With a thought, I called up the stats for both the implant in my head and the bike that rested in my Inventory.

Tier V Neural Link

Neural link may support up to 4 connections.
Current connections: Rudianos Class IV Outrider
Software Installed: Rich'lki Fire-wall Class IV, Rudianos Class V Controller

Rudianos Class IV Outrider

Core: Class IV Hephaestus Mana Engine
CPU: Class E Xylik Core CPU
Armor Rating: Tier V
Hard Points: 2 (1 Used for Nano Garage Module)
Soft Points: 2 (1 Used for Neural Link)
Optional: Neural Link for Remote Activation
Battery Capacity: 60/60

Satisfied that everything appeared to be in order, I looked back at Ryk.

"Everything seems great so far," I said, then looked at my remaining Credit balance. "Except my wallet."

Ryk chuckled at my complaint and ushered me toward the exit.

A flash of light, and I found myself back in the sanctuary. One of the teens from my escort earlier leaned against the wall as he waited for me. When I appeared, he pushed off the wall and beckoned me to follow him out of the church without disturbing the ongoing Mass.

I walked after the youth and left the church through the front doors. Once outside, I found the sun directly overhead. I said some quick goodbyes and thanked the young man who escorted me to the car barricade at the opposite side of the defensive structure from where I'd entered. I squeezed out through the small gate and waved to the defenders as I activated the new bike from my Inventory.

The sturdy vehicle appeared next to me on the street, and I swung a leg over it before I sank down into the low-riding seat.

The engine started with a touch and rumbled quietly. I enjoyed the gentle vibration for a moment before I punched in coordinates on the small terminal built into the center of the handlebars. The screen was a combined navigation and targeting system, but I didn't currently have any weapons paired with the bike. Once my destination was set, I revved the throttle and coasted down the street. I let the gentle grade of the downhill slope increase my speed naturally and swerved the bike from sidewalk to sidewalk as I got a feel for how the bike handled. I enjoyed having a clear street for once, as most of the vehicles in the area had clearly been added to the barricade that defended the church at the top of the hill.

I found the clutter in the roadway increased significantly after a few blocks as I wound my way down several streets toward the on-ramp for Interstate 376. Once on the interstate, I really opened up the throttle on the bike as I motored down the shoulder of the highway. Only a few times was I required to zig or zag my way through the snarled traffic of empty vehicles that littered the interstate.

Overall, I was impressed with the way the bike handled and glad I'd picked it up. It had power, speed, and responsiveness. I was curious to see how it would do off-road, but I wasn't in any hurry to test that out. I was just happy not to be walking everywhere.

It was a relatively short trip after I made it onto the interstate. About ten minutes later, I took the ramp onto I-79 North. I jumped off the highway at the next exit, then continued north on a road that ran parallel to the freeway.

I was a bit surprised that nothing had tried ambushing me during the trip, but as I neared the high school and heard the echoes of gunfire in the direction I was heading, I realized that nothing would ever be easy. The sounds of combat intensified as I neared the school, and it became obvious that a serious fight was taking place.

I ignored a gate with a Do Not Enter sign and cut across a grassy field with a gentle incline that sloped upward toward the school. Cresting the ridge, I found a school bus jammed across the rear entrance to the building and completely blocking the doors. I steered my bike onto the road that circled the building and followed it toward the main entrance.

When I rounded the corner, I braked to a stop as I took in the scene.

Two dark red fire engines—Moon Run Fire-Rescue emblazoned across their sides in gold letters—were pulled across the road that divided the two main high school buildings. A firefighter knelt on top of the tank with his hands glowing blue. It looked as if the man was channeling water directly into the tank.

Two more firefighters in bunker gear manned a hose that blasted a fierce jet of water into a canine shape that was bowled over by the force of the impact and tumbled a dozen or so yards before it skidded to a stop. The firefighters with the hose shifted the forceful stream of water to bat away another of the lanky pack of creatures that circled the area.

Between the two fire engines, a Pennsylvania State Police cruiser closed the gap. Two uniformed troopers stood in front of it with service pistols out, and they fired at any of the beasts that got too close. I could tell the standard firearms weren't doing much, if any, damage. The weapons were the source of the gunshots I'd heard as I approached.

I counted eight of the beasts, and on closer examination, they looked like coyotes. Unusually aggressive and larger than typical coyotes from before the System came online. Coyotes also didn't normally hunt in packs, but things hadn't been normal since the blue boxes started floating in my vision.

I wished briefly that I could have afforded a weapons system for the bike before I throttled up and steered at the battered coyote regaining its feet in a large puddle of water. It never saw me coming and only managed a sharp yelp as my front tire impacted it.

The crunch of snapped bones was faintly audible with each thump of my wheels as I rolled over the creature and left it broken in my wake.

The other coyotes heard the death of their packmate, and three split off after me. I turned sharply to avoid hitting the building and accelerated away.

I pulled a pistol and carefully aimed and fired over my shoulder as the canines pursued. My route led them past the stadium, then around the elementary school building as I controlled my speed to keep the pack interested enough to chase without really gaining ground. In between shots with the energy pistol, I cast my new Frostbolt spell for the first time.

With a few words and a rush of Mana, a jagged shard of ice about the size of a crayon materialized in front of my hand and shot directly toward my target. When it impacted the chest of the nearest coyote, the shard sank partly into its chest, and a white sheen of frost spread out around the wound. The coyote slowed, and its packmates quickly dashed past it.

I somehow managed to hit with most of my pistol shots and all of the Frostbolts. All of those points placed into Agility and Perception were paying off as I chipped away at my pursuers.

I had put enough shots into one coyote to kill it, and a second had been wounded badly enough that it limped far behind as I finished a lap of the complex. Since my beam pistol was over half empty, I swapped it for the full one from my Inventory as I stopped my bike and dismounted.

I set myself into a two-handed shooting stance as the third coyote rushed at me, and I dumped charges into the beast's muzzle until it face-planted into the ground, skidding to a halt several paces from me. Blood leaked from the fallen animal's ruined maw and it wheezed out a dying gasp before it went still.

Only a single creature remained following me, the one I had first used Frostbolt upon. The injured coyote had almost reached me, so I holstered the pistol and drew out my melee weapons.

With its front leg already wounded by my earlier pistol fire and Frostbolts, I used Hinder to slow the coyote even further and quickly dispatched the beast. I cleaned the blades of my weapons on the coyote's fur before I looted the bodies and remounted my bike.

I returned to the front of the school, where I found that the fight had devolved into another melee. One of the firefighters who had manned the hose lay still next to the engine, while the other rolled across the ground in a desperate attempt to keep from being mauled by the coyote on top of him.

The firefighter who had been on top of the engine now wildly swung a fire axe in an attempt to keep two other coyotes from piling onto the prone firefighter.

The final coyote was menacing one of the uniformed troopers, who fired at it with a standard firearm from close range. The coyote flinched with each shot but still stalked closer. The other trooper was on the ground behind them, one arm hanging limply as he attempted to crawl away.

The flailing axe seemed to keep the pair of coyotes at bay and the wrestling coyote didn't seem to be making much progress with the heavy material of the firefighter's turnout gear, so I headed to assist the deputy.

When I reached the coyote, I jumped from the seat of my still-moving bike and drew my knife as I landed on the back of the unusually large canine. I wrapped my left arm around the neck of the beast as I jammed the knife into the side of its head.

The coyote bucked then rolled onto its back, slamming me into the ground as it tried to dislodge me. I wrapped my legs around the coyote's torso and dug in my heels as I continued to stab my knife into the beast's neck. With every thrust, hot blood ran over my hand, and the creature's thrashing grew slowly weaker until it finally lay limp on top of me.

With a groan, I pushed the corpse off me and stood to find the wide-eyed trooper gaping at me. He was an older man with a deeply lined face and salt-and-pepper hair trimmed close on the sides.

"Pick your jaw up off the floor," I snapped. "We have work to do."

The pair of coyotes had gained the upper hand on the firefighter with the axe and had taken the man to the ground. One animal had the haft of the axe in its mouth, locked in a tug-of-war with the firefighter, who had managed to keep the weapon in his grip so far. The other coyote had its jaws locked onto the man's ankle, pulling him in the opposite direction.

My right hand was still covered in gore, so I pulled the pistol from my left hip with my off hand. The Luxor thundered as I put a round into the side of the coyote tugging on the axe, and it yipped sharply in pain as it jumped back and released its grip.

Before it could attack anyone further, I fired several more times. Each impact of the projectile rounds staggered the coyote until it finally fell over dead.

With the axe freed, the firefighter swung it at the coyote clutching his ankle. The blade of the axe sank deep into the back of the canine's head, and it instantly let go of the firefighter's leg. The coyote tried to jerk away, but the axe stayed lodged in the bone of its skull, and the beast only managed to drag the firefighter as it attempted to back away.

I activated Hinder again, since the coyote remained close enough, and the creature slowed further. I fired the Luxor once, and the round sank deep into the rear leg, which collapsed under the impact. The struggling firefighter used the opportunity to stand, and he pulled the axe free of the creature before slamming it back down into the beast's head.

I left the firefighter to pummel the crippled coyote and headed toward the only other fight that still continued. The last pair of combatants were locked together as they rolled across the ground. The weaponless firefighter clutched the coyote so tightly that the beast couldn't get enough of a purchase on the thick material of the firefighter's bunker gear.

That left me with a dilemma.

I couldn't shoot the coyote because the round might pass through the monster and hit the firefighter. I also couldn't stab the coyote, because the two were flailing so uncontrollably that I'd be just as likely to stab the person instead.

With a sigh, I stepped up beside them and hit the coyote with Hinder. Then I wound my leg back and levered a full speed punt into the back of the coyote as the pair rolled around. The coyote yelped at the sharp pain delivered by my armored boot, and I kicked it again. And again. I felt ribs break beneath my foot on the second blow, so I continued. Over and over.

I kicked the coyote to death by breaking its spine and crushing its torso.

The firefighter managed to roll away from the dying beast, but not before getting covered in gore that leaked from the coyote's mouth. Once free, the firefighter whipped off the helmet to reveal sweat-damped, shoulder-length black hair before the woman doubled over and emptied her stomach in revulsion.

By the time I finished off the coyote, the other one was dead too, and I realized that I had gained an audience.

A nurse in scrubs now knelt over the prone firefighter, but the rest of the newcomers watched me warily. The older trooper seemed to have recovered his composure and appeared cautious but relaxed. The injured trooper had made it to his feet and joined the group, but he still had his gun out at his side.

I looked at the nervous man and wryly raised an eyebrow as I glanced at the gun. I was pretty sure that with my Constitution, he wouldn't kill me with a single shot, and I wouldn't give him the chance for any more.

I cast the *Cleanse* spell on myself for the first time, and a rush of Mana swept over me from head to toe. I felt all of the gore evaporate from where it had clung to my hand. My whole body felt refreshed, and even my teeth felt as if they had been freshly brushed.

That spell had been worth every Credit.

Especially with the amazed expressions of everyone watching me. I couldn't hold back my amusement as I grinned. To further my demonstration that things were no longer the same, I walked over to my bike and stored it in my Inventory. The Nano Garage Module upgrade just paid for itself.

If I had amazed them with my ability to be instantly clean, disappearing the bike may have broken them.

"So who's in charge here?" I asked the group.

"I guess it's me," said the older trooper with a shrug as he stepped forward and extended a hand. "Trooper Nelson."

"Hal Mason," I replied and gave him a firm handshake.

"Thank you for your help," Nelson said. "I think things would have gotten much worse if you hadn't arrived when you did."

I nodded uncomfortably in acknowledgement. He was right.

"Well, what brings you here?" Nelson asked.

"I need to talk to a couple of students who were supposed to be here."

"What for?" the other trooper interjected suspiciously.

"I was with their dad yesterday," I replied.

"Oh, and you just need to take them to him," accused the trooper.

"No," I said solemnly and looked the man in the eyes. "I need to tell them that he didn't make it."

That shut the man up, and he turned away in embarrassment, unable to meet my gaze. He stomped over to the nurse, who had helped the injured firefighter up to his feet and asked that she look at his wounded arm.

Several school officials joined the discussion, and the topic turned to the System. I quickly explained everything I had learned so far. This conversation about Shops and loot was becoming a well-rehearsed spiel as often as I repeated it.

After the school officials had been brought up to speed, one of them guided me inside and sent someone off to find the two Thomas kids.

I could only imagine the pain I was about to bring into their world. With their mother long gone, I couldn't fathom how important their father had been to them.

It wasn't long before the pair were brought to where I waited inside the school's main entrance. The two teenagers were dressed casually in jeans and

T-shirts, but they shared their father's athletic build, and I easily saw the family resemblance to Zeke in their faces. When they reached me, the school official stepped away and left me alone with the kids for my unenviable task.

"Gabrielle and Jordan Thomas?" I asked. Their father had called them Gabby and Jordie in his stories, but I wouldn't presume that familiarity, not now and not like this.

"Yes," replied Gabrielle with hesitation.

"Please have a seat." I pointed the pair to a nearby bench.

The pair looked around nervously. Their eyes flicked between me, the school official who waited nearby, and back. From Jordan's expression, I could tell the young man knew something was gravely wrong.

Once they were seated, I took a deep breath and looked them in the eyes. "I'm sorry, there's no easy way to say this. Your father is dead."

"What?" Gabrielle blinked as she processed my words.

Tears slipped from the corners of her eyes and she leaned against her brother. Jordan wrapped his arm protectively around the young woman's shoulders, pulling his sister into a hug as she broke down.

Then he looked at me fiercely. "How did you know my father? What happened?"

Standing over the grief-stricken kids felt so awkward, as if I was talking down to them. Instead of responding to the question right away, I pulled a chair over and sat down in front of them as I gathered my thoughts. Now on their level, responding to Jordan's question seemed much more natural.

"I met your father yesterday morning," I said. "After we survived a swarm of monsters, all he cared about, with all of the insanity going on around us, was getting to you two."

Though her shoulders shook from silent sobs, Gabrielle's head turned toward me from where it rested on her brother's arm.

"We walked all the way across the city from Squirrel Hill. We fought monsters mostly, but there were some people who tried to stop us, so we fought them too.

"In the middle of the night, a massive creature appeared over the city and rampaged through downtown. This morning, the jabberwock attacked the place where we sheltered, and I tried to lead it away. I would have died then, if not for Zeke. His special ability broke through the creature's armor and diverted its attention from me.

"The monster's next attack left your father mortally wounded, then the jabberwock chased me through the city." I took a deep breath. "Eventually, I used the point your father broke in the monster's armor to kill it. By the time I got back to him, his health was almost gone. With his last words, he asked me to make sure you were safe."

Both teens had tears in their eyes as they held each other tightly.

"I'm sorry," I said finally. "Your father was a hero, and he deserved better. You two were all he talked about. He was proud of both of you and wanted to be here for you more than anything."

I stood, and a notification in the corner of my vision demanded my attention.

Quest Complete!
You have safely located the Thomas children.
1,000 XP Awarded

I closed the notification and left the kids alone to process their grief. That conversation was one of the hardest things I'd ever done.

The school official waited for me a respectful distance away as I moved away from the kids.

"Keep an eye on them," I said. "At least they know what happened to their dad, but others here may never know."

A sudden wave of exhaustion hit me as I wandered back to the entrance of the school building. On top of the emotionally draining conversation I'd just had, I had been up most of the previous night and then fighting or traveling for the entire day. My stomach growled, gnawing at my insides, but I felt too tired to even pull one of the ration bars from my Inventory.

I staggered to the side of the lobby and leaned against the wall before I sank down to sit with my back against a trophy display case. The afternoon sunshine that shone through the lobby windows warmed my skin pleasantly, and I relaxed as I listened to the firefighters and cops talk outside in the distance.

For the first time since the apocalypse began, I could do more than react to sudden changes in circumstance. I had finished Zeke's Quest and now found myself free to explore the new realities of our world under the System. I could grow stronger as I earned more Levels and learned new superhuman abilities. Then maybe, someday, I would put paid to the accounts of those who had consigned so many people here to their deaths.

My daydreams of the future relaxed me further, and it didn't take long before I nodded off completely.

A loud, heavy rumble deep in my chest that reverberated like the bass at a metal concert woke me, and I opened my eyes to find that it had grown dark outside the school lobby. I stood, still shaking off the abrupt transition from slumber to wakefulness, and stretched out the kinks in my back that were sore from my nap against the wall. As I twisted from side to side and looked for the source of the increasing vibration, an explosion detonated right in front of the building.

The shockwave shattered the window, covered me in razor cuts from broken glass, and popped my eardrums as I was picked up and flung through the air. The trophy case I had napped under was thrown after me by the force of the blast, and I hit the far wall just before it followed me.

When I hit the wall, my breath was driven from my lungs as several of my ribs snapped and several cement blocks crumbled under my impact as I was driven partially through the wall.

Then the trophy case hit and knocked me through the wall completely before it fell on top of me.

I gasped hoarsely as I tried to pull air into lungs, and my broken ribs screamed in agony. Distantly, I felt more explosions and debris falling on top of the trophy case above me, but I was too caught up in attempting to breathe to focus on what else might be going on.

Another explosion dislodged one of the heavy wooden shelves from the cabinet above me, and the shelf smashed down onto my forehead.

The world went dark.

Chapter 13

I woke in darkness, and I braced myself for the nightmares to begin once again.

Only the pains were different this time, and I wasn't struggling just to breathe. Aches suffused my body, and I remembered being catapulted across the school lobby. The miraculous powers of the System may have begun to heal my damaged body while I was senseless, but my health had been nearly depleted from the many wounds, and every inch of my body protested my injuries.

Memory warred with the reality of being trapped in a collapsed building for the second time in my life. Repressed emotions broke free of my control and ravaged me until I lost consciousness again.

The next time I awoke, a sharp pain dug a line deeply across my forehead. The pressure and pain helped me to focus, which allowed me to regain control of myself as I reined in my rampant memories.

Whatever else may have happened, I was still alive. I could still grow stronger and do something about these attacks on my world.

Silence filled the space around me. I could hear nothing, and I opened my eyes to find that I couldn't see anything either. I cautiously attempted to raise my hands to my face and sniffed, picking up the scents of smoke, blood, and dust.

Careful exploration by my hands revealed that a thick wooden shelf rested on my forehead and was angled above me to anchor somewhere above my lower half. When I lifted the wooden plank off my head, whatever held the other end gave way, and the full weight of the shelf slammed down onto my knees.

I groaned and cursed as I pushed the board off of me before I continued to feel my way around the dark space. It took a couple minutes to shift around in the tiny, rectangular space, but I eventually figured out that I was pinned underneath the sturdy wooden frame of the trophy shelf I had napped beneath for the afternoon.

The case angled upward toward my feet as that end of the case rested on the wall I had been thrown through by the explosion. From the rubble that littered the ground beneath me, I figured that the building had caved in on top of me.

That wall gave me an orientation of the direction I needed to go.

With a deep breath, I pulled one of my beam pistols from its holster and pointed it at a section of the wall that was not supporting the case. I didn't want to get crushed if this didn't work. I fired into the cement blocks that made up the wall and had to squeeze my eyes shut against the brilliance of the beam that lit up the darkened space. I blinked repeatedly in an attempt to clear the afterimage that had been seared into my eyes, then I reached out in the darkness to feel how effective the shot had been.

A tiny hole punched completely through the concrete, not even big enough to fit my index finger through.

I sighed; this would take a while.

By the time I had completely drained both of my beam pistols of charges, I had only managed to burrow through the cement blocks and barely scratched the pile of debris I found on the far side of the wall.

I supposed I was fortunate that this building had never been purchased and included in the System. I could only imagine how resilient the walls would have been then. Though it might also have shrugged off whatever attack had wrecked the building to begin with.

Tired of waiting for the pistols to recharge, I decided to try something that was probably a bad idea. I rolled sideways and pressed myself against one side of the trophy cabinet to maximize the opening I had managed to clear. Into the space beside me, I summoned the hybrid rifle from my inventory.

Wrapped halfway around the bulky weapon, I carefully pulled my body away from the hole I'd dug so far, then I double-checked that my legs were out of the way as I held the rifle across my chest and aimed in the direction of the lobby.

I squeezed the trigger.

The whine of the weapon spooling up deafened me in the small space, and I felt my eardrums pop as the rifle discharged. A spray of dust and sand back blast stung my arms and exposed skin as the shot tunneled far beyond where I'd managed to dig so far.

I swallowed and winced as I touched one of my tender ears. My fingers came away wet and bloody. I shook my head and brushed off the pain. Nothing I could do unless I got out of here.

I gripped the rifle firmly and fired twice into the crater I was digging with my weapons fire. Not seeing immediate results, I shifted my aim slightly upward and then fired twice more.

At the end of the tunnel I had just blasted, it seemed somewhat less dark. I stored the weapon back in my inventory as I bent in half, then inched my way into the narrow passage that I'd cleared. Sharp stones and jagged debris cut into my hands as I crawled through the tunnel. It was so narrow at points that I ended up removing my belt and holstered pistols, storing them in my Inventory so that I could slither through a narrow gap.

When I reached the end of the rubble, I pushed out into the open and stood to find that most of the sky remained dark and filled with stars. The faintest lightening hint of purple at the edge of the horizon indicated that dawn would soon come.

The smell of smoke was more intense, and I looked around at the still-smoldering rubble that had once been school buildings. Some places still stood, but they were isolated islands in a sea of wreckage.

Beyond the temporary damage I had already healed, the collapse of the school building on top of me had managed to add a few more tears to my already worn adventurer's jumpsuit. I dusted myself off and made a mental note to get higher quality gear when I could afford it. Or at least a few replacement sets.

All of the vehicles that had been parked outside, including the fire trucks, were also burned-out wrecks. I circled the area, searching for more information, and found several bodies had been laid out in a line in the grass away from the school.

On closer inspection, they were all of the adults who had defended the school building from the coyotes. They had all been put on their knees then shot repeatedly in the back. At the far end of the line, one of the figures lay on top of another, and I walked over for a closer look.

It was the younger state trooper who had been kind of a dick. At least trooper dick had somehow taken one of the attackers with him.

And the body under him wasn't human.

The creature was humanoid in shape with two arms and two legs. However, the legs were canted backward and ended in cloven hooves instead of feet. The flesh of the creature's sharply angled face was a dark red that shifted to purple-brown away from the center of its face. It had no hair on top of its head. Instead, two short, slightly curved horns jutted from the creature's brow like the horns of a goat. A tiny pair of horns, no larger than the tip of my finger, protruded forward and down from either side of the alien's chin. Its face was twisted in a rictus of pain and surprise that displayed sharp fangs within its mouth. The creature almost looked like a demon from any of a dozen different human mythologies. Even in death, the body had an unsettling aura.

Beyond where the bodies lay were several large rectangular impressions in the lawn surrounded by charred circles blasted into the grass. Something heavy had rested there, as if landing then taking off with rocket propulsion engines.

Spaceships.

I recalled the first of the welcome messages from the System, which had implied that aliens would be coming to Earth and that we humans should make friends. The evidence here showed that some of those Galactics had now arrived and didn't have humanity's best interests in mind.

At one side of each of the rectangles, impressions in the damp grass showed where numerous feet had walked up to the craft. I followed the tracks backward and toward where they seemed to point across the asphalt. When I circled the ruined school building along the line left by the prints in the grass, I found a section still intact amongst the rubble. The exterior wall here stood undamaged with only a single hole blasted through it, large enough to pass through. I cautiously approached the hole and peeked inside.

On the ground in front of the hole lay another human corpse. The body wore khakis, a button-down shirt, and a charred lab coat, so I presumed the dead man had been one of the teachers. Besides the body, backpacks and other school supplies littered the classroom.

But still no kids, living or dead.

Something tickled in my thoughts at that, so I walked back outside and continued around the building.

In several more places, I found classrooms that seemed to have survived the destruction of the school, but they were all empty, with the exception of bodies that looked like teachers or school administrators.

Despite a thorough search, I found no other survivors. Everything I could find indicated that the attackers had wanted the kids and had taken them all.

Back at the front of the school, I looked over the line of bodies once again. The clothing on their backs was scorched from repeated beam weapons fire, but the only one who had done something about it was the one trooper. From the looks of things, he had rushed at one of the executioners and beaten the alien to death with an extendable baton before the others had shot him enough times to finally bring him down.

I had rolled the trooper's corpse off the alien earlier, but now that I really looked at the man, I found that his sightless eyes were staring straight ahead, frozen in an expression of mindless fury.

The trooper, like the other bodies, carried nothing of value. The alien, on the other hand, still held an energy pistol that looked similar to mine. I knelt beside the alien and pried the weapon from the dead alien's grip before I added it to my Inventory.

The alien also had a ring on one of its fingers, and I worked the silvery band free with a few twists. I continued searching the corpse and added a few more interesting trinkets in the process.

A casting of Cleanse was needed to remove all the clotted purple blood from a necklace after I slipped it off over the sticky mess of the alien's ruined head. I also found a couple items that looked like grenades hooked to the alien's belt and a pouch that contained a Mana battery. I slipped everything into my Inventory so I could figure out how to get the items identified the next time I visited a Shop.

I couldn't wait until I finally unlocked my Class Skills. I was really looking forward to the Greater Observation ability in the second tier of the Pursuit tree.

Finished with the bodies, I stood and took another look over at the depressions where the spaceships had rested. Nothing new caught my attention as I roamed through the grassy impressions, and the early morning dew clung to my boots.

A few skill notifications demanded my attention, and I found that the System had credited me with having learned both forensics and tracking skills from my efforts in investigating the now-destroyed school.

A separate tab in my Status page listed all of the other skills I had accumulated so far, but they were just numbers, static measurements that rated various proficiencies. As far as I could tell, there were no actual bonuses attached to the numbers, so I didn't give much attention to the tab besides noting that my highest ratings seemed to be for energy pistols and knife proficiency.

A new Quest waited for my attention when I reached the bottom of my notifications.

Quest Received—Find the children.

The human remnants of the attack on Montour High School have been abducted by parties unknown. Locate the survivors.
Reward: Variable XP and Credits

I sighed as I read the vaguely worded Quest update. Of course, it gave me no hint of how to proceed.

I closed the windows and regarded the wreckage of the school around me. I should have felt angry. I had let down my guard, and now missing children were paying the price. Innocents, like the Thomas kids, who had just lost their father.

Everything that had happened over the past several days only strengthened my desire to get even stronger.

Sixty percent of humanity was dead, and all I could do was keep killing things in order to level up to get to the point where I could do something about it.

That goal lay years in the future. If I lived that long.

"You're a piece of work, Hal," I muttered.

I closed my eyes for a moment and leaned my head back.

There was nothing left for me here. I would need to find a new lead or catch a lucky break to find the school's killers.

I opened my eyes and stared at the stars of the Milky Way galaxy, bright in the night sky overhead. Up in the heavens, one star glowed far too brightly to be natural. I watched as it moved closer and dropped lower in the sky. At first, it almost looked as if the falling star was heading right toward me, but I soon realized that the descending object was tracking slightly to the west.

I thought about what was to the west and grinned as I pulled my bike from my Inventory and mounted it. Maybe it was more of the aliens, I thought as the Mana engine purred, and I throttled up.

Since my Class Skill, Keen Senses, boosted my night vision in all but complete darkness, the pre-dawn light provided more than enough illumination for me to clearly see the road ahead. Before long, I steered back onto the shoulder of the on-ramp for I-376 West once again. Staying on the shoulder allowed me to avoid most of the abandoned vehicles that still clogged the highway.

Above me, the falling star blazed even brighter. Soon it was nearly overhead. The light from it was bright enough that it could almost have passed for daylight. The object still moved west, but it steadily slowed to the point that my bike's acceleration soon matched its land speed.

I veered off the highway onto Exit 53, barely slowing as my bike climbed the hill. I grinned as I blew past the posted speed limit sign. Normally, before all this apocalypse stuff happened, there would have been a police officer hiding alongside the road, just waiting to give out a speeding ticket to drivers who went over the posted limit on the airport access road.

My expression sobered a moment later as I braked sharply to avoid a smoldering pile of wreckage that was strewn completely across all lanes of traffic and for over a hundred feet on either side of the road. When I noticed the tail fin that stuck up sharply from one end of the debris, my breath caught in my throat. I imagined what it must have been like for all the people in flight as the electronics failed. Most would never have had a chance.

Ahead of me, the falling star slowed then gently descended to land on one of the airport runways. The brilliant light source cut out immediately after it touched down.

I maneuvered the bike around the larger chunks of shredded airplane and carefully weaved down the access road. Fortunately, I found that the bike's thick tires held up just fine over the jagged bits of metal that littered the wreckage.

Once through the debris, I turned off the main drive just before the terminal where passengers used to be dropped off, and I angled out toward the tarmac.

I had to pull my bike into my Inventory when I reached a fenced and gated area, but with my improved stats, I easily leapt over the fence. A short jog and a few hops over additional fences later, I stood at the edge of the runway where the grounded spaceship sat.

The massive craft dwarfed the 737s that sat abandoned at the darkened airport terminals. The sharply angular ship was easily taller than the terminal itself, and the shape reminded me of the Washington Monument—if the monument were tipped over on its side and covered in gun turrets that poked out from the main body. The rear of the craft seemed to be made up entirely of engines and nozzles. Most of them still billowed steam. Bright lights shone down from the craft at regular intervals, illuminating the blackened runway underneath the ship and the surrounding area.

Ramps descended from open hatches along the side of the starship, and figures streamed out to gather in a large crowd at the base of the ship. Every one of the humanoids seemed to be carrying something off of the ship. Whether it was a case, a duffel bag, or a crate, a steady flow of cargo moved down the ramps to pile on the pavement. The humanoid figures huddled as close to the end of the gangways and their piled belongings as possible, only moving farther away when the press of the crowd pushed them from the ship. Those at the outer edges glanced around nervously.

At first, I thought the scale of the massive ship had thrown off my perception, but eventually I was able to make out that the issue wasn't my sense of scale. The figures around the starship were only about three feet tall, and their hair sprouted a dizzying variety of colors. Primary colors like red and blue seemed most popular, but a riot of neon and multi-toned shades also abounded.

They looked nothing like the dead alien back at the school. My longshot hope that these newcomers might be of the same race had failed to pay off. Part of me was disappointed.

Some excitement occurred when a figure at the edge of the crowd noticed me watching and pointed me out to others. Several individuals broke from the crowd and seemed to grow as they were covered in a metallic sheen. Three of the armored figures started toward me then halted about halfway between the crowd and me. The rest spread out in a perimeter around the throng.

The three figures were clad in wide-bodied armored suits and were close enough now that I could make out the variety of their weapons. Missile racks, gun pods, and crystalline laser emitters covered the torsos, shoulders, and arms of the mechas. I could also see inside the glass cockpit canopies and easily picked out the details of their pilots.

Gnomes. The first living Galactic aliens I encountered on Earth were gnomes.

Their armored suits were much more refined than the mecha I had encountered back in the library. That construct had looked unfinished with all of its exposed wires, gears, and pistons. These suits had a sleek, high-tech, and futuristic look. They were completely armored, and even the joints had added plates to minimize weaknesses over the articulation points.

A commotion pulled my attention away from the sleek mechas.

The nervous murmurs of the crowd had grown quiet, and I saw that everyone was focused on a confrontation at the top of the forward-most ramp of the ship.

A large four-armed, green-hued reptilian gestured and yelled at a much smaller gray-haired gnome who responded in kind, despite leaning on a cane that he jabbed down onto the deck plate of the ship for emphasis. I had no idea what the two were saying, but neither seemed happy with the other.

The gnome lifted his cane and jabbed it at the green alien, poking him in the abdomen. The alien stared down at the gnome incredulously for a moment. Then the green alien pivoted on one leg and booted the gnome out of the hatch.

The kick sent the gnome airborne, completely overshooting the ramp and out into the crowd below, where he landed on several others. The mass of tiny figures fell over in a pile of tangled limbs.

Before the gnome had even landed, the hatches of the ship all clanged shut, and the ramps retracted. A rumble grew from the ship, and the edges of the crowd backed away from the craft. The movement of the mob turned into a more panicked run as steam jetted out of engines underneath the ship.

As soon as the crowd had cleared away from the starship, small thrusters ignited at regular intervals around the ship. Fire streamed out from underneath the ship, and the craft rose slowly from the ground. Cargo dropped by the fleeing gnomes tumbled across the runway from the force of the thrusters.

Once the ship was fully in the air, it hovered for a moment until the rear engines flared. The added thrust pushed the ship upward and it moved away, accelerating faster and higher until it was only a dot in the dark sky above.

As the speck of light receded in the distance, I looked over the much-dispersed crowd. Quite a few had fled in my direction when the starship took off, while the three closest mechanized suits had moved even closer toward me in order to keep themselves between me and the crowd they protected.

Through the clear canopies of the suits, I saw the pilot's lips moving. Though I couldn't hear anything, I assumed they had a communications system built into the suits.

From behind me, the sound of teeth chattering and claws clattering across the asphalt tarmac pulled my attention away from the gnomes. I turned and found myself being rushed by a pair of groundhogs, each grown to the size of a shopping cart.

The two creatures were still over a dozen yards away, so I pulled my beam pistol from my holster and fired at the left-hand groundhog as I cast a Frostbolt at the one on the right. I heard the gnomes grow agitated behind me, but since they were still keeping their distance, I ignored them as I continued to pour energy beams and Frostbolts into the two creatures.

The left groundhog dropped quickly, and I activated Hinder on the last one. It slowed as I holstered my beam pistol and drew my combat knife. I spun the weapon in my hand as I pulled it, keeping the tip up but with the blade reversed, the edge pointing back toward me.

When the sole groundhog lunged toward me, I dodged the attack and jammed my knife into the side of its throat. Then I sidestepped toward the far side of the groundhog and pulled the blade toward me as the creature squealed. The blade tore through the flesh of the groundhog's neck and a torrent of blood gushed out as I spun away from the dying beast.

Using my new experience notifications, I confirmed the groundhogs were dead and cast Cleanse on my knife before I slid it back into the sheath. Then I turned back to the gnomes.

The faces of the armored suit pilots were pictures of shock and awe. It was the most perfect reaction I could have hoped for from my demonstration of "don't mess with the human." I couldn't have given myself a better introduction if I had tried.

Behind the mech suits, the crowd was getting organized under the direction of several elders who shouted commands in a language I couldn't understand. The gnomes scurried across the tarmac, gathering the containers scattered by the ship's departure.

As the belongings were assembled into neat stacks, two of the armored suits in front of me stepped aside and revealed a small gaggle of elderly gnomes led by an older gray-haired gnome with a fine beard that descended down to a belt filled with pouches and tools. When the bearded gnome stepped forward with a cane, I realized he was the gnome who had been punted off the ship. If the tumble had affected him at all, the dignified gnome now looked none the worse for the wear.

Close up, the gnomes looked very much like tiny humans with only a few differences. They had bulbous wide noses and large, rounded ears that stuck out from the sides of their wild hairstyles. Their bodies were pleasantly rounded, and I noticed that there seemed to be minimal deviation from their standard figure—none were either overly skinny or plump.

While I looked over the group, the older gnome approached within easy conversation distance before he stopped and jabbered something at me in a high-pitched voice.

I raised an eyebrow and shook my head. "Sorry, no idea what you just said."

I made a mental note to look into whether languages could be bought like spells or skills the next time I visit a Shop.

"Bah," spat the gnome. "Can you understand me now?"

"I can now." I nodded.

"Fantastic!" The gnome cheered up and a grin visibly split his beard. "I am Borgym Sprocketsworth. The Sprocketsworth clan has come to establish an advanced manufacturing center on this new world." He looked around nervously at the dark, quiet airport, then peered up at me intently. "Might I have your name, gentle being, and whether you represent the owners of this terrestrial transportation hub?"

"My name is Hal Mason," I replied. "I'm an Adventurer apparently, and I am not associated with any owners of this airport, if anyone does now."

Borgym's eyes widened in astonishment, and he turned back to the other elders. He said something in the language I didn't understand, and the others babbled back excitedly. They went back and forth for a couple minutes until Borgym seemed to remember I was still there and he turned back to me.

"Apologies, Adventurer Mason," he said. "We had nearly given up hope and have now been presented with an opportunity that may be the salvation of our clan."

My furrowed brow must have clued Borgym in that I had no idea what he was talking about.

"I can explain later," said the elderly gnome. "Right now, it is most imperative that we clear this airport of any spawned monsters and register ownership with the System at the nearest Shop."

I took the gnome at his word and explained the directions to the last Shop I had visited.

When Borgym called over a pair of younger gnomes and asked me to repeat the directions, I pulled up my map and shared the data of all the local Shop locations with Borgym and the couple with matching neon blue hair. I also warned them about the disabled vehicles that blocked the roads in many places.

A new notification popped up a second later and informed me that Borgym had tipped me a few hundred Credits for sharing the information. I nodded at him respectfully in thanks.

The older gnome grinned deviously. "How would you like to earn even more Credits, Adventurer?"

"You have my attention, Elder Sprocketsworth," I replied.

"Just Borgym, please," said the elderly gnome.

While we talked, the blue-haired couple stepped away from us and, after ensuring nothing else was nearby, placed a dark gray container on the ground. One gnome tapped the side of the box, then they both moved away from it as the sides unfolded. The thing expanded quickly and soon formed itself into a sled-like vehicle with side-by-side seats for a driver and a passenger.

Once fully assembled, the vehicle raised off the ground several inches to hover in place, and an energy shield shimmered faintly in the air around it. The two gnomes climbed into the sled, then the craft floated upward to hover in the air just over my head. The two gnomes waved to Borgym and me, then the hover sled jetted off to the south as they headed to the nearest Shop.

Borgym waved at the gnomes as they disappeared in the distance, then he turned to me. "Since I am sending several of my combat capable gnomes off to the nearest Shop to purchase this location, that will leave us shorthanded on forces capable of removing any hostile creatures that may have spawned here. I would like to hire you for your assistance and additional firepower."

"I'm always up for earning a few more Credits," I replied.

"Excellent!" Borgym exclaimed.

A moment later, a new notification appeared. I accepted the prompt, and the journal in my status screen updated with the new Quest.

Quest Received—Assist the Sprocketsworth clan with clearing the airport facilities.

Help the Sprocketsworth clan remove any monster spawns from within designated target structures.

Reward: Variable XP and Credits based on structure size and monsters encountered. 25% share of all loot obtained. Increased reputation with Sprocketsworth clan.

The old gnome turned and gestured toward the air traffic control tower that lay across the tarmac. "Let's start there."

"Sounds good to me," I replied and walked toward the distant building.

Borgym remained behind, but two of the mech suits followed me. The third suit sprinted toward where the other gnomes had gathered their belongings into evenly piled stacks.

The suit caught up before we were halfway to the towering structure and handed me a small bead that was slightly rubbery. The pilot gestured to me and indicated I should place the globule in my ear. When I pushed it in, the material felt cool for a second and distant sound disappeared, then the device warmed and all sound returned as the sensation of even having something in my ear vanished.

"Hello, Adventurer!" a feminine voice squealed happily in my ear. I looked around to see the suit pilot waving excitedly from within the clear cockpit.

"Hello," I replied.

"Oh, great," she said. "The earpiece works as both a communicator and translator so that you can be a part of our tactical net while we work here."

"That sounds useful," I said.

"Yep, especially in a fight," said a male voice over the comm. "I'm Ipbar. The excitable one who gave you the earpiece is Talliryna but just goes by Talli. Our third team member is Alryn, and he doesn't talk much."

"Hi," said a new male voice, presumably Alryn.

"It's nice to meet you all," I said. "It will be nice to fight with a team again."

"Have you been doing much fighting on your own?" Talli asked.

I thought about the best way to answer that question, considering they probably had analyzed my level by now.

"I was Level one yesterday morning," I said finally.

"Oh," said Talli, much of the enthusiasm drained from her tone.

After a pause, the three gnomes filled me in to the fact that they were not actually combat Classes. Talli and Ipbar were Engineer classes, which allowed them to build, maintain, and improve equipment like the mech suits they currently wore. Alryn was a Logistics Manager whose Class Skills allowed him to purchase limited amounts of materials, arms, and ammunition directly from the Shop despite not being at a physical Shop location.

It only took a few more minutes for the four of us to reach the lofty control tower.

The Pittsburgh Air Traffic Control Tower stood twenty stories tall, a building framed by four beige stone columns that rose the height of the tower. A metal skeleton within the columns made up the framework that housed the stairs, elevator, and infrastructure that allowed the control center at the top to operate. There was no entrance directly into the tower itself, and we had to go through the adjoining office building at the base of the tower.

Eventually, we found our way to the tower entrance, where we found a thick metal security door that was cracked open, as if the last person leaving had not bothered to shut the door behind them. I checked the door carefully and found no damage to it. The door had been released from the inside when the power had failed due to the Mana interference as the System came online yesterday.

I stepped through the door and listened quietly. Only silence filled the area, and I slowly crept my way over to the elevator. The elevator doors had been pried open, and a crowbar lay discarded beside them. I stuck my head cautiously inside and verified that the carriage was empty.

I gestured to the gnomes, who followed me toward the stairs, the metallic footsteps of their armor dampened to almost noiselessness. Flight by flight, they quietly followed me up the winding stairs of the superstructure and toward the control center at the top of the tower.

With only a few levels left to climb, a soft flutter beside me grabbed my attention. I turned to find a giant wasp clinging to the side of the tower column. Folded back along the insect's side, the creature's wings were almost as long as I was tall, and it was the gentle ruffle of those wings by the half-asleep creature that had alerted me to its presence.

I pulled my knife in a smooth motion and drove it into the insect's fist-sized eye. I yanked the blade toward me and rotated my arm as the insect screamed, grabbing the insect's mandibles with my other hand. I pulled and twisted, the insect's legs scrambling as they tried to retain their grip on the stone column. I jerked hard on the insect's head, and it tore free of the thin neck with a disgusting pop. The body of the insect tumbled away, and I was left with a wasp head in my hands.

My knife pulled free with a squelch, and I tossed the head over the side of the landing as a buzz filled the air above us with a steady drone.

The next few minutes were a flurry of energy blasts, gunfire, explosions, and spell bursts.

The gnomes used their combined firepower to engage the maddened wasps at range. Fortunately, the suits—and their weapons—were all created within the System and didn't have any of the weaknesses of native weaponry. Their beams burned away wing membranes, and their projectiles punched right through the insect carapaces.

With the gnomes handling the ranged attacks, I elected to save my ammunition as I dodged around the gnomes and attacked any of the wasps that dived in for stinger attacks. Between Hinder, Frostbolt, and my natural agility, I was able to deflect the diving wasps so that every dive always missed the gnomes, and I managed to dispatch several insects on my own.

One by one, injured and dying wasps dropped out of sight until none were left in the air and silence filled the tower once again.

The gnomes panted audibly over the communications link, so I waited for a minute to let them catch their breath before I continued up the stairs. I only made it up the next flight before I found the passage blocked with a brownish material. I pushed my hand against it and felt some give to the thick woody, paper-like material.

It was the wasps' nest, and it took up the top several floors of the tower directly below the control center.

My axe easily hacked through the material, and I pushed through to find myself in a small hexagonal chamber. More of the papery walls lined the sides of the compartment, and I followed the metallic floor plating to the far side of the chamber before I cut my way through it too.

I made it through three more chambers and had just started up the next flight of stairs when a massive black limb ripped through the wall and speared into my side. I managed to twist as the clawed leg hit me, but it still tore through my armored suit and into the flesh beneath. I cried out as I was flung aside from the impact.

The insect leg pulled back then stabbed through the wall at Talli, who had been on the stairs behind me. Fortunately, the gnome was already in motion, and the attack missed her.

Ipbar and Alryn leveled their arms toward the source of the attacks at the center of the tower and opened fire with their suit weapons. Their projectiles shredded the walls of the chamber and left it in tattered ruins that evaporated in flames as the beam weaponry punched through it. With the chamber walls nearly gone, we could all see the insect that turned within the heart of the tower and swung its clawed limbs down to swipe at us.

The huge wasp was easily twice the size of the previous wasps we had fought.

"It's the queen of the hive," I gasped through clenched teeth.

I pushed myself to my feet as the three gnomes dodged more attacks and poured fire into the wasp queen.

The weapons fire from the suits did damage, but not as effectively as it had against the other wasps. I opened up my Inventory and pulled out my hybrid rifle. I ignored the pain in my side as I brought the weapon to my shoulder. I lined up on the queen's head and squeezed the trigger.

The hybrid rifle whined loudly in the enclosed area before it fired. The electric thunder of the weapon stunned all of us as the round punched into the side of the queen's head. The impact knocked the queen from her perch, and she dropped almost a full level before her legs dug into the walls far enough to stop her sudden descent.

With her head now on our level, I aimed and fired the hybrid weapon at her again. This time, the round caught on the mandible and jolted the insect violently to the side as her head was twisted around.

The recovery from the attack was even slower. The queen's head turned to face us gradually, and I saw that one side of the insect's mandibles were completely sheared away. The queen lunged toward me with her maw gaping wide and lone mandible twitching. I fired the hybrid weapon once more. This time, the round blasted into the open mouthparts.

The queen was thrown backward and bounced off the far side of the hive chamber before she tumbled downward. The tower shook as the queen bounced off each landing before the body hit the ground far below.

I didn't feel or hear anything after that, so I checked my notifications. I only had experience gained for the wasps and none for the queen.

"Are you all right, Hal?" Talli asked with concern over the comm.

"I'll live." I sighed. "The queen's not dead yet though."

"I can fix that!" Talli shouted.

The gnome vaulted over the inside rail of the stairs, and thrusters fired from the feet of her mech suit, keeping her hovering as she centered herself in the middle of the tower. She twisted her suit toward me so that I could see her face lit by the glow of the instrument panel inside the cockpit. Talli winked at me, then her thrusters cut out.

The armored suit dropped like a rock out of sight. A crash echoed up the tower a few seconds later, followed by an experience notification for the death of the wasp queen.

I stored my weapons then sank down onto the nearest step.

"Show-off," Alryn grumbled as he looked over the railing toward the bottom of the tower.

"Are you still with us, Talli?" Ipbar asked.

"Yep," Talli replied cheerfully over the comm. "Buuuut my suit is stuck in the roof of the first floor."

Ipbar looked at Alryn, who sighed heavily.

"Yeah, yeah," Alryn said. "I'll go pry her loose. Again."

Ipbar chuckled as he walked over to me, and a small nozzle popped from the arm of his suit. A mist emanated from the nozzle as he directed it over the gash in my side. The mist sank into my skin and instantly dulled the pain as my health rapidly climbed back upward.

"There you go," said Ipbar. "I can't do anything about your jumpsuit now, but we should have people with the skills to fix it up later once we can get some of our equipment set up."

"Thanks." I stood and stretched experimentally, pleasantly surprised to find the wound not stiff or sore in the slightest. I rubbed the hole in my jumpsuit and looked at the skin. The flesh was slightly red where the wound had been, but it was smooth to the touch and I felt no lingering pain. "That's impressive stuff. What was it?"

"Healing potion," replied Ipbar. "The suit has a potion reservoir that can be injected internally or applied externally to allies."

"That sounds very useful," I said. "It seems like having high-quality consumables like potions or other utility items improves survivability."

Ipbar nodded. "A good alchemist is worth their weight in Credits."

"Does your clan have an alchemist like that?"

Ipbar gave me a smug smile and an unconvincing shrug through the cockpit of his suit before he turned to look at the hive material that blocked our path up the stairs.

"That cannon you've got there is impressive too," said Ipbar, intentionally changing the subject.

If he didn't want to share the info, then there was probably a reason, and I had no cause to distrust these gnomes so far.

Ipbar swept his arm across the hall from one side to the other as he fired a beam rifle attached to the arm of the suit. The energy seared through the papery wall, and flames flickered along it, not quite catching fire.

"It's saved my ass a few times already," I said as Ipbar worked on the hive.

"Oh?" Ipbar replied.

"Ever heard of a jabberwock?" I asked.

"No way," said the gnome. He stopped firing his energy weapon at the hive wall and turned back toward me. "That's a story I have got to hear."

I gave him the same smug look and shrug he'd used earlier. Ipbar clearly recognized the expression and glared at me in mock anger.

"How are you doing on charges for the beams?" I asked with my own subject change. "It might be better to save them for combat and just cut through the old-fashioned way."

Ipbar sighed over the comm. "You're right."

He stepped back on the landing to give me room to work. I drew my axe from the holster at my back and hacked at the wall. The blade tore easily through the hive material in most places, but it took more effort to cut through the thicker areas where the combs sections intersected.

I managed to carve my way up two flights of stairs to the next landing before Alryn and Talli rejoined us. The legs of Talli's suit were splashed with ichor nearly up to the waist, but the armor seemed otherwise undamaged.

There were no further incidents as I cut our way up to the bottom of the control center. The stairs led all the way up to an armored hatch in the center of the tower.

After a couple attempts at lifting the door, I let the gnomes work on the hatch with their energy beams. Alryn also had a small cutting saw that lowered from a boxy extrusion on one hand of his armor.

Eventually, the door gave way with a clang as it clattered to the bottom of the flight of stairs to rest on the landing below.

With the obstacle removed, I climbed up into the tower with the gnomes close behind. Only the mid-day light that streamed in through the angled windows allowed me to see clearly here, but there was no one in the control center, and all of the consoles sat dark. The windows gave a three-hundred-sixty-degree view of the airport and the surrounding area.

"All right," said Ipbar. "The tower is clear. We'll head down and figure out where to head next."

I looked out the windows for a moment and turned to Ipbar. "You should have a few people up here to keep an eye out for any problems."

The gnome looked at me speculatively then nodded. "I'll let Elder Borgym know about your suggestion."

The gnomes led as we tramped back down the stairs of the tower. When we reached the bottom, we found that the other gnomes had been busy too. All the equipment from the runway had been brought over to the base of the tower.

Elder Borgym waited for us by the assembled crates and containers. "Great work on clearing the tower."

He gestured toward the four of us and a quest update materialized for me.

Quest Update: Assist the Sprocketsworth clan with clearing the airport facilities.

PIT Air Traffic Control Tower cleared.

Rewards: 5,000 Credits and 2,000 XP. +100 reputation with Sprocketsworth clan.

"Thank you," I said to Borgym while I acknowledged the prompt.

"It's a good start," replied the gnome. "We'd like to clear the office building next so that we can set it up as our clan headquarters."

The three combat-suited gnomes followed me as we went back into the building. The building was only a couple stories tall and about a hundred feet square. We quickly swept through it and found nothing but empty offices.

When we returned to Borgym and reported the building clear, he provided another Quest update that gave me another thousand Credits and 500 XP. Clearly, my larger payout from the earlier update had been from the monster kills.

After we announced the building clear, a crowd of the gnomes streamed inside with all of their belongings in hand. The piles outside vanished quickly as many returned for multiple trips.

Next, Borgym directed our combat squad at some of the nearby hangars that had formerly belonged to American Airlines. It took several hours to make our way through each of the structures, though we only had two incidents with monsters.

The first was a giant hedgehog that had tunneled up through the cement floor of one hangar. The monster's fur had mutated into spikes like a porcupine, and it shot the stingers across the hangar.

During that fight, I ran out of beam charges for my energy pistols. Since I didn't want to get anywhere near the creature's spikes, I ended up forced into using my projectile pistols. That left me low on ammo when we found a nest of giant, acid-spitting spiders in the last hangar. The gnomes were short on rounds too, and we ended up in a brutal melee with the swarm.

By the time it was done, my jumpsuit was in tatters and there were actual holes etched through all of the armor suits. Nobody had any serious injuries, but we had all been splattered with acid. The four of us dragged ourselves back to the tower HQ in sorry shape.

Borgym took one look at our ragged appearance and told us to call it a night.

The three gnomes popped the canopies of their armor and a ladder unrolled down the front of each suit. Then the gnomes dismounted by turning around and climbing out of the cockpits.

Each of the three gnomes wore black, skin-tight coveralls, and I couldn't help but watch as Talli wiggled backward out of her armor. The knowing chuckle Borgym directed at me let me know that my observation hadn't been as subtle as I hoped.

I gave the old gnome a shrug, much too tired to feel guilty.

Another gnome directed me inside and had me swap out the rags of my armored jumpsuit after they guided me to an open space inside an empty office. I pulled the bedroll from the adventuring pack in my Inventory and laid it out in the corner. I flopped onto the thin but surprisingly comfortable pad and promptly passed out.

Chapter 14

The bright morning light that streamed in through the office blinds dragged me from the depths of slumber.

I blinked at the sunlight, then yawned and stretched my arms as I sat up to find my jumpsuit folded next to my head, along with a large box of ammunition for my Luxor pistols. The room was empty beside me and my bedroll, so I quickly dressed in the freshly cleaned and repaired suit.

I stowed my bedding, then I went through all of my weapons to check that they were recharged or reloaded with the ammunition left for me. While I loaded rounds into the magazines for my pistols, I checked my notifications. Besides the usual experience gains for monster kills and quest updates, I found one that caught my interest.

You Have Entered a Safe Zone (Traffic Control Tower, Pittsburgh Sprocketsworth Starport)

Mana flows in this area are stabilized. No monster spawning will happen.
This Safe Space includes:
Air and Space Traffic Control Tower
Sprocketsworth Clan Headquarters

Apparently the gnomes had made it to the Shop and purchased the building at some point during the night. I wondered how many of the other cleared buildings the clan had also bought.

Quest Update: Assist the Sprocketsworth clan with clearing the airport facilities.

Multiple facilities cleared.
Rewards: 12,000 Credits and 5,000 XP. +200 reputation with Sprocketsworth clan.

That mostly answered my questions.

And that was a huge chunk of experience. If I could continue to prove my worth to these gnomes and continue to complete these Quests in the process, it would go a long way to getting me to the Levels I needed in order to face threats like the jabberwock and whatever forces had blown up the school.

I finished my preparations and headed to the door, which I cautiously opened. I found the hallway filled with gnomes that hurried past in either direction. I wandered out of the office and worked my way through the flow of traffic to get back outside. When I reached the main entrance, I found it had been rebuilt overnight.

A guard post now overlooked the foyer, and the doors were now extended into two sets of double doors. The chamber within the pair of doors was like an airlock.

From the windows that looked outside, I couldn't see Borgym or any other gnomes outside, so I asked the guard who manned the post where I could find the Elder. The guard directed me to find the operations room on the second floor.

It didn't take me long to find the room, but it was only when I peeked inside that I realized the building now had power. Tiered rows of consoles faced a wall covered in large video monitors. The layout reminded me of footage from NASA mission control, but most of the monitors were dark, and the chairs at the terminals were empty.

Along the top tier at the back of the room, Borgym sat at a console and gave orders to the few operators throughout the room. The gnome elder saw me and beckoned for me to join him.

I climbed up on the platform carefully. I could fit, but it had clearly been designed for the much smaller gnomes.

"Good morning, Adventurer Mason!" Borgym bellowed as I eased toward him, turned sideways to avoid bumping the console equipment while I stepped along the elevated tier.

"Good morning," I replied. I never had been much of a morning person, but it always paid to be polite to your employer. "Thank you for the ammo and jumpsuit."

"It was nothing," Borgym said dismissively. "The least we could do for the help you provided to almost establish us as the first active starport on Earth."

"Almost?" I asked.

"Well," Borgym said hesitantly, "we have the traffic control tower, hangars, and support facilities."

"I sense a 'but' at the end there," I said.

Borgym sighed. "We own the terminal too. Technically."

I raised an eyebrow, and Borgym's expression grew dark for the first time since I'd met the cheery older gnome.

"It's full of monsters," he said. Worry creased his brow.

"So we clear it." I shrugged. "Like the tower and hangars."

"It's not that simple," he replied. "Buying a building from the System stabilizes the Mana in the location. When monsters infest the location as it is stabilized, those creatures become a part of that location. It's almost like a Dungeon. If killed, the monsters will just respawn after a period. Normally, you'd pay for it to be fixed, but we don't have the liquidity to do that."

"That's less than ideal," I said. I hadn't realized there was a downside to just purchasing a location.

"Right," Borgym said. "Unless all of the monsters are killed and someone with a specialized Class Skill can adjust the Mana flows while the area is clear, then the monsters will just keep coming back."

"Is that what happens in a Dungeon?" I asked.

Borgym nodded. "A Dungeon occurs in an area with high Mana density. That abundance of Mana allows the System to replace any slain monsters after a period of time. If the monsters aren't slain periodically, then they absorb that ambient Mana and become far more powerful over time. If they're left too long, then they can even create an Alpha monster or multiply exponentially."

"So assuming we can take out the monsters in the terminal, do you have access to whatever skill is needed to stop the monsters from respawning?"

Borgym hesitated as if reluctant to divulge his reply. "The clan does have an Architect with the necessary Class Skill."

"What's the problem then?" I asked.

"We're not Adventurers, Hal," Borgym replied. "We're a clan of Artisans."

"I'm afraid I don't understand the distinction."

"Artisans are crafters," Borgym explained. "We build and create things. The System gives us experience for innovation and efficiency in our designs. While we can receive XP for monster killing, our Skills and Quests are almost exclusively focused on furthering our crafts. The more and better things we build, the further we advance in our Class."

The elderly gnome waved in my direction as he continued. "Adventurers like you gain experience for destroying monsters and sentients that are a part of the System. There are whole Guilds devoted to that avenue of advancement, but it's a path our clan has tried to avoid."

"You're pacifists?" I asked.

The gnome cocked his head sideways as he contemplated his response.

"Something similar," Borgym finally replied. "We aspire to create and do our best to avoid the path of destruction. I'm reluctant to force any of my people along a path we would usually abhor."

"So how does a bunch of pacifists end up on a Dungeon World where they might have to fight for their lives?"

"Earth wasn't supposed to be a Dungeon World," Borgym said with a sigh. "It was supposed to be peacefully integrated into the System, and we booked passage in the hopes that we could be some of the first to get a foothold in manufacturing and development here.

"Since standard interplanetary travel takes weeks, we set out almost a month ago. Two days ago, when the Galactic Council changed the status of Earth to Dungeon World, we were too close to change course, and our charter insisted on following through his contract completely to land where we'd originally agreed. I believe you saw everything that happened when we landed, and the charter captain refused to renegotiate."

"It was some impressive airtime." I smirked at the thought of the gnome flying through the air.

Borgym narrowed his eyes, but the glare he leveled at me failed to dampen my amusement. His expression returned to normal as he continued. "When we found the airport here was practically empty, it was too lucrative to pass up. Since this is a Dungeon World, there will be a massive trade in loot being exported to crafters across the System, and that trade will need conventional transport. If we can be the first fully functional starport, then we'll have a head start and be the natural default for most large-scale transport."

"And to be fully functional, you need the terminal."

It wasn't a question, but Borgym nodded anyways.

"It sounds like you've already made up your mind," I said.

The old gnome met my eyes firmly, no surrender in his expression. With a gesture from Borgym, a new update appeared for me.

Quest Update: Assist the Sprocketsworth clan with clearing the airport facilities.

Assist with clearing monsters from the airport terminal.

Reward: 20,000 Credits and 15,000 XP

That was simply too much of a reward for me to pass up. The reward alone would bump me up a Level, on top of whatever experience I gained from killing monsters along the way. Growing stronger would be another step forward on my path to finding out what had happened at the school.

I accepted the notification and looked at the clan leader. "You need to talk to your Architect, I need more ammo, and I wouldn't mind some of those health potions if you have any to spare."

Borgym pulled two of the red potions from his Inventory and handed them over, then he told me to talk to the guard at the main entrance for more projectile ammo. I worked my way back across the tiered platform and climbed down to the door before I retraced my steps through the building back to the main entrance.

The guard gave me a crate of projectile rounds like the one I had found beside me when I woke. Since all of my weapons and spare magazines were already filled, I stored the case in my Inventory.

Ipbar, Talli, and Alryn showed up shortly after I finished with the guard, and they clomped down the hall, already suited in their armor. The four of us left the building through the security doors, and the first set sealed behind us before the second set opened to the outside.

Once we were outside, we stepped away from the entrance, and the three suits turned toward me.

"What's the plan, Hal?" Ipbar asked.

I considered the trio for a moment.

Talli's suit shifted from side to side in a movement that looked nervous at first glance, but I could see the bright-haired gnome grinning through the cockpit canopy, and she looked more excited than anything else.

Ipbar's armor stood still, though the way the gnome bit his lip belied the rest of his calm demeanor.

Only Alryn stared at me stoically, and the quiet gnome simply waited for me to respond.

"You're looking at me to be in charge?" I countered finally.

"You're the combat Class here," said Talli. "We just have suits that fit and can put the tech to work."

"Great," I said. "You do realize I've only been doing this for, like, two days, right?"

The three just blinked at me in surprise.

"Yes, but you're doing great!" Talli exclaimed.

I turned away from the overly optimistic gnomes and looked to the west across the tarmac. The airside terminal of the Pittsburgh International Airport consisted of four multilevel wings laid out in a mostly X-shape. The A and B Concourses of the two eastern-most wings had tips that angled straight east at the ends of the X.

While I contemplated the terminal building, several gnomes exited the headquarters building behind us and joined our group. I turned back to the others when I heard Borgym offer a greeting to Ipbar, Alryn, and Talli.

Then I started counting.

With the three armored suits, a full dozen gnomes stood gathered around the elder. Four of the new gnomes carried metallic cylinders that were almost larger than they were. A pair of the others carried gnome-sized rifles with a variety of attachments and tubes at the business end. The next couple carried staves with colored crystals at the top, one red and the other green.

"All right, here's the plan," said Borgym as he stepped forward and looked across the group, meeting each of our eyes solemnly. "We need to enter the terminal and clear any monster spawns we find. Our first pass through will be focused on removing as many monsters as possible. That'll take some time. But once we're done, we'll go through the terminal once more. The second pass will require that we hold the area for our Architect, Ospyr, to use his Class Skill to stabilize the Mana flows in the terminal."

Borgym continued. "Normally the Architect ability Structural Enfilade is used to expand the interior of System buildings beyond what their exterior dimensions would seem to hold. However, Ospyr is going to use it to channel Mana into the terminal. That should stabilize the Mana flows throughout the structure and keep the monsters in the building from respawning."

Borgym grew even more serious. "While Ospyr is channeling, any monsters left within that section will be enraged by the disruption to their environment. They will attempt to attack the source of that disruption, so it's critical that we clear out as many monsters as possible during our first trip through the terminal. Otherwise, you will have to defend Ospyr during his channeling process. It will take ten minutes of continuous channeling to stabilize each one-hundred-foot section of the terminal and any interruption means that he will need to start over.

"You all know why we chose to travel here. Even if we didn't expect Earth to be a Dungeon World, we have been presented with a unique opportunity. The Clan is counting on all of you."

The gathered gnomes seemed nervous, but their faces settled firmly in determination at his final words.

Borgym sensed the change in the group and nodded confidently. "Our new friend, Adventurer Mason, has agreed to assist us."

The gnomes all looked at me, and I waved casually. Talli excitedly waved back, and I couldn't help but grin at her antics.

A new notification appeared in my vision.

Borgym Sprocketsworth has invited you to join a party.
Accept: Y/N

I selected the affirmative option, and a new interface window showed up at the edge of my vision. Members of the party were listed in vertical blocks by name, with colored bars that displayed each individual's health, mana, and stamina.

The new party menu was unobtrusive, somehow discernable in my peripheral vision without limiting my perception. When I focused on one of the names, that block within the window expanded slightly and provided a better look at their status bars.

Borgym nodded at my acceptance of the party invitation and gave me a moment to adjust to the new interface before he led the group toward the nearest part of the terminal, the end of Concourse B.

There were numerous planes still parked at the terminal gates and a handful scattered along the runways, as if they had been in the process of taxiing between terminal and runway when the System came online and shut them down. All of the stranded planes out on the runways had their side hatches open with inflatable emergency slides deployed.

There were no signs of survivors, but a handful of bodies lay scattered around the tarmac, mostly closer to the terminal. Though some of them appeared to be fleeing passengers, the majority of the dead were clad in ground crew uniforms. The corpses we passed showed signs of scavengers in the way they were pecked apart, the lack of blood spatter indicating that the desecration had occurred postmortem.

When we reached the terminal, there were no obvious methods to access the building unless we wanted to go crawling through the network of conveyors in the bowels of the terminal that made up the airport baggage handling system.

I looked around for a moment, then up at one of the jet bridges that extended from the terminal before inspiration struck. I caught Borgym's attention and gestured to one of the open jetways that sat empty near the end of the terminal. The gnome picked up on my intent and guided the party to the narrow set of stairs built into the base of the mobile tunnel.

Normally the stair was used by ground crew to retrieve last-minute checked bags from overbooked flights, but in this case, it made a perfect way for us to access the terminal.

I drew my energy pistol from a holster at my hip and led the way up the rickety stair. At the top, I found the door into the jetway unlocked, and I cautiously cracked the door open to peek inside. The only sounds were the gnomes behind me on the stair and the wind that whistled through the open end of the jetway, where passengers would normally have boarded their flight.

No threats appeared, so I slipped inside. I moved up the passage to give the gnomes room to follow, and they clambered up after me, soon filling the corridor. Once I was sure they had all made their way inside, I cautiously continued up the jetway until I reached the security door that led into the terminal itself.

With a final look behind me to ensure the rest of the party was prepared, I tested the security door. The door opened easily, since the magnetic locking system had failed with the power.

The first thing I noticed once I stepped through the door was a gentle breeze. The wind flowed through the terminal from broken windows that lined both sides of the terminal. Most of the tall windows had left behind shattered glass, which covered the floors and the rows of seats nearest those windows.

If not for that draft from the empty window frames, the overwhelming scent of death would have filled the concourse. Bodies lay scattered in pools of blood, most of the corpses savaged into pieces.

I didn't see any immediate threats despite the dead, so I moved farther into the terminal. The gnomes followed, fanning out behind me as I moved slowly forward.

The concourse was eerily silent, which only made the charnel scene more disturbing.

I would almost have preferred the pre-System loudspeaker announcements that played on repeat about not leaving luggage unattended or reporting unattended baggage to the nearest Transportation Safety Administration personnel. I found the lack of such announcements especially ironic, since abandoned carry-ons and roller luggage now littered the concourse.

Food wrappers, drink bottles, and other discarded detritus lay discarded throughout the area.

After I'd moved up a couple dozen yards, I looked back at the group of gnomes who had spread out across the terminal behind me.

"This is good," said one of the new gnomes, who carried one of the big metal cylinders.

I somehow heard the words the young gnome had spoken, but they hadn't actually made any sound. I looked at him questioningly.

"Party chat," explained Ipbar, who had apparently noticed my look of confusion. "Just focus on the party window as you speak and only your party will be able to hear you, or even be able to tell that you've been saying anything."

"That seems pretty useful," I said as I attempted to follow his instruction and apparently succeeded. "Especially for anything requiring stealth."

Ipbar nodded.

While I had received an education on party chat, the gnome who had spoken, along with the other three carrying the large metallic cylinders, had moved to the four corners of the party. I watched as one placed the cylinder upright on the floor then slapped a hand down onto the top of the device before he stepped away.

Three legs folded down from the sides of the cylinder to stabilize it in a tripod position. The top split in two and slid around to create a half-moon shield as a barrel of a weapon raised from inside the cylinder and rotated down to rest on the level between the halves of the rounded shield. The automated turret pointed outward from the group, and the barrel of the weapon tracked smoothly from side to side as it searched for any threats.

All of the other gnomes had assembled inside the perimeter of a loose square, outlined by the four turrets. They clutched their weapons at the ready. Borgym stood at the center of the group and nodded at me once he saw that all the preparations had been completed.

I turned away from them and looked carefully down the length of the terminal before I stepped away from the perimeter the gnomes had set. I made it about twenty feet before a faint shriek echoed through the concourse.

I stopped, and the sound echoed again a moment later, this time louder and closer.

A winged blur streaked through one of the broken windows along the terminal, and the nearest turret behind me fired a beam at the fast-moving shape. The beam sizzled where it traced across the creature, and it shrieked loudly, the cry a louder match to the earlier distant screams, as the bird continued its flight.

I raised my right hand and cast Frostbolt at the darting beast. The shard of ice hit the bird and slowed it enough that I was able to follow up with Hinder just before it closed the distance. Despite slowing, the streak still slammed into my chest.

The impact barely staggered me, though talons punched through the armor plates on my chest, and I felt their sharpened tips dig into my flesh. I instinctively threw my arm in front of my face as the hawk's beak snapped forward. I barely managed to block the lunge as I jerked backward, and the hooked beak ripped into my forearm.

With my left hand, I jammed my beam pistol into the bird's chest along the underside of the wing and fired. A charred scent filled my nose as I held down the trigger, and the bird finally released its clawed grip on my chest and pushed off me.

It fluttered its wings to hover in front of me, but there was now enough space between us that the gnomes behind me could safely attack. Beam and projectile attacks passed narrowly on either side of me to slam into the hawk, and the creature tumbled to the floor. The hawk hopped right back up and spread its wings as it attempted to launch itself back into the air, giving me a good look at the whole creature.

Brown feathers covered the large bird, but it was the distinctive reddish tail feathers that identified it as a red-tailed hawk. Except that its six-foot wingspan was twice as large as a normal red-tailed hawk.

I joined in with more fire from my beam pistol as attacks poured into the hawk. It flapped its wings weakly for a moment then slumped to the floor.

Once it stopped moving, I stepped up beside the bloody raptor and looted it. I received a pair of red-tailed hawk talons, a handful of feathers, and some lightweight hawk bones. A notification informed me that similar items had been distributed to the other members of my party.

That was an interesting bit of information. It meant that only one person of an official party needed to loot something in order for the entire group to get their share.

I stood up from looting the corpse and resumed scouting ahead of the gnomes, still on the lookout for anything else that might aggress our group. Nothing else showed up as I crept forward another fifty feet. I moved slowly enough that I had healed back to full health by the time I paused again.

Two of the four gnomes who had activated the turrets initially reversed the process with the rear turrets before they scooped up the cylinders. Then they leapfrogged forward past the group and deployed the mobile weapons just behind where I waited.

We made it another one hundred feet without any monster encounters, the gnomes picking up and redeploying the turrets about every fifty feet. The group maintained a loose perimeter within the boundaries of the deployed turrets as I ranged out ahead of the group.

The cycle repeated itself twice more until we reached the point where the concourse angled forty-five degrees north, toward the central hub of the X-shaped terminal. This portion of the concourse was about three times as long as the section we had just cleared.

After another half hour, we had managed to move almost a third of the way through Concourse B with only intermittent monster attacks. The creatures had been easily put down, unlike the hawk we had encountered first. Almost all of them had been birds of some kind though, and I had the sense that this pseudo-dungeon was following an avian theme.

That theory was borne out almost as soon as I had finished the thought.

A hum filled the air as the two turrets were deployed once again. The noise grew slowly, pulsing louder then fading the slightest bit before ramping up again.

A writhing flock of birds poured through the windows on either side of us. They flowed in intricate patterns, swirling around each other to fill the entire width of the concourse. I recognized the mesmerizing aerobatics as a murmuration of starlings.

The turrets fired into the swarm, but there had to be hundreds of the creatures. No larger than my outspread hand, the birds were almost impossible to target individually. However, there were so many of the creatures that almost every shot hit something.

I joined in and fired at the swarm. Every shot of mine dropped a bird, but it was like spitting into the howling wind of a raging blizzard.

The birds whirled around us and dove into our group. I buried my face in the crook of my elbow as I flailed at the swarm with my free hand. I batted several of the birds with my blind swings, but the rest tore into me.

I felt almost no sense of impact from the starlings' attacks, but their tiny claws left behind a burning sensation as if I was being raked by a thousand paper cuts. Gradually, the assault slowed as the swarm passed on, and I cautiously lowered my arm.

My adventurer's jumpsuit was shredded in several places and hung in tatters around my arms and legs. The more heavily armored sections of my torso and greaves had held up to the onslaught, and I was surprised to find myself only down about twenty hit points from the attack.

Several explosions behind me pulled my attention back to the fight, and I holstered my ineffective pistol as I turned. The murmuration had swept over the entire party and passed into the area we had already cleared. The swarm was spinning and turning back toward us.

Everyone on the perimeter of the party shared my disheveled state except for the three armored suits. At the center of the group, Borgym had deployed a small shield that covered himself in a translucent dome.

Missiles launched from the armored suits erupted in the midst of the swirling flock. Every detonation tore out a chunk of the swarm and sent avian bodies tumbling from the air.

I summoned the hybrid rifle from my Inventory and aimed it at the densest portions of the murmuration, over the heads of the gnomes at the rear of the party. The rifle whined then fired a round that split the air.

The round's passage bore a circular hole about a foot in diameter through the dense flock, and even those not directly hit plummeted to the floor as the shockwave knocked them unconscious. My attack was less powerful than the gnome's explosive missiles but far more effective than the initial volley from my beam pistol.

"Switch to flechette," commanded Ipbar over party chat in a message that was clearly not meant for me.

The pair of gnomes with the multi-attachment rifles stopped firing long enough to make some quick adjustments to their weapons. When their fire rejoined ours, instead of individual rounds, each of the shots from the gnome's projectile weapons split up into a cloud of tiny darts that swatted swaths of starlings from the swarm.

The combined attacks whittled away at the murmuration, and the birds only swept over us once more before we managed to drop the last of the flock. Only when the birds were all dead did Borgym drop the shield that had protected himself from the attack.

Everyone in the party, except for Borgym and the three suited gnomes, had taken some damage during the fight. None of our injuries were serious, but we waited in our current position to heal up, instead of moving forward immediately.

So many fallen birds littered the floor that we ended up kicking them into piles as we looted, just to make sure we didn't miss anything. A mass of feathers, tiny talons, bird brains, and a few dozen starling eggs made up the loot.

Once everyone had rested sufficiently, we moved forward into the next section of the concourse. The next hour and a half passed uneventfully beyond the steady clacking of the automated turrets as they were deployed with each push forward through Concourse B.

Finally, we reached the end of the lengthy concourse where it opened up into the central hub of the terminal. The Airmall was an octagonal structure filled with a food court, numerous shops, and escalators that descended to an underground transit system. The tram ferried passengers between the airside terminal and the landside terminal that housed the airline ticket counters, baggage carousels, and security screening areas.

The air here smelled of smoke residue and rot. My nose wrinkled in disgust, and I stopped short, carefully looking over the area before I stepped out of the concourse and into the Airmall.

A few rotted corpses were scattered across the floor of the area, and I figured they were likely the source of the scent of decomposition that hung in the air. I saw no obvious signs of charring or soot, so the smoke must have come from somewhere else in the terminal.

I looked up and was surprised that I could smell much of anything since the skylights that supported a raised section of the central roof had all caved in and covered the floor in shattered glass. I figured that only my Keen Senses ability let me detect the odors, since the broken windows up above allowed a steady breeze of fresh air to swirl through the area.

I kept my gaze focused on the Airmall as I gestured for the gnomes to deploy the turrets along either side of where the terminal joined the central hub. The machines whirred as they deployed, and their silence told me when the task was completed.

I cautiously stepped out into the open area as the gnomes waited at my back. The wind that drifted through the broken skylights far overhead died down and left the area in an oppressive silence. I instinctively slowed, ensuring that my footsteps stayed quiet without the whistling breeze to cover my movements.

Something hard scratched faintly across the tile floor, out of sight below where the escalators dropped toward the lower level of the terminal. The sharp sound broke the eerie silence, and I froze, waiting to see if the noise continued. When I heard nothing else after the initial scraping, I cautiously approached the railing that overlooked the open stairwell and peeked over the edge.

The area directly below me consisted of two staggered flights of stairs that separated twin pairs of escalators. The stairs were brightly lit thanks to the skylights far overhead, but past the end of the stairs, the area was obscured in shadow.

The scratching sound had come from the darkness that led to the transit system, and I peered into the shadows to look for the source of the noise.

For a long moment, nothing moved. Then I saw a large shape move within the depths of the dim space and heard more of the scratching, now identifiable as claws, scraping across the hard tile floor. It was too dark to make out anything, but the figure that shifted within the shadows seemed quadrupedal. I peered into the darkness, hoping to make out more detail, and continued to listen as the creature moved about below. Then I heard a sound I could only describe as a soft, shrill screech.

An answering hoot came from deeper underground, and I realized the large creature was not alone.

I slowly backed away from the edge and returned to the gnomes at the edge of Concourse B. They watched my movements with apprehension, clearly nervous about whatever had made me so cautious.

"There are at least two of something large down below in the transit tunnels that lead to the groundside terminal," I said to Borgym. I kept my voice low but avoided whispering since the pitch of those sounds traveled farther, and I really didn't want to alert the beasts I'd spotted. Not until we were prepared, at least.

"Can you tell me anything else about them?" Borgym asked.

"They communicated by screeching," I said with a shrug.

"That hardly narrows it down." Borgym frowned. The old gnome looked lost in thought for a moment, then shrugged. "We still need to clear them out regardless. How do you want to do it?"

I looked back at the open area and the descending stairway. There was another set of stairs opposite the route down to the transit system, leading up to the mezzanine level where American Airlines had their VIP lounge.

"Suits on the backside of the stairwell, so they can shoot down and hit the creatures in the back when they're coming up the stairs," I said, then pointed up. "Everyone else goes to the upper level so they can shoot down from an elevated position." I grinned wryly. "Then I play bait and hope you can pick the things off before they catch me."

Borgym agreed to my plan, though he had a couple suggestions to improve it. The turrets were placed around the perimeter of the Airmall so that anything coming up the stairs would be caught in a crossfire. He also handed me two stacks of thin, beige discs, each about the size of my hand and a quarter-inch thick.

While the gnomes moved into position, I crouched low and scattered the beige mines across the space at the top of the stairs. After the mines were placed, the thin discs promptly shifted their coloring to match the tile floor and practically disappeared.

Once the gnomes were all in place, Borgym signaled me over party chat, and I creeped down the stairs. At the landing between the two flights, I lay down so that I was out of sight from below. Careful to keep quiet, I slowly crawled across the floor to spread out the second stack of mines across the landing.

With the mines emplaced, I pushed myself to my feet and started back up the stairs. A surprised screech from behind alerted me that my retreat hadn't been as unnoticed as I hoped, and I sprinted to reach the top of the stairs.

At the top of the stairs, I pulled the Banshee hybrid rifle from my inventory as I turned and got my first good look at the creature that had emerged from the shadows below.

A horrid, brown-furred quadruped was already halfway up the first flight of stairs. Each of the beast's four stocky legs ended in paws tipped with claws several inches long, though their sharp curves looked more like the talons of a giant bird of prey. The rest of the animal's body almost resembled a bear—smaller than the mother bear I had killed on day one of the apocalypse, but not by much. However, instead of a snarling bear head, this creature had a feathered, flat-faced cranium with a large hooked beak.

I pulled the rifle to my shoulder and fired. The hybrid weapon whined as it spooled up, then kicked sharply into my armpit as it discharged. The blast caught the bird-bear-thing in the face, and it staggered from the impact.

My shot was the signal for the gnomes to attack, and weapons fire rained down onto the creature from the armored suits positioned above it. Micro-explosions wreathed the monster in flames, and energy beams raked across its furred pelt. The creature stumbled under the sudden onslaught but continued to push its way up the stairs and onto the landing.

Then the beast stepped onto one of the mines. The tripped mine launched itself upward into the creature's underside before it exploded in a blast that lifted the creature off the floor. Fire engulfed the beast, and it let out an ear-piercing screech as it slammed back onto the floor. It feebly crawled back onto its feet as a flurry of answering screeches poured from the transit tunnels behind it.

I fired again, and another round of attacks from the armored suits poured into the injured creature. It keeled over as four more shapes charged up out of the gloomy underground.

Two of the new beasts were the same size as the one we had just managed to kill. The other two were even larger.

I shifted my aim to the first of the bigger bear-things that rushed up the stairs and fired the hybrid rifle as fast as it would cycle. The rest of the mines on the landing detonated under the big animal's thundering footsteps, but it pushed through the explosions with little more damage than singed fur as its hate-filled eyes bored into me.

Behind the creature I targeted, the other of the larger creatures saw the twitching corpse on the landing and stopped to nuzzle it. Then it leaned back on its haunches and gave a mournful screech that filled the air. The piercing sound echoed through the Airmall, and I winced as the shrill noise stabbed at my eardrums.

Mental Influence Resisted

The agonizing cries over party chat let me know that most of the unarmored gnomes had been affected by the shrill cry.

"They're birdbears," Borgym said over party chat, finally able to see the creatures from his position on the mezzanine above as the monsters climbed higher in the wide stairwell.

At least I now knew what the ugly beasts were called.

I quickly backed away from the stairs as the big birdbear reached the top and continued its charge toward me. The automated turrets activated, and all four fired simultaneously. Their beams caressed the massive beast and left behind singed fur.

I cast Frostbolt, then immediately activated Hinder. The combined movement-impairing effects slowed the creature enough that I stayed just beyond the reach of the massive beast's slashing claws.

I jogged backward, away from the center of the Airmall, as the big birdbear chased me, and I snapped off a shot from my hybrid rifle at the first of the smaller birdbears to reach the top of the steps in an effort to pull that creature into pursuing me as well.

The small creature looked around for the source of the attack. Then a pair of beam attacks from the gnomes on the upper level hit it in the side, and it charged toward the other stairwell that led to the mezzanine above. The mines scattered across the floor there exploded beneath it, and the beast tumbled into a skid. Its claws dug into the tile floor as it scrambled to its feet and headed toward the stairs ahead of it once again.

I fired another shot at the stair-bound birdbear, but the younger creature ignored my attack and continued toward the upper level. The gnomes would have to deal with that one on their own.

The second smaller birdbear crested the top of the stairs, and I cast Frostbolt. This time, my attack succeeded in catching the creature's attention, and it rushed toward me.

Still dancing backward, I returned my focus to the bigger birdbear and hit it with another blast from my hybrid rifle.

The repeated attacks were taking their toll on the large creature. The fur of its underside was singed from the explosions of the mines, and its face had become a matted, bloody mess from my repeated railgun shots. All that remained of one eye was a gaping, ragged hole where a lucky shot of mine had punched through the cheekbone.

The beast's remaining eye glared angrily and promised death if it reached me. I vowed to myself not to let that happen as I ran through the food court that took up a large portion of the Airmall.

Tables and chairs flew through the air as the two birdbears bowled through the food court and chased me. Every couple of steps, I twisted back to fire my rifle, and I activated Hinder when the smaller birdbear surged ahead of the larger one.

When Frostbolt finished its cooldown, I cast it again at the bigger birdbear. The creature shrieked angrily when the shard of ice burrowed into the thick flesh of its torso, and I fired the hybrid rifle into its open beak. The angry screech turned into more of a choking cough, and it staggered to a halt. The birdbear's head jerked down as it wheezed and hacked, blood spraying from its damaged maw to splash across the tiled floor.

I sped into a sprint and turned to circle the wounded creature, keeping its bulk between the birdbear youth and me. I ran around behind the creature and came up in the blind spot of its dead eye. The birdbear's shoulders stood nearly as tall as me, but with its head down due to coughing, the beast's face was near the floor, and I didn't have a good angle into the open wound.

I crouched and squeezed the trigger as I jammed the end of my rifle barrel into the hole in the birdbear's face. The creature squeaked in surprise as the rifle whined right beside it, and the birdbear swung a leg toward me just as the rifle discharged.

The powerful backhand crumpled the armor built into my jumpsuit, knocked the wind from me, and broke several ribs as the attack lifted me from my feet. I pinwheeled through the air, unable to breathe while the world spun around me. My rifle slipped from my grasp when it caught on something, and I only caught a glimpse of the weapon spinning through the air before it clattered out of sight.

Tables and chairs scattered, scraping across the tile floor, as I plowed through the food court. Each impact sent a stab of pain jolting through my chest as the offending piece of furniture skidded away. A table edge dug into my back before its legs gave way and I tumbled to the floor.

When I finally slid to a stop, I sat up with a groan and glanced at the birdbear. The massive creature lay slumped to the floor and looked as though it was missing half of its head. I glanced at my health bar and found that I was missing over a third of it from the single blow, so I felt as though that was a fair trade.

"One down," I gasped over party chat as the smaller birdbear barreled toward me across the food court. My chest heaved with the effort it took to breathe, and I felt a stabbing sensation as one of my broken ribs cut through my flesh.

I pulled one of the health potions from my inventory and gulped it down. A soothing sensation spread through my chest and dampened the pain, though the distant agony lingered. My health crawled upward, and I tossed aside the empty potion bottle as I felt the disconcerting sensation of my ribs shifting as they settled back into place.

I painfully heaved myself to my feet and drew my beam pistols to face down the onrushing juvenile birdbear. I opened fire as soon as my weapons were on target. The energy beams lashed across the beast's face, and it flinched from the assault. The attack wasn't enough to halt the creature, though the distraction slowed the beast enough for me to cast another Frostbolt before it reached me.

The birdbear leapt toward me, and I dove out of the way. I rolled to my feet and turned back to keep up my barrage of energy fire before the creature could halt its momentum. The beams lit into the birdbear's flank, and the smell of burnt hair filled my nostrils as the brown fur charred under my attacks.

The smaller creature was far slower than the larger one that had pursued me so ferociously, and I was easily able to avoid its claws. Still, the birdbear kept me occupied enough that I didn't have any attention to spare beyond a few quick looks around to ensure that none of the remaining beasts were trying to sneak up on me.

I had no idea how the gnomes fared, until a glance at the party menu showed one of the portraits grayed out with empty health bars.

Shit.

I still had an angry birdbear to contend with, and I couldn't do anything about helping the others for now.

My pistols emptied their charges with the beast still on its feet, and I had to stash the drained weapons in my Inventory. I pulled out one of my projectile pistols, along with the beam pistol looted from the dead alien.

The projectile pistol thundered as I fired, filling the indoor space with its sharp retorts and the acrid smell of gunpowder.

The creature collapsed under my renewed barrage and screeched pitifully as it clung to life. I holstered my weapons to conserve their ammunition and pulled my knife in a reverse grip as I jumped onto the birdbear's back. I stabbed down into the neck and shoulders of the beast.

The birdbear rolled in an attempt to throw me off and crush me beneath it. The movements were so slowed by Hinder, repeated Frostbolts, and the damage I'd been pouring into it that I easily leapt free. The roll onto its back exposed the underside of the monster's neck, and I lunged forward to stab my knife into it.

Despite the creature's tough skin, my knife plunged deep. Blood gushed from the neck wound to coat my hand and arm as I sawed the blade back and forth. When the creature tried to roll the rest of the way over, I twisted the blade and yanked it free in time to step out of range from a weak swipe of its claws.

Blood flowed freely from the gash in the birdbear's neck to pool on the floor. The creature slowed as the gory puddle spread around it, and the familiar tang of blood filled my nostrils while I watched the life fade from the birdbear.

A scream of terror over party chat pulled my attention from the dying creature in front of me.

I turned and found that the remaining large birdbear had been engaged by the three armored suits and the automated turrets. Two of the turrets were sparking wrecks, and the remaining two seemed to be out of energy charges.

One suit lay crumpled against the far wall and looked as though it was attempting to regain its feet despite the fact that one of the suit legs was twisted at a 90-degree angle above the knee.

A second suit, missing an arm, poured all of its weapon's fire into the birdbear's flank at close range. The suit's flamethrower burned through the thick fur and left behind charred, cracked flesh. Missiles from the suit's shoulder mounts dug into that burnt flesh and exploded, launching hunks of flesh across the area.

None of the attacks pulled the enraged beast's attention from its prey, the source of the panicked scream over party chat. The birdbear had the third suit pinned to the floor in a bearhug as it repeatedly hammered its beak into the cockpit canopy that had cracked under the assault.

Then the canopy shattered, and the scream cut off suddenly as the birdbear's beak plunged into the cockpit.

Another portrait in the party menu turned gray, and I noted it was the third darkened icon as a cry of despair and anger echoed through party chat.

I looked around the food court and located my dropped rifle before hurrying to the weapon and scooping it up. I gave the rifle a quick once-over to ensure it remained undamaged after being flung across the food court. I shouldered the weapon and fired at the birdbear.

My shot was far from alone.

Weapons fire poured into the beast from all sides. There was no sign of the other small birdbear and it must have already been slain, since all of the gnomes in the mezzanine now launched their attacks from above.

The birdbear lurched under the assault and staggered away from the fallen armored suit. The many projectile and missile attacks ripped chunks from the beast, and it finally collapsed under the storm of withering fire. The creature shuddered and twitched several times as the attacks continued. I stopped firing when the beast grew still, but the gnomes' fury remained unabated.

I pulled spare ammunition from my Inventory and reloaded my magazines. Then I looted the two dead birdbears that lay in the food court.

Even after the time that took me, several streams of fire still rained down on the corpse of the last birdbear.

"I think it's dead," I said over the party chat.

Gradually, the gnomes ceased firing.

I walked over to the blasted, gory corpse of the birdbear and looted it. Then I turned toward the downed suit.

The two other suit pilots had dismounted from their armor and looked down into the ruined cockpit of the fallen suit. Alryn had left his mangled armor tipped over on its side against the wall, never having stood back up on the twisted leg, and Ipbar's armless suit stood empty behind him.

Since I first heard the scream over party chat, I had known who the pilot of the fallen suit had been, but I had still avoided directly reading the gray icons in the party window.

Now the most cheerful of the gnomes I had met was gone. Somehow, Talli's loss made the clan seem diminished, even if I hadn't known her well enough to grieve like the two pilots in front of me.

Footsteps from behind caused me to turn, and I saw that a stream of gnomes were headed toward the fallen suit. I stepped out of the way and allowed them to pass in silence.

Borgym reached me and stopped.

The clan elder had always carried his age in a refined manner, even when punted through the air by a zealous starship captain. Now the Borgym I saw hunched over his cane just looked old and barely able to stand, as if the deaths of his clan members were weights placed on his shoulders to crush him. He stood quietly for a moment, trembling hands braced on the cane as if it were the only thing keeping him on his feet.

"There were always going to be losses once we set on this course," Borgym said. Then the old gnome sighed. "I just never expected my daughter to be one of them."

"I'm sorry," I said. "I can't imagine how you must feel."

"There's no time for grief now." Borgym closed his eyes to hide his unshed tears and shook his head. "We have to finish what we've started, or it will be for nothing."

The old gnome stood a little straighter, showing that he'd found the strength to continue on somewhere within himself. The father who mourned was set aside for another time, and only the resolute leader remained.

The elder stepped away from me and organized the group of gnomes. Tears flowed freely throughout the party, and several shoved at each other angrily until Borgym gave the troublemakers each a smack on the back of their heads.

The two functional turrets had their Mana batteries replaced before they were set to guard the area. The damaged turrets were gathered up, their wreckage placed next to the ruined armored suits and the trio of body bags that contained the fallen gnomes.

Everyone reloaded and rearmed themselves before all of the survivors left the Airmall behind, and we headed into Concourse A.

Chapter 15

After the struggle to clear the first concourse and the Airmall, the rest of the terminal went fairly smoothly.

Only a few minor creatures attacked us as we moved through the concourse. All of the creatures were birds, and none of them were as large as the hawk we had encountered when we first entered the terminal.

While we patrolled through Concourse A, the northeast wing of the terminal, we could see out the windows that there wasn't much left of Concourse D to the west. A plane had crashed into the terminal, and half of the concourse had collapsed into rubble.

Once we had cleared all of Concourse A, the party walked back the way we had come instead of going outside and working our way back to the central hub through the demolished Concourse D.

The final wing of the terminal, Concourse C, was similarly uneventful. The only attack came from a pair of rabid crows which alerted us with their caws and were put down before they managed to do damage to anyone in the party.

Once we had cleared the final concourse, I waited with most of the party as Borgym and two others went to retrieve the clan's architect.

When the trio returned, they escorted a young gnome. He was unarmed and looked much younger than the others. He stood at the center of the group with his thumbs hooked into the belt on his oversized jumpsuit, an outfit that was clearly meant for someone larger, and shifted nervously from side to side.

Borgym stepped up to the jittery young gnome and placed a hand on his shoulder. "Are you ready, Ospyr? We'll be here to protect you."

"Yes," the young gnome replied.

Ospyr knelt and placed a palm on the floor, then he closed his eyes. Beneath his hand, the floor glowed.

I turned away and looked down the length of the terminal as the rest of the gnomes formed into a loose circle around the architect.

I walked out of the perimeter and paced several strides down the terminal. Nothing stirred, and I was glad we had taken the time to clear the terminal before attempting to stabilize the Mana inside. We could be relatively confident now that the only monsters left would be stragglers. If we had ended up with more than the birdbears earlier, that fight could have ended up with far more dead gnomes.

I looked back at the party. The surviving gnomes had an edge to them, noticeable as each one watched their sectors intently for the arrival of any more monsters. It was a remarkable change in their demeanor from early this morning, when they had babbled in nervous anticipation.

Nothing stirred in the terminal and, about ten minutes later, the gnome finished channeling his skill. It almost came as a surprise when Ospyr gasped and sank down into a seated position, exhausted by the completion of the channeling process. We gave Ospyr a minute to recover before he shook himself as he stood stiffly. We moved down the terminal about a hundred feet before we reformed the perimeter.

Once we were in position, we were forced to wait for the young gnome's Mana pool to regenerate completely. The process, through which Ospyr activated his Class Skill and actively channeled it to modify the terminal, drained his Mana pool to nearly empty with each section.

We let Ospyr channel his skill. Moved to the next position. Waited for the architect to replenish his Mana. And then did it all over again.

The process continued uneventfully for almost an hour and a half until we finally finished securing Concourse C.

The rest of the day dragged on, a sharp contrast to the morning filled with adrenaline and blood. A few mutated small birds like sparrows and a solitary ruffed grouse were the only attacks throughout the day, and all were put down well short of the party's perimeter.

The central hub of the Airmall took just over an hour to lock down, followed by two hours each for Concourses B and A as we moved counterclockwise through the terminal.

Halfway through Concourse A, we passed a bar that didn't look completely trashed, and I made a mental note to come back when we were finished. I hadn't had a drink since the apocalypse started, and the amber bottles behind the bar practically called my name.

Dusk had fallen by the time we finished the last section of the terminal.

Ospyr finished channeling the final time and collapsed theatrically to the floor. His antics drew a few chuckles from the other gnomes, despite their exhaustion and the day's losses, and even as everyone stopped to read the new notification which had appeared for us all.

You Have Entered a Safe Zone (Terminal, Pittsburgh Sprocketsworth Starport)

Mana flows in this area are stabilized. No monster spawning will happen.
This Safe Space includes:
Passenger and Freight Terminals

Borgym passed orders to the gnomes, mostly sending them off to join other groups of gnomes who had started the laborious task of cleaning their new structure. Junk and bodies had been left throughout the area, all of which would need to be removed before the building could reopen as a functional starport.

I walked over to the old gnome, once the other gnomes had headed off to perform their various tasks and he was left alone. Borgym looked at me tiredly and gestured for me to join him as he walked toward the center of the terminal.

"Thank you," Borgym said and a notification popped up.

Quest Complete!

You have cleared the requested airport facilities of all hostile entities and allowed the Sprocketsworth clan to solidify their claim of the installation.

20,000 Credits and 15,000 XP Awarded. +400 reputation with Sprocketsworth clan.

I brushed aside the notification and looked at Borgym. "I wish I could have done more."

Even to me, the words seemed hollow and insufficient.

Borgym shrugged. "The System gives, and the System takes away."

Despite his casual acceptance of events, I saw the pain he attempted to bury in the depths of his eyes and had no idea how to respond to his statement. Instead, I let silence fill the air.

"What will you do now?" Borgym asked finally.

I was thrilled to let the gnome change the subject. "I was thinking of hitting that bar halfway down the concourse and seeing if any booze survived the apocalypse."

"I meant afterward," said Borgym. "But help yourself to the bar."

I debated how much to reveal. Borgym had provided me the opportunity to earn plenty of Credits and experience. Between the quests and the monster kills, I should have accumulated a couple Levels. At the least, he deserved my trust.

"I was actually looking for a group of Galactics," I confessed. "That's why I met your ship after watching you land, but you're not who I hoped to find."

"And who were you searching for?" Borgym asked.

I outlined the little I knew of the events from the school. The old gnome frowned when I told him how every adult had been slaughtered and that the schoolchildren were all missing. Then I described the dead alien I had discovered in the aftermath of the attack.

"Krym'parke," Borgym spat in disgust after I detailed the horns and fangs of the creature. Then the gnome looked up at my expression of confusion. "Bogeymen, you'd probably call them."

"Bogeymen?" I asked. "Monsters in the night that eat children who misbehave?"

A notification pinged and dragged my attention to the Quest page of my status screen.

Quest Update: Find the children.

The unknown attackers have been identified as Krym'parke. Find them and determine the fates of any human victims.

Oblivious to my attention to my Quest screen, Borgym nodded in response to my question and sighed. "The phenomenon is called Mana bleed. Even in places outside of the System, common myths and legends have propagated about some of the species that exist within it. It's as if the System is somehow preparing the universe outside it for eventual assimilation."

Elsewhere on my Quest status window, the System Quest tracker jumped upward a whole percent point.

Borgym placed a hand on his chest when I finally turned my attention back to him. "From what I studied of your planet on our way here, I imagine you would consider me a gnome. You probably think my people typically enjoy living underground with a natural aptitude for alchemy and mechanical ingenuity."

He was right. I had thought of them as gnomes. Especially given their inclinations as artisans from the mech suits I had seen and proven ability as alchemists.

"So you're not gnomes?"

"There are several different species that overlap with most of your mythological fantasy races, including gnomes," Borgym replied. "My people are actually known as the Pharyleri."

"Oh," I said. "I hope I haven't offended you."

The old gnome looked amused. "It's your planet, so humans will get a pass for most faux pas. You'll want to download a standard System cultural pack from the Shop if you ever leave Earth though. System etiquette generally follows common courtesy for the species whose homeworld you're on." He chuckled darkly and looked at me. "Always review the local etiquette before you set foot on a new world."

I nodded; message received. I made a mental note to pick up that cultural update as my next Shop purchase. My shopping list never seemed to get any shorter as my experiences grew and I learned that I always needed more knowledge, more equipment, and more Skills.

"So," I said. "Krym'parke, huh?"

"Pretty much what you would expect," replied Borgym. "Primarily nocturnal, their preferred source of sustenance is the youth of other sentient species. The young they don't eat are often sold as slaves. Most civilized races hunt them down when a band pops up, but their clans are as tenacious as

Feltha roaches. No matter how many times they get hunted down, they always seem to pop back up again later."

If a Feltha roach was anything like a terrestrial cockroach, it meant these things were hard to exterminate.

I frowned. "Not an easy group to track down then."

Borgym shook his head. "Not likely. It doesn't help that they tend to find other groups of dubious character and use them as a front. Gimsar or Hakarta renegades are popular choices, mercenaries who have forsaken their code of honor."

I had more information now, but it got me no closer to my goal of finding the attackers from the school. I knew who the attackers were, but not where they might be. For all I knew, they could be operating from the moon with their spaceships.

Borgym sensed my frustration and patted my elbow. "Give it time. They never just strike once, though that would be the smart play. There will be more sightings, and then you'll get your shot at them."

We reached the central hub of the terminal and found the entire clan gathered. Borgym patted my arm again then disappeared into the crowd.

I stood and watched the assembly. The somber gathering contrasted sharply with the lively group that had first arrived on Earth.

The bodies of the fallen had been arranged on biers at the center of the crowd. Small groups huddled around each of the dead—immediate family, I assumed from their wails and the way they clutched each other for support.

Soon, solitary voices rose from the crowd in a mournful song that echoed through the lofty space. I couldn't understand the language, the words coming through my earpiece were older and more primal than the dialect the system had been translating, but I felt the full force of the grief and heartache that suffused the lyrics.

Other singers added to the chorus, lending their support to the haunting melody. More and more of the assembly joined in. Even the family members lifted their voices as the refrain swept through the terminal.

At that moment, faced with the collective sorrow of an entire clan, I felt even more like an outsider intruding on their grief. The soulful harmony pursued me as I backed away from the gathering and slipped into Concourse A. I retreated to the bar I had noticed earlier when we had cleared the area.

Sleek paneling of dark wood lined the walls and the furniture surfaces of the airport restaurant. The somber tones of the wood were in sharp contrast to the teal-painted metalwork that provided the framework for the furnishings.

With no power, I resolved to find something I could drink without ice or mixers. I wandered behind the wood-topped bar and looked over the high shelf stock. If I wasn't paying for it, I was going to ignore the well drinks.

"This looks promising," I muttered as I lifted an amber bottle with a yellow label onto the bartop. This Pennsylvania Straight Rye looked like something I could drink without a mixer or ice.

I grabbed a rocks glass and poured a finger's worth of the whiskey into it. I swirled the golden liquid in the glass and took a cautious sniff as I raised it to my face. Notes of vanilla and black pepper filled my nose in a strangely appealing combination. I sipped at the liquor tentatively.

The first taste felt spicy and strong, with hints of florals and herbs that quickly gave way to a smooth, smokey finish as I let the liquor linger on my tongue. I swallowed and enjoyed the earthy aftertaste common to rye whiskey.

This would do, all right.

The bottle was nearly full, and I left it on the bar as I walked around from behind the bar to the front side of the counter. I perched on one of the high stools and sipped my way through the rest of the glass. I poured another round and kept drinking.

Four strong drinks later, the bottle was half empty, and I still hadn't felt the slightest tingle of a buzz from the whiskey. I double-checked the bottle.

Eighty-four proof.

I was drinking it straight, so I should have felt something by now. I frowned and checked my notifications. Nothing there besides the experience and question completion updates.

I then brought up my combat log.

Poison Effect Resisted.

The message repeated. Numerous times.

The System treated alcohol as a poison, and my increased Constitution combined with my Class resistances to nullify the effects.

Damn. So much for getting my drink on.

I poured myself another glass anyways and went back to the notifications I had accrued over the last day and a half.

Level Up! * 5

You have reached Level 13 as a Relentless Huntsman. Stat Points automatically distributed. You have 10 free attributes to distribute.

Class Skills Locked.

Woah. That was quite the jump.

While I knew I had gained a few levels, only earning two free points at a time seemed hardly worth the effort when I had been busy with the ongoing quest chain. Still, I had nearly doubled my level in just two days of near-constant combat. Over two levels had come from quest experience alone, and as a combat class, I had reaped the lion's share of the accrued group experience from all of the monster kills.

Clearly, I needed to find a way to complete more Quests if I wanted to gain Levels fast.

I really couldn't complain about my speedy progress, but that "Class Skills Locked" notification really was getting old.

Four of the free attribute points went into Agility, three into Strength, two into Perception, and the final point into Willpower. If my math was right and I put both free attribute points into Perception with my next level, I should hit the Class minimums after the automatic point distribution at Level 15, and finally unlock access to my Class Skills.

I confirmed my selections and reviewed my status one final time.

Status Screen			
Name:	Hal Mason*	Class:	Hunter*
Race:	Human (Male)	Level:	13
Titles			
Sharp Eyed (Title hidden)*			
Health:	450	Stamina:	450
Mana:	370		

Status			
Normal*			
Attributes			
Strength	29 (30)	Agility	56 (60)
Constitution	45 (50)	Perception	37 (40)
Intelligence	37 (40)	Willpower	28 (30)
Charisma	36 (40)	Luck	16
Class Skills			
Hinder	1	Keen Senses	1
On the Hunt	1		
Perks			
Gut Instinct			
Combat Spells			
Frostbolt (I), Minor Healing (I)			

I closed my status screen and took another gulp of the smooth whiskey as I looked at the last notification to await my acknowledgement.

Quest Update: Free the children.

You have identified the species responsible for the kidnapped school children.

Rewards: 1,000 XP and 1,000 Credits

I closed the update and hoped that the kids were all right, though given Borgym's tales of the aliens, I doubted it. I shook my head and sipped my drink.

The booze might not affect me, but the act itself brought relaxation, and I closed my eyes. I could almost imagine the murmur of bar patrons as they swapped stories before catching their flights as modern rock played from the speakers of the bar's sound system.

For a maudlin moment, I considered the fantasy. Would I go back to the way things were before, if I could? More than four billion people were now dead, if my back-of-the-napkin math was accurate for a planetary population of seven billion on day one. If that many had died the first day alone, I could only imagine what the death totals were at now.

Still, despite my many close calls, I seemed to thrive. I'd come out on top when it could have just as easily been someone else who lived in my place.

Maybe if my fire had drawn the jabberwock, Zeke would still be alive and I would be the one buried on the Point. Maybe he'd have reached his kids, none of them would have still been at the school when the Krym'parke attacked.

I dismissed the flight of fancy that my thoughts had taken. No second guesses could bring back the dead or reverse the course the world had taken under the System.

Would I go back, if I could? No. I had gained so much that to answer otherwise would be madness. I loved the abilities I had now and the way that my old injuries were only a memory. Still, a delusion remained buried in the depths of my mind, that somehow a lone individual could face down the might of the System and everything it represented. The blood of slain billions across the world called out for vengeance, and something inside me wanted to be an agent of that retribution.

Someday, if I successfully reached beyond a Master Class, then I could consider payback for what had been done to Earth. But today… today, I was just a gnat. A gnat that would be swatted if I didn't level higher and continue to push beyond my limits. I had seen how easy it was to fall against the monsters and spawns that the System threw at its inhabitants. Over and over, the System had reinforced the lesson that only the strong survived.

Determined to stay the course, I opened my eyes and drained the last of the whiskey in my glass. I was about to push back my stool and head out when I heard a pair of footsteps enter the bar.

Ipbar and Alryn looked around the dim space and tentatively stepped inside.

I stood and reached over the bar to grab two more glasses. I filled them and pushed the glasses down the bar toward the new arrivals before I refilled my own glass.

The two Pharyleri each climbed up onto a bar stool and sniffed at the whiskey skeptically. They glanced at each other then looked at me. I smirked at their expressions and gave them a toast before I tossed back a gulp.

Alryn just stared at his glass, but Ipbar attempted to mimic my actions. The gnome started coughing as soon as he swallowed.

I chuckled at the curdled expression on Ipbar's face and took a more normal sip. Alryn duplicated the more reasonable taste and nodded appreciatively. He smirked at Ipbar, who still opened and closed his mouth repeatedly as he tried to clear the taste.

"What the hell was that?" Ipbar finally asked.

"Whiskey," I replied. "Pennsylvania Straight Rye."

Ipbar just shook his head.

"Not bad," said Alryn.

From there, the conversation turned to Galactic spirits and comparing them with various liquors I managed to find behind the bar.

An hour and a half later, the two Pharyleri were well on their way to sauced. As crafters, their Classes lacked innate resistances, so they felt the full effects of the alcohol. Though I still wasn't feeling the buzz, the gnomes' antics raised my spirits.

While clearly not a fan of whiskey, Ipbar had discovered an appreciation for spiced rum and continuously failed to duplicate the raised leg pose of the red-coated privateer on the bottle. The tipsy gnome toppled over on every single try and giggled before standing up to take another drink. Usually he remembered to set the glass back on the bar before he attempted the pose again, to predictably hilarious results. Several cracked and broken glasses littered the floor from the times he'd forgotten.

"You're cleaning that up in the morning." I shook my head and chuckled.

Ipbar burped and pushed himself up off the bar floor yet again as Alryn laughed at him. Only then did I see Borgym standing outside the bar and watching the two drunk gnomes with a raised eyebrow. The old gnome turned toward me as if to ask what was going on, and I shrugged. He sighed and walked over to me.

"I sent these two to find out where you'd wandered off to," Borgym said.

"They didn't mention you sent them," I replied as I reached over the bar for another glass. The supply of clean glassware was running low thanks to Ipbar's destructive habits.

I poured Borgym a shot of the rye and handed it over. He swirled it and breathed in the aroma before he nodded appreciatively. Then he took a sip and held it in his mouth for a moment.

"Not bad," Borgym finally delivered judgment. "A little weak though."

"Weak?" I asked.

Borgym pulled a flask from his Inventory and handed it over. I unscrewed the cap and threw back a slug.

Fire swept through my mouth and shot down into my stomach in a raging torrent. Heat blossomed through my core and energy radiated out from my center to course through my body. Muscles quivered with anticipation, as if ready to explode into action at a moment's notice. The alcoholic buzz I had missed hit me full force as this liquid intoxicant rushed through my resistances as if they were nonexistent.

Borgym chuckled at my reaction. "That'll turn your whiskers pink."

"What was that?" I gasped and handed back the flask.

I rubbed the unshaven stubble along my jaw and hoped that Borgym's metaphor wasn't literal. After the genome treatment had erased my scars, I finally had a full five o'clock shadow for once. And while vibrant hues might work for the gnomes, I didn't think it would fit me.

He pushed the flask back toward me along the bar's counter. "Keep it, you looked like you could use a good drink. That's a forever flask of Argellian Fire Water."

"Uh, thanks," I said. "What's a forever flask?"

Borgym pointed at a rune carved into the outside of the flask. "Channel your Mana into that when the flask gets empty, and it'll fill right back up. Careful though, you may feel great, but your Willpower and Dexterity are both lowered when you're drinking it."

I checked my status. Sure enough, I had a timed debuff that lowered both Dex and Will by several points each. On the other hand, my health, mana, and stamina regeneration had all temporarily increased. No wonder I felt so great.

"Gotcha," I said. "Use after a fight, not before or during. Thank you."

I took another taste of the fiery liquid, and it burned just as much the second time. Then I put the flask away in my Inventory, lest I get too caught up with it.

Borgym joined me at the bar, and word soon spread to the rest of the clan. An impromptu wake formed, and this time, I was stuck firmly at the center of it. Fortunately, this gathering lacked the solemnity of earlier, and most of the Pharyleri had already returned to their normal cheery selves.

I ended up making several trips into the bar's kitchen and storage rooms for more glassware and booze as the crowd grew. My brief buzz cleared quickly while I worked to stack the pilfered supplies.

With the party in full swing, I stayed behind the counter and slung drinks. One gnome used a spell to fill an ice bin behind the bar with cubed ice, and I added chilled drinks to the rotation. I wouldn't claim to be a great bartender, but I could turn out passable drinks from the well stock. Long Island iced teas, gin and tonics, and black Russians were common, but I found that many of the Pharyleri shared Ipbar's affinity for rum.

I simply could not keep up with the drink requests and ended up leaving a case of rum out on the counter so they could experiment with the available combinations on their own. By the time I finally got a break, the bar was overflowing with the pint-sized Pharyleri. It was an odd sight, like a bar filled with kids.

The drinking continued long after sundown. By the time the last of the Pharyleri passed out, the padded seats at the terminal gates nearest the bar were filled with sprawled and snoring gnomes.

Even though I had been entirely sober for the last half of the evening, I still chugged water before I called it a night myself. Old habits died hard, and I had no desire to find out how ugly of a hangover Argellian Fire Water could leave behind.

I found an empty corner and slumped down against the wall before I quickly fell asleep.

Chapter 16

The next week passed in a blur.

I stuck around the burgeoning starport as the Pharyleri industriously developed the buildings they had claimed. Multiple engineers worked to install the infrastructure throughout the terminal that would support starship refueling and repair, as well as cargo and passenger transportation. The terminal gates that had formerly served the terrestrial aircraft industry were spread out to create larger bays so that massive transport ships would have wide berths with plenty of room to load cargo.

One of the biggest draws of a Dungeon World was the export of raw crafting materials to the universe at large. The starport was designed to facilitate the loading of those raw materials onto transport ships in order to get the cargo to the desired destinations as fast as possible. While the use of portals or teleportation technology was faster than the physical movement of the goods, the cost scaled with the size and number of items transported. Bulk transportation for any method besides physical movement quickly became prohibitively expensive.

I only picked up on all of those details peripherally though, since I wasn't involved in any of the building or logistical projects. Or the cleanup of the bodies that littered the grounds. The birdbears had pulled a number of bodies into the underground tram tunnels that had to be dealt with.

It turned out that the crashed plane on the airport access road was not the only wrecked aircraft. Several others littered the ground and the runways. It looked as though some of the pilots had attempted to somehow glide their craft onto the runways without any working engines. They had all failed, dooming their passengers when the planes smashed into the earth.

Instead of dealing with any of that, my job remained hunting monsters.

Even though the habitable buildings of the starport were now Safe Zones, none of the outside areas would receive that classification until the starport officially opened. So monsters roamed the outside, and the old chain-link fences that had bordered the airport did little to deter any remotely aggressive creatures. I patrolled regularly to eliminate anything that crossed onto the grounds.

I killed creatures until my Inventory filled up, then I dumped the corpses off at the airport fire station. The fire trucks had been cleared out of large truck bays, and the building had been repurposed as a crafting hub. Corpses went in one side and came out the other as processed raw materials.

I was more than happy to trade my kills to the clan crafters in exchange for Credits. It saved me the gory work of harvesting the useful bits myself. Though the clan paid a little less than I would get from the Shop, it saved me the hassle of making the trip, and I could make the exchange as soon as my Inventory was full. The difference was offset in that I was also being paid for the kills made on starport grounds.

Unfortunately, without the bonuses from Quests, my experience totals hadn't risen as quickly as my Credit balance. My leveling had slowed until I finally hit Level 15 almost exactly a week after we had cleared the airport terminal.

I had just dumped a pile of monster corpses off at the crafting station when I checked my notifications.

Level Up!

You have reached Level 15 as a Relentless Huntsman. Stat Points automatically distributed. You have 2 free attributes to distribute.

Class Skills Unlocked.

Finally, the notification I'd waited so long to see.

I had put my two attribute points at Level 14 into Perception, so the automatic distribution when I hit my latest level now raised me over the minimum requirements for my Advanced Class.

As I celebrated in my head, I allocated both of my new free points into Luck. The neglected attribute needed some love, and I'd certainly been lucky enough to survive so far.

With the attribute selection handled, I opened my Class Skill page. Without points to spend, I hadn't looked at it since enabling the Head Start perk all the way back on day one.

Class Skills unlocked

7 Class Skills Available to be Distributed. Would you like to do so?

I most certainly would! I selected the affirmative and started off by assigning a point to the only tier one ability still locked, the first Class Skill in the Utility tree.

Class Skill Acquired

Meat Locker (Level 1)

Effect: The Relentless Huntsman now has access to an extra-dimensional storage location of 20 cubic feet. Only deceased bounty targets or slain creatures may be added to this location and must be touched to be willed inside. Mana regeneration reduced by 5 Mana per minute permanently.

Since I now had a point in each of the tier one abilities, all of the primary trees for tier two Class Skills showed up as ones I could choose. There was a grayed-out tier two Class Skill between the Pursuit and Combat trees that looked to require that I take the primary tree Skills as prerequisites first.

That was easy enough. I put a single point each in the three main tree abilities and the grayed-out Class Skill became selectable. After I activated that Skill, a barrage of notifications appeared.

Class Skill Acquired

The Right Tool for the Job (Level 1)

Effect: The Relentless Huntsman now has access to an extra-dimensional storage location of 5 cubic feet. Items stored must be touched to be willed in and may only include weapons, armor, equipment, or supplies owned by the Relentless Huntsman. Any qualifying System-recognized item can be placed or removed from this inventory location if space allows. Cost: 5 Mana per item.

Class Skill Acquired

Greater Observation (Level 1)

Effect: User may now detect System creatures up to 50 meters away and is provided an analysis of the subject upon detection. Increased Skill levels may reveal additional System information not normally available. Depending on comparative overall level and Skills in effect, the target of focused Observation may know that the user has gained some level of information. Mana regeneration reduced by 5 Mana per minute permanently.

Class Skill Acquired

Rend (Level 1)

Effect: Physical weapon attacks that cause health damage apply a bleed effect, causing the target to bleed for 15 damage over 15 seconds. This effect can be stacked if the health damage occurs at a different location on the target. Cost: 10 Stamina.

Class Skill Acquired

Implacable Endurance (Level 1)

Effect: Reduces Stamina cost for physical exertion and activated physical abilities by 25%. Does not stack with other Stamina reduction skills. Mana regeneration reduced by 5 Mana per minute permanently.

I had spent five of my seven points and unlocked all of the available tier one and two Class Skills. Despite that, the third-tier abilities remained unselectable in the menu. When I tried to add the tier three Class Skill from the Combat tree, a message indicated that it would remain locked until I reached Level 30.

I decided to save the last two points for now, at least until I had a better idea of what my newfound Class Skills could do for me.

I looked over my status sheet once more and grinned at the new entries in the Class Skills section.

Status Screen			
Name:	Hal Mason*	Class:	Hunter*
Race:	Human (Male)	Level:	15
Titles			
Sharp Eyed (Title hidden)*			
Health:	510	Stamina:	510
Mana:	410		

Status			
Normal*			
Attributes			
Strength	31	Agility	62
Constitution	51	Perception	41
Intelligence	41	Willpower	30
Charisma	40	Luck	18
Class Skills			
Greater Observation	1	Hinder	1
Implacable Endurance	1	Keen Senses	1
Meat Locker	1	On the Hunt	1
Rend	1	Right Tool For the Job	1
Perks			
Gut Instinct			

Combat Spells
Frostbolt (I), Minor Healing (I)

Time to check out my new toys, such as they were!

I looked around the area and was surprised to note additional details picked up by Greater Observation. A tiny, translucent map now appeared in my peripheral vision, overlaid on the corner of my field vision and only visible if I focused upon it.

I oriented myself toward a green dot shown on the minimap and found that one of the Pharyleri was already slicing apart one of the monster corpses I had just dropped off. Her position aligned with the indicator on my display as a friendly entity.

Beyond that new ability to see creatures displayed on the map, I found another surprise to go with it. Instead of the faint green health bar over her head that I usually saw, the gnome had additional details displayed along with the status bar.

Emilyana Grindsaw (Harvester Level 34)
HP: 290/290

Fantastic. Now I wouldn't have to remember names. And I could think of multiple applications now that I could accurately gauge health. I frowned. Her health seemed really low when compared with mine, even though she was more than double my Level.

My focus on Emilyana caught her attention and she turned toward me.

"Oi!" Emilyana shouted across the blacktop. "What are you gawking at?"

I shrugged and waved her off as I made a conscious effort to fixate on something else. The gnome grumbled and returned to harvesting the corpse.

So that was what the ability description meant about alerting the target of my focus. I would need to practice my use of that Class Skill to avoid such casual detection. It seemed a likely candidate for one of the unused Class Skill points I still held, but I wanted to check out the rest of the abilities.

The Right Tool for the Job was the next Class Skill I tried out. When activated, the Class Skill popped open a new Inventory window in front of me. I moved all of my weapons, ammunition, tools, rations, and supplies into the additional space. That cleared out a number of spaces in my normal Inventory tab, which meant more spaces for loot and monster parts.

Speaking of monster parts, I tested out Meat Locker next. Like the previous skill, it also opened a new Inventory space. However, nothing would go into the open spaces in the grid as I went through everything left in my Inventory. Finally, I walked back to the pile of dead monsters and placed my hand on one.

The corpse dropped right into the new space without the slightest bit of resistance.

"Hey," a shrill voice called. "What are you doing? I already paid you for those."

I looked up to see Emilyana had turned back to me again.

"Sorry," I said defensively. "I was just trying something. I'll put it back."

With a mental tug, the corpse dropped out of the Meat Locker and back into the spot it had been initially, right where I'd dropped it off the first time.

Emilyana just glared at me.

I swallowed nervously at the angry gnome's look. "I'm just gonna go now."

The gnome watched with narrowed eyes as I walked away, and she didn't return to her work until I had put over a hundred yards between us.

I had tried out three of my new Class Skills. The added inventory spaces weren't earth-shattering or flashy but had significant practical application. I had quickly learned that equipment mattered in the System and that having a powerful piece of gear available could turn a critical threat into a trivial one.

Similarly, the ability to carry more monster corpses in the Meat Locker freed up my normal Inventory space for loot of other kinds. I could also just keep throwing in dead creatures, which meant I could stay out on patrol longer without the need to sacrifice kills I couldn't carry along.

Finally, Greater Observation was a game-changer, even though it wasn't showy either. As I'd been told multiple times now, knowledge was power. Any little bit of information about an opponent, their level, or their health points could be useful.

I still needed to try out Rend and Implacable Endurance, but those were more physical skills. I was sure to get the chance the next time I stumbled across a monster on patrol.

Overall, I was thrilled to finally have access to my Class Skills. I felt satisfied that the payoff for holding out had been worth it.

In the distance, I saw a waddling shape scurry across the tarmac, and I sighed. It looked as if I would get my opportunity to test my latest Class Skills more quickly than I thought. The damn giant groundhogs kept popping up all over the area. Unlike pre-System groundhogs, these had mutated into a breed far less solitary and would venture out in packs to scavenge for food. They had also become far more aggressively territorial to creatures outside their species—namely me. Then again, I had killed quite a few of them in the process of chasing them away from the starport.

I drew my axe and my knife, then I sprinted across the tarmac.

When I drew closer, I saw that there were only five of them, and the giant groundhogs stood above waist high, even when they were down on all four legs. As I reached the herd of brown-furred creatures, I focused my attention on the closest monster.

Thiccbody Whistlepig (Level 24)
HP: 870/870

The first few groundhogs were quickly dispatched, and I found that my stamina barely dropped in the brief altercation.

When the last of the plump rodents attempted to scurry away, I allowed it to flee, then I followed just closely enough to keep it within the range of Greater Observation. I was done with letting these things continue their attacks on the starport. This time, I was going to follow the survivor home and figure out where they kept coming from.

Several hundred yards beyond the fence line of the old airport, the groundhog dove out of sight into a hole in the ground. I slowed my pace as I approached the burrow, and a shrill cry whistled from off to my left.

I turned and saw another whistlepig atop a slight rise. It stood on its hind legs as it cried out an alarm at my approach. The piercing call was picked up by more of the creatures as they poured forth out of nearby burrows.

No wonder I could never seem to get rid of all of the groundhogs. There was an entire colony of the damn things out here.

I knew that if I stood my ground, the creatures would dogpile on me, so I jogged back the way I had come in an attempt to let the creatures string themselves out. They obliged, with the faster creatures racing ahead of the slower ones. While they might have been fast for groundhogs, none of them could catch me, and I let the leaders get far enough ahead of the pack that I would have time to deal with them.

When the fastest of the creatures had a good lead on their brethren, I darted back toward them. I repeatedly activated Rend as I passed the first groundhog and rained blows along its flank. The beast mewled painfully and turned toward me, but its reactions were far too slow. I left the bloody, dying creature behind, already engaged with the next monster.

A pair of large incisors snapped at me, and I deflected the bite with the blade of my axe before jamming my knife into the giant groundhog's eye. Its head jerked back, and I used the stuck knife for momentum to catapult myself, then I slipped the blade free as I landed on top of the beast. I stabbed the knife into the side of the groundhog's neck and rolled down the other side, pulling the blade down behind me as I activated Rend. Blood spurted, and I stabbed it a few more times as the creature weakly batted at me.

I ducked, dived, and dodged through the dozens of whistlepigs that pursued me. I led them in a giant circle, never allowing the enraged creatures to surround me as they attempted in vain to defend their home turf. I kept an eye on my stamina and never used Rend if I was below half. Fortunately, the cost for active fighting and ability usage had been reduced by Implacable Endurance, so my regeneration easily kept up with the demand, even in the drawn-out engagement.

At last, only the heaped piles of the dead remained on the surface outside of the burrows. I'd slaughtered at least thirty of the creatures by the time the last dropped to the ground. I wasn't the slightest bit winded.

Implacable Endurance was certainly useful, especially in a long fight. It was the ultimate pursuit predator ability, and I could use it to literally run someone into the ground.

I didn't think Rend had been great in this particular instance, mostly because I had been killing the mob too quickly to really stack up the damage from repeated hits on individual targets. I could see how it would be useful on something larger though.

Leaving the corpses behind, I walked over to the burrow the fleeing whistlepig had disappeared into. The opening was about five feet high, tall enough to enter easily if I crouched. The dark tunnel beckoned, and I knew I needed to enter if I wanted to be sure that the colony was no longer a threat.

Slowly, the light faded behind me as I crept forward into the darkness. I could see nothing and cursed my lack of foresight in ensuring that I had a light source, especially after how useful my flare had been back at the meth lab. I made myself a note to buy flares and a light spell the next time I visited a Shop. I wished I had one now, even if it would have revealed my obvious presence.

Instead, I made my movements as quiet as possible and slowed my breathing to the barest whisper. I focused on my senses, listening carefully for any sounds of movement within the tunnel.

I sheathed my axe and switched my knife to my dominant hand as I drew one of my beam pistols. If I sensed a target, I hoped that the flash from the beam would provide enough illumination for me to get a better sense of the threat. Though in the cramped confines of the burrow, my ability to outrun my opponent would be severely limited.

With my knife loosely gripped in my right hand, I trailed my index and middle fingers along the packed dirt wall to feel for any openings.

When my fingers felt empty air beneath them, I froze and listened. I heard nothing, but the rank smell that wafted from the side passage indicated that the chamber was the latrine for the giant rodents' lair.

I passed two more hollows that branched off from the main passage. The side tunnels were slightly smaller, and though I paused at each, I heard no evidence of movement within.

Just beyond the third junction, a red dot appeared on the minimap, and I halted. It was off to the side, enough that I figured another branch in the tunnel lay ahead.

I waited, and the dot moved toward me. It turned into an arrow that rotated to point toward me as the dot moved.

I fired the beam pistol from my left hand in the direction of the dot on my map. The flash lit up the tunnel, and the groundhog directly in front of me squealed at the burning energy ray that briefly illuminated the area. The sudden shot had surprised it, and I activated Hinder. With no room to run, I lunged forward instead. I ducked under the creature's jaw and planted my shoulder under its chin, then I drove myself upward.

The groundhog jammed its head into the ceiling of the tunnel, and dirt rained down upon us both. The impact stunned the creature, and I stabbed my knife into the underside of its neck over and over. The beast roused itself and clawed at me, but I fired the pistol into its side before using the weapon to bat away the paw on that side. Since my other arm was tied up stabbing the creature to death, the groundhog's other front limb raked across my arm and leg. Even slowed by Hinder, it still tore through my jumpsuit and ripped deep into my flesh.

I shut out the pain and continued my assault with the knife.

The second time the claws scraped over me, the attack was far weaker and only did damage in the places where my armor had already been breached by the first assault.

The beast twitched several times, then sagged limply in my arms.

241

I stepped back and allowed the corpse to fall to the ground before I checked on my wounds. The cuts hurt, but I hadn't been afflicted with a bleeding status effect, so my health points had stopped falling when the monster stopped attacking. Over two-thirds of my health bar remained, so I felt pretty confident continuing.

I felt around and found that the body almost completely blocked the passage. I really didn't feel like crawling over it, so I pulled the whole thing into my Meat Locker storage space.

With the obstruction removed, I worked my way farther down the tunnel. I passed the side chamber the groundhog had emerged from, but the passage seemed empty now.

I started to hope that maybe I had cleared out the last of the giant rodents and would soon be able to leave the tunnel system behind, looking forward to being able to stand up fully once more.

That wish ended as I approached the next chamber and heard sounds from within. Squeals and the sounds of bodies writhing against one another filled the burrow ahead of me. My minimap lit up red with a multitude of tiny dots and a single large one.

Swapping out my equipped weapons for the hybrid rifle, I selected the orange-tagged specialty magazine from my Inventory and loaded the weapon.

The deafening whine of the gauss coils cycling filled the cramped tunnel, and I used the minimap in combination with Greater Observation to aim in the direction of the larger threat. The weapon fired, and the incendiary round shot across the chamber and detonated in a massive fireball against a furry mass. The flames caught on the pelt of the largest groundhog I had yet seen, illuminating it and the entirety of the chamber.

Dummy Thicc Whistlepig Breeder (Level 37)
HP: 1148/1290

I blinked at the ridiculous name for a moment as I took in the sight of the disgusting creature that was easily three times the size of any groundhog I had encountered yet. Thick rolls of fat rippled under the beast's hide, and it warbled in pain as it became engulfed in flames.

The floor of the chamber seethed beneath the large creature. For a moment, I had a flashback to the swarms of sewer rats I had fought on the first day of the apocalypse.

Then I read the monster tag displayed by Greater Observation above the nearest one and realized that the hairless little creatures were the whistlepig young.

Whistlepig Chuckling (Level 2)
HP: 24/24

There were at least two dozen of the dog-sized pups on the floor of the room, and their mass prevented their massive mother from charging toward me. She bared her teeth at me and chittered angrily.

The warbling forced the baby groundhogs to retreat to the sides of the chamber, and many fled out another tunnel that I could see beyond the big mother. The movements of the young cleared a path between us, and the raging mama groundhog charged toward me.

The rolls of her fat rippled, and the clap of slapping flesh filled the burrow. I fired the hybrid rifle again, and an inferno blossomed around the whistlepig's face. The explosion halted the charging beast and charred several of the young monsters.

The mother groundhog threw back her head and let out a shrill whistle that reverberated through the underground space. The sharp noise bored through my left eardrum, and I winced as I felt it pop. A trickle of blood dripped out of my ear and down the side of my head.

A notification popped up that I had been deafened, and the only thing I could hear from my right ear was an echoing ring. I shook my head to clear it and gritted my teeth against the piercing pain.

Mental Influence Resisted

I focused on the threats in front of me and found that my distraction had nearly been fatal. I flung myself backward as large incisors snapped down where I had been. The teeth that slammed into the ground and dug into the dirt floor of the burrow were nearly as tall as my leg and would probably have bitten me nearly in half.

I scrambled backward on my elbows, dragging my rifle until I was out of range, then I pushed myself back to my feet.

The smoldering whistlepig frantically dug at the passageway, attempting to widen it enough to get at me, but the breeder was far too large to fit more than its head into the tunnel. I stood just beyond its reach and watched as it snarled at me. Then I shot it again.

The incendiary coated the face of the creature in flame, and it recoiled from the mouth of the tunnel. When it backed away, I saw that fire still flickered along the fur on its side.

It fled to the far side of the den and scrambled at the passageway there. The bulk of the creature worked against it again, far too large to escape down the narrow tunnel.

Confident that the thing would keep burning for a bit, I swapped magazines back to standard rounds and continued a barrage of attacks that eventually dropped the massive creature while I remained in the relative safety of my narrow tunnel.

Once I was sure the big whistlepig mother wouldn't get back up, I ventured into the chamber and dispatched the remaining young that hadn't managed to flee or already been burned to a crisp.

I stored the massive corpse of the breeder using Meat Locker, but it took up almost all of the available storage space. I'd have to make multiple trips if I wanted to haul all of the dead back to the harvesting station at the starport.

The chamber had plunged back into total darkness, since there were no more fires to light the area with the dead breeder now residing in my System storage.

I spent the next several hours stalking through the lightless tunnels as I mapped them out and hunted down the remaining whistlepig young. It was gristly work, but it had to be done if I wanted to ensure that this source of attacks on the starport ceased for good.

When I finally returned to the surface, I found that the sun had nearly reached the far horizon. The light still nearly blinded me after spending so many hours in complete darkness.

When I returned to the starport, my first stop was the creature harvesting station. The corpse of the breeder drew a small crowd of Pharyleri, and there were still several who stood around marveling at the size of the beast by the time I finished the half dozen trips back to the burrow to retrieve the rest of the dead.

After I'd finally dropped off the last corpse, I spent several minutes haggling with Emilyana over exactly how many Credits each one was worth.

I ended up giving in to a reduced bulk rate, since I really didn't want to have to take multiple trips to a Shop for just a handful more Credits for each corpse.

It had been a long day, and I decided to call it a night. I let Emilyana know that I was done for the day unless anything suddenly attacked the perimeter and headed off toward the terminal. I'd found an out-of-the-way place on the ground level and spent most of the nights there over the last couple weeks.

A pillow might have been nice, but I'd slept in far worse places over the years than the threadbare, but reasonably comfortable, couch in what had once been an employee break room for the airline ground crews.

As I stretched out on the couch, I reviewed my status screen. Despite the sheer amount of killing I had performed since my last level, quite a bit of it hadn't netted much experience toward my next level. The whistlepigs had given me reduced experience since they hadn't posed much of a threat, and the young ones hadn't gained me any experience at all. The breeder had netted me a fair amount, but that was because she had represented a significant threat.

Beyond the overall slight experience gained for the day, my mundane Skills tab had registered a few increases since I last checked. Stealth, tracking, and all of my weapons aptitudes had all been raised by one or two points from the heavy usage I'd made of them over the last weeks. Even my haggling skill had gone up a point, due to the constant negotiations over monster corpses.

I closed my status screen and relaxed while pondering how to spend my remaining pair of Class Skill points. Access to my Class Skills had proved satisfying and greatly improved my capabilities, though most of the gains were most useful outside of combat.

Between Meat Locker and Right Tool for the Job, my Inventory space had greatly increased. I could store whole corpses inside of Meat Locker, which meant I could sell more monsters and their parts for additional Credits. Since my normal Inventory space was mostly no longer being used for weapons, ammunition, and other combat gear, those slots could be used for more loot. I didn't really need more capacity since I could currently sell my hauls promptly, so I ruled out adding more points to those two Class Skills for now.

The rest of my abilities were far more difficult to exclude, since I could think of reasons why improving each of them would be a good idea. Another point added to On the Hunt would make it harder to penetrate, and I wanted to keep my unusual Class obscured. An increase to Keen Senses would improve my detection, overall movement, and aid my reaction speed. Greater Observation would get more range and added details about a focused target. Adding to Implacable Endurance reduced stamina costs further. Hinder gained range and increased the slow effect. Finally, improving Rend raised the damage and duration, while lowering the ability's recharge time between uses.

I mulled over my options as I lounged on the couch. In that half-asleep state, my thoughts kept returning to a phrase I'd heard repeatedly in this System world—knowledge is power.

If that was true, my best option for long-term survival was to reduce what anyone else could learn about me. Others would have their own versions of observation powers, so I needed to strengthen the ability if I wanted to continue hiding my full status.

That convinced me, and I dropped the point into On the Hunt. After I confirmed the selection, I checked the ability description for the Class Skills and found that it had updated.

On the Hunt (Level 2)

The Relentless Huntsman has a reduced System presence and increased ability to disguise their visible titles, class, level, and stats. Effectiveness is based on the user's Skill level and Charisma. Mana regeneration reduced by 10 Mana per minute permanently.

The updated Class Skill seemed even better than I'd thought. A reduced System presence seemed to indicate that I would draw less attention to myself, which was exactly what I'd wanted, in order to stay off the grid as I grew stronger.

That logic resonated with me so much that I doubled down on my dedication to the Skill and locked in the second of my free points there as well. Though there was no further update to the description, besides the additional reduction in Mana regeneration, the increased level alone left me with more confidence in the Skill.

Satisfied with my choices, I let myself drift off into sleep.

Chapter 17

Early the next morning, I sought to rectify some of the weaknesses in my repertoire exposed by my recent adventure in the underground whistlepig burrows.

The mass of younglings had reminded me of the sewer rats and showed that I still didn't have an effective counter for a swarm of monsters. Discussions with some of the Pharyleri alchemists in the crafting station and an exchange of Credits yielded me ten vials of alchemist fire. I would be able to pull a vial from my Inventory and throw it at a swarm of creatures. The combustible mixture would coat the area in flames when the vial shattered on impact.

I also bought a dozen flares. Those were much cheaper than the vials and almost exactly the same as standard red road flares. Both sets of purchases could be stored in the additional Inventory space provided by Right Tool for the Job.

When I left the building, I saw a team of Pharyleri assembling a structure at the edge of the tarmac and walked over to them. By the time I reached the group, the framework for a tower had risen over twenty feet. I greeted them as one of the gnomes clambered up the tower and placed a turret on the platform at the top.

Melton Quickwrench (Engineer, Level 38)
HP: 425/425

While the engineer climbed back down, I looked over the weapon that moved slowly atop the tower as it calibrated itself.

The system was larger than the portable turrets that had been used when we cleared out the terminal. The double-barreled energy gatling sat on a mount that rotated in a complete three-hundred-sixty-degree circle. A rounded sensor housing sat above the paired barrels and reminded me of the Phalanx weapons systems that had defended US Navy warships from missile attacks.

"Putting in static defenses for monsters?" I asked.

"Monsters mostly, yes. Once we get operations ramped up, the raw materials that pass through here will be tempting targets for pirates if the defenses aren't substantial enough." The engineer looked at the sky and glanced around. "Plus Dungeon Worlds tend to end up full of airborne creatures that are aggressively territorial and generally object to the spacecraft passing through their airspace." Melton pointed at the air traffic control tower, where I saw another crew hard at work on top of the building. "That beauty will be a threat to anything in the sky once we finish it."

I raised an eyebrow. "What's that?"

"An Icarus Mark VI Quad-barreled Suborbital Cannon," Melton said proudly.

"Sounds nasty," I acknowledged.

"It'll certainly handle most large flying monsters like chimeras or harpies," replied the engineer. "It should even make any dragons think twice before they mess with the starport or any ships overhead."

"Even dragons?" I replied with an arched eyebrow.

"Well, most junior ones at least."

Melton grinned as he and the others gathered up the tools they'd scattered about the base of the tower. I really shouldn't have been surprised that dragons were a thing in the System too. Not after finding out about gnomes, jabberwocks, and bogeymen.

"We've got six more of these to get put in today," Melton said. "Catch you later, Hal."

I waved goodbye as the group headed off toward their next installation site.

Then I looked up at the tower. Clearly most of my current job was being automated to a certain degree. It might be a good time to have another discussion with Borgym about my plans. I headed toward the traffic control tower and the administration building beneath it, where the clan head could often be found.

When I reached my destination, I found that the building itself hadn't changed much, but just outside the security door, a ratty canvas tarp covered something new. The grease-stained tarp looked as if it had been found in an old hangar, and stonework peeked through small tears in the fabric.

I left the covered object and went into the building. It didn't take long to find the old gnome, since Borgym was right where I expected to find him, in the command center on the second floor of the administration building.

In contrast to the first time I had visited the room, almost all of the terminals now sat occupied by uniformed Pharyleri, and a low murmur filled the room as the technicians monitored their active displays.

The big screens on the front wall showed radar displays of the surrounding airspace and security footage from throughout the starport, including the gun cameras of the new turrets that were even now being assembled around the perimeter. While the traffic control tower above was intended to manage the airspace over the starport, the center here would manage the operations of the entire facility on the ground.

A new glass-walled office had been added at the back of the operations theater, allowing Borgym to supervise the command center while still having the ability to conduct clan business in private.

Glad that I no longer had to crawl through the gnome-sized control center to speak with the clan leader, I knocked on the open office door, and

Borgym beckoned me in when he looked up from his desk. I stepped inside and closed the door. When I turned back to the clan leader, I found him watching me with a raised brow.

"It's going to be that kind of a conversation, is it?" Borgym said.

I shrugged. "The automated perimeter defenses are pretty much done. That doesn't leave much else for me to do around here. If the guns are killing monsters, then I'm not getting experience for them. And I have leads for a Quest to track down."

The old gnome sighed and nodded.

"Figured you'd be moving on soon," Borgym said and then pushed himself to his feet. "Come with me. I want to show you something."

He led me out of the office and back out of the building. The old gnome stopped next to the tarp-covered object I had noticed on my way inside. A few bungee cords held the cover in place with their s-hooks looped through grommets along the edges of the tarp, and Borgym carefully unhooked them before he pulled the cloth free to reveal the object beneath.

A chiseled stone obelisk stood nearly as tall as me. Embedded on the front face of the rectangular slab sat a bronze plaque with embossed figures rising from the metallic surface. It was written in a language that bore no resemblance to any written language I had ever seen on Earth. If anything, the scribbles looked more like wingdings.

I glanced at Borgym. "It's nice stonework, but—"

"You can't read it," interrupted the old gnome knowingly, and I shook my head. "Look again."

I returned my gaze to the plaque and blinked. First the letters blurred, then they shifted in a manner that almost made me dizzy. I shook my head and steadied myself before I looked back at the bronze plate.

I could understand it now, somehow. I knew that the plaque was not actually written in English, but that was what I saw. I gaped at Borgym, who smirked smugly.

"We enchanted it to be readable by the viewer in their native language," said the clan head.

I turned back to the plaque.

Our debt to those heroes
who lay down their lives
so that the clan might prosper
can never be repaid.
Rest in peace
knowing your sacrifices
were not in vain
and shall never be forgotten.

Birlez Grindsaw

Lieren Mechwrench

Talliryna Sprocketsworth

Underneath the names of the fallen gnomes, another section of the plaque listed all of the gnomes in the party who had survived the assault on the airport terminal. I read through the column, recognizing many of the gnomes I had come to know over the past week as they worked to construct a starport from the remains of the airport.

At the very bottom of the metal plate, a much smaller section held a single name and I felt Borgym step up beside me.

"The numbers in the first two lists would have been very different," Borgym said quietly, "if you hadn't been searching for answers and looking for a fight with the Krym'parke." The small gnome patted the side of my leg comfortingly. "I hope you find them."

I heard the clan leader's words, but my focus remained on the words etched into the final section on the monument.

> *Without the aid of our human ally*
> *the cost of our future*
> *would have been higher*
> *than our hearts could bear.*

Hal Mason

Chapter 18

Once again, I cruised along Interstate 376 on my all-terrain motorcycle. This time though, I headed east, away from the airport where I had spent the last week and back toward downtown Pittsburgh.

Unlike my previous trips down the interstate, I found the highway surprisingly easy to navigate, especially the closer I got to the heart of the city. Instead of occupying the traffic lanes where the cars had rolled to a halt as the System disabled them, the vehicles that littered the interstate were now tangled closer to the edges of the road. Smashed bumpers and crumpled quarter panels showed where the vehicles had been knocked out of the center lanes, seemingly bashed aside by a larger vehicle driven through them at full speed. Despite the evidence, I saw no sign of whoever or whatever may have been responsible for clearing the roads.

When I reached the entrance to the Fort Pitt tunnels, I slowed to a crawl and turned on the bike's headlight to peer into the gloom. Despite the vehicles piled up outside, I had no desire to barrel full speed into the darkened tunnels. Especially after my last underground adventure with the whistlepigs.

My caution seemed validated when my headlight illuminated a stopped vehicle ahead, and I brought my bike to a halt. The vehicle was a haphazardly assembled motorcycle with mismatched tires and an attached sidecar that appeared welded together from car doors. The vehicle was turned half sideways, and the front end was crumpled slightly from where it had impacted the side wall of the tunnel.

There was no sign of the driver or passenger though, and I brought my bike to a complete halt about thirty feet from the vehicle. Two faint red dots glowed dimly on my minimap in the darkness beyond the bike. Forewarned by Greater Observation, I dismounted and drew a beam pistol with my left hand.

The walls glistened with wiry strands that shimmered in the glare of my headlight and also hung ominously from above the damaged vehicle in front of me. The hanging strands wavered slightly, wafting upon the slight breeze that flowed through the tunnel and sent a chill down my spine.

I pulled a flare from my Inventory and lit it with a quick strike against the pavement at my feet. The red glow revealed more strands of the webbing above me, apparently torn by the passage of the crashed motorbike. I stepped forward and flung the flare in a toss that arched over the stopped bike ahead of me and into the darkness beyond.

The infernal glow of the flare illuminated a pair of large, multi-legged figures that loomed just beyond the stopped motorbike. The limbs of the spidery creatures were large enough that they spread across an entire lane of the tunnel, and I tagged the closest of the spidery creatures with Greater Observation.

Mottled Recluse (Level 31)

HP: 930/930

The spiders skittered away from the flare, and their chitinous armor flashed in the gloomy tunnel as they jumped up into the safety of their webs, high along the sides of the tunnel walls. Two tiny figures lay unmoving, left behind on the ground by the startled spiders, but I had no time to spare for the creatures' previous victims.

In fact, now that I saw the bodies, I was almost certain that the only reason the ambush spiders had shown on my map at all was due to the prone figures lying beneath them. If I had been a few minutes earlier, it might have been my corpse there on the ground instead.

Up on the tunnel walls, the two recluse spiders scuttled toward me. I swapped out my equipped weapons with a quick activation of Right Tool for the Job, and my hybrid rifle whined as I squeezed the trigger while swinging the muzzle in line with the first recluse. The blast from the rifle punched into the side of the monster and sheared off the forwardmost two legs along one side before it punched into the carapace. The impact combined with the loss of its legs to knock the spider from the wall, and it tumbled to the pavement below.

I cast Frostbolt at the second spider as I shifted my aim toward it. The chunk of ice jammed into the slight gap between the thorax and one of its front legs. Rime glistened around the wound, the cold radiating outward from the point of impact. The spider's advance toward me slowed, and I fired my rifle again.

The shot punched through one of the centermost of the spider's six eyes and pithed the brain. The giant monster fell from the wall and landed on its back, where it lay with legs twitching in the air.

Despite its wounds, the first recluse had lurched toward me and nearly crawled within range while I had dealt with its partner. The spider's remaining front leg shot out with incredible speed, and my attempted dodge was far too slow. The spider's claws ripped through my armored jumpsuit and into the meat along the outside of my thigh. I gritted my teeth against the sharp pain and jumped away.

I staggered backward, and the recluse advanced to match. I swung the hybrid rifle level and squeezed the trigger, but the monster's foreleg flashed out, smacking the weapon from my grip before it could discharge. Already off balance from my injured leg, the blow that disarmed me spun me to the ground.

I activated Hinder on the recluse and crawled backward on my elbows, leaving behind a trail of blood that leaked from my wounded leg. I quickly saw that the recluse, as lopsided and slowed by Hinder as it was, still moved faster than me. I gave up on my attempt to put more distance between us.

Instead, I pulled a pistol from my Inventory into each hand and opened fire as soon as the weapons materialized. I quickly realized that one of my attacks was failing to have much of an effect as the beams from the energy pistol failed to burn through the reflective carapace. I focused on my shots from the projectile pistol instead and poured fire into the joints of the legs on the already crippled side of the spider. When the last two legs on that side gave way, the body of the recluse sagged to the ground.

Now with a little room to breathe, I cast Minor Healing on myself and a tingling sensation filled my wounded leg. In moments, the flesh knitted together over the worst of the damage to my thigh. The wounds still pained me, but I could at least use my leg now.

With my mobility mostly restored, and the recluse missing half of its legs, I easily dodged the monster's clumsy attacks and finished it off. Once the final monster was dead, I confirmed my kill on the first before I stored both of the giant spiders within Meat Locker and retrieved my hybrid rifle from the side of the road.

Only once assured that the threats had been dealt with did I check on the prone figures by the oddly constructed bike. The tiny, green-skinned humanoids might have measured nearly up to my waist if they had been able to stand. The aliens had larger-than-average round heads with long noses and pointed ears that stuck almost straight out to the sides. Their wide mouths were filled with rows of sharp teeth.

Both bodies lay along the wall at the edge of the tunnel as if they had been thrown from their vehicle by its collision with the wall. One's head had been caved in by the impact with the side of the tunnel, and there was a matching spatter on the wall above the oddly built motorcycle. The other fragile-looking creature had limbs twisted at unnatural angles and a bloody gash in its torso from one of the recluse's clawed limbs. The wound was a clean slash carved deeply into its chest that even cut through the bones of its ribs, and I was thankful that the monster had never caused similar damage to me. I knew the goblin-looking creatures were beyond help, between the sorry state of their bodies and that Greater Observation reported both creatures at zero hit points.

I checked over the bodies, but I only found one interesting thing besides standard Adventurer gear. Both goblins were armed with what appeared to be crudely built human firearms designed for someone with child-sized hands. The roughly machined metal work felt blocky, with edges still sharp enough to dig into my hands as I held them experimentally.

The only thing that made me question the observation that the weapons were human-designed were the words painted in white block letters along the barrel of both pistols.

"What the hell is a 'YEET CANNON'?" I muttered when I read the text.

On a whim, I attempted to stow the weapons in my Inventory. Surprisingly, both pistols slid into my Right Tool for the Job inventory space, and the only explanation for that would be that the weapons had been System-made.

With the weapons stashed, that left me with an odd bike and a pair of bodies in the middle of the road. Without a better plan, I tried to put the goblin corpses in Meat Locker and found myself pleasantly surprised when the bodies disappeared into the ability's storage.

Twisted from the impact with the tunnel wall, the front frame of the bike and the wheel no longer properly aligned. Fortunately, I found that I could also stow the vehicle within the extra System storage provided by Right Tool for the Job. It took up a significant amount of space, but I really didn't have that much equipment yet. My own bike soon followed, stored in my Inventory rather than risk a continued drive through the potentially monster-infested tunnel.

While I looted, I used Minor Healing on myself every time the sixty-second cooldown timer expired. Only after I had healed myself to full health did I proceed forward, though my pace through the rest of the tunnel slowed significantly.

I scooped up the still burning flare and chucked it as far down the tunnel as I could throw it. Even though no red dots appeared on my minimap, I waited to see if the flare revealed any movement along the walls or ceiling before I cautiously moved forward. Once I reached the flare, I repeated the process and continued through the length of the tunnel.

I found a few dried-out husks of humanoids and various monsters discarded along the walls of the tunnel. Bones and skin were all that remained of the spiders' previous victims. There wasn't any loot to speak of, but no more creepy-crawlies appeared out of the gloom.

When I finally made it to the end of the tunnel, I looked over the Fort Pitt Bridge and found that the sun hung high in the sky. Retrieving my bike from my Inventory, I straddled the comfortable seat and throttled up.

The cars along this stretch of Interstate 376 were also smashed to the side of the road, and I had no problems crossing the bridge. I looked to my left as I crossed the Monongahela River and saw the four-cornered star of Fort Duquesne several stories below. The walls of the fort were completely repaired and showed no signs of the damage left behind after the jabberwock's attack. They stood significantly taller now than when I had left the fort over a week ago.

I saw no movement inside the structure and wondered if something had happened to the ranger and the others left behind there, though my curiosity lacked enough motivation to change my current plans now to check it out.

I veered left onto the exit ramp for I-279 North, then across the Fort Duquesne Bridge over the Allegheny River.

The green and black fireworks, first noticed from across the river a week ago, still continued to detonate overhead at regular intervals as I followed the signs for the North Shore exit and left the highway.

After that ramp, I took the next exit onto Reedsdale Street, then turned left onto Casino Drive, immediately noticing the long line of people who stood waiting on the sidewalk. From the intersection, I could see that the queue started at the casino entrance, took up the entirety of Casino Drive, and wrapped around to disappear down the length of Reedsdale Street.

The gate at the entrance to the casino was new, as was the ten-foot-high wall that separated the waiting people from the casino itself. The wall had been welded together from sheets of metal and disassembled car parts. Guard towers supported the wall at regular intervals, their viewports only a narrow horizontal slit in the crude armor that protected the structures. The ramshackle construction of both the wall and the towers appeared very similar to the layered armor plates bolted onto the bike I'd found in the tunnel.

The entrance gate was a main vehicle entry completely closed off by a smaller personnel gate off to the right-hand side. The line of waiting people began at the smaller door, which swung open while I watched to let out a man who left empty-handed before the next person in line was granted access.

Instead of turning toward the casino entrance down Casino Drive, I drove straight through the intersection and coasted down the street along the line of people who went down the block. My slow pass down the line gave me time to assess the people who waited.

Almost all of them carried monster parts or other loot, as if they had no more room in their Inventory or they were saving that space for more valuable items. All of their clothing was stained, ragged, and torn. The System might have healed the wounds these people survived, but their ripped garb told the story that they were barely hanging on.

Those with free hands clutched baseball bats or crude, homemade weapons. It looked as if no one had upgraded their gear since day one, which made no sense if there was a Shop right here.

In fact, now that my attention was drawn to it, I saw few pieces of System gear throughout the crowd at all. That lack of proper equipment and the glares that many in line directed my way were obvious tells that something was very unusual here.

Also troubling were the Levels and health quantities I found on the few individuals I carefully inspected with Greater Observation. Or more precisely, the lack thereof. They were so far below my level that none of them even flinched as my activated Class Skill pried apart their System status to view names, levels, and health. Most people held Basic crafter or non-combat Classes, and the few combat-focused Classers I saw were the only ones who had reached double-digit levels.

I reached the end of the line and climbed off my bike, which I stored in my Inventory as I joined the queue. I caught a few grumbles of surprise from those who were watching me as my bike disappeared, but other than that, the people at the end of the line pointedly ignored me and continued to face forward.

Everyone seemed clustered into little groups of people who knew each other or seemingly worked together. The parties kept a bit of space between themselves and those around them, with almost no intermingling or talking to others outside of their family or friend group. An aura of distrust filled the air, and each party kept glancing around furtively as if they expected to be robbed or assaulted at any moment. More of those glances seemed directed at me than anyone else, and I wondered if it was because I had better gear, if it was because I had shown up on a vehicle instead of on foot, or if it was because I was completely by myself.

The line crawled forward slowly.

As time passed, more people wandered into the line behind me with their arms full of monster parts. Bones, antlers, teeth, pelts, and carapace sections made up their bounty. I recognized parts from some of the creatures I had faced, but just as often, I had no idea what monster had died for the loot.

My empty hands got a few side-eyed looks from the newcomers, but nothing near the bitter glares I had initially received. The new arrivals seemed a little less guarded than the people in the line ahead of me, and I soon overheard parts of their conversations that led me to believe they were hoping to trade their raw materials with the casino owners for better weapons and armor.

That struck me as odd. The longer I was here, the more questions I had.

Why were the people here trading with the casino owners instead of getting gear from the Shop?

I turned to the group behind me in line to broach the question, but they pointedly turned away when I tried to introduce myself. I waited for a moment for a chance to insert myself into their conversation. A couple times the men and women on the far side of the group glanced at me but quickly looked away. The rest kept their backs to me, and the only time one of the group members spoke to me, it was to point out that the line had moved on ahead.

Rebuffed, I turned away from the group and closed up the open space in the line. I had been more than willing to pass on the System knowledge that these people clearly lacked, but I wasn't going to force myself into their group.

In a way, I understood the trust issues these people might have. Forced into a fight for survival, with only immediate friends and family for support. My early encounters through the city with Zeke had proved that there were still those willing to threaten and kill. Best not to put faith in anyone who might stab you in the back.

It took a half hour to get back to the corner at the intersection I had passed through earlier, then another forty-five minutes to reach the gate. As I approached the gate, I saw a second line on the far side of the street. That line wrapped around that block in the opposite direction and led into a city parking lot with an entrance across from the casino gate. People in that line manually pushed along battered cars or other non-working vehicles of one sort or another.

Through the trees that lined the lot, I saw that the line of cars led up to a huge truck sitting in the middle of the cleared parking space. That massive vehicle may have started life as a PennDOT snowplow, but now, after all the modifications the truck had received, it more closely resembled something out of a post-apocalyptic movie where drivers fought over gasoline, bullets, and women. The plow blade lowered in front of the truck was reinforced and had heavily patched over scrapes and paint smears.

From the appearance of the plow, it looked as though I'd found the group responsible for clearing the local highways.

The hydraulic lift bed that the plow truck would have used to dump road salt had been replaced with a robust crane arm that reached out over one side from behind the cab, and the bed behind the crane had been extended by several drive train units with paired wheels. The extended bed held an open bay contraption that looked like a car-crushing grinder often found in junkyards.

As I watched, a group pushed a car up next to the bed of the truck, and a person got out from behind the wheel before waving up at the crane. The claw at the end of the crane extension grabbed the car and lifted it over the bay of the crusher. Then the crane dropped the vehicle into the crusher's gear-like wheels, which ripped the car apart in seconds. At the rear of the crusher unit, tiny green-skinned workers swarmed as they sorted the resulting components into large bins. From what I could tell, those disassembled vehicle components were repurposed into things like metal plates that armored the walls around the casino or the motorcycles that were parked next to the giant wrecker. Motorcycles that looked like the one stored in my Inventory.

The owners of this operation and the Shop inside were more goblins like the bodies I'd found on the highway, I realized as I reached the gate that led into the casino.

A heavily armed goblin stood in the open doorway. I scanned the creature lightly with Greater Observation, carefully pulling only basic information from the System in order to see what I was dealing with.

Gribbari Bruiser (Level 31)
HP: 290/290

The System name for this race of goblins was Gribbari, just like how the gnomes from the starport were actually a race called Pharyleri and the bogeymen from the school were Krym'parke.

My earlier estimations of the Gribbari's size based on the corpses I'd found in the tunnel proved accurate. They were of a similar height to the gnomes, standing to mid-thigh on me. Their bodies were scrawnier than the more rotund gnomes, but their heads were larger and much less human. A sharp chin knifed down and forward beneath a wide mouth filled with yellow teeth, and a pointed nose jutted out from the center of the goblin's face. The base of the creature's ears was nearly as large as the goblin's entire head, but they stuck straight outward from the head in a nearly triangular shape that narrowed to a thin point at the end.

The bruiser gave me a questioning look when it noted that my hands were empty, unlike everyone else who carried monster loot in through the gate. The alien's gaze flicked to the weapons holstered on my belt and it cocked his head, as if confused by my armed appearance. Still, the guard waved me inside when it saw that I was holding up the line.

A notification appeared when I stepped through the gate.

You Have Entered a Safe Zone (Rivers Casino Pittsburgh)
Mana flows in this area are stabilized. No monster spawning will happen.
This Safe Space includes:
Village of North Shore, Pittsburgh City Centre
A Casino (+1% Credits Gained from Wagers)
The Shop

In addition to the notification that appeared as I passed through the walls, I almost didn't recognize the area under the wide, multi-lane awning that covered the space where the old casino entrance had been. When the next person in line stepped through the gate after me, I moved off to the side, out of the way of the traffic that flowed through the personnel gate. Once sure that I wouldn't draw attention to myself from my spot beside the outer wall, I examined the area.

Only a single lane of clearance remained open through the former valet and drop-off zones under the covered portico that sheltered the space outside the casino entrance. Beside that single lane blocked off for vehicles, most of the space was filled with tables, where humans were exchanging monster parts or whole carcasses for goods. Beyond the organized chaos of the tables strewn across the trading floor, I saw another of the wrecker truck contraptions at the end of the cleared traffic lane, and a squad of armed goblins kept any gawkers from the trading area clear of the vehicle.

A slight commotion nearby pulled my attention from my inspection of the surroundings. I watched as one towering man in full hockey pads dropped an entire Razorhorn deer carcass onto one of the wide tables. The goblin behind the table looked over the carcass carefully then nodded before it vanished into the goblin's Inventory. In place of the dead monster, the goblin pushed a knife across the table toward the tall man in the Pittsburgh Penguins jersey.

I focused Greater Observation on the knife as it sat alone in the center of the table.

Tier V Knife

Base Damage: 4
Durability: 25/25
Special Abilities: None
Cost: 50 Credits

The man glared at the goblin and spat something ugly in what sounded like Russian before he scooped the knife up from the table and stormed off toward the gate.

I couldn't blame the man for being upset. The knife was trash.

The goblins appeared to be doing the same thing to humans that European explorers had with natives the world over during the Age of Sail. The colonists had traded cheaply made, mass-produced goods like blankets, beads, and knives to the natives. In exchange, they'd received raw materials like furs or spices that were far more valuable back in their home nations.

I'd learned from the gnomes that the monster parts were raw materials with high value, just like the animal pelts in Earth's past. With Earth as a Dungeon World, the products created by the monsters that spawned here were in high demand out in the galaxy. Every bit of a monster that could be harvested was a valuable commodity that could be sold through the Shop or transported in bulk off world. Trade and transportation hubs were lucrative businesses across the other Dungeon Worlds, and competition would be fierce here also.

That was one of the reasons the Pharyleri had risked, and sacrificed, so much to get their foothold in at the starport. Goods, like the ones these Gribbari had to be amassing with their exploitation here, would soon flow out into the galaxy through the Pharyleri's starport.

Beyond the organized chaos of the tables strewn across the trading floor, a handful of guards stood at the main entrance into the casino itself. The Shop had to be inside, so I worked my way through the throng toward the doorway. Only once, on my way through the crowd, was I forced to bat away an attempt from grabby hands that attempted to slip one of my pistols from the holster on my hip. The would-be pickpocket grew wide-eyed when my reaction to their fast fingers was faster than theirs, and the grubby kid scampered off in a panic when I glared at them menacingly.

A notification after that interaction informed me that my skill at Intimidation had increased.

I reached the casino entrance shortly without any further incident and found my path blocked by a stocky goblin with a tiny rifle strapped across its chest.

Gribbari Goon (Level 27)
HP: 210/210

The goblin ignored me at first, seemingly intent on a conversation with one of the other guards and unwilling to acknowledge my presence or let me pass. I folded my arms across my chest and affixed the tiny creature with the same dangerous gaze I had used on the sneak thief.

The goblin finally glanced at me from the corner of its eye. Then its head snapped around in alarm, and it half raised the rifle toward me, my clearly armed and armored form recognized as a threat that stood out from the other humans milling around the trading area.

"Whatchyowant?" the goblin spat the shrill words in a rapid-fire cadence.

I nodded toward the door behind the goblin. "I want to go inside."

"Why?"

I raised an eyebrow. "Why do you think?"

The goblin looked nervously at the other guards. None of them appeared as threatened as the goblin in front of me, but none of them seemed interested in speaking up either. They looked back at it and shrugged one after another.

"The trade area is out here," the goblin finally replied.

"Do I look like someone who trades out here?" I asked.

The goblins all looked nervous at that.

"No," the goon in front of me muttered.

I tapped my foot impatiently. "Well?"

The goon sighed and lowered the rifle. Then it turned around, pulling open the door and holding it for me.

I raised my chin and snorted imperiously as if my valuable time had been wasted before I passed the goblin, stepping through the door and into the casino. The creature quickly let go of the door, allowing it to swing closed behind me and sealing out the noisy commotion of the trading area.

Inside, the casino entrance had been renovated in a completely different manner than the ramshackle appearance of the walls outside.

Chandeliers still hung over the circular basin-like flower beds that stood waist high and bordered the entryway that funneled arriving guests into an interior security checkpoint manned by an additional half dozen or so goblin security guards. Besides the goblins, the largest change to the space was the floor-to-ceiling wall behind the stone planters that separated this new lobby from the gaming floor. The wall matched the marble and red stone of the planters.

And those chandeliers overhead were lit, indicating that the goblins had a System power source.

The goblins at the checkpoint were even lower Level than the ones outside and paid even less attention to me as I walked inside. I caught a bit of side-eye from a couple of the more alert goblins when I passed through the checkpoint, but they made no move to stop me.

Beyond the checkpoint, the gaming floor remained largely untouched by the arrival of the System and the change in casino management. Row upon row of gilded and brightly lit slot machines filled most of the available space.

Many of the machines were occupied not just by goblins or humans, but by species I didn't recognize in the slightest beyond a few that seemed straight out of standard fantasy fare.

Gnomes and goblins were real. I shouldn't be surprised by the appearance of dwarves or elves.

Beyond my casual appraisal of the casino patrons, I noted that even the humans inside were finely dressed—far better than the bedraggled people outside. Even my System-made, Shop-purchased adventurer's armor felt shabby in comparison. I only relaxed after I saw several people in what appeared to be tracksuits.

I wandered past the slot machines and the table games as I looked around for any sign of the Shop. I managed to circle halfway around the casino's main floor before I reached the cashier window for patrons looking to cash in their chips. There I found the Shop crystal up against the wall, off to the side, and with its own waiting line sectioned off from the cashier by gilded stanchions and burgundy guide ropes. Several people and a handful of aliens were waiting in both lines.

The sight of the alien species queued up and casually interspersed with the humans seemed entirely surreal to me despite my experiences with gnomes and goblins so far. My steps faltered, and I halted as I forced myself to look away from the strange figures who waited in the various lines.

When I turned to avoid staring, my gaze found itself drawn to the wall beside the cashier window. A number of portraits were posted there on single sheets of paper, standing out from the otherwise fine decor of the casino. I stepped over for a closer look at one of the postings.

A picture of a spectacled man took up the top left corner of the page. To the right of the image was listed a number of personal details like name, age, height, weight, and hair color. Beneath the picture and description, a short paragraph explained that the man had stolen a number of casino chips and that a reward was offered for his apprehension, with a bonus for the retrieval of the purloined chips. The fine print detailed the poster of the bounty, the location where the subject was to be brought if captured, the amount of the base reward, and that the bounty status was public.

My eyes focused on the five thousand Credit reward. That was a fair number of Credits just to bring in a subject.

A glance at the other pages confirmed they were also bounty postings for a variety of misdeeds. The offenses ranged from petty theft, as on the first sheet I had read, to breach of contract, where the subject had fled from their indentured service.

My brow raised at that last one. I hadn't known that indenture was a thing under the System, but it seemed to be the highest paying bounty on the wall. The status of that bounty was different from the others though. Instead of public, that bounty had a status of "limited." Nothing on the sheet itself defined the status, so I figured I needed to get more information on System bounty hunting.

On the heels of that thought followed another.

What if I got into bounty hunting?

In fact, it sounded like the perfect next step on my Quest. If I went back to utilizing the talents I had been using prior to the apocalypse, perhaps I would be able to make some contacts that could lead me to more information about the Krym'parke.

With that goal in mind, I stepped away from the bounty wall and slipped into the line that waited to use the Shop. Once I saw that no one had reacted when I joined the line, I turned my attention toward the strange sentients who shared the line with me. I focused on not examining them too obviously and instead subtly extended my awareness with Greater Observation, so gently that not even the typical name and level were displayed.

The first alien in the line was a massive humanoid with the head of a bull and towered over everyone else in line. The eight-foot-tall creature was thick with muscle and took up the entire width of the lane roped off between the stanchions. Greater Observation informed me that the creature was from a species known as the Yerrick but provided no further context. However, the massive two-headed battle axe strapped across the Yerrick's back was a clear enough signal that the giant minotaur was not to be messed with.

I shifted my focus to the next alien, a creature of average height that looked like a three-legged mushroom. A pair of scrawny arms stuck out from above the tripod legs, just below the conical cap that was a third of the creature's overall height. The gaps between the plates of light armor worn by the creature revealed pale, off-white flesh, but the mushroom head was a deep red with yellow spots. After my examination, my Skill filled in the species name of Frulegur for the fungus-like creature.

The final alien in line was a lithe elf with pointed ears, midnight-black skin, and silvery white hair. The luxurious platinum mane was streaked with hot pink that reminded me of the gnome's neon-hued hair. Amber eyes filled with hate stared out of a sharply lined face with rather bitter features, but it was possible that the elf's face had contorted into that harsh expression. It was only the intensity of the Truinnar's glare that revealed I had missed an alien in my initial evaluation of the crowd.

The subject of the dark elf's ire was another elf in the next line over, though this one had blended in with the humans at first, due to its milky white skin and golden-blond locks. The light-skinned elf had to be aware of the vitriol directed its way, but it ignored the intense gaze and deftly flipped a casino chip from fingertip to fingertip. The elf's other arm carried a rack full of chips as it waited in the cashier line.

I wasn't the only one who noticed the tension between the elves. Several goblin bouncers by the cashier's window nervously glanced between the two elves as if they expected an altercation to break out.

From the evidence, I'd say Mana Bleed had ensured that our fantasy stories of bad blood between the various elven races held more truth than fiction.

With my look over the various aliens completed, I turned my attention to the others waiting in the lines near me. Like the light-skinned elf, those at the cashier window carried trays filled with casino chips from the blackjack and poker tables. Conversely, pretty much everyone who waited in the Shop line seemed to be mostly empty-handed.

Both lines moved fairly quickly, and it wasn't long before I was next to access the Shop. I stepped forward and touched the Shop crystal. My fingers grazed the surface of the orb and reality dissolved around me as I was transported by the System to my Shop.

Chapter 19

The long, museum-esque hall of the Shop materialized around me, and the expected voice greeted my arrival.

"Greetings, Adventurer Mason," Ryk stated. "Welcome back. I had worried I might not see you again as it has been some time since your last visit."

"Good day to you, Shopkeeper Ryk," I replied. "No, my travels just kept me away from a place where I could access the Shop for a while."

The Bariadur nodded at my words.

Only then did I realize I had picked up the actual species name for the ram-like creature, in addition to finally getting a read on his emotional state. On my previous visits, the shopkeeper had been a blank slate due to how far his level outstripped my own. While my levels had only increased slightly, Greater Observation seemed to gain synergy with Keen Senses and the two abilities were combining to give me a greater awareness of everything in my nearby surroundings.

"Do you have any goods for trade today?" Ryk asked.

"Only a few," I said.

I really only had the recluse corpses as loot, since I felt reluctant to reveal the goblin corpses that remained tucked away within my Meat Locker.

The shopkeeper and I quickly haggled through an exchange for the giant spider parts. When we were done, I was ready to have myself a nice shopping spree. I felt pretty flush with Credits after unloading all of my harvests onto the gnomes for the last two weeks. I wouldn't be purchasing a Settlement anytime soon, but I had significantly more Credits now than I had at any point previously.

Ryk left to sort out the gooey spider bits, and I turned toward the console where most magical, Class Skill, and information could be purchased. After several searches, I selected the items from the mental list I had assembled since my last trip to the Shop.

Welcome to the System

This etiquette primer provides an introduction to the commonly followed practices amongst Galactic civilizations. This handbook is highly recommended for newly assimilated species as they integrate into the System and Galactic society.
"Four out of five spears up"—anonymous Galzon reviewer

The Book of the Species of the System

This cultural and physiological guide provides a high-level overview of major species and their factions. Only generic details are included and specifics will need to be researched separately in focused guides that specialize on individual species in order to receive more detailed information. For the subject of this book, major species are defined as those who have elected membership on the Galactic Council. Note: This directory does not include Sects, Guilds, or Corporations.

Fundamentals: Pharyleri

This book gives a detailed look into the Pharyleri species. Their physiological and psychological composition are examined, as well as a species history from System assimilation until the present.

Fundamentals: Gribbari

This book gives a detailed look into one of the variant goblinoid species. Their physiological and psychological composition are examined, as well as a species history from System assimilation until the present.

Fundamentals: Krym'parke

This book gives a detailed look into the depraved Krym'parke species. Their physiological and psychological composition are examined, as well as a species history from System assimilation until the present.

I started with a generic System etiquette handbook, followed by a cultural guide for the most major Galactic groups that would likely have an interest on Earth. Then I purchased more detailed information on the factions I had encountered so far: the gnomes, goblins, and the Krym'parke.

The last item was the most expensive and cost as much as all of the previous information downloads combined. I purchased books to read for myself rather than direct downloads that would integrate into my mind because there was an even more staggering increase in cost to have the knowledge implanted in my mind as if it was something I had always known.

Another search about locations on Earth where I could find Krym'parke returned a result that required an eight-digit Credit deposit. I blinked and counted the zeros on the window again. Whatever Class Skills protected the despised aliens clearly raised the cost required to find any information about them.

I would have to do it the old-fashioned way, hunting for clues and tracking them down myself.

Finally, I added a comprehensive database of common Dungeon World creatures as implanted knowledge.

Bestiary I

This compendium of commonly encountered creatures is a must-have for any Adventurer. Note: Paezo, Inc. is not responsible for any mutations of the creatures contained herein and cannot be held liable for deviations from Adventurer expectations.

The knowledge within would give added context to the raw identification I currently received from Greater Observation. Beyond just having a name, now I would have an instinctive grasp for what the creatures might be capable of. However, the warning in the description made me wary of relying too much on the implanted knowledge as it could turn out to be inaccurate. It was better than nothing though, so I accepted the fees for knowledge transfer.

While those purchases completed the initial list I had put together, I had one more need. Another quick search turned up the guide I wanted, and this time I splurged on the full download.

Bounty Hunting for Dummies

Galactic bounty hunting made easy!

Here's a plain-speaking reference guide to the profession, whether you're a hardened veteran of law enforcement or an Adventurer looking to make a few Credits on the side.

Bounty Hunting for Dummies, 23rd Edition, avoids all of the industry jargon to cut to the chase with clear, easy-to-understand explanations and step-by-step instructions for:

- *Obtaining Bounty Hunter Guild certification*
- *Dealing with Guild paperwork*
- *Accessing the Galactic Bounty Network*
- *Understanding bounty classifications*
- *Accepting posted bounties and claiming the reward*

The knowledge filled me when I completed the purchase, and I knew that the next thing I needed to obtain was a certification from the Bounty Hunter

Guild. A few hundred Credits later, I had bought the license and earned myself a new title, Galactic Iron Bounty Hunter.

Since iron wasn't even close to being a precious metal, I was obviously at the starting tier with the lowest rank possible. However, the title meant I could access the Galactic Bounty Network to find work and was eligible for taking bounties with statuses of Limited and Reserved.

While a Public bounty could be taken by anyone, a status of Limited meant that only registered Galactic Bounty Hunters could claim the reward. Reserved bounties were a step up from there, limited to specific individual hunters or requiring the hunter to be a certain rank in order to pursue.

Now that I was registered, I could freely hunt down the contract breaker listed on the casino wall for the maximum Credit reward.

At the initial rank, the title provided no other bonuses. Hopefully, if I ranked up to a higher tier, that would change.

With my information needs met, I left the kiosk and obtained restocks for all of my various ammunition needs. With all the added storage I now had from Right Tool for the Job, I might have purchased a slightly excessive number of projectiles and other explosives.

While I filled my inventory with ammo, I had a few more ideas on how to further my newfound professional goals and I returned to the terminal for spells and Class Skills. It only took a cursory search through the Shop's spell interface menu to find the first of what I was looking for. I wanted a way to alter my appearance, and the Lesser Disguise spell would do nicely.

Since I could use On the Hunt to alter my System status, the new spell would give me more flexibility when pursuing targets who might be on the lookout for me specifically. I had already encountered bounties who ran as soon as they spotted me, so anything that let me get closer before they bolted could only help.

When I completed the purchase and the knowledge of how to cast my newest spell filled my head, I left the console and went hunting for some additional equipment to aid in my return to bounty hunting. There were all kinds of high-tech surveillance toys that I would have loved to have had before the Apocalypse, and now that I could afford them, I added them to my list.

In addition to that gear, I picked up a variety of individual restraint systems that ranged from single-use zip ties, to handcuffs, to shackles. Just in case, I picked up some rope, a coil of nanosteel cable, and a few lengths of chain. You never knew when you might need some rope.

I also added a solid supply of energy drinks, meal replacement bars, and a variety of potions to my order. No more gas station coffee on stakeouts for this investigator.

Before I finalized my selections, I picked up spares for most of my armored attire, as well as nanotechnology patch kits that were designed to fix up armor at a cheaper cost than full replacement. Several of my fights had left my jumpsuit with slashes and holes, so it made sense for me to fix those whenever I could.

The equipment, armor, and tech devices all fit comfortably in my expanded gear storage provided by my Right Tool for the Job Class Skill, which left plenty of room for the food and consumables in my normal Inventory space.

Finally satisfied with my purchases, I stepped back from the terminal and nodded in satisfaction.

Despite the fair amount of Credits I had just spent, for once I would actually be leaving the Shop with funds to spare. I bid goodbye to Ryk, who returned my farewell cheerfully since I had spent so many Credits. His earlier advice and investment in my survival clearly paid off. I then found myself transported back to the casino floor.

I arrived in an open space off to the side of the Shop crystal, well clear from the lines that waited for both the Shop and the cashier window for the casino. I circled around the queues and returned to the bounty board on the wall.

This time when I looked at the info sheet on the contract breaker, I received a prompt from the System.

Would you like to accept this bounty? (Y/N)

There are currently...0...registered bounty hunters in pursuit of this subject.

I accepted the prompt and received a notification that the Quest panel in my status now listed the same details that were shown on the bounty sheet from the wall. I brought up that report and found that the information on the target only included the man's name and the location of employment from which he had fled, breaking the terms of his indenture contract. It wasn't much to go on, but at least the site was local, and it gave me a place to start my investigation.

The bounty contained a waypoint for the employment location, so I activated it, and a ping lit up on my minimap.

Now that I had a bounty to complete, I didn't have any other reason to hang around the casino, so I headed straight across the gaming floor toward the front doors. I walked through the security checkpoint on my way out, still without drawing more than a cursory glance from the inattentive goblins who manned the checkpoint.

I pushed open the front door and stepped past the guard who had let me inside initially. The goblin saw me and turned away to ignore me again, but only after making sure he wasn't in my path.

I worked my way through the crowded trading area to join the line of disgruntled hunters and gatherers who were lined up to leave through the main gate. None of them paid me any mind while we took our turns leaving the personnel gate one by one.

I turned left outside of the gate and remained on foot once I was outside. I walked north in an attempt for my departure to blend in with the others leaving the casino and to avoid the same scrutiny prompted by my earlier arrival.

At the intersection, I turned left again to head west along Reedsdale Street. I followed the road when it transitioned into Beaver Avenue and curved north. Within several blocks, the people leaving the casino had mostly dispersed, and I was left on my own.

Off to my right, a tall, reinforced berm supported the highway above and blocked the view of the rest of the city. I could smell the Ohio River off to my left, only a block or two away. Between the street where I walked and the river was the Chateau industrial district. This section of town contained manufacturers and warehouses that ranged from marine supply and auto parts, to building material and appliance repair. Or it had before the System's arrival.

The streets here were strangely empty, with none of the disabled vehicles that had littered the streets and sidewalks throughout the rest of the city.

I soon reached an area that stretched for several blocks and was walled with the same haphazard construction and towers as the casino. The location in the bounty for the subject's employer, and holder of the indenture contract, was inside the walls.

A five-minute walk along the perimeter later, I found a sealed gateway outside of a building that had a collapsed Mack truck sign just outside. I knocked on the closed panel with my fist, but the sound barely carried. I gave it a moment, in case one of the guards in the towers on either side of the gate were actually paying attention, but I didn't hold much hope if the goblins here were as inattentive as the casino guards.

Drawing my knife, I rapped the base of the hilt against the metal gate. This time, the clash of metal on metal echoed loudly, and I sheathed the knife before anyone could get the idea that I was trying to be threatening.

"Oi," shouted a shrill voice from the tower on my left. "What are you doing?"

"I'm here about a bounty," I replied, looking up at the guard tower.

I couldn't see inside the firing slit that ran around the tower, but I saw several weapon barrels now pointing out of the narrow gap and aimed down toward me. I opened my hands and spread my arms away from my waist to show that all of my weapons were holstered.

"Wait there," commanded the voice after a long pause.

Several minutes later, one panel of the gate rolled back with a grinding squeal to provide an opening just large enough for me to walk through. An armed goblin waited just beyond, and I examined him with Greater Observation as I stepped through the gate.

Kild Fastflare (Gunslinger Level 19)

HP: 190/190

MP: 110/110

Like me, the goblin wore a pistol holstered on each hip, but that was where any similarity ended. The tiny green-skinned alien also wore bandoliers of ammunition that crossed his chest and a ridiculously wide-brimmed hat that made him look like a bandito out of an old western.

"You here about a bounty?" Kild, the bandito goblin, asked as the gate closed behind me with a clang.

I pulled up the System information window on the bounty I had accepted at the casino and flicked it toward the goblin so it could view the bounty for itself.

While the goblin read the information, I looked around the area inside the walls. A half-constructed wrecker sat in the open bay of the former truck garage directly in front of me. A dozen or so goblins swarmed over the vehicle, assisted by a smaller number of humans, as they welded armor plates and affixed a claw to the end of a crane arm on the back of the contraption. This looked to be where the wrecker trucks I had seen at the casino were assembled. Several cars and trucks lay half disassembled around the wrecker, their frames being stripped for parts by the workers and added to the larger vehicle.

"Ah, Archer Hayes," said Kild, reading the bounty's name from the info screen. "Why don't you just buy his location from the Shop?"

I hadn't realized that was an option. Still . . .

"That would cost Credits," I replied. "I would rather try to track him down the old-fashioned way first."

"I guess that makes sense," Kild said slowly. "How are you planning to do that?"

"I thought I would start here," I said. "Someone might know something since it's where he was supposed to be working, right?"

"We can check." The goblin shrugged, beckoned me to follow, and turned away from the gate.

I accompanied the tiny alien around the side of the industrial truck garage. We crossed an empty street then a parking lot before entering an office at the front of another long building. The brim of the goblin's ridiculous hat brushed against both sides of the doorway as we stepped into the building. Once inside, the clamor of heavy machinery clanged and rattled from deeper in the structure, muted slightly by the office walls but still loud enough to be distracting.

The office held three more goblins, none of whom paid much attention to our arrival. Two of the three were involved in a card game at a desk near the back of the room, and the third drooled with its head down on a desk of its own as it somehow managed to sleep despite the noisy machine shop on the other side of the wall.

Kild walked over to the desk where the goblin lay sleeping and jumped up to slam its hand onto the desk. The smack of flesh onto the flat surface echoed through the small office, even over the background noise, and the two card-playing goblins in the back jerked their heads toward the sound. The sleeping goblin bolted upright and toppled backward out of the chair behind the desk.

My escort howled in laughter as the fallen goblin tumbled across the floor and rolled to a stop against another desk. The two other goblins joined in with their own shrill laughs as the fallen goblin struggled to its feet and staggered unsteadily.

Now that the goblin was no longer hidden behind the desk, I could get a better look at it and gave the creature a quick once-over.

Gribbari Overseer (Level 17)

HP: 150/150

MP: 180/180

Between the goblin's class and the whip coiled at its hip, I started to get a clear picture of the type of operation the goblins were running here. Especially when combined with the fact that the bounty I had accepted was for a broken indenture contract.

In addition to the whip, the goblin had a chromed pistol stuck into its belt. While the metal was brighter, the weapon still looked like the same model Yeet Cannon I had seen on most of the goblins so far.

The overseer finally gained its feet and glared at Kild, who still heaved with laughter.

"Aren't you supposed to be on gate duty?" demanded the overseer.

Kild jerked a thumb back over his shoulder in my direction. "Got a bounty hunter looking for one of your strays."

All three of the office goblins turned to examine me. I returned their looks, using the moment to scan the remaining pair and finding that their Classes were Foreman and Taskmaster.

The overseer chuckled and looked at the other two goblins. "A human hunting humans. How fitting." The goblin turned back to me. "Which bounty do you have?"

"Archer Hayes," I replied. "What can you tell me about him?"

The overseer shrugged. "Sold himself into a fifty-year serf contract but then didn't show up for work this morning. I activated the penalty clause of the contract, so he's not going to be doing much. But he's still alive, otherwise the contract would have dissolved."

"Penalty clause?" I asked.

The goblin looked at me, looked at Kild, then back at the pair of goblins and snorted derisively. "Clueless."

The two other goblins snickered while staring at me.

While shaking its head, the goblin said, "If ya break a properly written System contract, ya get hit with all kinds of nastiness like lowered attributes, lower experience gains, and increased Mana cost for spells and Skills."

"Thank you," I said, ignoring the condescending tone. "Do you know any personal details or where he could be staying?"

"If we knew where we could find him, we wouldn't have posted a bounty." The goblin snorted.

"Was he friends with any of the other workers?" I asked.

The goblin frowned. "Don't think so, he was pretty new. Only worked a day before he pulled a runner."

I sighed. Of course. "Did he have a vehicle?"

After a moment in thought, the goblin finally replied. "I don't think so." Then the goblin chuckled darkly. "Most people who can afford a vehicle don't sell themselves into serfdom."

"That makes sense." I nodded in agreement.

"I don't think there's anything else," said the goblin. "We're very busy, so you'll have to let us get back to work."

"Of course," I said. "Thank you for the information."

I turned and left the office, holding the door open for Kild, who followed. Before the door swung closed after the goblin, I saw that the overseer had already laid its head back down on the desk, and the other two goblins in the back of the office had returned to their card game.

Kild walked me back to the front gate without further conversation, and I felt as though the trip inside had almost been a complete waste of time. Sure, I knew more about the goblin operation and that they were building machinery of some kind, but that got me no closer to finding the bounty.

Or further toward my ultimate goal of figuring out what had happened to all of the kids from the school.

Chapter 20

The compound gate crashed closed behind me with a loud clang, and I sighed. My trip inside the operation had failed to provide any new information about my target.

I started up the street, still headed north, as I let my thoughts wander. A block later, I had passed the end of the walls that circled the goblin industrial enclave. The roads here were empty too, stripped of disabled cars by the compound's labor crews for the raw materials used to build the goblin's walls and their kooky vehicles.

I continued on, crossing another street to reach the start of the next block, then I stopped to stare at the brown-and-yellow sign next to the sidewalk.

The shield-shaped logo of an international transportation company of the same colors adorned the sign, and a thought struck me. Shipping companies kept records, right? It might not have the information I was looking for, but it wasn't like I had any better leads at the moment. I crossed the parking lot and started looking for a way into the building.

An empty parking deck made up the first story on the end of the building nearest to me with a number of freight docks farther down the front side of the structure. Since all of the docks looked to be shut tight, I headed for the parking area.

Above the single level of parking were windows that looked as if they could be for an office area, so that's where I needed to be.

My eyes quickly adjusted as I stepped out of the afternoon sunlight and into the parking garage. On the far side of the shadowy area, I saw the outline of a door and crossed to it. A quick push and pull on the door confirmed it was locked. Some mechanism must have remained engaged when the power failed. A card reader and an intercom sat on a panel set into the wall beside the door, so I poked the buttons there. When nothing happened, I rammed my shoulder into the metal door, bouncing off the door with no effect. I wasn't getting in this way.

I left the garage and went around the back side of the building, easily hopping over the chain-link fence that blocked my way.

My next attempt to access the building came when I tried to dig my fingers under a closed garage door but had no luck. The door was shut tightly enough that my fingers couldn't get a purchase under the metal frame, and even when I pressed upward on the door's panels, the door refused to rise in the slightest.

I hopped another chain-link fence into an area the goblin work crews had not yet stripped. This stretch of the warehouse-like building contained recessed bays that held a fleet of the company's distinctive chocolate-brown delivery trucks. I squeezed between two of the trucks, pushed myself up onto the dock behind them, then I stopped to look around.

The loading bays had seen better days.

The dim warehouse was lit only by the sunlight that filtered past the tightly parked trucks, but I could clearly see the collapsed stacks of parcels strewn across the floor. Many of the boxes had been ripped open, the contents spilled out. Toys, tools, and dozens of other household objects littered the few open spaces that I could see from where I stood.

I could almost trace the path of destruction through the warehouse.

Deep in the room, I heard a box fall to the floor with a slam, then something shifted in the dimly lit depths. Light glinted from a glossy, segmented surface that rippled through the shadows, and I heard the skittering of hundreds of legs across the concrete floor.

I focused on the movement and activated Greater Observation.

Giant Thousand Legger (Level 41)
HP: 2186/2186

"Oh, hell no," I muttered and pulled the railgun from my inventory, aiming toward the front of the writhing carapace that snaked through the storage depot.

The rifle whined as I squeezed the trigger, then it bucked back against my shoulder. Light flared from my weapon, and its hypersonic projectile streaked across the room before blasting completely through the arthropod. Gore splattered from the wound, and a chunk of the creature's health disappeared.

The flash from the weapon also gave me a better glimpse of the monster I faced.

Cylindrical in cross section, the millipede stretched through the warehouse. Its body consisted of hundreds of segmented sections with each segment containing a pair of spike-tipped legs protected by an armored exoskeleton.

The creature had a rounded head with a pair of jagged mandibles that gnashed together menacingly. Above its maw, a pair of antennae swung from side to side as the monster searched for its attacker.

Then the antennae pointed in my direction, and the massive millipede surged toward me. It flowed up and over the mountains of packages littering the warehouse. Its sharpened feet tore through boxes and sent cardboard flying.

I fired the hybrid rifle at the approaching monster, and it reared up, twisting away from the attack. Instead of a decapitation shot, the projectile impacted several segments below the raised head. The blow ripped away several of the legs along the giant insect's side before it lanced deep into the body of the millipede.

The monster shrieked in pain, and I took the opportunity to cast Frostbolt. The icy bolt flung from my open palm and pierced the carapace. The attack did little damage to the armored creature, but lines of rime spread from the impact point and slowed the monster further.

I darted down the loading bay, putting more distance between myself and the approaching millipede. As I ran, I tossed out a handful of flares to light the darkened warehouse. The crimson light from the flickering flares cast eerie shadows around the space, but it was far better than running face first into a wall and knocking myself senseless.

The creature pursued, but slower now that it had taken serious damage to the forward sections of its body.

I proceeded to lead the monster on a merry chase through the warehouse. I took shots when I had a clear line of fire and stacked applications of Frostbolt to slow it more.

In desperation, the creature flailed its lengthy body, and a number of shelves around the warehouse collapsed. One after another, shelves topped like dominoes as I sprinted to get clear.

I almost made it.

A powerful blow battered into me from behind and flung me through the air. I hit a support column and groaned as I slid limply to the floor.

Hearing the monster's skittering legs grow closer, I pushed myself up and staggered to my feet. It had almost reached me when I activated Hinder. I dodged the mandibles as they snapped closed where I had just been, taking a chunk of concrete out of the support column.

I had lost the hybrid rifle at some point, either when I had been hit by the falling shelving or when I had crashed into the pillar. I cast Frostbolt again, the ice materializing before my raised palm before shooting out to hit the arthropod. This time, the force behind the jagged icicle pierced through the weakened carapace that protected the monster's head. Green goop dripped briefly from the shattered carapace before freezing from the spell's chilling effect.

Without my most powerful weapon, I hoped that my other ranged weapons would finish the job.

I pulled my pistols from their holsters and opened up on the monster, even as it recovered and lunged toward me once again. I stepped backward and focused my fire on the weakened part of the carapace on the creature's head, looking to exploit the cracks where the Frostbolt had punched through the monster's armor.

The hard chitin dissipated the damage from the first several energy beams and deflected the first round from my projectile pistol. Then the second round punched through, and the following rounds widened the opening. With the armor breached at that point of attack, the energy beams finally added damage to the destruction begun by my projectile weapon.

The millipede chittered and changed tactics. It looped its lower body around itself to put a fresh section of its trunk between my assault and the exposed area of its head. Then it flailed the rear third of its length around the area in an attempt to crush me beneath the writhing plates.

I swapped out my pistols for fully loaded weapons from Right Tool for the Job and ran toward the thrashing monster. I leaped onto the end of the tail as it bashed into the floor, then I vaulted higher on the monster's frame, using its momentum as it lifted the section of the body back up. The leap brought me from the rear third of the millipede to land on the middle section it was using as a mobile shield.

Then I launched myself airborne once again, flipping over to fire straight down into the millipede's already broken head. The barrage of fire shredded the last of the health from the monster, and it collapsed below me.

Gravity reasserted itself as my reckless acrobatics ended, and I crashed back to the floor. I tumbled through something that could only be called a landing if I was being especially generous, and I slid across the cement warehouse floor, my body battering itself through stacks of boxes until I finally rolled to a stop.

Confirming the monster's death from my latest experience notification, I lay still for a minute and reveled in the silence. My health had taken more damage from the damn boxes in the warehouse than from the actual insect attacks, though the impact with the support column had also hurt me a fair bit.

The concrete floor quickly became uncomfortable, and I forced myself to get up. I looted the giant millipede, then I spent the better part of twenty minutes searching through the dimly lit warehouse before I found my dropped hybrid rifle.

The weapon had taken a few hits to its durability, and a few scuff marks now marred its glossy shell, but everything still seemed to be in working order when I inspected it. The rifle reloaded without any problems before I activated Right Tool for the Job once again and stuffed it back into my specialized System armory space.

The flares I had tossed out during the fight were burning out, and the light in the loading bay grew dim as I headed through it, looking for a way up to the offices I had seen from outside.

I passed from the wide-open warehouse section of the building into a small hallway that showed no sign of the millipede's passage. The short hall contained bathrooms, a janitor's closet, and an employee break room with a small kitchenette. Nothing drew my interest, so I continued through a door at the far end of the hall and into a dark stairwell.

I held the door cracked open and stood silently, listening for any sounds in the darkness. I heard nothing, so I pushed the door open and stepped onto the landing. Dim light filtered down from a skylight in the building's roof far above, providing enough light for me to see that stairs led both up and down. I already knew that I needed to get to the level above the ground floor.

All light cut off as the door behind me swung closed, and I reached out with one hand to grab the railing. With the rail as a guide, I climbed two flights of stairs before reaching the next door out of the stairwell. I pulled the door open a crack and peered out.

Natural light filtered through tinted windows to reveal a maze of cubicle walls just beyond the doorway. Still hearing nothing to hint that something else might live within, I slipped quietly into the office and let the stairwell door latch closed behind me.

I walked around the floor, looking for any indications of a record archive and finding nothing obvious. With no other ideas, I picked a cube at the end of the row and began a more methodical search.

The desk was covered with standard office computer peripherals, like a keyboard and a mouse with the mousepad showing a cute cat picture. A pair of dark LED monitors were centered in the workspace. The desk itself held the typical variety of office supplies but a frustrating lack of paper records.

I glared at the dead monitors. Or course everything had been electronic. With the arrival of the System, terrestrial computer equipment was little more than junk, and I had no hope of retrieving any records from the lifeless electronics. I shuffled through the desk drawers anyways, hoping to find some kind of records. My search turned up personal effects, a few manuals for various shipping applications, and an employee handbook.

No shipping records.

I sighed and moved on to the next cube. Then the next. And the next.

It took about five minutes to rifle through each cubicle, and there were about twenty cubes in the office, plus a half dozen closed-door offices around the outside walls that I went through after I finished the cubicles. None of them contained any paper records.

As I headed toward the last corner office, I saw an alcove that I had overlooked during my first lap around the office. One side of the cubby held a large copier and scanner unit. Across from the copier sat an industrial shredder with a full bin of waste beneath it, which explained the lack of hardcopy laying around the office.

Shelves at the rear of the alcove contained stacks of paper stock in different sizes for the copier. On the lowest shelf, half hidden behind the bulk of the copier itself, a thick tome lay flat under several discarded magazines. I almost dismissed it as another manual, but something made me take another look.

I bent down and poked the dust-covered book enough to make the spine visible from the front. My eyes widened when I read the text printed along the spine, and I snatched the heavy volume from the shelf.

I flopped the phonebook onto the top of the copier and flipped through it, searching for the name of my bounty. It didn't take long to find the name, and I could only hope that the one "Hayes, Archer" listed on the page was the man I sought. The phone number in the directory would be useless, but I read the address several times until I had it memorized before I closed the yellow tome.

I stared at the closed phonebook. The date on the cover revealed the volume as several years out of date, so I hoped my quarry hadn't moved in the intervening time. Still, it was a far better lead than anything I had managed from the goblins or anywhere else.

I tried to put the phonebook in my inventory, but the item refused to enter my System storage. It gave the same red flash that the shotgun had all the way back on the first day, so it looked as if I still couldn't store non-System items. I pulled a backpack from the survival supplies I had piled in my Inventory and dumped the phonebook within it, prepared to carry it on my back in case I needed it in the future. On a whim, before I slung the straps over my shoulders, I tried to return the backpack to my Inventory and blinked in surprise when it successfully went.

I shook my head. The System made no sense to me sometimes. Someone far smarter than me would have to figure out that System Quest because it just sounded like a headache waiting to happen.

I used a different stairwell to leave the office, which brought me out of the door in the parking deck that I had first tried to use to enter the building. It opened easily from the inside when I pressed the push bar, of course. That's how my luck ran sometimes.

By the time I left the building, I found that the sun had dropped low in the sky. My search inside had eaten up the rest of the afternoon, and it would soon be dusk.

With the address of my quarry in mind, I left the shipping center and walked another block to the north. A cross street ran under the state highway here, and I was able to turn east without needing to climb the vertical berm to reach the residential neighborhood beyond.

The farther I headed into the neighborhood, the more quickly it became obvious which houses were still occupied. The homes here mostly fell into three categories.

First, and the rarest, were the structures where the owners had purchased them from the Shop. These stood out from the System-assisted upkeep that kept them clean and in good repair. Some of these structures even had some obvious System upgrades, built by their owners or purchased directly from a Shop. Solar collectors, Mana batteries, and upgraded defenses in the forms of reinforced walls and armored windows were all integrated seamlessly into the structures.

Few of the non-defensive improvements were on the ground floor of most buildings, and most were only visible from their attachment points on the sides of the upper stories or as glimpses where they peeked over the edges of a building's roof.

The second category of homes were slightly more numerous than the System-owned houses but just as distinct in their own way. Whether their owners couldn't afford to purchase the building from the System or just stubbornly refused to, these structures had more homemade defenses. Boarded-over windows, welded shutters, chain-link fences, and layered strands of barbed wire covered these homes and made them look like something out of a zombie apocalypse movie.

The final, and most depressingly common, class of homes sat empty and dark. Broken windows and shattered front doors gaped open ominously. Occasional crashes or snarls echoed from the abandoned buildings before silence, only hinting at what horrific dangers might lurk within.

The people I passed on the sparsely populated sidewalks gave me a wide berth, but I noted that everyone seemed on edge. It was the wary tension of those prepared to fight or flee at a moment's notice. The locals had been forged in the crucible of the apocalypse, honed to react with the finely tuned instincts of survivors, and I once again felt the eerie similarity to the combat zones of my past.

The few monsters that poked out their heads were quickly dispatched by combined attacks from everyone nearby. Spells and shots from multiple angles stunned the creatures long enough for melee users to pile into the conflict. I limited myself to only a few shots from one of my beam pistols the two times I was close enough to be involved, first with a mutated squirrel, then with an eight-legged alligator that crawled out of a sewer grate.

Each time, I waved away offers of loot as I continued on foot. The locals needed the drops far more than I did, and I was more preoccupied with finding the address listed in the phonebook for my bounty.

Instead of loot, I did take the opportunity to ask the locals who stripped the dead monsters if they knew directions to the street I needed. The first two attempts were a bust, but the third time I asked, the woman told me to go north two blocks then turn left. I thanked her and left her to the bloody work of skinning the alligator corpse.

A short walk later, I reached the address from the phonebook and stood on the street, looking up the empty cement driveway that led to the house. The two-story home was one of the self-improvement types without System upgrades, so it looked as though someone lived here.

I walked up the stairs to the front door and pounded my fist against it. After I'd waited for about a minute with no sign of response, I knocked again. I heard faint movement on the other side of the door following the second knock, but it quieted quickly, as if whoever was inside couldn't decide whether to answer the door or not.

While I normally preferred to be ignored by most people, I didn't appreciate it when it got in the way of finding my target. I hauled back my armored boot and delivered a solid kick to the door that rattled the frame.

A shout of alarm cried out from behind the door, "Who is it and what do you want?"

I stopped my foot just before I unleashed a second kick. The voice was thin, frail, and unmistakably male.

"Are you going to open the door, or do I need to keep knocking?" I asked, ignoring the man's question.

Silence greeted my question, so I pounded my boot into the door again. This time, a few splinters shattered free from the impact and skipped off to either side along the cement patio.

"Fine," cried the voice from inside. "Fine, I'll open the door."

A wooden crossbar scraped along the inside of the door as it slid free from mounting brackets and a pair of deadbolt locks were thrown open before the door cracked open inward to reveal a narrow opening with a single eye that glared out fearfully from the gap.

"What?" The single word came out in a gasp, as if it exhausted the man to even speak.

I looked pointedly at the mostly closed door then back at the speaker.

I clearly heard the man sigh, then I heard the rattle of a security chain being removed before the door eased open a little further.

The man inside leaned heavily on the door frame as if he were unable to stand without the structure's support. The pale skin of his face had a jaundiced hue that highlighted his sunken cheeks and bloodshot eyes. His clothing hung loosely on his body, as if he had lost a significant amount of weight recently.

I activated Greater Observation to confirm the man's identity, but I could clearly see the effects of the System disabling this man. The attribute drain from the broken contract had an obvious effect.

Archer Hayes (Machinist Level 5)

HP: 40/40

MP: 30/30

A strong breeze could take this guy out. Why had he even tried to flee his contract?

"Why did you run?" I asked.

His eyes widened in surprise, then he looked nervously to either side. He had all the hallmarks of a man ready to bolt.

"What?" Archer said with a twitch. "Run? What are you talking about?"

"Your contract," I stated.

The man stepped back and tried to slam the door closed as he turned to flee, but he'd given me plenty of warning with his evasive behavior. Even beyond that, he moved painfully slowly.

I lunged forward and shouldered open the door before it could shut. I bounded forward and caught Archer in a single step, grabbing the man by the shoulder and one wrist. Our combined momentum carried us forward, and I jacked the man against the wall just inside the entryway to the house.

The man's health dropped by a huge chunk from the impact, and I eased up slightly as Archer wheezed painfully. I twisted his wrist up behind his back into a hammerlock, then used my free hand to summon a set of zip ties from my Inventory with a quick activation of Right Tool for the Job.

I secured the zip tie around Archer's wrists to bind his hands behind his back before I stepped away from him. The man sagged against the wall, tears streaming down his face.

"Please," he cried. "Don't make me go back. I don't want to go out there. I can't."

I sighed. I didn't really care, but I asked the question anyway. "Why can't you?"

"I'll die," he wailed. "Everyone dies."

"That's true," I said. "Everyone dies eventually."

I grabbed the back of Archer's arm and tugged on it to pull him toward the door as he stared at me in surprise.

"No," he shouted and fell to his knees. "Please, I can't leave my family."

I left the man on the floor and closed my eyes, focusing on my other senses. I cocked my head as I listened for sounds throughout the house. I heard nothing besides the man at my feet. I sniffed to breathe in the scents of the home's occupants. I smelled unwashed human, spoiled food, and burnt cooking.

"Your family?" I said. "There's no one here but you."

"They're hiding," Archer mewled unconvincingly.

"No," I said with a shake of my head. "You're just a liar who will say anything."

I stared at the man with crocodile tears and lamented that my foresight in buying bounty hunting supplies had not included the potential need for a sedative.

I dragged Archer to his feet. He tried to go limp in my grip once again, but the man was so frail that his struggles failed to break him free. Tired of this ridiculous situation, I swung the flailing man up onto my shoulder and walked out of the open front door. I didn't bother to close it behind me.

It said something about the neighborhood that none of the neighbors had stopped by during our altercation or came outside to investigate the noises Archer continued to make.

I summoned my bike and used a coil of rope to tie my bounty on top of the storage rack mounted behind the seat. A few extra loops of the rope might have gone into the man's mouth to cut down on the whining.

Then I climbed onto the bike and started it. The Mana engine purred as I powered the throttle and headed down the street.

Night had fallen completely by the time I returned to the goblin industrial compound. I pulled up to the gate and knocked.

The gate squealed as it swung open. The goblin in the sombrero-like headgear waited beyond.

"You back already?" Kild asked.

I jerked my thumb over my shoulder to where I had Archer tied up on the back of the bike.

"Oh," said the goblin, peering around me to where Archer remained bound. "That was fast."

"I have a particularly useful set of skills," I replied. "Now how do I get paid?"

"Uh, the boss'll have to do that," Kild beckoned me to follow. "C'mon."

I motored along on the bike; the motor rumbling barely above idle as the goblin walked back to the office I had visited earlier.

"Bring him on in," Kild said when it reached the office door.

I glared at Archer in warning as I untied him. The man remained mercifully silent when the ropes came off, and I twisted the line into a neat coil before I stored it in my Inventory.

When I had the man back on his feet, I pushed him in front of me toward the office while keeping a hand on his shoulder in case he decided to run again. Archer sullenly stepped past Kild, who held the door open for us.

Noise still echoed from the machinery beyond the office, and I was a little surprised to find that the overseer still sat behind the office desk, apparently working even at this late hour. But then I realized I was still applying human logic to yet another alien culture. The goblin was alone in the office this time.

"Well, look who it is," the goblin overseer boomed when Archer set foot inside the office.

"He's all yours," I said over Archer's shoulder. "As soon as the bounty is marked completed and I get paid."

The overseer waved toward me, and a notification pinged for attention at the bottom of my vision.

Bounty Completed!
You have successfully returned the subject of a broken indenture to the principal contract holder and completed the outstanding bounty request.
500 XP and 6,000 Credits Awarded

When I finished reading the notification, I pulled my knife and cut through the zip tie that bound my bounty's wrists. I sheathed the blade and pushed Archer toward the overseer, who grinned gleefully as it jumped down from his chair behind the desk.

"Let's go, slacker," commanded the overseer. "You have a quota to meet."

"But it's getting late," whined Archer.

"Shoulda thought about that before ya tried to skip out on work ya agreed to do." The goblin snickered and led Archer through a door at the back of the office.

The noise in the room grew deafening until the door shut behind them.

I finally gave in to curiosity.

"What is that racket?" I asked Kild, who waited at the entrance behind me.

"Machines," replied my escort.

I didn't think the goblin was being intentionally evasive, but it was still an alien.

"Doing what?" I asked.

"Making boom sticks," Kild replied.

My escort looked at me gleefully from beneath the brim of its wide hat. Then the goblin crossed the office to open a wide cabinet near the door the overseer had just taken Archer through. The door swung open to reveal racks packed full of firearms. Human firearms.

Between my time in the service and my experiences as a bail bondsman, I had seen or fired a fair number of weapons, and I recognized most of the locker's contents instantly as I stepped in front of the collection. Some of the handguns appeared shrunken to fit goblin-sized hands, but most, and all of the rifle-length weapons, were the same as any found behind the gun counter at any local sporting goods store. The majority of the weapons shared the rough construction and unpolished look of the weapons I had found back in the tunnel.

When Kild pulled one of the pistols from the locker and held it up, I could see the white lettering on the barrel. It matched the firearms I had found earlier and proved that the goblins were indeed manufacturing them.

I nodded in appreciation and Kild replaced the pistol in the cabinet.

"You hummies have so many types of guns," Kild babbled excitedly. "It's so amazing to have all of these options for dakka!"

"Impressive collection," I said.

The goblin beamed at my praise, then pulled the pistols from the holsters on its hips and aimed them toward the wall.

"Dakka, dakka, dakka," shouted the tiny goblin as it shook the weapons, pretending to fire them at an imaginary target.

Then the pistoleer spun both pistols around the index finger that remained through each weapon's trigger guard. The gunslinger flipped the guns forward then backward before rotating its hands sideways and spinning the weapons horizontally. It was like watching an old western, if the lone gunslinger had been a green, three-foot-tall alien.

Finally winding down the impromptu show, Kild jammed both pistols back into the holsters on its belt at the same time before he looked at me as if seeking approval.

I nodded appreciatively, not trusting myself beyond that to keep a straight face at the ridiculous sight.

The door from the workshop behind the office opened, and the overseer walked out. The goblin saw Kild showing off the open gun locker and frowned at my escort. Kild remained oblivious until I nodded toward the overseer, at which point my escort caught sight of the boss goblin's disapproval and scrambled to close the cabinet.

"Why you still here?" demanded the overseer.

"Got any more bounties?" I asked hopefully.

"No," barked the goblin boss. "Get out."

Kild looked embarrassed as the tiny alien pointed me toward the office door. I walked out ahead of the goblin and looked back when the door closed behind us. While its face remained hidden by the brim of the hat, I saw the goblin's shoulders shrug when I glanced back.

"What was the problem?" I asked.

"Humans." Kild chuckled. "Your kind always puts the boss in a bad mood."

"But not you," I said.

"Yous makes the greatest dakka," chirped Kild.

The goblin pulled a bullet from one of the crossed bandoliers on his chest and fiddled with it as I climbed back onto my waiting bike. Kild tossed the bullet from hand to hand and continued to fiddle with the round as I rolled my vehicle toward the gate, slow enough for the short-legged goblin to keep pace.

When we reached the gate, it creaked open just wide enough for me to roll through, and I motored my bike out of the goblin compound.

"Come back if you have any more bounties here," Kild called.

"Will your boss like that?" I asked, looking back at the goblin.

"If you're doing something to benefit the boss, like bringing in another runner."

"Well, we'll see," I said.

I gave Kild a small wave as the gate shut. The sun had finally set, and flood lights from the guard towers above illuminated the area outside the compound walls.

I throttled up and left the compound as I headed back toward the residential neighborhood where I had nabbed the bounty. One of the abandoned houses would be a decent place to hole up for the night so I could catch some sleep.

A sudden weight landed on me, and the impact knocked me from my seat. I caught a brief glimpse of claws flashing from just behind me as the bike toppled over and I tumbled free. The motorcycle skidded along the pavement, and I rolled to my knees to find a massive feline crouched with its gaze locked on the still-moving bike frame as it slid to a halt halfway down the block.

The mottled gray, brown, and black cat watched the unmoving cycle for a moment, and its tail twitched with anticipation as I looked over the creature. The beast was a short-haired tabby cat grown beyond the size of a greyhound and looked as though it could easily weigh a couple hundred pounds.

Alley Tomcat (Level 39)

HP: 976/976

At my use of Greater Observation, the cat's head swiveled toward me. A baleful yellow glare gazed at me from its sole good eye, the other matted closed by scar tissue that crossed over the cat's face.

When the cat gathered itself, crouching lower as it prepared to pounce, I muttered the spell to cast Frostbolt. The jagged shard of ice flew from my outstretched hand to imbed itself in the cat's leg, and it yowled in pain.

I drew my pistols and fired both weapons in unison. A crimson beam burned a slash across the feline's chest as blood blossomed from the impact of a projectile round. The beast bared its fangs as it hissed in pain then bounded toward me. I activated Hinder as the cat entered the range of the Class Skill. The ability slowed the creature's movements ever so slightly, but its claws still flashed at me in a furious flurry. I danced backward out of reach of the slashing attacks.

For the first time, I fell into a flow state, the combat surprisingly smooth as I twisted and spun through the street. With every step, I swung a pistol into line with the furious cat and squeezed the trigger. With each trigger pull, a round bored into the cat or fired a ray of brilliant energy that burned away at my target.

I pushed myself to move faster and sweat dripped from my brow as I blinked to keep my vision clear. The tomcat's health dipped lower and lower, its desperation growing as I evaded each attack it launched.

Finally, the beast turned and leapt away from me. With most of its pelt singed, burned, and bloody, it became obvious the tomcat had decided to flee.

"Oh, no, you don't," I growled.

I ran after the cat as it hurtled down an alley to head deeper into the industrial district, and I continued to fire once I had it back in sight. A beep from the beam pistol alerted me that the weapon had depleted its charges as the slide locked back on my empty projectile pistol. I pushed them both into my Inventory and pulled out another beam pistol. I kept up my barrage as I sprinted along behind the cat, but my haste threw off my aim, and while my shots still hit, they only left burned streaks on non-critical areas as the feline continued to flee.

My attacks still chipped away at the creature's health, and after another block, I had closed the distance between us as it finally stumbled. Another flurry of shots dropped the feline, and it twitched once before it lay still on the ground. Only after it completely stopped moving did I double-check that the tomcat's health had zeroed out before I crouched over the body.

I picked up a nice-sized pelt, a handful of fangs, and a half dozen wickedly curved claws. I slipped the items into my Inventory and stood once again. I looked around the empty alley but found nothing that stood out before I headed back the way I had come.

While I retraced my steps back to my fallen bike, I thought back over the fight that had just occurred. I might have been a combat veteran, but this proved that I had more to learn about fighting in new ways under the System. The old Earth tactics of fire and maneuver were not effective at combating monsters who could strike from ambush without warning or close any intervening distance in the blink of an eye.

I had started out the fight well, but I clearly needed more practice at firing on the move. My combat style was starting to look like some kind of action sequence out of a Hollywood action blockbuster. Even though the System had boosted my accuracy to preternatural levels with my Perception and Agility, it still took skill to hit anything while running at a full sprint.

My bike lay in the middle of the road, where it had slid to rest after the cat had launched its ill-fated attack. I stood the vehicle back onto its wheels then walked in a circle around it to look for any signs of damage. I found none. Not even the paint was scraped from where it skidded along the pavement.

"Good bike," I muttered and gave the frame of the armored vehicle an affectionate pat as I swung a leg over to mount it.

The rest of my ride back to the residential neighborhood stayed uneventful, and I pulled up to the first abandoned house I saw when I noticed that the front door was cracked open. Hoping that nothing too problematic had found a home inside, I stored my bike in my inventory and drew my beam pistol. With my free hand, I pulled an item from my equipment storage.

Starburst Tactical Flashlight

This high output light source casts a brilliant beam of light, adjustable to fit your needs in a variety of situations. The ruggedly engineered frame of this tool can be used as a weapon of last resort, held comfortably by all species with opposable thumbs, or affixed to any standard weapon attachment point.

The tactical flashlight had been one of the plethora of gear I'd picked up during my last visit to the Shop when I'd grabbed anything I thought I might find useful. I held the small cylinder in my free hand and thumbed the activation switch before I pushed open the door.

I paused in the doorway, pistol raised to confront any threat.

Signs of a struggle greeted me within the front room of the house as furniture lay broken and cushions were scattered over the floor. There were no bodies though.

I scanned the room, but nothing moved in my sight, and I heard nothing throughout the rest of the house. I closed the front door and latched the deadbolt before I searched through the rest of the house for any signs of occupancy. Besides the state of the front room, and the smell from whatever was rotting in the fridge, the rest of the house seemed to be in fair condition.

The first floor cleared, I cautiously approached the stairs to the second level as a tiny pair of red dots appeared on the minimap in the corner of my vision.

No sound came from the upstairs, but I crept upward with my pistol raised. The wooden stairs creaked as I climbed, but I continued despite the small noises. The stairs turned ninety degrees at a landing halfway up, and I slowly cleared the corner pistol first before I continued the climb.

A patter of tiny, padded feet across the wooden floor brought me to a halt as I drew even with the top of the stairs. A streak of white flashed in front of me at eye level, past the top of the stairs. I jerked my weapon to track the movement and another streak followed, though this one was more brown.

The brown blur stopped suddenly, and ominous, glowing red eyes faced me.

Then I blinked, and I snorted. It was a rabbit.

The rabbit quivered and launched itself toward me. I fired my pistol, but the rabbit somehow twisted in flight to dodge the energy beam.

Then the creature landed on my chest. The rabbit's claws dug and scrambled for purchase on my armor as its sharpened front teeth snapped toward my neck.

I stumbled back down the stairs and crashed into the wall at the landing as I batted at the demonic beast with glowing eyes that had latched onto my chest. Finally, I dropped the flashlight and used that hand to grab hold of the creature. The fabric of my jumpsuit ripped as I pulled the monster free, then I threw it to the floor. The impact stunned the tiny beast, and I quickly smashed my foot down on the prone rabbit.

I stomped again and again until the beige fur of the creature was matted red with its blood. When the creature finally stopped moving, I stood panting. The monster's blood had spattered onto my dropped flashlight, which lay angled on the landing and cast the stairwell in a dim, eerie light.

Glancing up at the top of the stairs, I saw a pair of glowing crimson eyes staring down at me, and I realized it was the first monster that had streaked past the top of the stairs.

The white rabbit sat, watching me.

Arrrghhh Beast (Level 18)
HP: 175/175

I lit into the beast with my beam pistol as it charged down the steps. This time, my flurry of shots all hit and burned into the rabbit before it could get close enough to leap like the first one had. The body of the small creature tumbled down the last few stairs and flopped limply to a stop on the landing at my feet.

I shook my head and brushed the front of my ripped jumpsuit. Those little creatures had seemed far more of a threat than they'd actually turned out to be.

A quick looting of the bodies turned up some small pelts and a pair of rabbits' feet, all of which I stored in my Inventory. Then I collected my dropped flashlight and headed back up the stairs.

The acrid stench of urine and accumulated animal filth drifted out of the first bedroom at the top of the steps. Just inside the door sat an elevated rabbit hutch with a hole chewed through the wire cage, which revealed how the animals had escaped their confines. I shut the bedroom door to block the worst of the smell and wondered who would keep a hutch like that inside their house.

The remaining rooms of the upper level were empty, and I picked one that looked like an unused guest room at the opposite end of the hall from the foul-smelling rabbit room. After I closed the door, I slid an empty dresser in front of the door in the hope that it would block anything that tried to batter through the door in the night.

I pulled out my pistols and set them next to me on the bed as I lay down on top of the comforter. Staring at the dark ceiling, I contemplated my plans.

In the short term, the goblins had more bounties posted at the casino. Working through those would help me obtain Credits and experience. The exposure to more of the Galactics in the region might open up further opportunities for reward.

Beyond that, I still hoped I could find clues to the whereabouts of the Krym'parke. If they were even still in the area. I had to assume they were, since if they weren't, then I had little chance of doing anything about them.

I also wanted more levels and more Class Skills. Using my abilities brought with it an almost addicting sense of power and purpose. Despite the dangers of this changed world and the constant need to fight for my life, today's successful hunt for a bounty had filled me with immense satisfaction. I wanted more of that challenge.

Content with the thoughts and plans that circled through my mind, I soon drifted off to sleep.

Chapter 21

"We have an ice machine, you know."

The goblin bartender's shrill admonition almost interrupted me as I fed Mana to the jagged spike of ice that coalesced in the air over my upraised palm. Sweat dripped off my brow despite the frigid aura radiating from the end of my arm. Satisfied with the size of the icicle, I cut the flow of Mana and tipped my hand to the side. The miniature Frostbolt tumbled into the rocks glass on the bar in front of me with a satisfying clink.

Unamused with the bartender's interference in my little experiment, I glared at the spectacled goblin. The bartender blanched and quickly retreated to the far end of the bar.

With no one left to bother me, I swirled the Mana-created ice in my glass half full of amber liquid under my nose as I sat at the bar in the casino and contemplated the whiskey's oaky finish. I took a sip and savored the rich, golden liquid as it flowed smoothly over my tongue. With a sigh, I set the glass back on the bar, almost disappointed despite the quality of the liquor. The improvements to my Constitution meant that feeling any buzz from booze was now nearly impossible.

The pricey drink was a little reward to myself, since I had just finished the last posted bounty and the goblin job board on the casino wall was now completely cleared. It had only taken me four days, and the rewards from the various jobs had added up to a tidy sum of Credits.

The jobs themselves had been more tedious than difficult or dangerous. The majority of the tasks involved humans too clueless or too lazy to completely read through the details of the various contracts to which they had bound themselves. I got hired to hunt them down when they invariably ended up in violation of the contract because they had not read the fine print.

The hardest part had been tracking down the various offenders, and fortunately, they had all been local. The phonebook I'd liberated from the shelves of the dusty copier kiosk had led me true more often than not. The few who weren't in the book took longer, but I'd still managed to hunt down leads while I trekked all over the North Shore and then farther north into the city environs. In those cases, my questions from interviewing the locals pointed me in the right direction, then the bounty fled when they caught wind of my approach, which only served to paint a target on their back.

Even while out hunting, I'd kept my eyes and ears open for clues about the Thomas kids, the missing children, or the mysterious attackers from the school, but nothing had turned up so far.

The downside of my bounty hunting was the negative reputation I was picking up from the local townsfolk. Most of it was relegated to dirty looks or muttering as I passed by, but the fact that I was a human hunting other humans on the behalf of the exploitative aliens who had taken over the area was drawing significant vitriol from the population.

On the plus side, slightly offsetting the negative reputation, the loot and experience from the monsters slain along the way as side tasks on my hunts only added to my overall take. Since the fights typically took place in the middle of the street, my rep as a monster slayer was almost on par with that as a bounty hunter.

In fact, the experience gained from the bounties, combined with what I had earned from slaying various monsters along the way, had pushed me to the next level, and I brought up my latest notification now that I had time to deal with it.

Level Up!

You have reached Level 16 as a Relentless Huntsman. Stat Points automatically distributed. You have 2 Free Attributes to distribute.

A quick look over the attributes on my status sheet at the points that had been added automatically showed that Agility remained my highest stat by far, with a level in the mid sixties. Constitution sat just behind that in the fifties, then Intelligence, Charisma, and Perception were all in the low forties. Strength and Willpower were the two attributes that lagged far behind, with their levels in the low thirties. My highest attribute was nearly double the value of my two lowest, and that made me uncomfortable.

I added a free point to both Strength and Willpower in an attempt to shore up the lack I felt there. Satisfied with my choices, I confirmed the changes and reviewed my updated status.

Status Screen			
Name:	Hal Mason*	Class:	Hunter*
Race:	Human (Male)	Level:	16
Titles			
Sharp Eyed (Title hidden)*			
Health:	540	Stamina:	540
Mana:	430		
Status			
Normal*			

Attributes			
Strength	33	Agility	65
Constitution	54	Perception	42
Intelligence	43	Willpower	32
Charisma	42	Luck	18
Class Skills			
Greater Observation	1	Hinder	1
Implacable Endurance	1	Keen Senses	1
Meat Locker	1	On the Hunt	3
Rend	1	Right Tool For the Job	1
Perks			
Gut Instinct			
Combat Spells			
Frostbolt (I), Lesser Disguise (I), Minor Healing (I)			

"Excuse me, Adventurer Mason."

The nasally voice grated on my ears and pulled my attention from my status. I closed the window and looked over to the source of the interruption.

A goblin in a tailored suit waited a few paces away from my seat at the bar.

Meqik Blastlock (Concierge Level 32)
HP: 310/310

MP: 360/360

A pair of armed guards stood behind the sharply dressed goblin, and a quick scan with Greater Observation pegged the pair as a Bruiser and a Bouncer. The two bodyguards had levels in the mid twenties, making them lower leveled than their charge.

"You have performed great services for the Goldmiser Cartel with your completion of our posted bounties," said the goblin in the fancy suit when I turned toward it. "So I wanted to thank you personally."

"You're welcome," I replied.

The goblin remained standing there, and I got the sense it had more to say.

"Is there something else?" I asked with an eyebrow raised.

Meqik took a half step forward and leaned toward me. "There is a further opportunity that may be available for someone of your skill set, but that discussion will require some discretion."

The goblin pointedly looked around at the other occupants of the bar, and I understood that the concierge wanted to talk business somewhere more private. I nodded to the goblin and finished my drink in a single swallow, lamenting the lack of liquid fire that would have burned its way down my throat back before the System. I stood from the bar, completely unfazed by the alcohol in my system.

I waved for Meqik to lead on and joined the goblin as it walked across the casino's gaming floor. The two bodyguards let me get ahead of them then trailed after both of us.

"You mentioned the Goldmiser Cartel," I said while we crossed the casino. "I haven't seen that name anywhere except the fine print on the bounties I've been collecting."

"The illustrious leader of the Goldmiser Cartel, Trade King Fezz Goldmiser IV, purchased this outpost as an expansion to be managed by his son, Trade Baron Fazz Goldmiser," explained my goblin guide. "If Baron Fazz can manage this facility into turning an ample profit, then he will have proved himself worthy of being named heir to the Cartel."

"Seems like you've got a brisk business going here so far." I gestured to the bustling gaming tables around the floor.

"Projections for this quarter are exceeding expectations so far," the goblin replied.

In other words, they were fleecing the local rubes for every Credit they could, and I almost snorted in disgust. I'd been lucky that my first visit to a Shop hadn't turned out like the farce the goblins had set up outside the casino.

Still, there was little I could do about the situation. The goblin forces were numerous, even if they were mostly low Level. If I engaged them directly, I would just be swarmed by overwhelming numbers. And now, I had learned that the Cartel presence here was only a part of a larger Galactic organization. Any actions on my part would have to be subtle.

"Many of the Cartel's youngest members joined this expedition," Meqik continued, oblivious to my cynical thoughts. "They hope to take advantage of the profits and experiences gained by the Cartel setting up a resource monopoly in this city."

The goblin lapsed into silence for several paces.

"However, we have had some setbacks recently," the goblin finally admitted. "Instead of relying on our trade bazaar for System weapons and supplies, the local population is obtaining equipment from a source across the rivers from downtown."

While the goblin talked, we went up a flight of stairs and toward the location of the casino's Grand View Buffet restaurant. Another pair of goblin guards waited on either side of the open doors, but neither of them batted an eye as my suited escort walked me between them. One guard was too busy picking his nose to even look up, but the room beyond quickly pulled my attention from the careless guards.

Despite the lackadaisical demeanor of the guards, I felt a brush of static across my skin as I walked through the doors.

Meqik caught my puzzled expression and looked up at me. "Privacy field. Anything said in this room should be difficult for any enemies to obtain details about."

My attention was pulled from my escort by the massive golden throne that had been raised in the center of the former buffet style restaurant. A well-padded cushion took up the seat, but the rest of the structure looked to have been built from slot machines. Lights blinked over the frame in attention-grabbing sequences, and I figured out that the effect was intentional when I had to exert mental effort to focus on the throne's occupant.

Seated on the throne was a large goblin with slicked back black hair. The goblin wore a purple tracksuit with the jacket unzipped to reveal several gold chains that circled the goblin's neck and rested over a bulging gut that hung out from under a stained white undershirt. The goblin played idly with the slot machine in one of the throne's arms and repeatedly pressed the button to spin the reels every few seconds.

Meqik guided me in front of the throne then took an additional step forward after I halted.

"Trade Baron, I bring you the human adventurer, Hal Mason." Meqik bowed as it spoke.

I nodded my head respectfully but did not bow. Instead, I observed the goblin on the throne as the goblin cocked its head and looked away from the slot machine to examine me in turn.

Fazz Goldmiser, Sticky Fingered, Corporate Climber (Trade Baron Level 3)
HP: 890/890
MP: 970/970

The sobriquets after the goblin's name were something of a first, or they would have been, if I wasn't hiding a title of my own.

The ridiculously low level contrasted significantly with the high health and Mana values, which informed me that I'd finally met another Advanced class. This goblin was someone who had received their Class by earning the full fifty levels of their Basic Class first, instead of being granted the Class as a shortcut by the System. If I had to guess, the higher Mana value indicated the goblin focused less on physical attributes and more toward intellectual gains. That assumption fit with the name of the Class itself, which seemed to indicate a focus on leadership and mercantilism rather than combat.

Interestingly, it seemed that the goblin's Class was treated as both a title and a Class from the way my escort addressed the Gribbari leader.

The Trade Baron looked down at me and over at the concierge who had brought me, then raised an eyebrow in surprise. "This is the human who completed all of our bounties?"

"Yes, Baron," replied Meqik.

The goblin leader harrumphed in disappointment.

"He's just a Hunter," Baron Fazz said dismissively, giving away the fact that it had been able to read my status and Class. At the same time, the slip told me that despite also possessing an Advanced Class, the Trade Baron was unable to penetrate my On the Hunt skill.

"A resourceful one," Meqik chirped. "He located many quarries that our own hunters were unable to track down."

"Fine then, give him the Quest." Fazz sighed. "If he fails, at least it won't be one of ours that goes missing this time."

That statement hinted that the problem the goblins had encountered with their business was a dangerous one, but that was far from surprising. Even in the pre-System world, disrupting the logistics of a foe was a tried-and-true battlefield tactic. Without anyone owning enough of the city buildings to create an area-wide Safe Zone, the continued spawn of monsters meant that most of downtown Pittsburgh remained little different from a warzone.

Meqik gestured toward me, and a new notification appeared.

Quest Offered—Locate Interference

Goldmiser Cartel plans for trade monopoly in the Pittsburgh area are in danger of disruption due to an outside source of equipment entering the city. Locate the supplier of these goods and inform the Cartel.

Rewards: 10,000 XP and 15,000 Credits, increased reputation with the Goldmiser Cartel

Optional: Actions taken to counter the mystery supplier may result in additional rewards.

Optional Reward: Variable

Accept Quest—(Y/N)?

The experience and Credits awarded for completing the quest were too good to pass up, but before I accepted the quest, I looked at Meqik.

"Is there any more information you can give me?"

The concierge wordlessly held out a hand, and a pistol appeared in the palm. The goblin offered the weapon to me. I instantly recognized the weapon as one of the popular firearms of the last century, the 1911 model pistol. However, unlike the weapons I had seen produced by the goblins, this weapon had a polished and complete appearance.

Since Meqik had offered the weapon to me, I picked it up and checked the chamber to ensure it was clear before I gave it a more detailed inspection.

The pistol grip felt comfortably angled in my hand, with none of the sharp edges or rough machining I had noticed with the goblin weapons. I understood why the goblins felt threatened if these high-quality firearms were the kinds of weapons showing up.

I nodded and accepted the quest. I didn't particularly care for the goblins or their treatment of the locals, but I also couldn't turn down the potential goodwill from the largest Galactic power in the area.

"Thank you, Adventurer Mason," Meqik said. "You may keep that as a token of our generosity."

I stored the pistol in my Inventory as Meqik tossed me a box of ammunition for the firearm that I also stowed. Then the goblin gestured for me to leave the throne room.

I nodded respectfully to the Trade Baron before I turned away, but the goblin leader had already resumed playing with the slot machine in the arm of the throne and paid no mind as I left the room with Meqik.

The goblin concierge's bodyguards formed up after us when we exited the throne room and followed behind as we headed downstairs. Meqik stayed quiet as it escorted me through the casino and back to my empty seat at the bar where the goblin had initially approached me.

"I bid you well on your quest, Adventurer Mason," Meqik said.

Meqik hustled off to do whatever tasks a concierge usually performed. Standing alone at the bar, I briefly debated whether to have another drink, and the thought of the rich whiskey tempted me onto the barstool despite my outstanding quests.

The goblin bartender quickly filled my drink order in exchange for my Credits, then retreated back to the end of the bar to resume a murmured conversation with one of the casino floor managers.

I sipped the drink absently, without really enjoying the taste, while I plotted out my next moves. Since I only had the requirement to find information as part of my newest task, it actually dovetailed nicely with the need for more information that I still had from my older quest.

The unfinished Quest to find the kidnapped children remained active in my logs. Unlike the System Quest, which I simply felt no compulsion toward advancing, my task to locate the missing children chafed with the sensation of unfinished business that demanded to be resolved.

My recent work had kept me exclusively on the north side of the city since that was where the local population that interacted with the goblin Goldmiser Cartel lived, all without finding any new clues to the whereabouts of the Krym'parke over the last several days. Investigating the new source of equipment coming up from the south seemed a logical next step in that quest too, as I had now spent time in the west and north parts of the city. If nothing for that turned up, then I would sweep out farther from the city.

Once finished with my drink, I slid from the barstool and left the casino. The constant explosions of the advertisement fireworks overhead greeted me as I walked out the door and crossed the trade area to the gate.

After I left the casino walls behind, I turned right and walked over to the paved path that ran along the river. The Three Rivers Heritage Trail had once been a popular walk for the city residents, but I imagined that enthusiasm had significantly lessened with all of the river-based monsters that now constantly crawled out of the water to harass the locals.

As I headed east along the trail, the Ohio River stretched out to my right. I had just passed the Carnegie Science Center on my left when a splash from the water's edge alerted me to a new danger.

A giant turtle lunged out of the water and scuttled over the rocks toward me. A beaked snout barely extended from the cavernous shadow of its protective shell as the creature charged at me. The beast moved surprisingly quickly for its large size.

Hardshell Snapper (Level 45)
HP: 1994/1994

I cast a Frostbolt to slow the monster, and it hissed as the jagged icicle slipped into the joint at the base of the turtle's neck. Despite my spell, the turtle swiftly drew closer, and I backpedaled along the trail as I pulled my weapons and opened fire at the hard-shelled quadruped.

When my energy beams landed on the creature's head, its scaly skin glowed at the points of impact. Armor fragments splintered and spalled away as my projectile rounds chipped away at the beast's protection. The few shots that missed the monster's head deflected off the shell, failing to damage the heavy carapace there.

It was fast for a creature of its size, but I was far faster and managed to stay ahead of the turtle's snapping beak.

Then the head shot forward, extending on a serpentine neck, and only a last second dodge kept the monster from biting me in half. The end of the beak snapped closed on the back of my calf as I dove aside, and I screamed in pain. Flesh tore and blood sprayed as the turtle jerked its head to the side, ripping completely through my armor and tearing away flesh as it flung me through the air toward the river.

I managed to hold on to both of my weapons as I used the momentum from the throw to roll shakily to my feet several paces from the water's edge, and I gritted my teeth against the pain from my leg. I belatedly activated Hinder on the giant turtle, then emptied my pistols at the monster as it slowly retracted its lengthy neck, the damage from my attacks evident in the ichor that seeped from the wounds on its head and flowed together with my blood that dripped from the monster's maw.

Both of my weapons went dry at the same time, the beam pistol indicating its depletion with a beep as the slide locked open on the projectile pistol. I banished both empty weapons with Right Tool for the Job and summoned my hybrid rifle in their place.

I fired from the hip, the rifle whining as it spooled up then bucked in my hands as it discharged. The blast punched through the turtle's armored head and dug deep, the force of the impact slapping the creature's head to the side.

The monster snarled, still moving despite the damage dealt to its battered face. Shaking off the damage, the monster lumbered back into motion toward me. I limped backward along the uneven terrain of the rock-covered riverbank and fired again, dragging my wounded leg more than really walking on it. Something squelched under the foot of my wounded leg with every step, and I couldn't tell whether it was mud from the riverbank under my boot, or if my boot had filled full of the blood that poured down my leg from my mangled calf.

With my powerful hybrid rifle steadily dishing out damage, the fight swung in my favor and ended soon after. A final handful of shots wrecked the rest of the monstrous turtle's head, and only a gory lump remained of the sinuous neck that protruded from the shell. The stump leaked a stream of bloody goop that trickled down to the water's edge.

I cast Minor Healing on myself and pulled a healing potion from my Inventory, chugging it down as soon as the turtle slumped to a halt. Between the spell and the potion's effects, the pain from my wounded leg faded by the time I finished emptying the vial down my throat. The missing flesh from my calf knitted itself back together as I watched.

My boot still squelched with each step as I walked over to loot the turtle corpse. The unpleasant liquid feeling between my toes confirmed that my boot was indeed filled with blood. I parked myself on a bench alongside the trail and took off the offending footwear before dumping out the gristly contents.

Then I stopped and sighed. Sometimes I still forgot that I lived in a video game.

A cast of Cleanse cleaned up my gear, and I swapped out my ruined jumpsuit for a spare I had picked up in my last visit to the Shop. I had picked up replacements for most of my equipment at that time, just in case something happened, and I was now even more glad that I had shown some foresight.

Despite the damage taken, I felt pretty good about the fight. The monster had been nearly three times my Level, but the combination of my abnormally high attributes and the variety of damage types available to me from my gear selection provided advantages not immediately obvious in the differences in Level between myself and a foe.

I'd come a long way from smearing tomato plants into the asphalt.

I chucked the turtle corpse into my Meat Locker storage to deal with later and continued east along the trail.

Heinz Field stood quiet and empty off to my left as I passed by, and I realized that there would probably never be another football game. I stopped when that thought crossed my mind and looked up at the towering structure. The horseshoe-shaped stadium faced roughly south, opening up on the end toward the river where I stood, and I could see the empty yellow seats in the stands of the upper levels.

Thousands upon thousands of empty seats that would never again be filled. And that was the least of humanity's losses. If sixty percent of us had died on the first day, how many more had perished since?

I tried to look away from the stadium, but when I turned my back to the structure, my stare fell across the river on the stone walls of Fort Duquesne. Another site of destruction and death, where yet another brother in arms had fallen in battle.

The weight of loss pushed down on me. For a moment, I felt as if another building had collapsed over me, leaving me trapped where I stood. My breath caught in my throat, and I braced myself for the haunting accusations of the fallen.

None came.

Finally, I forced myself to breathe deeply and I filled my lungs with fresh air.

I shook my head and left the silent structure behind. Gravel crunched under my feet, breaking the foreboding air of solitude as I took a step along the trail, but my thoughts kept trying to return to the former home of the Pittsburgh Steelers at my back.

I felt something harden within me.

Sometimes the fate of the whole world was too much for any one person, and you had to just let it go. It was enough to just survive. To go on living. To take one more step.

So I let the dead go.

My squad.

The police officer, buried under a swarm of rats.

The would-be thieves downtown.

Paula.

Zeke.

All of them.

I let them go and anchored myself to the sounds of my feet on the trail, moving forward one step at a time.

And I continued on.

Chapter 22

By the time I hiked up the stairs beside PNC Park, another deserted stadium, and passed the statue of baseball great Roberto Clemente at the corner of the ballpark, I had put my thoughts of the dead behind me and focused once again on my quest to find the new source of equipment in the city.

A surprising number of pedestrians moved freely in both directions on the bridge, and for a moment, I stood still while I adjusted to the notion. The street could hardly have been considered crowded, but the number of people who dotted the street were a sharp contrast to the deserted trail, and it took me a minute to adjust to the movement around me.

I caught some strange looks from the nearest pedestrians, who glanced nervously behind me at the stairs beyond. Considering my encounter with the giant turtle monster on the trail, I wasn't surprised that most people stayed well away from the waters below.

Beyond the looks, no one bothered me as I slipped into the southbound lane to cross over the Allegheny River on the iconic yellow bridge named for the Baseball Hall of Famer whose statue I had just passed.

While there were more bicycles here than I had ever seen—outside of watching the Tour de France on TV—most people were relegated to getting around on their own two feet. The lack of ready access to a Shop clearly prevented most people from the most common ways to obtain Credits or purchase vehicles. If I wanted to blend in, then my beast of an all-terrain motorcycle needed to remain hidden in my Inventory.

Once across the bridge, the foot traffic split up at the intersection, and I flowed along with those who went straight ahead along 6th Street into the heart of downtown. Only the main thoroughfare seemed open as I passed the first couple blocks. The alleys between buildings were blocked off with rubble or vehicles that had been pushed aside.

Two blocks later, I passed between Heinz Hall for the Performing Arts and a parking garage that had partially collapsed in on itself. I continued for another block then turned left on Liberty Avenue.

Clumped scraps of ragged clothing, most commonly the blue of denim jeans, lay littered around the area and marked the demise of some of the people in the area. Bleached bones stuck out from the scraps, broken and gnawed on by all manner of scavengers.

The streets smelled faintly of decay, smoke, and decomposing garbage. No more would the scents of the numerous downtown eateries fill the air, since the restaurants were all dark and abandoned.

My path wound through downtown without purpose, and I had to backtrack several times when I found streets blocked completely by rubble. I wondered what could have caused such destruction, then I mentally kicked myself after I saw the massive claw marks torn into the side of the downtown DMV.

I was in the area where the jabberwock had first arrived.

My wandering led me around the city until I found myself on the north side of the US Steel Tower, where the areas around the building were heavily cratered by wreckage fallen from above after the jabberwock had mauled the sixty-four-story tower during its descent from the portal in the sky. I looked up toward the top of the tallest building in the city, and the huge white letters stood out against the dark brown steel of the building's exterior. One of the letters waved precariously in a slight breeze that I barely felt at the street level.

I shuddered and moved away from the base of the skyscraper. I had no desire to get crushed by that giant letter when it finally fell away from the building. Not after I'd survived the monster that had wrecked the building in the first place.

332

The nearby roar of automatic weapons fire pulled me from the reverie and centered my attention back in the present. I listened for a moment to figure out the direction of the sounds that echoed off the tall downtown buildings, then I circled around to the skyscraper, toward the source of gunfire.

On the south side of the towering skyscraper, the two-block stretch of Steel Plaza and Mellon Green provided a bit of greenery and separated the tallest building in Pittsburgh from the second tallest, BNY Mellon Center.

A pair of translucent blue monsters rampaged around a fountain in the center of the green. Foam swirled through the figures like waves cresting on open water. The top half of the figures were roughly humanoid, with a rounded head, a torso, and a pair of waterspouts in the shape of arms. The torso rested on a cylindrical column of water that churned all the way to the ground beneath the figures. As the monsters flowed around the square, their arms lashed out and sent pavestones and shrubs flying.

Lesser Water Elemental (Level 28)
HP: 674/682

Lesser Water Elemental (Level 29)
HP: 709/718

The source of the gunfire and the minimal damage to the elementals sat parked in the street alongside the green with a clear line of fire toward the park. A ring-mounted turret on top of an odd vehicle spat tracers and solid ammunition toward the pair of watery figures.

A light machine gun chattered rapidly as the rounds snapped through the air, while the steady *thunk*ing sound of an automatic launcher remained audible even over the detonation of the exploding grenades. The pair of weapons barrels in the coaxial turret mount were both pointed at the elementals, and from my time deployed, I recognized the weapons as a Mk 19 grenade launcher and a M240G machine gun between the sound of the gunfire and the silhouette of their profile.

The rest of the vehicle was something I had never seen before, and I swept over it with Greater Observation.

Wolverine Peace Officer Protection Unit (Class IV)
Armor Rating: Tier V

Painted a glossy black with gold stripes that ran down the sides, the vehicle was marked with the shield insignia of the Pittsburgh Police. The front of the vehicle angled sharply down to the ground and gave the sleek impression of a high-performance sports car. The dark-tinted windshield and side windows only reinforced that impression. A push bar stuck out from underneath the front bumper, and the heavy-duty ram detracted from the sporty appearance.

Above the angled windshield, the roof sloped upward until it leveled off just before the turret. From that point onward, the rest of the vehicle more closely resembled an up-armored Humvee. A series of armored plates in an octagonal formation with slight gaps between each plate made up a gunner's shield. Each plate had a narrow strip of more tinted glass that protected the turret's occupant while allowing a view in every direction. If I had to guess, the gaps between the plates were to allow the gunner to deploy Class Skills or personal weapons separate from the mounted machine gun.

While I examined the vehicle, it continued to attack the pair of elementals to little apparent effect. Neither the machine gun nor the Mk 19 grenade launcher had much more impact on the monsters than the slight damage I had seen when I initially examined the creatures. The projectile rounds from the weapons punched straight through the figures, imparting minimal damage that rapidly healed, and the grenades failed to detonate until they hit the ground beyond the creatures. Even when the grenades landed at the feet of the monsters, the blasts splashed water away from the creatures that only flowed back toward them to be quickly reabsorbed into the frothy columns at their base.

The vehicle occupants clearly also drew the conclusion that the gunfire was useless, as the turret weapons ceased fire. Then the front doors on either side of the vehicle swung open, and a pair of armored figures stepped out.

The two officers wore jumpsuits similar to mine, except both had silver shield-shaped badges pinned to their chests. The pair also wore helmets with tinted visors that hid their faces behind a reflective sheen. Besides the System jumpsuits and helmets, the duty belts at their waists held the typical assortment of gear I would have expected to see on an officer before the apocalypse. Their equipment was an odd mishmash of pre- and post- System, and I wondered whether the gear design intentionally looked as though it hadn't been upgraded.

Pearce Williamson (Guardian Level 15)
HP: 150/150
MP: 110/110

Zoey Kemper (Patroller Level 14)
HP: 140/140
MP: 100/100

Pearce, the officer who had climbed out of the driver's side of the vehicle, led the attack and charged forward. The man easily vaulted over the waist-high shrubs that bordered the square as a riot shield of red energy snapped into existence in front of him. The shimmering energy covered the officer from knee to shoulder and had a slightly curved face that seemed to originate from a bracer the man held up at chest height as he ran forward. With a shout, the officer used a Guardian class ability to grab the attention of both elementals.

The elementals responded to the shout almost instantly, and water swirled like a whirlpool at the center of their chests before a pair of watery streams gushed out toward the charging officer. Even after it left the elementals, the forceful water blasts swirled in a tight spiral that surged out to impact on the officer's shield and stopped him in his tracks. Like water blasted from a high-pressure hose, the water deflected out around the curved shield to splash harmlessly to the ground once the attack was spent.

With the elementals focused on the man with the shield, Zoey pulled a pistol and opened fire. At the sharp report of the weapon, I shifted my focus from the elementals to the firearm. The deep bark of the weapon indicated a larger caliber, and I grinned as I realized that the pistol the officer held was an exact match for the one stashed in my Inventory.

I had stumbled into a lead for the quest the goblins had given me. Now I just had to find out where the police had obtained the System weapons of human design.

"Dammit, Zoey," yelled Pearce, his head turned back toward his partner. "Use your beamer. You just saw that guns were no good."

With the distance between us, the officer was barely audible over the roar of rushing water, and I missed it if the other officer replied. The second officer holstered the firearm and drew out a sleeker looking pistol, one that appeared similar to mine.

The officer leveled the beam pistol at one of the elementals, and a ray of energy stabbed out to lance into the creature, which hissed as water flashed into steam.

Then the officer's next two shots missed, and I blinked in surprise.

I was pretty sure I could count on one hand the number of missed shots I had made since the whole apocalypse started, so the lack of marksmanship reminded me that most people simply lacked the raw Perception and Agility attributes I had lucked into with my Advanced Class. As I had that thought, one of the middle doors of the police vehicle opened and another officer climbed out.

Kevin Beatty (Deputy Level 9)
HP: 80/80
MP: 120/120

The new arrival stretched a hand toward Pearce, and the shield that protected the officer glowed brighter. Whatever the lower-leveled officer had done had reinforced the first officer and allowed him to move forward once again.

Still, this seemed like an opportunity to make new contacts and potentially learn more about the goblins' rivals. The three cops were overmatched by the monsters, and even if they could take them down, it would clearly take them a while.

I circled the block so that I approached from a right-angle to the embattled officers, and I drew only a single beam pistol from one of my holsters. I targeted the same elemental Zoey had already damaged and opened fire.

All three officers glanced toward me in obvious alarm when my attack landed on the elemental, so I grinned and gave a friendly wave before I fired at the elemental again.

The officers hesitated and watched me warily while they continued to defend themselves from the water elementals. They were clearly concerned I might use the monsters as a distraction, so I shrugged and continued my shots on the same target that had already taken damage.

A cloud of steam rose from the elemental as my fire flashed into the watery figure over and over. The constant damage soon pulled that elemental's attention from Pearce and onto me. I circled away from the officers as the elemental's stream of water stretched toward me. The water surged faster than I expected, so I sped up until I reached a full sprint. Even then, I just barely managed to stay ahead of the rushing torrent, but I turned sideways to fire at the elemental as I ran.

Zoey, the officer with the energy pistol, finally added her attacks to my target again, though several of the shots went wide, despite the fact that the officer stood still and fired with a two-handed grip on her pistol.

Meanwhile, with only a single stream of water pushing against the riot shield, Pearce managed to push his way forward to stand in front of the other elemental. The last deputy, Kevin, continued to offer support, his Mana reinforcing the riot shield and preventing the water from damaging it.

When Pearce advanced to only an arm's length away from the elemental, he pulled a cylinder from his duty belt and extended the baton with a flick of his wrist. Jolts of electricity flickered between prongs on the weapon before the officer swung the weapon in a horizontal strike that slammed into the side of the elemental.

Light flared where the baton impacted, and visible bolts of electricity shot through the elemental's translucent frame. The monster shuddered, and the stream of water that had gushed endlessly from the monster lost force. With the water pressure lessening, Pearce continued to batter away at the water elemental with the charged baton. Water splashed off the elemental with each hit, and tiny bolts of electricity sparked out from the site of the blow to flash the droplets to steam before the elemental could reabsorb them.

Unwilling to reveal my full capabilities, I stuck with attacks from my beam pistol and kept up a constant barrage of energy fire at the elemental still directing its liquid cannon toward me. With only myself, and the beam pistol-armed Zoey attacking the monster, and no stun affecting it, the second creature continued to pursue me as I circled the square.

I took another two laps around the small park before Pearce finished off his target with a flare of light from his shock baton and turned to assault the elemental targeting me. Already heavily damaged from energy weapon fire, the remaining monster fell quickly after all four of us focused our attacks upon it.

I slowed to a halt and holstered my pistol as I watched the officers pull back to stand beside their vehicle. When the low-level deputy crawled back inside, I checked the fallen elementals for loot and picked up a handful of watery elemental essences. I felt a slight chill emanate from the jewel-like crystals that were soft to the touch before I stored them in my Inventory.

Then I slowly approached the two officers, their faces hidden behind the reflective visors of their helmets. Both officers still carried their weapons, though they were lowered to point at the ground, clearly prepared to defend themselves if the need arose.

"You're carrying pretty heavy gear," said the first officer, the man with the shield who had gotten out on the driver's side of the vehicle. From the triple chevron on the sleeve of his jumpsuit, he was also the higher ranking of the pair.

The second officer stared at me with her head cocked to the side as she considered me intently.

"The city is a rough place these days, officer." I shrugged and gestured toward the fallen elementals. "A man has to look out for himself."

"Let's just waste him and get back to the barracks," said a voice from the vehicle turret.

The pair of weapons barrels in the turret mount were both pointed in my general direction, and the casual indifference in the man's tone almost concerned me more than the threat of violence itself.

Both officers outside of the vehicle jerked their heads toward the turret in alarm, which made me think this wouldn't be the first time their gunner had acted on that threat.

"Chill, Kevin," ordered the sergeant. "You can't just go gunning people down in the middle of the street."

The clear implication was that the gunner had already opened fire on someone in the past. When the two officers turned back toward me, they both hesitated when they noticed that my hands now rested on the grips of my holstered pistols. The verbal threat from their gunner had been met by an unspoken warning of my own.

I felt pretty confident I could handle the two officers outside of the vehicle as long as I avoided the stun effect from the sergeant's shock baton. However, the one in the turret would be a challenge. My defensive abilities were all geared toward single targets, and I had no idea how Hinder might affect vehicle-mounted weaponry. Nothing I had encountered so far had been protected by armor that heavy, except for the Jabberwock, which had had its armor shattered by Zeke's Class Skill.

"Easy," cautioned the sergeant.

"What do I have to be easy about?" I asked, my words deceptively calm. "I've just been threatened by armed men who are pointing a machine gun at me. And after I gave them a helping hand."

Awkward silence reigned for a moment before the second officer stepped toward me and held up both hands in a calming motion. "Wait a second, is that you, Hal?"

I raised an eyebrow in response, unsure how the officer would know my name.

The second officer pulled off their helmet, revealing a woman with a shaggy head of brown hair. The woman's face looked vaguely familiar.

Then it clicked into place.

I did recognize the woman, but I had never known her name. Fortunately, I had Greater Observation to help me cheat.

"You're one of the guards from the Allegheny County Jail," I said. "Zoey, right? You took prisoners for booking when they were dropped off."

"Yeah, man," said Zoey, clearly pleased to have been remembered. The officer turned toward the sergeant and pointed at me excitedly. "This guy is one of the best bail bondsmen in the city."

"Oh?" The one-word response carried the sergeant's skepticism clearly.

"He never failed to bring in a bail jumper," Zoey continued. "The intake crew regularly bet on how long it would take him to bring one in. There was actually a bet outstanding for a guy who skipped his court appearance when this whole apocalypse happened." Zoey frowned, then looked toward me. "What happened with that one?"

"Well, he had a meth lab," I replied.

Zoey's eyes grew wide. "No way."

"The situation went downhill from there." I shrugged.

The officers waited for me to continue, but I let the silence drag on. I really didn't want to get into the fact that I had actually killed the man. Or fought giant bears before blowing up the meth lab. The whole story sounded ridiculous in hindsight, but I had lived it.

Zoey's exuberant outburst and the ensuing discussion seemed to defuse the initial hostility of the situation, the tension dropping to the point where I was far less worried about the turret gunner lighting me up with the 240G. I still kept an eye on the turret, since it seemed the third officer was a bit of a loose cannon.

With Zoey's removal of her helmet, the professional demeanor of the officers faded into something more casual. The sergeant also pulled off his helmet and ran a hand through his matted blond hair before he absently scratched at the stubble on his chin while he looked me over critically.

This time the look was more of an assessment than an obvious threat evaluation. It felt like he somehow knew I had left things unsaid about the fate of the bail jumper and had drawn an accurate conclusion.

"Kevin, keep watch on our backs," commanded Pearce. "I don't want anything sneaking up on us."

With a sigh audible from where I stood, the gunner complied with the order, and the turret gave a faint hum as it spun smoothly in its housing to point its paired weapons behind the vehicle.

"You obviously know Zoey," said the sergeant. "I'm Pearce."

"Nice to meet you, Pearce." I nodded respectfully.

Now that both officers had their headgear off, I could plainly see the telltale signs of exhaustion. Dark circles under their eyes and matted hair gave them an unkempt appearance previously hidden by the uniforms.

"What are you doing out on patrol?" I asked Zoey.

"There's not really much left of the law enforcement in the city," she replied with a tired shake of her head. "Those who remain have sort of merged together. Police, Bureau of Prisons, Marshals, FBI, DEA, we're all just doing what we can to hold things together. Warden Hughes is organizing whoever is left and everyone is working overtime just to try to keep the streets the slightest bit safe. Sometimes, it seems like it's a losing battle." She gestured to the vehicle. "We've got a supplier for high-tech gear, but between the monsters spawning and people going crazy, we just can't keep up."

The listless tone and thousand-yard stare were all too familiar from my time deployed. Pearce clearly caught the tone and stepped over to the depressed officer before placing his hand on his partner's shoulder in an attempt to comfort her.

"Oh, come on," Kevin whined from inside the vehicle turret. "Yinz better not be having another emo moment out there."

"Cut it out, Officer Beatty," Pearce snarled toward the vehicle.

I barely heard the mumbled reply with my enhanced senses from several paces beyond where the sergeant stood, but it was definitely not the cooperative response the officer wanted from his subordinate.

"What was that, Officer Beatty?" Pearce asked. The sergeant stared at the backside of the turret, his eyes boring into the armor and his voice cold.

"I said, 'yes, sergeant,'" came the belligerent reply from inside the vehicle.

Pearce glared at the turret for several long seconds then looked at Zoey. The tired officer shrugged. Pearce sighed and gave the woman's shoulder a reaffirming squeeze before he let go. Seeming to ignore the issue with their third partner for now, the two officers turned their attention back to me.

"As you can see, Hal, we're in need of good officers," said the sergeant. "Would you be interested in a job?"

The sudden shift in behavior after their initial antagonism had warned me to expect something, but I had not anticipated a job offer.

"Just like that?" I asked cautiously. "You just met me, and now you're offering to let me join up?"

Pearce bit his lip, and I could see the man struggle with whether he should speak.

"We need more people to hold the city," he finally explained. "Unless we can get eighty percent of the buildings bought from the System, then the monsters will just keep spawning. We've got some aliens supporting us with vehicles, weapons, and Credits, but they don't want to take an active role in any combat." The sergeant sighed. "You're clearly competent enough to get by on your own, but we need all the help we can get. We've got our families protected at our compound, so if you've got anyone you care about, then we can shelter them too."

I brushed off his initial proposal with a wave. "I've got no one, so safety doesn't hold any value. What can you offer *me*?"

The sergeant frowned at my casual dismissal, but he quickly schooled his features to hide his displeasure. "We also have a bounty program offering Credits and equipment for monster kills."

"Now that's more like it." I gestured for the officer to go on.

The officer outlined the reward structure that paid a premium for materials in good enough condition that crafters could use them to level their professions.

After he'd finished speaking, I said, "Hmm, so you'd pay well for intact monster corpses?"

"Yes." Pearce nodded.

"I do like the sound of Credits," I said.

"What Class are you?" Pearce asked.

"I've got a Hunter Class," I lied. "It turns out that hunting monsters isn't so different from hunting men most of the time. I'm pretty good at bringing down monsters and harvesting their corpses."

I had no interest in fully revealing my actual Class or abilities. I certainly did not trust them, especially after the threat offered by the officer in the turret. The fact that the streets had remained empty around us for the duration of our fight and the ensuing conversation so far meant that the locals were not particularly pleased to see the police officers either.

Fortunately, Pearce seemed to buy my explanation.

"That's useful," he said, and I saw an opportunity.

"It would be, if I could find a reliable place to sell monster carcasses after I take them down," I replied.

"I'm sure our crafters would pay well for them," Pearce said.

I paused to let the officers think I was contemplating the merits of their deal. "All right, I'm interested enough to see what your crafters will pay."

"Credits by the fistful," Zoey interjected. "I'm sure of it."

Pearce shook his head at Zoey's words but waved toward the vehicle behind them. "Would you like to ride with us?"

"Sure," I said.

"We've got to finish our patrol route," cautioned Pearce. "But once we're done, we can take you back to the compound and get you set up."

"That's fine." I shrugged indifferently.

I followed Zoey around to the passenger side of the vehicle. There were three doors along either side with a slight gap between the middle set and the door farthest to the back. In the center of that space sat the turret housing. Zoey was already climbing into the first, so I approached the middle door and pulled it open when I found it unlocked. I glanced inside and found a relatively comfortable interior.

"Wait," the voice of the third officer demanded from the turret as I looked inside. "You're bringing this guy with us now?"

"If I wanted your opinion, then I would have asked for it, Beatty," Pearce responded.

I easily picked up that the sergeant's intentional omission of the man's honorific highlighted his displeasure. The turret gunner missed the hint and continued to grumble.

"Shut your mouth, Beatty," ordered Pearce. "If I hear another word out of you, you won't be leaving the compound again no matter who your daddy is! I'll ensure you're stuck on barracks duty and spend all of your time cleaning toilets!"

The stream of obscenities from the turret abruptly cut off as Kevin finally clued in that his superior had lost any semblance of patience.

The inside of the vehicle was broken up into three main compartments. In the forward compartment, the vehicle controls looked like something out of a science fiction movie and included holographic displays projected onto the inside of the front windshield. There was enough space between the seats that someone could climb between the middle section and the front without too much trouble.

Between the middle compartment and the rear section, a raised circular platform supported the turret housing above and saw the legs of the third officer ascend up into the turret itself.

It was interesting to me that the most aggressive member of the group was also the lowest leveled. Was he pushing hard to catch up or to impress his superiors? I pushed aside my thoughts on the group dynamic for now and returned my attention to the rest of the vehicle's interior.

A fine mesh divided the rear compartment from the rest of the vehicle— clearly the prisoner transport section of the upgraded police cruiser.

Since the inside of the vehicle didn't look like an obvious trap, I swung myself into the bucket seat and closed the door. Then I leaned forward to poke my head between the pair of front seats and look over the controls as the officers settled into the forward compartment.

When the vehicle moved forward, the acceleration was so smooth that I barely felt any sense of motion. While Pearce focused on the road, Zoey explained the vehicle's controls and features. The officer's lecture about the features of the vehicle continued for the entire length of the patrol, only interrupted during the times when monster spawns attacked.

The most notable encounter occurred when a handful of fire-breathing squirrels were easily mowed down after Pearce allowed Kevin to open up with the 240G. The weapon thundered, the chattering echoing down into the vehicle compartment, accompanied by the tinkling of empty shell casings that fell from the gunner's station overhead. When the stream of machine gun fire raked over the beasts, I felt relief that I hadn't ended up on the receiving end of that fire during our initial meeting.

Pearce eventually drove south along Grant Street, passed the Boulevard of the Allies, and almost to the end of the street before he turned left onto First Avenue.

After a couple minutes of quiet driving, Pearce said, "We're here."

I leaned forward and looked over Zoey's shoulder to see out through the front windshield as we drove beneath Crosstown Boulevard and into the parking lot outside the Pittsburgh Municipal Court. The imposing, fortress-like structure of the Allegheny County Jail stood just beyond the courthouse, and it was immediately obvious that the prison had received some upgrades since I had last seen it before the System's arrival.

The jail building itself still looked almost like an interconnected complex of a half dozen rectangular, red brick apartment towers. The upper levels of the building were offset, like a pair of rows of red squares on a red-and-white checkerboard, connected only at their corners. Only the narrow windows of the structure—with specially constructed cement housings partially obstructing them—hinted at its true purpose.

Where a chain-link fence had once surrounded the complex, now a rectangular wall of smooth stone stood, complete with a two-story watchtower that overlooked the parking lot we had just pulled into. The wall around the jail also wrapped around the adjoining area that included the Pittsburgh Municipal Court building.

Far above, the transformed roof of the prison now held lights and guidance systems for a series of landing pads that sat above the rooftops. A scaffold framework extended out wider than the building itself to support the wider platform. Due to the elevation of the roof, I only got a brief glimpse of a single aircraft that sat close to the edge, but something about the vehicle jarred my memory, and I more closely examined what I could see of the craft. The boxy aircraft appeared to have engines that could rotate for vertical takeoff at each corner of their rectangular frames.

Then I realized it wasn't the aircraft itself that had drawn my attention but the profile of the craft's footprint. The distinct shape of a rectangular outline with nozzles at the corners would leave circular down blast burns beneath them.

That layout matched the impressions burned into the grass at the high school weeks ago.

I had finally located where the Krym'parke were based.

And I was being practically chauffeured directly inside.

Chapter 23

"You guys have spaceships?" I asked.

I pointed toward the roof of the jail as the officers and I climbed out of the Wolverine. Kevin ignored the rest of us and quickly walked toward the gate that stood between the parking lot and the main entrance to the Pittsburgh Municipal Court building. Pearce and Zoey seemed content to let the young man rush off, so I matched their relaxed pace while I looked around.

A matching vehicle sat parked several empty spaces away, though the rest of the lot stood empty. The other transport bore signs of heavy use, with the paint heavily scratched and the push bar attached to the front bumper bowed inward before it twisted downward to almost touch the pavement.

"Not really," replied Zoey. "Those belong to our suppliers. They're aliens, but their equipment allowed us to put down a riot on the first day after prisoners started using their abilities to escape from their cells."

"Sounds like a rough day," I said.

It took a surprising amount of effort to fake sympathy after how that first day had started out for me.

"Our radios stopped working, so we couldn't coordinate," Zoey continued. "Any guard on their own got overwhelmed as the inmates gained control of one wing and pushed into the next."

The officer trailed off, her eyes distant as the memories played out in her mind. After a moment, Zoey shook her head and continued. "Then the warden showed up with a bunch of high-tech gear, and nobody questioned it when several aliens joined her in pushing back the inmates. The warden and her new allies cut through the front line so fast that the bodies were unrecognizable, and the rest of the rioters surrendered quickly after that.

"Once we had things under control, the warden explained that she had struck a deal to exchange the dangerous prisoners for technology that would help us build this area into a fortified compound to keep us and our families safe."

While Zoey told the tale of the first day from the perspective of a guard at the Allegheny County Jail, we crossed the parking lot and reached the gate in the wall that surrounded the compound. The metallic portal noiselessly split open in the middle at Kevin's approach and remained open until we had all passed through. Both sides of the gate had retracted into slots set in the stone wall, unlike the goblin fortifications where the gates were hinged and swung open inward.

Beyond the gates, the courthouse remained largely unchanged. Roughly rectangular in shape, the front entrance into the gray stone building was on the short end that faced north. The three-story structure had successively smaller footprints for the second and third floors, while the long sides of the building bowed slightly outward like the curved sides of a rugby football. Tall windows rose above the front entrance, but to either side of the center, the far narrower windows along the wings gave the building a fortified atmosphere.

Kevin had long disappeared through the glass front door by the time the rest of us reached it and entered. A notification appeared as I stepped through the doors, and I scanned it quickly.

You Have Entered a Safe Zone (Pittsburgh Municipal Court)

Mana flows in this area are stabilized. No monster spawning will happen.

This Safe Space includes:

Pittsburgh Municipal Court

Allegheny County Jail

By the time I read and dismissed the System message, we were inside, and I saw Kevin standing just behind a man in a black robe. Arms folded across his chest, the youth stared at us over the man's shoulder with a smirk that radiated smugness.

"Sergeant Williamson," thundered the black-robed man. "You will explain yourself this instant."

"Judge Beatty," Pearce replied coolly. "What exactly do you expect me to explain?"

"You can begin with why you have been holding back opportunities for my son to level and why you are allowing a stranger into the safety of our refuge." The man lifted his chin upward so that he looked down his nose toward us, and I saw the similarities in the facial structure between the older man and the youth behind him.

While he had his attention focused on the sergeant beside me, I took the chance to examine the arrogant man.

Maximillian Beatty (Judge Level 12)

HP: 110/110

MP: 140/140

Pearce looked silently at the official, then shifted his gaze to the young man behind him. Kevin paled slightly and his smirk faded before the youth looked away from the sergeant's intense stare.

A few people in civilian clothes loitered in the long entrance hall beyond the father and son, clearly listening to the drama as it played out. Another police sergeant, equipped similarly to Pearce and Zoey, leaned on a reception desk to the side of the entrance and watched the showdown with a bemused air.

"Don't ignore me," Judge Beatty ranted, his face growing red. "I—"

"Our mandate is accountability, integrity, and respect, Judge," growled Pearce. "Not shooting pedestrians with machine guns because we don't like the way they look."

"That was one time," scoffed the older man.

"If I had my way, your son would be in a cage with the other animals. Warden Hughes, for some inexplicable reason, still likes the boy and wants him trained, so I will continue to follow orders." Pearce stalked forward and jammed his index finger into the chest of the older man. "But be warned, my patience for putting up with him is almost out." The officer gestured toward me. "And this stranger is a registered Galactic Bounty Hunter. Do you know what that means?"

The judge mumbled a sullen response, and a vein throbbed in the forehead of his reddened face. Far more interesting to me was the information that Pearce had seen something of my status. Some ability or Class Skill had allowed him to read enough about me to at least identify my title. That revelation filled me with a sense of vindication that I had been right to disguise so much of my status.

I still didn't trust this group, especially now that my hunch that Kevin had murdered civilians had proved accurate. While I felt that I could justify my actions, at least to myself, for those I had slain, every sense I possessed told me that Kevin would lack any justification whatsoever for his actions. My intuition led me to believe the young man was an arrogant narcissist who followed in his father's footsteps, and that neither man had any qualms against killing in cold blood if it benefitted them.

The judge huffed at the sergeant's aggressive stance and opened his mouth to retort, but a pair of tiny figures rushed out of a courtroom and streaked across the hall.

"Daddy, Daddy!"

Only after the two blurs had wrapped themselves around the officer's legs and stopped abruptly could I see that they were a pair of little girls, neither more than five years old. They wrapped their arms around the officer's legs so that one was on each side and clutching him desperately. The blond hue of their pigtails matched the sergeant's hair, so their cries weren't much of a surprise.

The judge seemed unwilling to continue the verbal altercation in the presence of the sergeant's children and promptly turned away before stalking off. Kevin followed his father, and Zoey snorted in disgust beside me.

Pearce took a moment to pry the two children from his legs before he scooped them up into a bear hug and held them tight. After a moment, he set the girls back down, but they latched onto his arms like they had his legs moments earlier.

"Girls, you know I love you, but what have I told you about running off from your mom?" the sergeant said, his voice warm but stern.

"To always stay within sight of her," muttered the slightly taller of the pair.

The two girls finally released the officer and reluctantly stepped back. Abashed, they fidgeted with their heads down and stared at their feet.

"That's right," replied Pearce.

He affectionately rubbed the tops of their heads then dropped his hands to their shoulders. He turned them back the way they had come.

"I need you to go back to your mom now," Pearce said. "Dad has to finish some things for work, but I promise I'll come spend time with you once I'm done."

"Okay, Dad." "Yes, Dad."

The two bolted off after their hurried replies.

"I love you, you little munchkins," Pearce called after the girls as they ran down the hall and disappeared through one of the open doors.

The sergeant stood still and watched for a moment after they were gone, then he sighed and turned back toward us.

"Sorry about that," Pearce said. "I know that wasn't exactly a warm welcome."

"You don't have to apologize for the kids," I said with a shake of my head. "Though seeing Kevin's father, it pretty much explained his attitude. It must run in the family."

The sergeant who had stood beside the reception desk walked over and shook his head.

Brian Conrad (Sharpshooter Level 15)
HP: 160/160
MP: 170/170

"You have no idea." Brian chuckled darkly as he joined the conversation.

"The judge called in a few favors with the warden to get his son assigned to one of the patrol groups so that his college-dropout son could gain experience faster," Pearce explained. "And that was after using one of his Class Skills to pass a judgment on his own kid to leech a percentage of the boy's experience gains back to himself, all so the judge doesn't have to go outside the walls at all."

"Is that why Kevin has such a low level?" I asked.

Pearce nodded. "Neither of them will go out alone to put in any extra effort that might endanger themselves, so we're left to babysit a kid who is behind and gains levels slower than everyone else."

The bitterness in the officer's voice was apparent to everyone, and silence fell over the group. No one wanted to speak up after that.

The fact that this organization tolerated the actions of the judge and his son justified my wariness and proved my lack of trust well-founded.

"Let's go see the warden," Pearce finally said, his words ending the awkward silence.

Brian waved a farewell and returned to his post at the reception desk as we headed down the hall. The central corridor had offshoots that led to various courtrooms, including the doorway the girls had run into earlier, and I could see into them since all of the doors into the hall remained open. People were packed within, though they weren't crowded to the point of being uncomfortable from what I could tell.

"We turned the courtrooms into dormitories," Zoey explained when she saw where I was looking. "That's where the families are staying." She was quiet for a moment, her aura of depression palpable. "Those who survived, that is."

"I'm sorry," I said.

There wasn't much I could say. It was obvious the officer had lost someone close to her.

We passed the courtrooms and turned left before going through a security checkpoint manned by a pair of guards with levels just out of single digits. While it seemed that the patrol groups, like Zoey and Pearce, were picking up levels regularly, those who stayed behind to guard the facility were falling behind.

Once through the checkpoint, a narrow passage connected the courthouse to the adjoining jail building. I followed beside Zoey as Pearce led the way to the warden's office.

After a short walk, Pearce knocked on a nondescript wooden door in the middle of a long hallway.

"Enter," a piercing voice called from the other side.

Pearce opened the door and stepped through as he beckoned me to follow. There were two figures inside, one human and the other most definitely not.

The back wall of the room was filled with a well-stocked bookshelf. Centered in front of the shelves sat an elegant desk, behind which sat a sharp-featured woman with black hair pulled into a tight ponytail and dark eyes that bored into me as I stepped into the room. I met the woman's scrutiny, and a chill ran down my spine. Soulless depths peered out at me from her hooded gaze, and I glanced away to take in the rest of the room.

A couch took up most of one side wall. The pillow and blanket that lay neatly on the couch indicated that the warden probably slept there most nights.

Perched on one arm of the couch was an alien with one leg on the floor and the other resting on the couch. Even though I had expected to see one in here at some point, encountering one of the purple-brown-skinned Krym'parke face to face still unnerved me.

The horned alien blinked at me with amber eyes then smiled, revealing jagged fangs.

Mental Influence Resisted

I raised an eyebrow then hid my amusement at the wide-eyed surprise that crossed the alien's face after I failed to show any sign of the intimidation effect it had activated. Instead, I schooled my expression into blank neutrality as I looked over the gear it carried. Several knives were sheathed across its body in belts that circled its waist and chest over a standard adventurer jumpsuit.

Jahgg'd Ot'lyke (Flesheater Tactician Level 5)
HP: 1680/1680
MP: 1500/1500

Low level combined with the insanely high health and Mana values, dead giveaways I had found another Advanced Class. The alien recovered from its surprise and curled its lips back in a silent snarl as it stared at me.

"Cut it out, Jahgg'd," commanded the same sharp voice that had told us to enter the room.

The alien closed its mouth to hide the fangs, but its lips remained twisted in displeasure that I had resisted its intimidation effect. I looked back at the speaker and found that the warden's attention was firmly focused on me now.

"Sergeant Williamson?" Unspoken in the woman's tone was the implication that there better be a good explanation for my presence.

"Warden Hughes," Pearce said, "this is Hal Mason. He's a Hunter who is also a registered Galactic Bounty Hunter. He assisted us while on patrol, and I thought he might be useful."

From the corner of my eye, I saw the Krym'parke on the couch stiffen at the mention of my Galactic Bounty Hunter title, but the alien made no further move toward me, so I kept my focus on the warden behind her desk.

The warden sized me up as I returned her appraisal with a frank stare of my own.

Madison Hughes (Warden Level 25)

HP: 280/280

MP: 300/300

The warden was the highest leveled human I had yet seen.

"Officer Kemper recognized him as a bail bondsman from back before the System happened," Pearce continued.

The warden glanced at Zoey for a moment before she returned her attention to me. "Mr. Mason, you seem like a competent individual. What are you looking for with us?"

"I'm mainly looking to kill monsters to gain experience and materials," I replied. "I'm also open to working on any bounties you may have posted."

The warden exchanged a look with the alien on the couch when I mentioned bounties.

It was the alien's second strange reaction to the word "bounty." Something odd was going on here behind the scenes.

Then the words of the gnome clan leader echoed in my mind, from when Borgym had identified the dead alien from my description of the corpse at the school. I recalled that the Krym'parke were often hunted for their barbaric practices. If there was an open bounty on the aliens, my presence threatened them and endangered the warden's supply of high-tech equipment. The warden's reactions so far indicated that the woman understood the nature of the Krym'parke and also knew that they were Galactic pariahs.

I was already in too deep. I needed to find a way to be useful to the warden and the aliens, at least until I could complete my quest. Both of my quests actually, since I now seemed fairly certain that the Krym'parke were the mysterious suppliers of the high-quality goods that threatened the goblins' trade monopoly, though I still lacked information on how they manufactured the weapons locally.

Those thoughts prompted an idea. The two factions were already poised for a trade conflict. What if I gave things a little push?

"If you've got any bounties on those goblins across the river, I'll take those with great pleasure," I said.

The warden cocked her head and considered me carefully. "You have a bone to pick with the goblins?"

"You could say that," I replied with a sneer. "Those cheapskates. If there weren't so damn many of them, they'd be easy pickings."

The warden leaned back in her chair and considered my words. "I think we can work something out that will be mutually beneficial. Stick with Sergeant Williamson for now."

"Sure," I said. "The sergeant runs a good team."

The warden waved us off, clearly dismissing us from the office. I followed Zoey out into the hall and waited for Pearce, who pulled the office door closed behind us.

"Thanks for the good words about the team," said Pearce. The sergeant led us away from the office and deeper into the jail.

"It's the truth." I shrugged. "We wrecked those elementals, even with the kid being under leveled for the fight."

Zoey snorted. "I'm not sure which is a bigger problem, his lack of levels or having to rein him in before he tries to kill everything he sees."

We passed other officers in the halls only twice, and each time the officer hurried by, too tired to give more than a nod in greeting. Besides those two occurrences, the jail hallways were silent and empty. We also walked through a few open and unmanned security gates, something I found unusual if prisoners were still housed in the jail.

Halfway down a hall, Pearce stopped and turned toward me. "You have some monster corpses you're looking to sell now?"

"I've got a couple," I replied.

The sergeant nodded and led me through the door we had stopped beside while Zoey waited in the hallway.

My nose crinkled at the acrid metallic scent of blood which filled the room. The small gymnasium had been emptied of most fitness equipment and repurposed as a slaughterhouse. The floor had been stripped of the rubberized mats, which were now stacked in a corner of the room. A pair of power cages, once used for free weightlifting, had monster carcasses hung within. Blood dripped from the bodies and ran in rivulets across the floor to a drain in the center of the room.

A Krym'parke stood inside one of the squat racks with its back to us as it deftly carved slabs of meat from one of the monsters with a knife held in one hand. The alien's other hand held a platter beneath where it worked and caught a filet each time the knife flashed through the monster.

After several slices, the alien flicked the knife upward after it completed one of the cuts and a bite-sized chunk of raw flesh flipped into its fanged maw.

Krahg'k Am'tyve (Flesheater Butcher Level 37)
HP: 780/780
MP: 850/850

The alien was the second one I had seen with the Flesheater designation included in its Class name. Since this one was clearly not highly Leveled enough to be an Advanced Class, I had to assume that the Class was somehow related to the aliens' barbaric practice of consuming sentient life whenever they could get away with it.

"Yo, Krahg'k," said Pearce. "Got some fresh meat for you."

At the officer's words, the alien spun toward us with eyes that glowed an angry red and raised the knife toward us threateningly. The Krym'parke paused as it looked at us, then slowly lowered the knife. After a few seconds, the haunting crimson glow in the alien's eyes faded into a dull yellow.

"Thiss one iss ssorry," the alien hissed, opening its mouth to display its sharpened teeth.

Despite the words, I didn't think the alien felt particularly sorry.

"What can thiss one do for you?"

"Our new friend here has some monsters to sell," Pearce explained.

There simply was not enough space for the carcass of the turtle I had slain earlier, so I only summoned a couple of the other monsters I had kept inside Meat Locker.

The alien examined the pair of dead monsters and spat an offer. I countered higher, and we haggled for a bit until we reached a decent price. The agreed upon sum was less than I would have gotten from the gnomes, but still more than I would have received at the Shop.

After the Credits appeared in my Inventory, we left the butcher to his work, and Pearce guided me back out of the room.

"He seemed like a nice guy," I said once the door closed behind us and we rejoined Zoey.

Pearce looked at me with narrowed eyes as we walked, apparently unable to tell if my words contained sarcasm. Zoey just snorted as we continued down the hall.

After we passed several more doors, the hall opened up into a moderately sized cafeteria filled with long tables and benches bolted to the floor.

Murmured conversation echoed from the half dozen officers in black armored uniforms who sat clustered in small groups with a handful of civilians who seemed to be support staff as they ate from compartmentalized plastic trays.

Pearce pointed toward a stairwell beyond the cafeteria. "If you're here without us later, don't go up the stairs. That area is off-limits to everyone."

"The aliens run the prison now," explained Zoey. "We're just here for exterior security against the monsters outside."

"I understand." While I verbally agreed, I kept my face blank. The forbidden staircase likely led to the missing kids.

Confident that his warning had been received, Pearce led us to a narrow window set in the wall that separated the cafeteria from the kitchen beyond. A cook on the far side wordlessly filled three trays and slid them over. I collected the last of the plastic platters and followed the officers to an open table.

"This sure beats the slop they're giving to the refuges in the other building," Zoey said, though she still sniffed her tray cautiously before taking a seat. "Even if it's mystery meatloaf again."

I caught the hint of a frown from Pearce at that remark, but it vanished by the time I joined the pair at the table. Perhaps the sergeant held some resentment that only officers were able to eat here, while his family remained stuck with the rest of the displaced survivors.

Once seated, the two officers dug into their food ravenously. I lifted a cut of mystery meat and sniffed it cautiously before my stomach growled in hunger. From the way the meat had been cut, I was pretty sure I knew exactly where it had come from. Still, my stomach demanded fuel, and I soon joined my tablemates in scarfing down the unidentifiable protein. In addition to the mystery meat, likely cooked from one of the monsters butchered in the former weight room, the trays had been generously piled with standard institutional fare that could have been found in any military barracks or hospital cafeteria.

Rice and beans were heaped in one corner section of the plastic tray, and applesauce filled the next compartment. Two pieces of wheat bread and a pad of butter completed the meal. The final compartment had an upside-down plastic cup, which I flipped over and filled from a pitcher of ice water on the table.

It was nothing fancy, but after several days of cooking monster bits over a Shop-bought camp stove, the simple meal was heavenly. Sometimes, there was pleasure in just not having to hunt and cook your own dinner.

I realized halfway through inhaling the meal that I couldn't remember the last time I had eaten surrounded by this many people. Before the apocalypse, my diet had mostly consisted of fast food and pre-packaged gas station sandwiches as I constantly pursued bail bounties to keep myself busy. In fact, the last time I had eaten with others may have been in a VA hospital cafeteria not dissimilar to this one.

I dismissed the thoughts of the past and focused on finishing my meal. I had more pressing issues to deal with than my antisocial tendencies.

The brownie in the dessert compartment was a little dry, but I washed it down with another glass of ice water. I wasn't going to complain about free food.

Once my plate was empty, I sipped my water and looked at Pearce and Zoey. They had almost finished, though Zoey had left the applesauce on her tray untouched.

"So what's next?" I asked.

Pearce cut a bite-sized piece of his brownie with his fork. Up until now, I had thought that the sergeant was a decent guy, between his affection toward his family and clear opposition to casual murder, but what kind of a person eats their brownie with a fork?

After he finished his bite of dessert, Pearce said, "We're off duty until dawn tomorrow."

"Unless monsters swarm the walls." Zoey sighed. "Again."

Pearce nodded tiredly. "Then it's all hands on deck no matter the hour."

"So what do you do with your evenings when you're not fighting at the walls?" I asked.

"I spend them with my family," Pearce replied with a look that dared me to find fault with that.

"Sleep mostly," said Zoey.

"I don't sleep much these days," I said. "Is it cool if I go out and keep hunting?"

Pearce snorted. "Nobody is going to complain about you reducing the local monster population."

The conversation turned to more small talk until our plates were clean. Once the pair had finished everything they were going to eat, we cleaned up our area of the table and returned the trays to a slotted window that led back to the kitchen. Zoey split off once we left the cafeteria, and I followed Pearce back to the courthouse.

The sharpshooter, Brian, still stood as informal guard at the reception desk when we returned to the courthouse entrance. Pearce gestured toward me when we reached the desk.

"Go ahead and clear Hal for gate access," Pearce explained. "He's going hunting and will be back to join us on patrol tomorrow morning."

"Hunting solo?" Brian raised an eyebrow skeptically and shook his head. "Ballsy."

A holographic panel appeared over the desk, and Brian swiped through several menus, presumably adding me to some kind of authorized user list.

"It's the best way to gain experience," I said.

"It's the best way to die alone," Brian retorted. "I'll stay inside the walls, thank you."

"See you in the morning." I waved to Pearce as I ignored the officer's comment.

Pearce waved back then hurried straight toward the courtroom his kids had scuttled into earlier. I pushed open the glass doors and stepped outside. The exterior gate parted to let me walk into the parking lot before it slid closed behind me.

The sun had dipped behind the skyline to the west and covered the city in the long shadows of the tall buildings that filled downtown. Cognizant that the guards in the watchtower were probably keeping an eye on me, I remained on foot when I left the parking lot. I walked west along First Avenue as I retraced the route by which I had arrived.

Once out of sight of the complex after walking the better part of two blocks, I turned north onto Ross Street. After another two blocks, I circled east onto Forbes Avenue.

Only a few people were hustling about on the street, intent on finishing whatever tasks they had before night fell. With few Safe Zones free of monster spawns, the streets were especially dangerous to non-Combat Class civilians at night. I tipped my head in greeting to the few people I saw and they nodded back as we passed each other, but it was more a wary acknowledgement that we weren't going to attempt to kill each other than any actual sign of respect.

My walk through downtown went quietly, and I soon reached the edges of the Duquesne University campus. I turned south when I reached the campus, bypassing the many buildings that sat dark and abandoned, most of the ground floor windows and doors broken. I headed to the southernmost part of the campus and entered the shattered glass doors of Mellon Hall.

Since I'd only ever driven past the university and had never been inside any part of it, I was forced to spend a bit of time exploring the inside of the structure. On the top floor, I disturbed a nest of giant, acid-spitting mice that ruined another armored jumpsuit before I managed to put them down. Once I dealt with the mice, I was able to locate an access point that led onto the roof of the four-story building. When I reached the roof, I closed the access door behind me and headed to the southern side of the building. As I approached the edge, I crouched so that anyone looking toward the building wouldn't see me easily. Few buildings in this section of the city were tall enough to give any watchers enough elevation to see me crouched on the roof, but there was no sense in tempting fate.

I crawled to the edge and sat with my back against the short wall that ran around the perimeter of the roof. Once seated, I accessed Right Tool for the Job and pulled out one of the pieces of gear I had purchased from the Shop when stocking up for my return to bounty hunting.

Ommatidia Tactical Surveillance Camera

This tactical surveillance camera consists of a headset viewing unit and a variety of attachments that can be used to obtain live visuals of a target location. Optional remote cameras can be synced with the viewing unit to give multiple perspectives or allow a user to watch different locations with a single receiver.

I strapped on the viewpiece and adjusted the fit until it rested comfortably on my face, then I extended a linked fiber-wire camera remote up and over the edge of the wall behind me. In the viewscreen, I saw over the roof and the streets below toward my target.

The imposing, fortress-like structure of the Allegheny County Jail sat on the far side of the four-lane Boulevard of the Allies. From my elevated position, I now had a much better view of the rooftop landing pads, even though the highway blocked the view of the lower levels from here.

A handful of figures moved between the craft parked on the rooftop landing pads, but while they were definitely Krym'parke, I couldn't tell right away if those were guards on patrol or aircrew performing maintenance for the ships. In the pre-System world, aircraft required extensive maintenance to stay airworthy. Even now, with most items having a durability measured under the System, it made sense that these ships would require skilled workers to keep them airborne.

I secured the camera in place near the corner of the rooftop and stored the headset back in my Inventory before I crawled along the roof to the southeastern corner. When I got there, I pulled another camera from my equipment storage and fixed it in place before I headed back to the access door. I slipped off the roof and secured the door once I was in the narrow stairwell that led down to the interior of the building.

Even if I never came back for the cameras, having a visual on the aircraft could provide intel later.

Since I was supposed to be out hunting anyways, I left Mellon Hall and worked my way through the other campus buildings. Almost every building had some kind of monster infestation that I cleared with little trouble. I stuck to my beam pistols and melee weapons for the fighting since shooting projectiles meant that I would need to spend Credits to resupply, which cut into any profit gained from selling the monster loot.

The monsters I found on the defunct university campus ranged from additional nests of the acid-spitting mice to a mutated boa constrictor that hunted them. The giant snake might have been more of a problem if it hadn't been already locked in combat with one of the mice nests.

Judging by the lumps that bulged throughout the middle of the snake, it had managed to swallow several of the rodents before I used my axe to hack through scales weakened by the mice's acid attacks and sever the reptile's spine. Finishing off the rest of the mice was trivial.

The rest of the monsters I faced were more mundane variations of common rodents, pets, and insects. Most of the creatures had levels that were at least double mine, but I found that I could quickly dispatch most foes by targeting vulnerabilities like joints, necks, and other areas with little protection. My high attributes of agility and perception allowed me to precisely aim my beam weapons at those points. When I switched to melee attacks with my knife and axe, those same attributes gave me the speed to exploit any weaknesses I discovered. That attack style synergized well with the slowing effects provided by Frostbolt at longer ranges and Hinder at close range.

When I did take hits, my Constitution gave me the hit points to be able to absorb those blows, provided I wasn't careless enough to let myself get surrounded or swarmed. I stalked through the campus until the wee hours of the morning.

Finally, I decided to take a break from the killing so that I could be ready for a patrol with the police at dawn. I barricaded myself in a janitor's closet on the ground floor of a campus administration building and curled up on some couch cushions I had taken from a lounge down the hall. Then I let myself fall asleep.

Chapter 24

The first light of dawn peeked over the eastern horizon and filtered down past the buildings of downtown Pittsburgh to where I sat on top of the Wolverine police cruiser parked outside of the municipal courthouse. The morning air was crisp and cool, just warm enough that the strip of grass alongside the parking lot glistened with dew instead of frost.

I yawned as I lounged, one leg dangling, on the roof of the vehicle while I waited for the officers to appear. I might not have been a stranger to late nights and early mornings, but I didn't particularly enjoy them. Fortunately, it seemed I needed less sleep the higher my Constitution climbed, so I had woken up with plenty of time to spare. My pre-dawn stroll back to the parking lot from the university campus had been uneventful.

Heavy thoughts had occupied my mind as I returned to the prison. People would likely die today, if I succeeded in my plans to set the alien forces in the city at each other's throats. Casualties would be caught in the crossfire.

I didn't have anything against most of the officers. Like Pearce and Zoey, most seemed to be trying to survive in this crazy world and going along with the warden.

That woman was a different story. I was sure that she knew about the dark side of the Krym'parke. She had, quite literally it seemed, made a deal with the devils. She needed to be brought down, even if those who had signed on with her paid the price.

It was largely a selfish decision on my part. I could see no other way through the defenses of the prison in order to complete my Quest to find the missing children. Part of me still dared to hope the Thomas kids would survive to be rescued. Zeke's offspring deserved the chance to flourish in this new world, and if I could make that happen, then I would.

I might not have a quest for that, but it meant more to me than the camaraderie of the officers I had fought beside yesterday.

The compound gates slid open not long after my arrival, and the trio of officers I had met the day before walked out together. They all carried their helmets instead of wearing them, so I could see by their facial expressions that none of them were particularly surprised to see me waiting. The tower guards on the wall must have warned them.

The three appeared more rested than they had the previous day, which I attributed to a decent night of sleep. Kevin stomped behind Pearce and Zoey. He still looked rather sullen though.

"Good morning, officers," I called as the three approached.

"Good morning," replied Pearce, while Zoey waved and Kevin continued to ignore me.

"What's the plan for today?" I asked as I hopped down from the roof of the vehicle.

Zoey sighed. "The same thing we do every day."

I looked at the officer and raised an eyebrow. "Try to take over the world?"

"What?"

The three all looked at me with confused expressions.

"Never mind," I said with a shake of my head. "Old cartoon reference."

The sergeant glared at me, narrowing his eyes.

"I don't need any more snark on this team," Pearce warned me with a glance at Kevin.

"Fine," I said. "More monster killing then?"

Pearce nodded and climbed into the driver's compartment of the Wolverine. The rest of us boarded after him, and Kevin clambered up into the turret housing. Pearce drove out of the parking lot and down First

Avenue, almost retracing my steps when I left the previous evening. Instead of turning right though, which would have taken us into the heart of downtown, Pearce continued another block and turned left. He drove south, the wrong way onto the off-ramp from US-22, the Penn-Lincoln Parkway. The ramp sloped as it curved down to merge into US-22, which ran along the river. We were soon headed westbound in the eastbound traffic lane, the closest street to the river's edge.

"There's always something crawling out of the river," Pearce explained. "So we try to get down here a few times a—"

Thunder from above interrupted Pearce as Kevin opened fire with the 240G.

Through the front viewscreen, I saw a cluster of large lizard creatures clumped up around something in the middle of the road ahead. The dark green reptiles had long V-shaped heads like a crocodile with protruding teeth visible all along the jaw. While the creatures also had lengthy bodies and a thick tail similar to a standard terrestrial crocodile, the six-clawed legs that were longer and more agile than normal made it clear that these were System-mutated creatures.

Tracers highlighted the line of fire from the turret overhead and stretched out to the cluster of lizards. Kevin raked the hail of bullets from the 240G through the cluster, but only a couple were knocked down by the barrage. The beasts were surprisingly agile, and they scattered in several directions. While a handful dived away over the railings that bordered the road to drop ten feet to the riverside below, the rest charged toward us. Pearce jerked the vehicle to a halt and into reverse, backing up to keep the range open between us and the approaching mass of lizards.

Explosions tossed a couple of the reptiles airborne when Kevin added the Mk 19 to the stream of fire he poured toward the advancing monsters, but there were too many of them, and they moved too fast for the young gunner to target them. With Kevin's low level, the youth simply lacked the combination of Agility and Perception to track the creatures accurately, in sharp contrast to my relatively high attributes that had allowed me to remain deadly accurate with ranged weapons.

"They're going to catch up," I said, my voice low enough that only Pearce and Zoey could hear me over the roar of the weapons overhead.

"I can see that," Pearce replied tersely.

The Wolverine shook as something slammed into it from the side, and I glanced over to see one of the lizard creatures just before it rammed a shoulder into the passenger door opposite from me a second time.

Daggermaw Racer (Level 29)

HP: 726/726

The vehicle rocked to the side from the blow, and Pearce cursed from the driver's seat as he attempted to continue driving backward while struggling to maintain control. Another racer popped up over the guardrail next to the first lizard and joined its companion in battering against the side of the cruiser.

A moment later, the rear of the Wolverine bucked upward as we hit something behind us that thumped against the underside of the cruiser as we rolled over it at speed. The momentary loss of traction on that side, amplified by the lizards ramming into us, caused Pearce to lose control completely, and we bashed into the cement roadside barrier.

The impact turned the vehicle into a spin that twisted us three-fourths of the way around before we hit the barrier on the opposite side of the road and punched through the concrete. The front tires dropped as the bottom of the vehicle scraped over the rubble and brought us to a halt with the front of the vehicle over empty air a story above the river's edge.

There was no time to celebrate the fact that we had managed to not flip the vehicle or end up in the river. Since we were no longer moving, the pack of lizards quickly surrounded us and swarmed the vehicle. Claws scraped the Wolverine, digging into the armor and filling the air with piercing screeches as the armor gradually peeled away. The frenzied monsters bit and snapped their large maws at any exposed edges, and the vehicle shook as the creatures battered it.

"They're too close," Kevin shouted from the turret. "I can't aim low enough to hit anything without hitting us too."

Pearce yanked on a control lever beside the driver's seat, and I felt the vehicle heave beneath us as the sergeant tried to get the vehicle to pull itself back from the edge. Tires spun but failed to gain enough purchase to pull free.

"We're stuck," Pearce said.

"That armor isn't going to hold," Zoey said, worry filling her voice.

"Then we do this the hard way," Pearce replied grimly.

The sergeant grabbed his helmet from where it had been sitting between the two officers in the front seats and pulled it over his head. Zoey sighed and put on her own helmet.

Pearce reached up to a button on the dash next to the steering column, then paused to look back at me. The sergeant cocked his head in a wordless question.

"Ready when you are." I grinned as I pulled out my knife and axe. This would be a close quarters fight.

Pearce punched his finger onto the button, and hair stood up on the back of my neck as I felt a jolt pass through the vehicle beneath me. Outside the vehicle, electricity swept from the surface of the Wolverine in a jagged wave. Brilliant blue arcs of energy jumped from lizard to lizard, and the creatures shook, seized into place by the electric attack.

"The shock stun won't last long, go now!" Pearce shouted as he jerked open his door and leapt toward the nearest lizard, baton extended and lighting up with energy as he swung.

The daggermaw against my door tumbled over as I pushed the door open and jumped out. I wasted no time in shoving my knife through the eye and into the brain of the prone lizard that I had just knocked over, activating Rend to create a damage over time effect even though I was pretty sure the wound was fatal, before moving on to the next monster.

I dropped three of the daggermaw lizards before they showed signs of shaking off the effects of the stun from the Wolverine. Slowly at first, but once the creatures started moving, it became much more challenging to land critical hits that would keep the monsters down.

Thick, scaly hides protected the daggermaws, but both of my melee weapons tore through their defenses to inflict grievous wounds with every attack as I darted through the mass of lizards and activated Rend to maximize my damage. Just as the beast in front of me steadied itself, I sprinted past and delivered a blow with my axe that hacked into the creature's neck at the base of its skull. The weapon sliced through scale and muscle to splinter the vertebrae of the spine. Blood sprayed from the wound as I yanked the axe free, and the lizard crumpled as I planted my foot and turned to stab my knife into its side.

I kept moving, even as I landed a pair of blows on the daggermaw before I moved on to another target. The beast wasn't dead, but it was down and suffering from a quad stack of bleeding debuffs from my Rend that would further weaken it. I needed to get clear of the scrum before the monsters completely recovered from the stun that had given us the opportunity to get clear of the vehicle.

While I slipped through the throng of lizards, Pearce and Zoey remained near the stuck cruiser. I had no attention to spare for the pair as the daggermaws snapped and clawed at me, so I judged their status from the sounds I could hear. The impact of Pearce's heavy blows carried to where I fought even though he was on the far side of the Wolverine, and I heard the jolt of his baton discharging with each hit. From the sharp cracks of gunfire, Zoey had pulled her firearm to assist her partner.

I reached the outside of the scrum and worked around the edges of the mass of lizards. They may have been deadly and agile opponents, but so was I. My speed gave me just enough edge that I dodged the worst of their attacks, now that I had the room to maneuver.

Clawtips still slashed through my jumpsuit and sliced into my legs as I harried the fringes of the monster pack. Blood seeped from the cuts, and though none of the wounds were critical individually, the damage added up. My health dropped as blood trickled down my legs.

My stamina dipped lower as I unleashed Rend after Rend on the monsters. The creatures I attacked turned their attention from the Wolverine and circled around me. If they surrounded me completely, the lizards would tear me apart.

I dodged their attacks, slipping between the enclosing monsters, before I led the pursuing creatures off down the road and back in the direction from which they had first charged toward us.

Blasts from the earlier grenade launcher fire had left the street a pitted mess, and I danced sideways with half of my attention on my path through the rubble while the rest remained focused on avoiding attacks from the daggermaws that ran after me. Three of the six-legged creatures easily navigated through the cratered debris in pursuit.

Once a dozen paces separated the lizards that followed me from the rest of the monster pack, I pivoted and used the guardrail as a springboard to leap onto the daggermaw on the left. The creature threw its head back to snap at me as I landed on its spine, and I hooked my axe under the lizard's long chin to hold it in place as I raked the blade of my knife across its throat. The daggermaw bucked beneath me as blood poured from the gaping wound, and I jumped free of the creature, careful to place the dying creature's body between the two other monsters and me.

The pair of lizards clambered over the fallen daggermaw, consumed by their fervor to reach me and heedless of the lacerations their sharp claws left behind. Still unwilling to utilize my full skillset with the officers nearby, I circled quickly enough that one was briefly behind the other, then I darted forward.

I feinted toward the creature, and the monster snapped its jaws where I should have been but caught only empty air. I had pulled back at the last second, then I swung my axe onto the creature's snout. The blade punched through the monster's upper jaw completely and lodged in place. I lost my grip on the weapon when the lizard jerked away. The monster twisted away from me completely and writhed against the guardrail in an attempt to dislodge the stuck weapon.

That left me to face a single daggermaw with only a knife in my left hand. I tossed the knife to my main hand and summoned a beam pistol from my equipment storage into my open palm. I squeezed off a pair of shots, and the beast instinctively recoiled as the hastily aimed energy beams scored hits dangerously close to its eyes. In the creature's moment of hesitation, I focused my aim at one of the eyes, and this time the shot punched into the orb with a sizzling pop. The daggermaw hissed and flinched to the side. I lunged into the exposed blind spot and stabbed my knife into the blackened hole that had contained the beast's eye. The long combat blade pierced the monster's brain then slid out, coated in gore, as the beast fell twitching to the ground.

I stabbed it several more times before I finished off the other two wounded animals and retrieved my axe.

A shriek of terror cried out from the continued fight at the cruiser, and I looked back to where the others still battled the remaining monsters. Zoey stood on the hood of the vehicle and fired into a swarm of daggermaws that clustered on the ground beneath her. For a moment, the vista gave me a flashback to another officer firing down toward a monster swarm from the hood of his vehicle. Another panicked screech helped me shake off the mental image, and I realized that the cries echoed from the turret.

Blocked from Zoey's support by the bulk of the turret itself, a pair of daggermaws ripped and clawed at the shield from the back of the vehicle. Even as far away as I stood, I saw that repeated attacks had weakened the armor. The gaps between the plates grew wider as the monsters tore their way inside.

Despite the fact that I thought Kevin was a little turd, I opened fire on the pair of monsters on top of the turret as I rushed back toward the fray. The energy beams burned into the lizards, but they ignored my attacks and continued to dig into the vehicle. One managed to get a clawed limb through a gap, and the screams from the turret turned from panic to pain.

A pair of lizards snapped at my heels as I vaulted over them and landed heavily on top of a third. The creature instinctively tried to heave me off, and I used the momentum to catapult myself the rest of the way onto the Wolverine.

Zoey fired behind me as I leapt, her shots raining down on the lizards I had just hurdled. The rounds snapped through the air right next to me, but I had no time to consider how close the officer had been to hitting me.

I stored my weapons into my Inventory and rotated midair so that I impacted feet-first into the daggermaw without a limb stuck into the turret.

My kick launched the creature into the air, and it flipped twice before I lost sight of it on the other side of the vehicle. The monster with a claw stuck into the turret swung its head toward me, and I swung my boot into the side of its snout before it could take a bite at me. The attack knocked the creature's head against the turret, and I spun around as I rebounded from the blow. I flipped onto my stomach and crawled onto the monster, pulling my knife once again. It weakly tried to throw me off, but with one limb still reaching into the turret, it failed to do much more than arch its back beneath me. I wrapped my legs around the creature to hold myself firmly onto its back while I plunged the knife into it repeatedly.

The monster went limp eventually, and I pushed myself off of it to stand on top of the vehicle. I looked over the turret just in time to watch as Pearce crushed the skull of the lizard I had kicked off the vehicle with a devastating swing of his shock baton. Blood dripped from a number of wounds all over the sergeant's lower legs and forearms, but nothing looked critical. The bracer that had generated his energy shield in the elemental fight sparked and trailed a faint haze of smoke as if shorted out.

Zoey still stood on the hood, and her hands shook as she tried to awkwardly reload a pistol magazine while also holding the box of ammunition. Rounds pinged off the hood as her shaking hands dropped more than she managed to successfully load into the magazine. The officer's pistol lay empty at her feet with the slide locked back. Now that I finally had

378

a good look at the weapon, I noted that it definitely matched the firearm the goblins had asked me to track down.

I glanced around to confirm that none of the daggermaws remained a threat. I saw only corpses. I wiped the blade of my knife on the scaly underside of the dead creature slumped beside me on the roof of the vehicle before I sheathed the weapon and tugged the dead monster's front limb free from the turret's bent armor. I ignored the faint sobs that babbled from within the turret as I kicked the carcass to the ground and jumped down from the vehicle to loot.

"Is he okay?" Pearce asked me with a nod toward the vehicle.

I shrugged. "Sounds like he's still alive."

I returned to looting the monster carcasses, and it took me a few minutes to puzzle out my indifference to the young man's survival.

Besides the couple of daggermaws Kevin had taken out in his initial barrage, the youth had been relatively useless in the fight, especially once the Wolverine had crashed through the guardrail. While I understood that the sergeant had had the young man foisted on him by his superiors, Kevin was clearly not cut out for combat. I understood that sticking him in the turret was meant to offset his relatively low level with the turret's firepower, but he lacked the skill to use the weapons effectively.

The fight would have been much easier on all of us if the turret had adequately whittled down the lizards before they had surrounded us.

The loot from the fight turned out to be fairly generous with a number of high-quality reptile skins, claws, and teeth. Even with the materials split four ways, I had enough for a good return on my next trip to the Shop. I also dropped a trio of the least damaged carcasses into Meat Locker for a donation to the kitchens back at the jail.

By the time I finished looting, Kevin had emerged from the shelter of the Wolverine. His eyes were red, and tears streaked his face. Ugly red slashes covered his hands and forearms—defensive wounds from his attempts to fend off the daggermaw that had reached inside the turret. The sidearm remained holstered in his belt, not even drawn to be fired in his own defense.

"Thank you, thank you," Kevin babbled and stepped toward me, his arms wide for a hug.

I pulled a weak health potion from my Inventory and pushed it into the young man's hands to fend off his attempted hug. "Here, drink this. You'll feel better."

Kevin blinked at me without understanding for a moment, then stared at the bottle of red liquid in his hand.

Pearce arrived and took the young man by the shoulder. The sergeant helped Kevin drink the potion before escorting him over to the side of the road for a chat. I walked over to Zoey, who had finished her reload and gathered up all of the dropped rounds. The officer rubbed the back of her neck and holstered her pistol as she peered at the front of the Wolverine where it stuck through the guardrail and hung out over open air.

"That looked like a nice pistol." I nodded toward the weapon secured in the officer's holster.

"This?" Zoey asked and pulled the weapon back out.

She ejected the magazine and cleared the chamber before handing it to me. I hefted it experimentally, as if for the first time, but now that I had my hands on it, I was confident it was an exact match for the weapons the goblins had wanted me to find.

I just had to get the information I now possessed back to the casino to get paid for the quest.

"It feels good in the hand," I said. "Where did you get it?"

I released the action and aimed it over the river, then nodded in satisfaction and cleared the weapon before I returned it to Zoey.

"We've got an armory back at the jail on the second level. It's got a bunch of System variants of traditional firearms that the warden's benefactors have helped construct. Though we can only go up there with an escort. I'll have to show you when we get back." Zoey reloaded the pistol and holstered it once again. "How are we going to get this thing out?"

"Pull on it?" I suggested.

Zoey blinked.

"With increased stats, we have superhuman strength, right?" I asked.

"Right," she replied.

I could tell she was unconvinced, so I walked to the back of the Wolverine and tugged on the rear bumper. It seemed solid enough despite the claw marks gouged into the surface. I squatted and wrapped my hands around the underside of the bumper. A lip on the bottom of the fender made for a comfortable grip, and I heaved backward. The vehicle swayed toward me.

Zoey stood alongside the vehicle watching, and I realized I had an opportunity. With my hands hidden beneath the vehicle, I pulled a translucent wafer the size of my thumbnail from my equipment storage and pressed it on the top side of the lip on the backside of the bumper.

Ixodada Nanopatch

This tracking device fuses with a target surface when applied and takes on both the surface appearance and texture of the target. The nanopatch uses ambient Mana to report the target's location and movements, remaining in place until receiving a self-destruct command—after which the patch will disintegrate and leave no trace of its placement.

Duration: 7 Galactic standard days

"Come on," I told Zoey once I no longer felt the wafer beneath my fingers, nodding to the space on the bumper beside me.

The officer shook her head but joined me anyway.

Together we pulled and felt the vehicle rock back noticeably. Pearce saw our attempt and joined us with Kevin. The four of us pulled on the rear of the vehicle, and it slowly scraped backward onto the street.

Finally, after much sweating and a not-insignificant amount of cursing, the group of us managed to get all four tires of the Wolverine back onto the road. Pearce climbed into the driver's seat and started the vehicle.

"I think we're good," the sergeant called.

The rest of us boarded the vehicle, but once inside, I saw that Kevin stared at the turret with fear and reluctance. He was clearly unwilling to take his previous position in the gunner's seat. Pearce looked back and saw the look on Kevin's face. The sergeant frowned and looked at me. We needed someone up there, so I shrugged and crawled from my seat up into the turret housing.

Daylight shone into the turret through the gaps between the armor plates. Those plates were twisted and slashed in places, but most of the armor remained in good shape. The weapons barrels protruded from the armored housing, but I had access to their bodies inside the turret, and I quickly went through the process to clear the weapons for action. I was a little surprised by how much of the checklist remained muscle memory as I checked the ammunition feeds and chambered rounds in the pair of belt-fed weapons.

Once I felt confident that the weapons had taken no damage from the fight, I settled into place. A pair of clips held a hammock-like sling attached to the inside rim of the turret, and I repositioned them slightly to hold myself comfortably in position at the weapon controls.

A joystick on the rim beneath the weapons controlled the rotation of the turret, and I experimentally twisted it in either direction to get a sense for how the weapons would move.

"Are you all good up there?" Pearce called from below.

"Yep," I replied. "I can handle this."

The Wolverine rolled into motion a second later and headed west down the street, in the direction we had been headed before running into the daggermaw lizards. Pearce steered around the worst of the craters that had been blasted into the street, but the vehicle bounced through the ones he couldn't avoid.

Beyond the craters, we passed the spot where the lizards had been gathered when we first spotted them. Blood and viscera lay smeared over tattered scraps of fabric on the pavement between the scattered remains of what had once been a person. Below me in the cabin, I heard Kevin retch at the horrific sight.

"If you puke in here, you get to clean it up," Pearce yelled. "Open the door."

The door cracked open, and Kevin upchucked even as Pearce drove down the street. Despite the vehicle's movement, the acrid stench of bile filled the cabin and wafted up into the turret. I quickly rotated the turret so that the largest hole the lizards had pried between the armor plates faced forward, and fresh air flowed through to dampen the smell.

After a few minutes, Kevin managed to get his stomach back under control and shut the door. Silence filled the vehicle after that, broken only by the wind that whistled through the turret as we continued the wrong way down the highway.

Chapter 25

We cruised along the empty stretch of highway as the road sloped upward before the lane of traffic curved south to cross over the Fort Pitt Bridge. Instead of following the road and continuing the wrong way, Pearce turned us sharply to the north and took the Liberty Avenue exit ramp that headed back toward the heart of downtown.

I swung the turret left to see if I could catch a glimpse of Fort Duquesne as we coasted down the ramp, but the trees along the edges of Point State Park were in bloom and obscured the view beyond. I continued the rotation to point behind us to check our backtrail before I swept the turret the rest of the way around to point forward once again.

With the lack of vehicle traffic throughout most of the city, pedestrians flowed on both the street and sidewalks along Liberty Avenue. The throng slowed us to a crawl as we left the exit ramp. Quite a few bikers pedaled through the crowded streets, but everyone cleared away from our path as we pushed ahead. Even though I made sure to keep the turret weapons pointed upward, we still got plenty of side-eyed glances.

We had only gone about a block when movement above and to the left caught my eye, and I instinctively swung the turret toward the motion. An orange tentacle descended from a window high on the side of a gray brick tower to grab a woman from the brick pathway next to the building. The woman screamed and batted the fleshy appendage wrapped around her as she was pulled upward.

"Contact left," I shouted as I raised my aim to a point on the tentacle well above the struggling woman and squeezed the trigger on the 240G.

The weapon roared and a stream of tracers punched into the tentacle. The rounds splattered green ichor onto the building, and stray rounds raised clouds of shattered brick around my target. Enough shots landed that the tentacle twitched and released the woman, who fell a story and a half to land heavily on the sidewalk below.

I had absently noted that the crowd around us had mostly dispersed when I opened fire, so no one was close enough to provide immediate aid when the woman crumpled to the ground and dragged herself away from the building. Since I could do nothing for the woman from here, I kept my attention, and weapons fire, on the tentacle retracting into a window about halfway up the skyscraper. Sporadic attacks from some of the few other people who remained around belatedly joined the stream of fire that spat from the machine gun, but the tentacle retreated before most bystanders reacted into anything beyond immediate flight.

Once the tentacle had disappeared, I eased up on the trigger. A few more gunshots echoed from others on the street before a ball of fire erupted against the wall next to the window, the detonation blasting out flames that scorched the gray stone of the tower.

I glanced around and found that the street was almost completely clear, with the exception of the handful of people who had attempted to assist us once we had engaged the threat. A white-haired man in a leather vest hurried over to the injured woman, who had managed to crawl into the street while we had been attacking the monster. The man looked to be performing first aid or healing, but I lost sight of them as Pearce pulled the Wolverine over to the side of the split-lane road next to the building the monster had retreated into.

"Are we going after it?" I called into the vehicle's cabin.

"We can't very well let it continue grabbing people," Pearce said.

Unfortunately, the thing had been too far away for me to use Greater Observation on it, so I had no idea what we might be facing. I unhooked myself from the turret and dropped into the main compartment.

"Oorah." I grinned and pushed open the door to exit the vehicle.

After I gave myself a quick once-over, I realized that only Pearce and Zoey were also checking over their gear. Kevin remained inside the Wolverine. I looked at Pearce, who shrugged when he saw me nod questioningly toward the vehicle with a raised eyebrow.

"Someone's got to keep an eye on our ride," Pearce said.

I shook my head and rolled my eyes. If I was in charge, I would never have let the young man out of my sight. Even beyond his dubious moral character, he had proved decidedly unreliable in a serious fight.

When the two officers left the vehicle, I followed them across the wide brick sidewalk toward the main entrance to the building. A pair of revolving doors that led into the lobby were the only places where the glass had not been completely shattered. The lobby itself consisted of an arch set between two of the four equally sized wings of the cruciform-shaped building, and it was labeled in silver letters across the rotunda as Three Gateway Center.

Broken glass crunched underfoot as we stepped inside with weapons drawn. Trash and other debris littered the area, but no immediate signs indicated the presence of any monsters. We passed an empty security desk at the rear of the lobby and passed a bank of elevators which sat with their doors partially pried open. Only one had an elevator car in place. The rest opened into empty shafts filled with darkness. Beyond the elevators, we found two sets of stairs, each set in opposite corners of the central column of the building where the wings of the cross-shaped building intersected.

Pearce paused before he headed toward the southwestern stair doors, and I took the moment to read the signs by the stairs, noting that there was an underground parking structure beneath us.

"This is more than a three-person job, but we work with what we have," the sergeant said over his shoulder, gaze focused on the door in front of him.

"We're going to clear floor by floor. I don't want anything sneaking up behind us when we get to that tentacle thing."

In an ideal world, we would have had at least two much larger teams to clear the building and assault up each stairwell simultaneously in a coordinated fashion. The rearguard from each team would secure each set of stairs so that nothing could slip past while the individual floors were cleared. But as Pearce said, we worked with what we had.

"Sounds good," Zoey agreed.

"I'll bring up the rear," I said.

It felt odd for a moment, and I only realized why when I had a sudden flashback to before my medical discharge, my last combat operation as a Marine. I had been the tail-end Charlie then too.

I shook off the feeling as Pearce stepped up next to the door. The sergeant held his wrist out in front of him as he reached the door, then nodded to Zoey. She pulled open the door for Pearce as the energy shield from the sergeant's bracer snapped into place. Pearce stepped into the dark stairwell, and light flared from his bracer to illuminate the stairs. I held the door open with my foot for Zoey, who followed behind the sergeant, then I pulled my own tactical light as I entered the stairwell and closed the door quietly behind me.

We climbed two flights of stairs before we reached the door that led to the next level. Pearce and Zoey stacked up on the door while I stepped past them to pull the door open. The two officers led the way, and I flowed through behind them.

The officers had both turned left after they went through the door, toward the central intersection of the floor, so I went to the right. The hall ended just beyond the stairwell door and opened into a long rectangular space filled with rows of cubicles. Four support columns provided structural support for the wing, and there were no interior walls throughout the wide-open area. Sunshine poured into the space through large, evenly spaced square windows that ran the whole length of the structure's three walls. With the light provided by the windows, I no longer needed my tac light, so I put the tool away and drew my knife instead. Anything that popped up from within the cubes would need to be dealt with at close range.

I quickly checked each cube as I swept down one aisle between the rows to the far end, then returned back up the other side. When I got back to the stairs, Pearce and Zoey were just coming back to the main intersection from their checks of two other wings. I gave a quick shake of my head to the two officers. There were no signs of monsters here.

After a quick check of the final wing, we went back to the stairwell and climbed to the next level where we repeated the process to clear the floor. For ten floors we found no living creatures, but evidence pointed to something having been through the area at some point.

Each level showed increasing signs of damage, with holes opened up between the levels more and more frequently as if something had burrowed through in random places. At first the holes were small, no larger than the size of my closed fist. The farther we climbed in the skyscraper, the larger the holes became, and we had to carefully watch our steps as we cleared the floors.

The holes grew large enough that we could soon see through them to the levels above, and our pace slowed. Each floor took longer and longer, as we had to check our footing while looking overhead to be sure nothing waited above to pounce on us.

The floors blended together, and we lost ourselves in the monotony of clearing every level. Despite the repetitive nature of our task, the tension grew as we climbed. We knew that a threat lurked somewhere in the building, and we just had not found it. Yet.

On the sixteenth floor, I had just finished inspecting a bunch of admin offices filled with file cabinets when I heard a shout followed by gunfire. I raced back toward the center of the tower. Pearce dashed across the intersection before I reached it and disappeared toward the sounds of combat. Seconds later, I heard the discharge of the sergeant's shock baton, and I turned the corner at a run to join the fight.

The first thing I noticed was that Zoey hung upside down from the ceiling.

A barbed tentacle as thick as my wrist encircled the officer's leg and was trying to pull her upward through a hole to the floor above. Zoey had braced her free leg next to the hole in an effort to keep the tangled leg from being pulled through while she fired her pistol at the orange appendage that had descended through the ceiling.

Pearce jumped up with a shout and smacked his baton into the tentacle. The shout was the same as the one he had used to keep enemies focused on him during our previous battles. It seemed to have no effect here though, and the tentacle remained wrapped tightly around Zoey. However, the limb shivered from the shock of Pearce's baton attack. Zoey screamed also as the shock from the baton traveled through the monster to her leg.

"Don't shock me," yelled Zoey, her teeth gritted in pain and exertion as she pulled against the tentacle that threatened to rip her leg through the gap in the ceiling.

"My taunt didn't work," Pearce called with a glance at me. "The actual creature must be out of range."

"On it." I nodded and darted toward the stairwell. The monster had never appeared as a red dot on my tracker, so it had to be at least two floors above us.

I clambered up the two flights of stairs and shoved open the door so hard that I nearly knocked it loose from the hinges. I raised my pistol as I ran toward the spot where Zoey struggled below, expecting to find a monster when I turned to face that wing of the tower.

There was no monster though. Instead, the orange tentacle stretched from the floor up into another hole in the ceiling. The space here was mostly empty, only a few boxes and scattered debris littering the wing as if the previous tenant had moved out and left a bit of mess behind.

I snarled and dropped my pistol into my equipment storage space as I used my free hand to pull the axe from the sheath behind my back. I planted my foot and spun as I reached the tentacle, using my full momentum to swing the axe into the barbed appendage. The axe head carved completely through the tentacle with a disgusting squelch and only the slightest hint of resistance. Green ichor splattered from the severed tentacle, and the lower part dropped through the hole in the floor.

A pair of voices shrieked briefly, followed by a heavy thump, and I chuckled as I imagined Zoey falling onto Pearce.

The upper part of the severed tentacle swung toward me, and I slashed the wound with my knife. I applied Rend to the attack and noticed an immediate increase in the flow of green ichor that dripped from the wound.

The ceiling rumbled, and a cloud of debris exploded above me as two more tentacles punched down to lash toward me. Spikes at the ends of the feelers dug into the floor as I danced and dodged through the open level, thankful there were no cubicles here to hinder my movements.

I circled the building support columns, using them to block the trio of tentacles from trapping me in place as I twisted back on my previous path. With the appendages stretched across the space and wrapped around the columns, I attacked the tentacles well away from the pair of jagged barbs at their tips that raced after me. I noticed that the tentacle I had originally severed had pulled back up through its hole as I hacked and stabbed at the limbs that remained.

These two tentacles were thicker, faster, and resisted my attacks far better than the one I had cut through at first. With the ends in pursuit, I landed a couple blows then weaved around to give myself enough space to attack the same spot again. The pair of tentacles managed several slashes that ripped through my jumpsuit and dropped my health, but neither managed to wrap me up like Zoey had been.

Gunshots from the mezzanine by the stairs indicated that Pearce and Zoey had finally caught back up.

"The body isn't here," I yelled. "Go up another level."

The gunshots cut out, and I focused on avoiding the tentacles while getting hits in whenever I could.

It took several minutes of intermittent attacks, but I finally managed to chop completely through one of the thicker tentacles. With only one tentacle as a threat, I combatted it more directly. The tip of the feeler ended in a jagged spike as long as my hand that held up against my attacks, but just beyond that hardened material was the rubbery orange flesh that took damage from my weapons.

I alternated between parrying the spike with the blade of my knife and the sharpened edge of the axe head, using the free weapon to land hits each time I deflected a blow. I had chopped most of the way through the tentacle when suddenly the whole limb went limp.

I stood alert for a moment, just waiting for the monster to move again, before I realized that Pearce and Zoey must have killed the body of the creature somewhere above.

I headed back to the stairwell. It took a climb of three floors before I found the officers.

Gunfire and cracks of jolting electricity echoed from the level when I caught up, indicating they were still fighting something, but it sounded as if they were handling it.

A glimmer of an idea blossomed. Instead of rushing out to join the fight, I cautiously peeked out from the stairwell. The empty lobby section for the floor was all I could see, and it sounded as though the fight was around the corner in one of the wings.

With the officers distracted, this could be my chance to turn the cold war into a hot one between the goblins and the Krym'parke-backed police.

I slipped out of the stairwell and crossed to the door that led to the opposite set of stairs, the northeast stairwell we had avoided so far. I pulled a device from my Right Tool for the Job storage space, another one of the cool System items I had purchased for my return to bounty hunting.

Cacophony Decoy IV

This remotely activated noisemaker can be programmed to generate a variety of sounds across a wide range of audible frequencies.

The noisemaker was a gray, rectangular block the size of my index finger. I set the decoy to mimic the sound of the door swinging shut and stuck the device to the underside of the door handle.

Then I pulled up the details for a spell I had bought at the same time as my bounty hunting equipment but had yet to cast.

Lesser Disguise (I)

Effect: Creates an illusory visage over the target of the spell that changes the target's appearance. The caster's familiarity with the desired form of the disguise increases effectiveness. The spell does not provide any abilities or mannerisms of the desired form, nor does it alter the perceived audible or tactile features of the target.

Cost: 75 Mana plus 10 Mana per minute to maintain the illusion

I frowned as I reread the spell description. I needed familiarity with the target, and I really needed to get the details right.

I brought up my Inventory status and swiped past my Right Tool for the Job section filled with equipment and weapons. Instead, I looked over the section dedicated to Meat Locker and spent at least a minute in study of one of the corpses as I memorized every detail. I dismissed the status screen and listened to the fight still going on.

My Mana dropped as I cast the spell, and I felt a sudden sense of dissociation as my body shifted to translucence before it became completely invisible. I looked down, and at waist height, I saw a goblin also looking down. I shifted my head from side to side and the visage matched my movements.

The sounds of combat from down the hall died off, and I pulled the goblin yeet cannon from my Inventory, the same gun I had found next to the goblin figure I now imitated. I checked that the tiny weapon was loaded and ready to fire, even though my index finger barely fit through the trigger guard. I raised the firearm, and the illusory goblin at my waist, now armed with a matching weapon, pointed its gun in the same direction.

Satisfied with my preparations and with my appearance now masked by magic, I crept back across the lobby area and peeked around the corner.

Pearce and Zoey fought through another empty suite, this one filled with a tangled mass of tentacles that mostly lay limp and unmoving. I finally glimpsed the main body of one of the creatures we had been fighting, but only a single monster remained standing in the nest.

Tentacled Grabber (Level 29)
HP: 126/626

The orange-skinned monster limped backward on four short, stocky legs that reminded me of a rhinoceros or hippopotamus. The creature had no head, just a large tooth-filled maw in the center of its front torso. A thick tentacle extended from a shoulder joint on either side of the monster's thick body above the front pair of legs. The creature moved backward slowly, one of its forwardmost legs dragging lifelessly as the quadruped retreated from the officers who attacked it relentlessly.

The monster was an ambush predator that captured prey with the lengthy tentacles that held victims helplessly as they were fed into the cavernous gullet. Only there was no disabled prey here. Even as I took in the scene, beam weapon fire from Zoey laid down cover fire for her partner's assault. Pearce took advantage of the support and leaped over the body of a fallen creature toward the last monster, his baton raised for a powerful overhead attack as he landed in front of it.

With both officers preoccupied by the monster, I aimed the goblin pistol at Zoey and opened fire. Six shots cracked out from the weapon as I walked my fire across the officer's back, intentionally missing with my first and last two shots.

Zoey spun toward me and blinked in surprise when she saw the goblin firing at her. I squeezed off another round that hit the officer in the chest before Zoey managed to return fire. The beam from her shot scorched the wall next to me, and I ducked back around the corner.

Once out of sight, I dropped the tiny goblin pistol at the same time I dispelled the magic from Lesser Disguise. With my own figure now visible and the illusory goblin vanished, I punched the wall at waist height. The drywall crumpled beneath my fist, and I summoned the corpse of the goblin with the smashed skull from my Meat Locker storage space. I jammed the head of the broken body into the hole that I had just smashed. Blood and brains drenched the cratered sheetrock as I let the corpse sag to the floor.

I no longer heard combat from beyond, but footsteps rushed toward me from around the corner, and I flicked the pistol away from the body with the tip of my boot. The pistol skidded out across the floor, visible to whoever rushed toward me.

"You guys okay?" I called.

Zoey swept around the corner a moment later, her pistol leveled. The officer stopped in surprise when she saw me, then she looked at the goblin corpse. Her eyes flicked to the gore-splattered wall, and she lowered her weapon, accepting the evidence as presented. She knelt over the body as if to search it, and I activated the decoy.

The sound of the door across the lobby closing echoed in the silence, and I drew a pistol as I spun toward the sound. As I expected, I saw nothing and looked back at Zoey. The officer still knelt beside the goblin corpse, but now she also had her weapon aimed toward the far stairwell, and she glanced at me.

"There's another goblin," Zoey whispered.

"On it," I exclaimed and charged toward the door.

With my body blocking Zoey's line of sight to the door, I slipped the decoy from the handle and back into my Inventory as I yanked the door open, then I charged into the darkened stairwell.

So far, my plan seemed to be working, but this was the most dangerous part. The deception could still crumble apart depending on how quickly the two officers followed me.

With my tac light at full brightness, I raced down the stairwell and listened for sounds from both above and below. We had not cleared this stairwell, so it was possible that something might lurk within.

I made it down about a half dozen floors before I heard movement above me. From the echoes of booted footsteps pounding through the stairwell, it sounded as if Pearce and Zoey were trying to catch up.

Since I was running at full speed, the trip down was much faster than our climb up, and I soon reached the ground floor. Instead of leaving the stairwell, I continued down another level to the underground parking garage. I sprinted out of the stairwell and passed the elevators to the parking area itself.

I didn't have much time.

I summoned the goblin bike from my inventory and frowned when I examined the bent front wheel in the light of my flashlight. It would never pass for functional.

I turned the bike toward the exit from the garage then tipped the vehicle onto its side, as if I had flipped it to keep the driver from fleeing. I pulled the second goblin corpse from my inventory and placed it beyond the bike. A casual examination would make it seem as if I had tackled the goblin and flipped the bike in the process.

Then I straddled the body and drew my knife before running the blade through the slash that bisected the goblin's chest and coating the weapon with blood.

Just as I finished, I heard the door crash open behind me, and I pushed myself to my feet before I turned to face the sounds. Pearce and Zoey gasped for air as they stumbled to a halt, their Constitution not up to the pursuit. They took in me, the wrecked bike, and the blood that dripped from my knife.

"I told you." I grinned darkly. "I don't like goblins."

I bent and wiped my blade clean on the corpse at my feet.

"I can see that," Pearce said as he caught his breath.

I sheathed my knife and kicked the body. "If they're starting to attack in the open, things might be worse than I thought."

"We need to inform the warden." Pearce frowned.

"You guys do that," I said. "I bet these goblins are with that group from the casino, but I'll backtrack them from here and see what I can learn anyways."

Zoey righted the bike and noticed the bent front wheel.

"Piece of junk," Zoey said dismissively as she kicked the wheel, which only twisted it further.

"Leave it," Pearce said. "We need to move. See you back at the courthouse, Hal?"

"I'll see you back at the courthouse." I nodded as the two officers started back toward the stairwell.

I left in the opposite direction and headed toward the parking garage exit, the illumination from my tac light leading the way.

Chapter 26

Late afternoon sunlight streamed down into the tunnel entrance as I walked out of the underground garage and climbed the slight incline of the dual-lane ramp that led into the parking structure. The alley opened up before it ended abruptly at street level, and I found myself on Fort Duquesne Boulevard.

A pile of rubble on the street to my left made me take another look at the partially collapsed building. Something incredibly large had burrowed through the front entrance to the structure.

I winced as I examined the debris and realized that I had been the cause of the destruction here. This was where the jabberwock had pursued me into the condominium towers, and I had lucked out with the specialty ammunition for my hybrid rifle.

Like most of the damaged buildings throughout the city, until someone claimed System ownership, the structures would continue to fall into disrepair. If I recalled correctly, a city-wide Safe Zone required that residents have ownership over something like eighty percent of the buildings in an area before monsters would no longer spawn.

I shook my head, and my resolve hardened. I had already committed to a path, but this realization only reaffirmed my decision. I might not care for the Gribbari and their exploitation of the locals who could not afford to access the Shop, but the goblins were investing in the city and expanding their operations. Eventually they would control enough of an area for that Safe Zone to manifest, and the citizens would no longer face the dangers of monster spawns.

It didn't hurt that the choice would let me finish a Quest for significant rewards in both Credits and experience. At least one Quest. There remained a strong possibility that I could complete a second if I took some risks.

I turned away from the ruined condos and trekked up the street. There were a few pedestrians out, but I noticed that there were fewer people the farther I walked.

Only half paying attention to the area around me, I pulled my map interface and zoomed out until all of downtown was displayed. A glowing dot was headed south, farther and farther away from me. The tracking unit I had placed on the Wolverine showed the location of the vehicle on my personal map as it raced toward the courthouse. I had been pretty sure that Pearce and Zoey had bought into my deception, and the tracker confirmed that they hadn't stuck around to keep an eye on me.

I turned north two blocks later and crossed back over the Allegheny River on the Roberto Clemente bridge. Had it only been yesterday morning that I had come south over the bridge?

Once I reached the far side of the river, I stepped off the street and turned around to watch the foot traffic that flowed across the bridge. Nobody seemed to be paying extra attention to me, but I really wanted to ensure no one followed me back to the casino. After a couple minutes of crowd watching, I slipped back onto the road and continued alongside the ballpark. I took the next left after the park, then I cut across several parking lots shared by the nearby stadiums. With my longer route, I hoped to make my destination less obvious to any potential watchers as I worked my way back west.

When I reached the casino, I headed to the main entrance, where a line of people waited to enter the trade square inside the gate. By this time late in the afternoon, the hunters had usually filled their Inventory to capacity and were looking to unload for whatever equipment they could barter for at the goblin-controlled market.

I made it through the gate and the tumultuous trade square without incident before I reached the casino proper. The front door guards passed me through after they recognized me from previous visits. Once inside, I stopped at the security checkpoint and tried to get the attention of the closest guard. The goblin sat in a tall chair behind the counter that ran alongside the checkpoint and had its feet propped up while it read from an information tablet.

"I'm looking for Meqik," I said when the bored goblin finally noticed me.

The goblin frowned at me. "What you want with Meqik?"

"I have information for him," I replied.

"Tell me what ya got, I'll pass it on," said the goblin.

"No," I said. "But I'll be sure to let Meqik and the Trade Baron know why they didn't get the information they asked for right away."

The goblin's eyes went wide, and it bolted upright. "Come, come."

The goblin jumped down from the chair, and I followed it through the casino until we reached a hallway that led to a series of offices in the rear of the building. The guard led me to the end of the hall and knocked on an unmarked door.

The door swung open to reveal a well-appointed office with the concierge behind a desk at the back of the room. Meqik waved me into the room, then cocked its head to stare at the guard who had followed me in. The guard gawked at the various decorations around the office, completely inattentive to the gaze Meqik had fixed upon him. That intense stare quickly showed hints of the concierge's annoyance.

"Ahem." Meqik glared.

The guard finally looked at the concierge. "Yeah, boss?"

"Get. Out," Meqik demanded.

The guard blinked at the furious expression on the concierge's face, then dashed out of the room. The door swung shut behind the fleeing guard, and Meqik sighed.

"Competent help is so hard to find," the goblin whined. "I hope you have good news."

"I have news, at least." I shrugged. "I found the weapons supplier."

"Do tell." Meqik leaned forward on the desk, hands steepled under his chin.

"There are a group of well-equipped aliens holed up at the Allegheny County Jail," I began.

I continued on to describe the physical appearance of the Krym'parke and the aircraft parked on the roof of the jail—without actually using the name of the alien species. I certainly did not want the goblins to realize exactly how much I knew about the Krym'parke or how close I had managed to get to their operation.

"The aliens seem to be utilizing survivors from the local human police forces as their enforcers and distribution network," I finished my report.

Meqik nodded, fingers steepled beneath his pointy chin, and sat in silence for a moment. "Thank you. That was an excellent report, and we now have a target we can deal with."

Meqik waved his hand in a complicated gesture, and a notification appeared before me, which I took the time to read through.

Quest Complete!

You have successfully located the supplier of the mystery weapons and informed the Goldmiser Cartel of the source's location.

Optional objective not met; no bonus rewards granted.

15,000 Credits and 10,000 XP Awarded. +100 reputation with Goldmiser Cartel.

I nodded in thanks to the goblin concierge.

"If you will excuse me, I have plans to make," Meqik said.

"Of course," I replied. "Thank you again for the quest."

The concierge reached for an ivory-and-gold phone that rested on the corner of the desk, and I heard the goblin's shrill voice issuing orders even as the office door closed behind me. I left the hallway of casino offices and headed over to the Shop.

While I didn't intend to get much beyond restocking ammunition and consumables, I needed to replace or repair damaged pieces of my gear. That mostly meant the armored jumpsuits that had acquired slashes and holes over the course of my adventures, but my melee weapons were low on durability, so I needed replacements or upgrades for them. I also wanted to pick up a few extra backup weapons now that I had the Credits to spare and the available space afforded by Right Tool for the Job.

At the cashier window, a variety of aliens and a few well-dressed humans waited with racks of casino chips, but there was no line for the Shop. I walked up to the crystal and placed my hand on it, which teleported me to the Shop.

"Welcome back, Adventurer Mason," Ryk greeted me a moment later.

"Thank you, Shopkeeper Ryk," I replied. "It's good to see you."

"You're only saying that because you have things to trade." The shopkeeper squinted at me in suspicion.

I grinned when Ryk pointed at the stasis table where I usually unloaded my monster bits for trade.

"Got a bigger table?" I asked.

Ryk raised an eyebrow, still managing to glare at me with fake suspicion at the same time, though I could tell it was an act. After giving me the look for a few seconds, he waved for me to follow as he led me through a door that appeared where only a blank wall had been seconds before.

The temperature dropped significantly, and an energy field tingled over my skin as I stepped through the door into the room beyond. A high ceiling with exposed metallic rafters far overhead contributed to a warehouse feel. The smooth floor angled slightly downward toward a series of drains that ran in a line down the center of the large room.

"Is this big enough?" Ryk asked as he stepped to the side and allowed me to examine the room.

"It'll do," I said and summoned the carcass of the hardshell snapper from my Meat Locker.

Ryk jumped backward as the dead monster materialized directly in front of him and flopped limply to the floor with a splat. The shopkeeper fixed me with another glare, and I chuckled as I continued to pull dead monsters from the bonus System storage. When I finally emptied the Meat Locker completely, dead monsters covered the floor of the large room while blood trickled into the grates that covered the drainage system.

"You've been busy," Ryk commented.

"Earth is a Dungeon World." I shrugged. "Plenty of monsters for the killing."

The shopkeeper and I haggled over the carcasses for a minute. I ended up with an offer slightly higher than Ryk's opening bid but far lower than my counteroffer. I didn't begrudge the shopkeeper too much though; Meat Locker gave me a huge advantage as far as earning Credits went, and I didn't want to abuse the goodwill Ryk had shown me so far.

Once my Credit balance reflected the transaction, I went about the business of lowering it back down with purchases from the Shop. First, I topped off my ammunition levels. I hadn't used much in the way of grenades or mines yet since I had been keeping my full collection of weapons and abilities hidden, so I didn't need to purchase any more.

With my low tier jumpsuits, it turned out to be more cost effective to sell the ruined ones back to the manufacturer to be recycled than to have them repaired.

I looked into armor with self-repair functionality and winced at the price tag. I bought a single self-repairing jumpsuit and picked up several much cheaper versions of the more disposable options.

The one other thing I splurged on was a next tier hybrid rifle. The weapon had been one of my most effective weapons in all of the fights I had been in so far, so it made sense to upgrade.

Banshee II Hybrid Gauss Rifle
Base Damage: N/A (Dependent Upon Ammunition)
Ammo Capacity: 18/18
Battery Capacity: 40/40
Recharge Rate: 8 per hour per GMU
Cost: 15,100 Credits

Then I looked for melee weapons that were not bound by durability limits, but my search results only turned up a limited number of results with insanely high prices. That seemed wonky, so I turned toward the shopkeeper who waited a discreet distance away.

"Hey, Ryk, what's up with the lack of weapons that don't have a durability rating?" I asked.

"Only summoned or soulbound weapons do not use durability because they are temporary Mana constructs that refresh each time their wielder draws them," explained the shopkeeper. "Most of the time, these weapons are transformed using a Class Skill from a mundane version, so those that don't come from a source like that are rare and expensive."

"So that's why all of the ones listed have unique-sounding names?"

"That is correct," said Ryk. "Each of those weapons is hand-crafted by a Master level weaponsmith so there will never be another like it. Even if the smith follows the same process, the creation will be different in subtle ways."

After that explanation, I gave up on finding a weapon without durability in my price range and settled on Tier III melee weapons instead. I picked up a spare axe and several knives to replace the weapons I carried in my sheaths, both of which had had their durability reduced down into single digits.

Finally, I added another spell to my repertoire. Frostbolt complemented my fluid combat style in that it helped me keep enemies at range by slowing them while they were still a long distance away. However, if an enemy closed that range before I got off Frostbolt or Hinder, then I needed something to let me break the engagement and control the distance once again.

It only took a few minutes of reading through available spells before I found one that fit my needs.

Frostnova (I)

Effect: Creates a ring of Frost from the user's Mana which blasts outward in a 3-meter radius centered on the user. The ring does 12 Ice damage and may affect enemies with a Freeze effect, rooting them in place for up to 8 seconds. Cooldown 30 seconds. Cost: 50 Mana.

The spell met all of my requirements. It was an instant cast spell centered on myself that could catch an enemy that had managed to get too close, even if that enemy was behind me or if I was threatened by multiple foes. I purchased the spell and felt the magical knowledge fill my brain.

I also purchased the next tier of the Frostbolt spell, which increased both the damage and the slow effect.

Once I finished spending a good chunk of my Credits, I took the time to catch up on my notifications before I returned to the casino. Besides the usual assortment of experience gain updates for the monsters I had killed, there was one that required my attention.

Level Up!

You have reached Level 17 as a Relentless Huntsman. Stat Points automatically distributed. You have 2 Free Attributes and 1 Class Skill Point to distribute.

With all of the monsters I had killed in the past twenty-four hours, I was almost to Level 18, but I wasn't all the way there yet. I would have to take what I could get now. The two free points were again assigned into my lowest effective attributes, Strength and Willpower. That brought my total Strength up to 35 and my Willpower to 34.

The increased Willpower helped bump up my Mana Regeneration, which had been reduced by the permanent reduction from the Implacable Endurance Class Skill. The added Strength improved my melee damage, something I had relied on more frequently as I attempted to spend fewer Credits replenishing my depleted ammunition. Every bullet fired cost me, so if I could save them for dicey situations, then I was willing to get a little beat up stabbing monsters to death.

With the attributes set, I was left with one new Class Skill Point to spend.

The improvements that On the Hunt had picked up when I added a second point there earlier were nice, but I didn't feel the need to add yet another point there just yet. When viewed from that perspective, I used one ability in almost every fight to give myself an edge. I added the point to

Hinder, raising it to the second level. The only change to the ability was that the range slightly increased.

Once I had finished with my status updates, I waved farewell to Ryk. A moment later, the Shop faded around me to be replaced with the casino floor, and my sensitive ears were assaulted by the noise of chaos from throughout the casino.

Heavy metallic shutters closed over the cashier window next to the Shop and sealed the counter shut. Goblins rushed to and fro, mostly from the hallway back to the rear offices, with little organization. Unarmed goblins ran from the casino into the hallway and came out armed with both weapons and shoddy armor.

The goblins were preparing for a fight.

One hapless goblin ran from the back hall while carrying a rifle and wearing an olive-colored bucket helm that would have been right at home on an American GI on the beaches of Normandy during World War II. The overly large helm flopped loosely on the goblin's head before it dropped down over the goblin's eyes. The blinded goblin promptly tripped over its own feet and slammed face-first into the floor. The rifle it had carried tumbled away across the casino where it slid across the floor to lodge between a pair of slot machines.

The goblin pushed itself back to its feet and wiped at a broken nose as blood dripped freely before it raised the helmet so it could see once again. Then the goblin frantically looked around for the dropped rifle with one hand pinching its nostrils to stem the flow of blood from the broken nose. Other goblins streamed past the hapless goblin as it searched in vain for the lost weapon. The frustrated goblin gave up the cursory search and turned around to run back down the hallway.

It wasn't long before the bloody-nosed goblin reappeared, a new weapon in hand. I just shook my head as the creature dashed off with the other goblins, completely unaware I had witnessed the whole thing.

I slipped through the crowd, towering over the running goblins who parted around me. I casually made my way to the bank of slot machines by the dropped rifle and made sure none of the goblins paid me any attention as I slipped the discarded weapon into my equipment storage. Confident that no one had noticed my act of pilferage, I left the bank of slot machines. I kept an eye on the chaos while I worked my way around the periphery of the casino until I reached the exit.

Once outside, I saw even the trade market had been largely emptied. Only a handful of dealers remained in business, and the few people who remained in line nervously glanced around at all of the goblin activity.

Most of the tables and trading stations had been cleared from the traffic lanes, two of the large wrecker vehicles now occupying most of the space. The massive vehicles idled with their engines running, the thunderous noise echoing under the awning that covered the trade area, as a line of goblins carried artillery shells to the wreckers. Behind the cannon mount on each vehicle, a crane arm picked up the oversized rounds from the goblin porters and stowed them in an ammunition compartment attached to the cannon turrets.

Around the wreckers, at least a dozen of the goblin-built motorbikes were also being prepared. Only a handful had sidecars like the damaged bike I had left in the underground parking garage, but the sheer number of the vehicles pointed to the goblins' preparedness for a conflict.

Unlike my previous visits, both wide doors of the vehicle gate out of the trade market were now wide open in preparation for the wreckers to roll out. Since the gates were open, there was no line to exit, and the few people who had completed their trades were in a clear hurry to leave. I joined them and strolled out of the compound without a glance back.

Chapter 27

Events were in motion, and I was on the clock now.

Tension filled the air and the streets were surprisingly clear, as if the city somehow sensed the conflict to come and the surviving people had hurried to shelter out of sight.

It was the calm before the storm.

A block after I left the casino, I summoned my bike from my Inventory and mounted it in the middle of the street. Tires squealed beneath me as I accelerated down the road until buildings flashed past.

I cornered sharply, and my knee almost kissed the pavement with each turn. It was the fastest I had ever driven, far beyond anything I had dared to try before the System, and I reveled in the sensation. Before the apocalypse, riding through the streets this recklessly would have been pure insanity, but my attributes were now far beyond the old human norm. I found a rush to the precision afforded me by the increases to my Perception and Agility that allowed me to push the bike, and myself, to the limits.

I existed in a zone where nothing mattered outside my link to the bike between my legs and the connection to the road beneath me.

In that moment, I realized something about myself.

Maybe it was the conflict I had endured, maybe it was the changes the System had wrought upon me, or maybe it was the System itself, but I had discovered a fundamental need to push myself to my limits and grow beyond them.

There was always another quest to complete now, or another level to gain. I needed to reach those milestones, to push beyond them, and to grow stronger.

I crossed the Clemente Bridge in a flash, the light of the setting sun flickering off the river below. Still crouched low over the handlebars of the bike, I eased up on the acceleration as I shot into downtown.

Motion on the display superimposed in the corner of my vision drew my attention, and I slowed further as I took a quick glance at my minimap. The dot of the tracker placed on the police cruiser blinked on the map as it moved away from the jail.

I rolled to a stop at the intersection of 6th Street and Liberty Avenue, then I put down my feet to hold the bike upright while I stayed seated. Half of my attention remained alert to the streets around me while I watched the dot on my map move across the city toward me.

When the dot turned onto Fifth Avenue, I figured I could seem as if I were just returning from scouting and let them run into me almost naturally. I dismounted from my bike and returned it to my inventory before I jogged across the intersection, angling south around the small Triangle Park and onto Market Street.

When I stepped out to turn onto Fifth Avenue, just before the dot on my map reached the same intersection from my left, a line of tracers and bullets skipped off the pavement in front of me, and I danced backward as automatic weapons fire thundered from the same direction as the dot on my map.

Bullets chipped through the glass at the corner of the building beside me as I backed around the corner and ducked below the windows. My brief glimpse of the source of the gunfire made me realize my mistake. A second Wolverine drove ahead of the one I tracked, which threw off my timing and apparently startled the gunner in the turret mount of the vehicle at the front of the column.

"Cease fire," someone called, the command audible even over the thunder of the machine gun.

The voice sounded familiar, but it took me a moment to place it.

"Come on out," said Warden Hughes. "We won't shoot."

I poked my head around the corner for a quick peek but pulled back before anyone could get a shot off, just in case. After my glance failed to draw fire, I stepped out from behind the building, prepared to duck behind cover at the first sign of another attack.

Nobody shot at me this time, and I took my time to get a better look at the vehicles stretched out down the road. The pair of Wolverines led the convoy, followed by a more heavily armored quad-axle vehicle with a sleek twin-barreled turret. The first, larger barrel was some kind of cannon, while the coaxial weapon appeared like a smaller energy weapon. Though the vehicle had the same black-and-gold color scheme, the armored vehicle towered over the pair of smaller vehicles in front of it, and I gave it a quick once-over.

Grizzly Urban Assault Vehicle (Class III)
Armor Rating: Tier IV

A few seconds after I stepped out from around the corner, the rear doors of the lead vehicle swung open, and the warden herself climbed out, followed by Jahgg'd, the Krym'parke from the warden's office at our first meeting. Pearce quickly ran up to the warden's side as they stepped forward to meet me in the middle of the intersection ahead of the convoy.

"Sorry about that, Hal," the sergeant hurried to explain. "We're a little on edge after that goblin attack earlier."

"Understandable," I replied. "No harm done, but I might have to change my shorts."

Even the alien chuckled darkly at my comment. Several other officers walked up to join our gathering in the street. The first two to approach wore pristine uniforms, as if their gear had never seen combat, while the rest of the police were clad in gear marred with scratches and dents. It was easy to see which of the group most actively patrolled in the monster-infested city.

"Thank you for the warning you sent back with Pearce. We might have been caught unprepared if you hadn't taken out those scouts that attacked you. Did your own recon turn up anything?" Warden Hughes asked after everyone gathered.

"The goblins were swarming over at the casino like a kicked-over beehive," I replied. "They're gearing up for something big."

Several frowns appeared throughout the cluster of officers, followed by muttered worries over the goblin threat.

Surprisingly, Jahgg'd spoke up to silence the concerns. "We have provided you with new armored vehicles. Their vehicles are assembled from scrap and nowhere near as advanced as the weapons you possess. Your attacks will tear through them like one of your paper tissues."

The mumbles faded away, and the Krym'parke nodded confidently.

"If there are issues, which I doubt," Jahgg'd continued, "we will stand by to provide air support." Then the alien focused on me. "What vehicles did you see prepared?"

"Maybe a dozen or so of the bikes and two of the bigger trucks with the gun platforms," I replied. "None of them had left yet when I started back to report in, but it's probably been fifteen to twenty minutes."

"They have more, but that is within expectations," the alien commented. "Though the real threat will be if they deploy any Advanced Class forces within the expedition that use the regular troops for cover." The alien looked serious as it pointedly glanced around the assembly. "If any of their higher tier individuals join the conflict, they must be immediately engaged."

The alien paused to let its words sink in. With the exception of the alien tactician, I had seen no Advanced Class fighters amongst this group, so the

414

threat of one showing up amongst the enemy force sobered everyone. Since everyone still thought I was a Hunter and my true Class remained a secret, hopefully no one would expect me in the center of the fight.

Tension built in the silence, and I realized that even the distant fireworks from the casino had ceased. The lack of the regularly fired explosions felt almost unsettling after days of listening to them whenever I'd been outside.

Then my ears caught the high-pitched whine of a distant motor as it grew louder, the source drawing closer. The noise grew as other engines joined it, and Jahgg'd cocked its head as the alien also picked up on the sounds of the approaching goblin motorbikes.

Hughes looked at Jahgg'd and nodded. The alien pulled a device from its belt and growled something unintelligible into the silver box. A voice growled back from the handheld communicator in the same alien language, and Jahgg'd grinned at the warden.

Then the whine of the engines peaked as a squad of goblin bikers raced out from behind the parking garage at the corner of 6th and Liberty, the direct route into downtown and the same path I had taken from the casino. The squad split up when they hit Liberty Avenue, and a trio of bikers headed in either direction.

Two of the three bikes headed toward us were standard two-wheeled motorcycles, but the third bike had a sidecar with a second rider. The rider in the sidecar held a gadget in front of its face that it peered through as it looked from side to side. Through the thin trees planted in Triangle Park, it caught sight of where we clustered in the street and called out to the other riders as it pointed toward us. All three bikers followed the pointing finger and swung toward us.

Lights blinked along the side of the sidecar passenger's binocular-like device, indicating it was more high-tech than most gear the goblins used. I swept Greater Observation lightly over the pair of goblins on the bike to get a feel for the incoming forces.

Gribbari Spotter (Level 24)
_HP: 170/170_

Gribbari Scout (Level 25)
_HP: 190/190_

While I processed the goblins and their Classes, I ducked out of sight behind the lead Wolverine as everyone also scattered for the cover of their vehicles.

Spotters had two main uses within a military organization. Though often paired with snipers as rangefinders and overwatch, I didn't think that was the case here. That increased the likelihood of the second option—that some kind of artillery needed the goblin as an observer.

The Wolverine in front of me pulled forward to clear the corner of the building beside us, then it stopped once it had a clear field of fire across the open expanse, the roof-mounted turret opening up on the goblins as they darted through the small park. Shots from the machine gun splintered trees and chipped cement as the trio of bikers spread out. The bikers wove around the benches and planters that covered the plaza as they attempted to avoid the hail of fire.

Then tracers from the Wolverine's machine gun punched through the front wheel of the lead bike, and it disintegrated under the attack, flinging the rider through the air as the bike flipped end over end. The sidecar motorcycle turned away sharply as the damaged bike plowed into a planter and exploded, while the other biker veered off to angle in front of the lead Wolverine.

The second Wolverine pulled into the empty oncoming lane and drove around behind me as I circled to the rear of the first vehicle. The pair of machine guns bracketed the oncoming scout and perforated both the bike and rider.

I crouched beside the hotel and peered through the already broken windows of the building lobby as a cheer went up from the Wolverine gunners. The machine gun fire slacked, and the mangled wreck of the goblin bike coasted to a halt in the middle of the street, but the scout's death took long enough that the spotter vehicle disappeared out of sight around the block ahead before the gunners could retarget.

Thunder ripped through the square, and fire blossomed along the side of the forwardmost Wolverine. The impact of the surprise attack lifted the vehicle from the ground and tipped the vehicle onto its side with the armor panels along the passenger doors crumpled inward, though they remained in one piece.

Across the plaza, one of the goblin wreckers pulled out from the street where the goblin scouts had first emerged, and its cannon belched deafening fire as it took a second shot. This time the attack hit the undercarriage of the Wolverine. Screams echoed from the vehicle as it rolled over onto its roof, flattening the turret with the vehicle's own weight.

The remaining Wolverine advanced to place itself between the wrecker and the toppled vehicle. With the space to move forward, the Grizzly UAV pulled up behind the pair of smaller vehicles and engaged the wrecker with both turret weapons. A flurry of ruby energy beams streaked across the park and left spots of molten metal across the plates welded to the wrecker's armor.

Behind me, the police force dismounted from the transport vehicles at the rear of the column and entered the buildings facing the developing firefight. Across the park, similarly deployed goblins opened fire from the second and third floor of the parking garage that blocked the line of sight to anything behind the armored wrecker. Bullets and energy beams crisscrossed the plaza as the ground forces from both sides fully engaged. Nobody hit much of anything, but the center of the park quickly turned into a free-fire zone.

A side door on the flipped Wolverine opened, and a person flopped halfway out onto the pavement. Before I could regret my decision, I sprinted toward the prone officer.

A cannon shot impacted the Grizzly as I darted behind it, and the shockwave of the attack staggered me. I stumbled past the UAV, barely keeping my feet beneath me as the Grizzly returned fire. When I reached the flipped vehicle, I leaned down to grab the collar of the man who lay half out onto the street.

The man screamed in pain as I dragged him from the vehicle, and I looked down to see that below the thigh of his left leg, only a mangled mess of blood and shattered bone remained. Despite his cries, I kept moving and heaved us backward through the window of an apparel store behind us.

I barely heard the sound of the glass shattering over the weapons fire around us, and I pulled the sobbing man down behind the cover of the raised level of the window display shelves. The officer's helmet fell off when he hit the ground, and I recognized the wounded man.

Kevin groaned in pain, barely conscious from the injury to his leg. If Kevin was here, then Pearce and Zoey were probably still trapped inside the rolled vehicle.

I glanced at the flipped Wolverine but saw no movement. I gathered myself to run out to check the vehicle when a series of blasts detonated over the plaza and the upper stories of buildings around us.

None of the explosions hit the armored vehicles, but they pitted the pavement in several spots across our side of the plaza, all well away from the goblins. From the nearly circular impact craters, the barrage had to have come from almost straight overhead. The indirect nature of the fire meant the goblin spotter had returned and was directing fire toward us.

The arrival of the artillery support shifted the tempo of the firefight in favor of the goblins.

Before the other side could capitalize on the additional firepower, the air over the plaza shimmered, and one of the boxy Krym'parke aircraft became visible as it opened fire with a pair of energy cannons set beneath the cockpit.

The blasts tore chunks out of the parking garage that sheltered the goblin infantry, then punched into the armor of the wrecker's cab. Smoke billowed from the driver compartment, but the turret behind the cab continued to fire.

With the aliens on both sides now fully engaged, I needed to slip away while the battle raged and kept everyone too busy to pay any attention to me.

A groan from beside me reminded me of one other little thing.

Pain clouded Kevin's expression as the young man looked at me. "Thanks." He gritted his teeth against the pain of his injuries. "This is twice now you've saved my life."

"Maybe you can tell me something in return," I said.

Kevin just looked at me in confusion.

"How many people did you gun down in the street before we met?" I asked.

Kevin recoiled at the chill in my voice, but I grabbed a fistful of his collar before he could push himself away. I leaned over, half on top of him to stay behind the cover of the front window ledge. My forearm pinned him in place, and my weight held him despite his struggles.

"How. Many?" I repeated.

"Six." His voice wavered, and his gaze flicked nervously from side to side, as if looking for someone to bail him out of his precarious situation.

Gunfire, explosions, and beam fire continued to rage in the plaza, but I had Kevin's complete attention.

"I don't believe you," I said.

Kevin flinched as I rested the cold edge of my knife against his throat just under his chin.

"Ten," he blurted in panic. "I needed to level up faster, so I killed them when I found out I could get more experience from people than monsters."

"Hmm." I pressed the knife a little harder. "And how many of those ten were in self-defense?"

"None," Kevin whispered.

"None," I stated. "All of them just shot down on the street in cold blood."

"Yes."

Tears streamed from Kevin's tightly closed eyes, and I held still for a moment.

Then one eye peeked open to look at me, as if to gauge my reaction, and I realized that the young man's reticence was entirely faked. My expression caused Kevin to jerk both eyes open, and he struggled beneath me.

There were no courts or real prisons in this new world ruled by the System. Only the will of the strong, imposed on the weak. Maybe it wasn't much, but I could make sure that this excuse for a human being would never kill another undeserving soul.

The blade of my knife rammed up under Kevin's chin and slipped into his brain. The body twitched as the last of his health drained away, and I pulled out the blade as the stench of death rose around me. I wiped the blade clean on the dead man's uniform and filched the few useful pieces of gear that remained on his belt.

I glanced up over the cover of the storefront just in time to see a wave of magic wash over the hovering Krym'parke gunship. Fireballs, shards of ice, and electrical blasts battered the airborne craft, and one of the engines failed under the assault. The ship drifted to one side of the plaza and jerked around as the pilot overcorrected. It twisted as it swung back across the park and bounced off the parking garage.

The impact, combined with the continued magical attacks, overwhelmed the protections on a second thruster, and the craft drifted back across the park as it sank toward the ground. The pilot managed to spin it completely around so that its chin-mounted turret kept pointed at the goblin forces, and the weapon continued firing even after the craft crashed into the ground.

Despite the grounding of one craft, another gunship shimmered into view and continued to attack the goblin positions.

Confident that I remained unnoticed, I scooped up Kevin's helmet and left the body behind as I crawled through the racks of clothing that occupied the store until I found my way to the back wall. Though there were several hallway storage rooms, there was no rear door.

I cursed my luck and stayed low as I worked along the back wall until I reached the far side of the store. An off-target mortar had shattered the windows on that side of the building, so I vaulted over the ruined display mannequins and turned left to sprint down the road toward Market Square.

I expected to be shot in the back as I ran since any goblin in the parking garage would have a straight shot down the street toward me, but either they were preoccupied with more immediate targets, or they deemed my retreating form no longer a threat.

Just when I thought I was in the clear, a mortar detonated in the street behind me and knocked me a dozen feet through the air. My left knee hit the ground first, and I felt bone crack from the impact with the pavestones.

Bruised and battered, I tumbled into the otherwise empty Market Square and wiped a bloody nose. I painfully crawled to my feet and hurried to break my line of sight to the battle that continued behind me.

Fortunately for my pride, I saw no one around to witness my airborne exit from the conflict as I hurried down another side street.

Chapter 28

Explosions and gunfire echoed through the streets behind me as I limped away from the battle. The fact that I had managed to walk away was a win in itself, and I now needed to use their distraction to my advantage.

I cast Minor Healing on myself and chugged down a healing potion to deal with my injuries, and the worst of the effects were healed by the time I reached the end of the next block.

Just before I reached the jail, I cast another spell on myself. Since I already wore the helmet I had lifted from the fallen officer, Lesser Disguise only needed to make minor changes as it shifted the color of my jumpsuit to the shade of black used by the police force and a badge appeared on my chest that read "Williamson." The holstered weapons at my waist were camouflaged as the standard duty belt worn by the officers.

Now that I looked like Pearce, I faked my leg injury when I came into view of the courthouse parking lot and staggered toward the gate. I couldn't tell if the guard towers were even still manned, with the number of officers I had seen back at the ongoing fight, but no one seemed alarmed by my approach. The heavy gate doors retracted when I reached them, so no one had removed my access yet. I quickly limped over to the courthouse entrance and stepped inside.

"Pearce, is everything all right?"

Brian, the guard at the front desk, pushed himself up from his seat behind the counter, and I waved him back without speaking. The man paused, still behind the counter, and looked at me in confusion.

If I spoke, my voice would not sound like Pearce's and would give away my illusion. I hoped that the officer would stay behind the desk. I had no desire to kill the man just because he was in my way.

A scream echoed down the hallway, and we both turned toward the sound.

A black robed figure stalked down the hall toward the lobby, face twisted in an expression of rage. The judge clutched the upper arm of a young blond-haired girl in one hand. Tears ran down the girl's face as she was practically dragged behind the man, and my blood ran cold at the sight.

"Why is my son dead, Pearce?" Beatty shouted. "I felt the link break. Why are you here and not my son?"

The judge pulled a recognizable handgun, another of the ubiquitous pistols that almost all of the cops carried, from under his robes as he stopped less than a dozen paces from me and pressed the muzzle to the side of the little girl's head.

"Judge Beatty, what are you doing?" Brian said in horror.

"I've lost my son, and now Pearce here is going to feel what it's like to lose a child too," the man snarled at the officer.

"There's just one problem with that," I said.

Brian's head snapped toward me, clearly recognizing now that my voice was not Pearce's.

Before the officer could react, I stretched a hand toward the black-robed judge and cast Frostbolt. The shard of ice flew across the short distance and stabbed into the man's shoulder. The impact knocked the gun forward, out of line with the girl's head, and forced the judge backward a step.

That step put space between the judge and his hostage, though he still held her firmly. I activated Hinder to slow the man and lunged across the distance between us as I drew my melee weapons.

By the time the man had recovered his balance, my axe swung down into the space between the pair. I carefully angled the blade of the weapon just above his wrist to avoid the hostage, but the blow still sliced deep enough to chop into the bones of the forearm, and I heard an audible crack as both the radius and ulna shattered beneath the force of the strike.

The judge instantly lost his grip on the girl, and she stumbled away with a shriek as blood spattered her face from the nearly severed arm. I pivoted and stepped around the judge to place my body between him and the child. I dropped the spell that disguised my appearance, since this conflict would ruin my cover however it turned out.

Pain warred with hate on the man's face as my appearance shifted, and he tried to swing his gun toward me, but I was inside his reach. The firearm discharged from the jarring impact as I batted the weapon aside with the knife held in my offhand. The shot was nowhere near me, and I grinned beneath the visor. That single shot was the only one he would manage.

My next attack sliced the blade of my knife through the tendons of the judge's wrist. The hand that held the gun flopped limp, the weapon falling to the floor before he could threaten to hurt anyone else.

Despite the fact that the man was disarmed, I continued my attacks to keep him from activating any of his abilities. I certainly did not want to end up cursed with a judgment like the one on his son that reduced experience gains, so I could not afford mercy.

When the judge only had a sliver of health remaining, I knelt over the gasping ruin of a man and leaned down beside his ear. My final attack had sliced the man's throat and blood spurted as it pumped out of his body with each heartbeat. A tide of blood covered the floor beneath him. The man had only seconds left to live.

"Pearce didn't kill your son," I whispered so quietly that only the dying man could hear me. "I did."

The man blinked and breathed his final breath before his body went still.

I wiped my weapons on a mostly bloodless section of the man's robes and sheathed them as I stood to face Brian, who still stood behind the desk with a shocked expression.

"Daddy?"

I glanced to the side and saw the tearful young girl cowering at the side of the hall. She looked around for her father with a confused expression. My disguise spell had faded, but she deserved to know I wasn't her father. I pulled off the helmet.

The little girl stared at me, and I saw fear fill her eyes once again.

"Your dad isn't here. Go find your mother," I commanded softly, my eyes back on the officer in front of me.

Tiny footsteps pattered away down the hall as the girl fled, and I continued my staredown with Brian.

"You killed him," the officer said.

"Some people just need killing." I shrugged. "It was him or the girl, so don't pretend he didn't deserve it. He was an even bigger piece of garbage than his son."

The man looked conflicted, and I saw the truth of my words hit home.

"What do you want here?" Brian finally asked.

"The Krym'parke," I replied.

The officer went pale and looked away nervously.

"You knew," I said after I saw the officer's reaction. "You knew what they were and what they did to the prisoners."

The man seemed to deflate before my eyes.

"We suspected," Brian said hoarsely, but he refused to meet my gaze. "We didn't know for sure. We had our families to look out for. They were more important."

"It was only a matter of time before they turned on you." I shook my head. "They would have come for your families as soon as you couldn't meet their demand for the flesh of others."

I turned away from the officer and put the helmet back on as I left the courthouse entrance. I wasn't worried about Brian following. He might not have stood up for anything right, but he wouldn't stop me now either.

The halls were quiet, and I encountered no one as I followed the passages that led from the courthouse to the jail. Once in the prison complex, I took the same route I'd used when Pearce had led me through the building to the cafeteria.

I froze in the middle of the hallway as a door swung open in front of me, and the alien butcher stepped out of the converted slaughterhouse room, a full platter of monster filets in one hand. The other hand held a keycard that the alien swiped over the lock beside the door, which flashed red.

The Krym'parke paused when it saw me, then gave me a closer look. The alien's yellow eyes narrowed, and it snarled. The alien dropped both the keycard and the platter as it lunged toward me, a knife suddenly appearing in hand. The wide blade looked like a thick butcher's knife, but it extended to a sharp pointed tip.

The platter bounced off the floor and scattered filets across the hall as the butcher reached me, but I had activated Hinder as soon as it lunged. The Class Skill slowed the alien just enough that I could draw my own weapons in time to parry the assault.

The alien slashed at me with the butcher knife, and I hooked the alien's wrist with the bottom of my axe blade as the knife slashed past. I tried to use the alien's momentum to spin it around, but the Krym'parke nimbly twisted its arm and disengaged before I could apply any force.

Side to side movement within the hallway was limited, so we could really only advance and retreat to control the space of the fight.

I managed a slash across the alien's tricep before it stepped back out of range and considered me. I'd triggered Rend, so the wound on its arm dripped blood. The cut was so minor that the butcher's health bar had barely dropped from the attack, even with my Class Skill active.

The alien nodded to me and grinned menacingly before it launched back onto the offensive. Blades flashed between us, and we were soon covered in minor nicks that bled through the slashed fabric that had once covered our arms and torsos. The flurry of attacks slowed, and we broke apart, both breathing heavily.

The pair of us were almost evenly matched on speed, and while I had an advantage in overall strength, the Krym'parke showed a raw mastery over the blade that I lacked. If I hadn't kept Hinder activated on the alien, I would have been sliced apart already.

With a moment of reflection afforded by the break in combat, I noticed that my wounds were bloodier than I would have expected for such shallow cuts. Clearly, my Rend was not the only bleed effect Class Skill in use here; the alien had used something similar on me. I cast Minor Healing on myself, and the bleed effect dissipated. Though the majority of my wounds remained, my health no longer continued to drop.

The alien snarled when my wounds glowed slightly from my use of the healing spell.

With no idea how the battle in the city might be going, I needed to end this fight before it dragged out too much longer.

The alien obviously felt similarly, and we charged toward each other at the same time. Just before we clashed, I noticed that the alien had equipped a weapon in its offhand. The handle had a ring for the index finger to help secure the weapon in the alien's grip, and the small blade was held in a reverse grip, curved forward like a claw.

The alien's arms blurred with speed as the Krym'parke crossed blades with me once again. The added speed must have been from another Class

Skill, and this time I could not keep up. I barely managed to deflect the larger butcher knife with my own weapon, but the curved blade in the alien's offhand slashed across my torso, ripping completely through my armored jumpsuit and digging through the muscles of my chest.

I winced as pain tore through me, but I could not let the wound distract me now. Before the alien could follow up from the attack, I kicked the alien square in the chest and used the momentum to flip myself backward down the hall. The alien had been knocked from its feet by the blow and recovered by rolling backward. With both of us backing off, the space between us opened considerably.

The alien grinned hungrily as blood from my chest wound dripped down my front and spattered onto the floor. The Krym'parke crouched in a ready stance, content to let me continue to bleed while my healing spell remained unavailable due to the length of its cooldown.

I grinned back at the alien and sheathed my weapons. The alien's brow furrowed, and its head tipped to the side in confusion.

Then its yellow eyes grew wide as I flicked my wrist toward it, and my upgraded Frostbolt shot across the space between us to hit the alien in the chest. The Krym'parke staggered backward, rime spreading from the site where the spell had impacted and left a jagged shard of ice implanted in the center of the alien's torso.

When the alien recovered, it looked at me with an expression of fear, and I knew the fight was all but over. I opened fire with the pair of projectile pistols I had summoned while the alien took the hit from my spell.

Slowed by the combined effects of Hinder and Frostbolt, the nimble alien failed to dodge my attacks. I offset my shots so that I alternated between the weapons and kept up a steady barrage of bullets. Each shot hammered into the alien with a deafening roar in the narrow hallway.

The Krym'parke jerked with each impact even as it attempted to rush me under the fusillade of fire. With each step it took toward me, I backed off down the hallway to keep the range open as it advanced. When a pistol slide locked back with the magazine empty, I swapped it for a loaded spare from my Inventory. When the battered and bloody alien finally toppled to the floor, I poured a few extra shots into it until its health bar completely blacked out.

Then I stood in the hall and reloaded my emptied weapons with the spare ammunition I carried. Only once I was prepared for another round of combat did I approach the fallen alien and loot the corpse.

Since the alien's blades were still clutched in its hands, I pried them free and added them to my Inventory. I noted that the claw-like blade was a karambit, but I would take the time to check out the full stats later.

Once I had looted the few useful pieces of kit from the alien corpse, I chucked the body into my Meat Locker. It would take far too long to clean up the blood and empty brass that littered the hallway, but at least I wouldn't leave a body lying around to mark my passage.

I then scooped up the keycard the alien had dropped before the start of our fight, since I figured it might come in useful.

Another cast of Minor Healing and a quick potion later, my health was recovering, so I left the area. The banging of pots and pans from the kitchen beyond the cafeteria meant that the non-combat staff still remained in the building, so I would need to avoid them unless I wanted another fight like the one I'd just had with the alien butcher.

I crouched low and slipped past the cafeteria doors, then I headed up to the next level when I found the forbidden set of stairs just beyond the kitchen.

I hadn't been this far into the building previously, so this was new territory and my progress slowed once I reached the next floor. Most of the rooms were empty, but halfway through the floor, I found a locked door that failed to open when I tugged on it.

When I swiped the butcher's keycard over the lock plate beside the door, the light flashed green, and I heard a click. This time when I tugged on the door, it swung open, and I whistled in awe when the lights inside the room kicked on automatically.

I couldn't help myself.

"Guns, lots of guns," I said in my best movie quote voice despite my situation.

I stepped through the door and into what had to be the armory mentioned by Zoey after the lizard fight.

Racks of firearms behind clear glass doors ran along either side of the room. A futuristic but recognizable milling machine took up most of one corner, next to a similarly sleek drill press, and a massive Mana battery sat on the floor between them with connections running to both pieces of equipment. Next to the drill press sat a workbench that took up the rest of the rear wall. Above the workbench, a pegboard held a variety of differently sized hammers, screwdrivers, punches, calipers, and assorted other hand tools.

Two tall tables filled the center of the room with just enough space around them for a half dozen or so people to clean their weapons at the same time. The center of each table held a caddy filled with bore snakes, solvents, oils, stacks of square cotton patches, and a variety of other gun cleaning supplies. The table's surfaces were spotless and reflected the bright overhead lights.

The neatly organized cleaning supplies and the pristine tables were in sharp contrast to the clutter that covered the workbench at the back of the room. When I walked over, I found pieces of metal scattered over the open work surface. A partially assembled weapon rested in a vise attached to the end of the worktable.

I recognized the weapon as the standard sidearm used by the officers out on patrol, but this one was in poor condition. Pitted spots all over the weapon marred its surface, and there were a few areas of rust along the edges of the slide. The cracked grips made it almost look as though the weapon was about to fall apart.

On the floor beneath the vise holding the ruined weapon sat an opened crate. I lifted the lid and peered inside to find it half filled with identical firearms in similar condition, all wrapped in thick, filmy waxed paper.

I closed the lid and noticed the circular logo on the top of the crate. The emblem consisted of an eagle clutching a sheaf of arrows in its claws with a shield in the foreground. The circle around the eagle read "Civilian Marksmanship Program."

The CMP Sales program distributed government surplus firearms that had been in storage for decades, most commonly M1 Garand rifles. From the crate at my feet, I guessed the crate had come from a looted government storage depot.

My eyes flicked from the crate, to the weapon in the vise, to the components on the workbench, and the puzzle pieces fell into place.

The weapons started in a ruined condition and were disassembled. Someone with a System ability or Class Skill restored the individual components before everything was put back together as a functional System weapon.

I admired the ingenuity.

So much so that I would show my appreciation by liberating some of their work. From the collection around the room, someone had looted a government depot or a private collection. More than likely both.

I turned to the racks and swiped a handful of the restored pistols for myself. Next to the pistols, the most common firearm in the glass cases were police issue AR-15 rifles. I grabbed a couple and added them to my weapon storage. The Right Tool for the Job Class Skill really paid for itself here, though I took the time to load each of the new weapons before I stored them away.

Fortunately, beneath the weapons were shelves of ammunition in neatly stacked boxes that corresponded to the calibers fired by the weapons above them, which helped me ensure I had enough to fully load all of my loot. Then I pretty much cleaned out the rest of the supply.

Ammo that didn't cost me Credits? Score.

When I reached the end of the rack, I found that the CMP depot wasn't the only unusual source of weapons here.

At the very end were a number of guns I had seen only in movies. I scooped up a pair of machine pistols, a couple Uzis, and even a massive hand cannon that was the largest revolver I had ever seen. I didn't recognize the model by sight, since revolvers weren't in use by the military and I hadn't trained with anything that massive. The boxes of ammunition underneath the rack for the hand cannon were labeled as ".44 Magnum," and I grabbed them all.

My extra equipment storage provided by Right Tool for the Job was nearly full by the time I finished my looting spree through the armory. There were noticeable gaps in the shelves that marked where I had liberated either weapons or ammunition, but I hoped to be long gone before anyone noticed.

I turned toward the exit and froze when a loud click echoed from the door just before I reached it.

As I drew my pistols, the door swung open to reveal two figures. Their eyes widened in surprise when they saw me inside the armory with my weapons raised.

A gray-haired man with a thick metal collar around his neck stood in front of another Krym'parke. The blinking lights on the device around the man's neck made me think of those movies where a villain threatens to use an explosive to blow off a prisoner's head if they try to escape. The alien behind the man wore a skintight beige shirt and brown cargo pants with a utility belt covered in pouches and handheld devices.

Robert Wilson (Gunsmith Level 11)
HP: 90/90
MP: 150/150

Rahrn't Eh'pyxe (Slaver Level 35)
HP: 720/720
MP: 820/820

The old man threw himself to the side, which gave me a clear shot at the alien who had only just begun to pull out its own weapons as it recovered from my unexpected appearance.

The alien stood well within my range for Hinder, and I activated the Class Skill along with a cast of my Frostbolt spell. The jagged shard of ice slammed into the chest of the Krym'parke at the same time as I opened fire with my pistols. Gunfire echoed loudly in the enclosed armory, and the alien staggered back from the impact of the pistol rounds.

Blue-black blood spread from the wounds across the alien's torso and leaked through the round holes in the alien's tight-fitting muscle shirt. Driven back against the far wall of the hallway by my attacks, the alien managed to draw its own weapon and returned fire with a beam pistol.

The energy burned into the sleeve of my jumpsuit, but the armored fabric held up against the attack. I still took damage from the shot, but I had come out ahead on the exchange. If the alien kept its distance and continued this fight of attrition, I would win.

I stepped forward until I stood in the doorway of the armory and fired until my pistols were empty, then I changed them out for a loaded pair from my Inventory. The alien blinked in surprise at my seamless weapons swap, and a look of panic crossed its face as it drew the same conclusion I had about the eventual end of the fight.

While the damage from the beam pistol hurt me, the burns were mostly surface level since each shot had landed on a different part of my body and only charred my skin in the spots where my earlier skirmish had left my armor sliced open. I could push through the pain to continue my attacks.

On the other hand, the Krym'parke's chest was a bloody mess. The projectile rounds I fired were doing internal damage and breaking bones within the alien's torso. Even now, it struggled to keep the beam pistol aimed at me.

The alien looked around frantically, then paused with its head turned slightly to the side as it saw something in the hallway just outside the door. It was the same direction that the gunsmith had moved to get clear of the fight, and I realized the old man must still be on the ground.

The alien looked back at me and showed its fangs in a maniacal grin.

Not good. I had to stop it before it could act on whatever idea it had just come up with.

I lunged across the hallway even as the alien reached for something at its waist. I dropped my pistols and latched onto the alien's hand as it fumbled to pull a device clipped to its belt. I kept the alien's wrist locked in place with one hand and drew my knife with the other. Pinned to the wall, the alien tugged on the device but lacked the leverage to overpower me.

I realized that despite the difference in our Levels, I was more than a match in any single attribute for most Basic Class foes. Since they typically received fewer attribute points per level, most Galactics would focus on a single attribute that played to their Class abilities. Though my attributes were more spread out, my overall attribute totals would be at least close to matching the specialized total for a Basic Class up to double my level.

The alien reacted to its predicament by placing its pistol next to my ear and firing directly into the side of my head. I screamed as the stench of burning hair and flesh filled my nose. I twisted my head away so that the energy beam seared its way across the back of my head instead of the side.

I dropped my shoulder and rammed it forward without releasing the alien's wrist, slamming into the alien's already wounded chest. The Krym'parke gasped, the wind knocked out of it by the impact, and the pistol fell out of line with my head.

In the moment of respite, I followed up the body blow by stabbing my knife into the side of the alien's head. The tip of the knife found the ear canal and bone crunched as my knife sank to the hilt. The alien jerked in my arms, but I pulled out the blade and stabbed again until the slaver went limp. Only then did I release my grip on the dead alien's wrist and allow the corpse to sag to the floor.

My knife slid free with a disgusting squelch, and I stumbled backward as the adrenaline rush of combat faded. I dropped to one knee beside the dead alien and wiped my blade clean on the cloth of its pants before returning it to my sheath.

While I could have used Cleanse to remove the blood from the weapon, I preferred the old-fashioned way and instead used the saved Mana to cast Minor Healing on myself before I gingerly explored the blistered side of my head that still radiated heat and throbbed in pain. Little more than a charred flap of flesh remained of my ear, and a line of burned flesh the width of the beam pistol barrel ran around to the back of my head.

Movement in the hallway beside me pulled my attention away from my wounds, and I looked over to find the gunsmith crawling to his feet. I saw pain in the old man's eyes, but his gaze was fixed on the dead alien as he limped over and dropped to his knees beside me. He reached over to the device the alien had attempted to grab before being slain and pulled the boxy item free of the belt.

I pulled out and drank a health potion as the man fiddled with the device, lights blinking across the surface of the silvery box. Then the box gave a beep, and the gunsmith froze with a look of utter panic on his face. A second later, the collar around the man's neck gave a metallic click and unlatched.

The man sighed with relief and dropped the box to pull off the collar. He flung it at the corpse with an expression of revulsion and spat at the corpse.

"I owe you my thanks, young man," the gunsmith said as he rubbed his throat. The skin was red and raw underneath where the collar had sat.

"You're welcome," I replied.

"I'm Robert," he said, hand extended toward me.

"Hal," I said, giving the outstretched hand a firm shake.

"I take it you're not with the owners of this fine establishment," Robert said.

"No," I replied with a shake of my head.

Robert nodded and slowly pushed himself to his feet. "I'm sure glad to have that slave collar off my neck."

"Slave collar?" I asked. "How does that work?"

Robert pointed at the thick metal ring that lay on top of the dead alien. "You do what they say, or they press a button and your head goes *pop*."

"That's the first time I've seen something like that."

"They've got them on the kids too," Robert said.

"What kids?" I asked sharply.

"They've got a bunch of kids stuffed into the cells upstairs. Ain't hardly none of the original prisoners left." Robert pointed upward and shuddered.

"Sounds like I'm going upstairs then," I said.

The old man considered me in silence for several seconds.

"Why would you do that?" Robert finally asked. "Everyone is out for themselves these days."

"I won't claim to be much different." I met the old man's gaze. "But I've got a quest to free the kids, and I mean to see it through."

The gunsmith nodded. "Gimme a sec. Let me get armed up, and I'll tag along."

He turned away from me and went into the armory.

I scooped up the slave collar and control device, storing them in my Inventory before I shoved the entire dead alien into Meat Locker, then I stood back up. The worst of my injuries faded as I heard the old gunsmith cursing about missing weapons through the open armory door behind me.

I had no plans to reveal myself as the culprit.

While the gunsmith got ready, I prepared myself. I reloaded the weapons I had used throughout the last fight. Once satisfied with my weapons, I checked over the state of my armored jumpsuit. Though now charred in several places, it hadn't really picked up too much more damage since my fight with the butcher. It was looking pretty ragged, but it remained serviceable enough for now.

By the time I finished prepping my gear, the gunsmith still puttered around in his workshop, so I leaned back against the wall to wait and kept an eye out for any movement in the empty hall.

After a couple more minutes, the old man walked out of the room with one of the police-issue AR rifles slung over one shoulder with a sling strap and a sidearm holstered at his waist. He gave me a once-over and then nodded.

"Most of them aliens took off in their ships not too long ago, so we might have time to get the kids out of here if we hurry," Robert said.

"Where are we going?" I asked.

"Three floors up," he replied. "That's where the kids are kept. Above that is a housing floor for the aliens, then a level for their gear and maintenance equipment for their ships."

"Sounds like you got around here a fair bit," I commented.

"Somebody had to fix their crap," the man replied. "They were mostly too lazy to maintain their own equipment when they had someone to do it for them. Besides, I had a babysitter."

He gestured toward where the alien had fallen, then frowned when he saw the body missing. Only blood spatter on the walls and floor remained to mark the slaver's demise.

"I took care of the corpse," I said before the gunsmith could ask about the missing body.

The old man nodded, but the frown remained, likely since the slave collar had disappeared too.

"Ready?" I asked, drawing a pistol from a holster.

"Let's go," Robert replied.

The old man swung the weapon off his shoulder and readied it with the clear competence of someone with years of experience. Either the old man was a veteran, or he had regularly practiced with his equipment. Probably both.

I turned my back to the man and headed toward the stairs. If he was going to shoot me in the back, I'd rather know now, though I didn't think he would. I thought I was a fair judge of character, and I got the sense that the gunsmith was looking to pay back the aliens who had enslaved him.

I opened the door to the stairwell and led the way as we climbed to the higher levels of the prison.

Chapter 29

Fortunately for my health, my judgment of Robert held, and my back remained without bullet holes by the time we reached the level where the kids were held.

I stepped out of the stairwell and found myself in a gated corridor that functioned like an airlock to limit access to the rest of the floor. Unlike the previous floors, this one very much looked and felt like a prison.

The butcher's keycard let me through the security gates, and Robert followed with his rifle raised. The gunsmith hadn't swept me once with the muzzle of his weapon as we crept down the hallway, and I had to admit that I was impressed so far. I just hoped he could shoot as well as he moved if we ran into anything.

Once through the security gate, the hall split with one corridor at a ninety-degree angle to the right and the other stretched out straight in front of me. At the end of the hall ahead of us, the corridor turned right. A glance down the right-hand hall showed that it turned left, which meant that the floor plan for this section resembled a square.

A map of the floor next to the security gate confirmed my guess on the layout. Cells lined the outside wall of the hallway while the center of the floor held an exercise area, laundry facility, a small kitchen, and a prisoner cafeteria. With the entire level a self-contained facility, prisoners never needed to move between floors. In theory, at least, that was how it would have worked before the arrival of the System.

In reality, the smell of unwashed humans assailed my nose the moment we left the security gates. My nose wrinkled in disgust, and I looked at Robert, who appeared unfazed by the stench. The old man glanced at me with a blank expression then turned to cover the open hallway to the right without a word, daring me to comment.

I kept my mouth shut and moved forward to glance inside the nearest cell. My unasked questions about the condition of the floor were answered by the sight.

The cell contained a bunk bed, a small shower, a sink, and a toilet. In the space designed for two adult prisoners were a half dozen kids who spoke to each other in hushed whispers. The children were of mixed ages and sexes, as if whoever had imprisoned them had never bothered to sort them out, but they were all younger than eighteen.

The six youngsters fell silent when I stepped to the door of the cell, then they instinctively shrank back in dread. Confusion replaced worry when they gave me a closer look, seeing that I wasn't an alien or a uniformed officer, but the sight of the children recoiling in fear seared itself in my mind even more than the overcrowded and unsanitary conditions.

"Where's the control room for the floor?" I asked as I turned away from the cell, my voice little more than a growl.

"This way," the old man said over his shoulder as he started down the hall.

He led and I followed, turning to check the hall behind us every few paces. I avoided looking into the other cells. We reached the end of the corridor and rounded the corner to the next section of the hallway.

Robert halted before we reached the next intersection and waved me up against the wall. I planted my back against the bulkhead and made sure our backs were clear before I looked up ahead.

Just past Robert, the solid metal door indicated the entrance to the control room. Armored glass made up at least one wall of the room and explained why the gunsmith had me hugging the wall.

Beyond the control room lay the intersection where the corridor wrapped back around the square of this tower, then another set of security gates separated the cell block on this floor from the next tower. The offset layout of the towers, like matching colors on a chessboard, prevented the cells around the outside walls from sharing an exterior wall with another cell.

Robert motioned me to the door, and I pulled out the stolen keycard as I slipped past him. The gunsmith stacked up behind me with one hand on the door handle when I paused with the keycard in front of the lock. I glanced at Robert, and he gave me a confident nod. I nodded back and swiped the keycard past the lock's reader.

The door clicked and Robert swung the door open, which allowed me to charge through. The Krym'parke inside the checkpoint lay back in an office chair tilted at a dangerous angle with hands folded behind its head and feet up on the edge of the console that sat under a wide bank of monitors. If the alien hadn't been napping, it would have watched us move through the halls on one of the many screens.

Certlk'n Af'ryve (Slaver Level 36)
HP: 730/730
MP: 840/840

When I stepped through the door, the Krym'parke cracked open one eye as if mildly annoyed by the interruption to its nap. Then the alien jolted awake at the sight of my leveled pistol and swung its feet off the desk.

Before the alien's feet touched the floor, I fired with my pistol and kept moving into the room. I cast Frostbolt when I cleared the doorway, and Robert opened fire with his rifle from behind me. Our combined attacks slammed into the alien as it tried to stand against the force of the incoming projectiles. It failed and only managed to tumble backward when the tilted office chair tipped over.

The alien landed on its knees, and I activated Hinder before it could do anything else. Its reactions slowed even further. The alien never even pulled a weapon before it collapsed as the last of its health evaporated under the barrage of gunfire.

Robert rushed to the console the alien had used as a footrest and quickly typed at a keyboard while I checked the body. A holstered knife and beam pistol were soon stashed in my Inventory, but I found nothing else useful.

Robert pressed several buttons next to the control console, then he rushed out of the room. The old man moved surprisingly fast, and I hurried after him.

Out in the corridor, the cell doors had all swung open, and several children bravely peeked out of the cells.

Robert ignored them all and darted through the security gates that led to the adjacent prison tower. Whatever he had done with the control room console to open the cell doors had caused the security gates to open at the same time.

I followed him through to the next cell block, where the hall was filled with children who had left the cells. They quickly retreated from our path, and Robert ignored them as he pushed through the throng. He continued through the hallway, through another security checkpoint, and into the next cell block.

Robert began looking at the kids about halfway through the next hall. He glanced from face to face, as if searching for someone specific.

"Mickey," Robert yelled. "Mickey, where are you?"

"Poppop," cried a voice from a nearby cell.

A young boy dashed into the hallway and rushed toward Robert. The old gunsmith swung his rifle onto his back and dropped to his knees to wrap the boy in a bear hug. The boy couldn't have been older than twelve.

Michael Wilson

HP: 50/50

The two clung to each other desperately, even as more children stepped out into the hallway. I walked over to the pair and gently shook Robert by the shoulder.

"We need to go," I said. "It probably won't be long before the rest get back."

The gunsmith pushed himself to his feet and hoisted his grandson onto one hip when the boy refused to let go of his neck.

The boy's attachment to Robert seemed to relax the kids around us and lower their suspicions. The fact that we had freed them from their cells also helped.

Somehow the two of us managed to get the kids rounded up and moving toward the stairs. Rigged by whatever Robert had done to the security, the gates by the stairs were both open now, so I led the way down the stairwell.

A quick stop at the armory left the weapon racks there empty of the remaining weapons and ammunition, all stuffed into my equipment storage and nearly filling it to the brim.

I felt like the Pied Piper as I led the procession of children out of the prison and through the courthouse.

When I reached the front desk, Brian stared at the kids with a shocked expression. "Where did all of these kids come from?"

"Your alien friends were holding them in the jail," I replied.

"What? No, that's impos—" The officer's jaw clamped shut as children continued to stream into the hall, and their very presence confronted the man's denial.

Soon, well over one hundred kids filled the lobby and the crowd finally slowed as Robert pushed his way through them to reach the desk where I stood waiting. As the gunsmith worked through the mass of children, I saw a pair of faces I recognized.

The Thomas kids had survived.

I felt a sense of relief, as if a weight I hadn't even realized I carried had been lifted. Zeke was long gone, but his kids were still here.

Robert stepped between the two kids and me as he approached, still carrying his grandson protectively, and I saw Brian blink in recognition at the gunsmith.

"Robert, I haven't seen you in weeks. Do you know what the hell is going on?" Brian asked. "Where did all of these kids come from?"

"Those alien jagoffs had me in a slave collar," Robert spat. "They locked up Mickey here with the other kids to keep me cooperative. They were planning to ship most of these kids off world as slaves and breeding stock for a black-market network."

"There's no way all these kids were in the prison," Brian said. "There were too many prisoners here, even after the riot on the first day."

"There are no prisoners left," Robert said with a shudder. "The aliens ate them first."

Brian stood still for a moment as he wrestled with the information, but I felt the weight of time press down on me once more. I had no idea how long the battle in the city might continue, and I wanted the kids long gone before any survivors returned.

"We need to get these kids out of here," I said. "Open the gate, Brian. I don't care what you decide to do after we leave."

The officer pressed a control on the desk, and the front gates swung open outside the glass front doors of the building. Night had fallen outside and shrouded the parking lot beyond the gates in darkness.

"Come with us, Brian," Robert said quietly. "You're a good man, and the kids are going to need more good people looking out for them. I have a place where we can go, but I could use your help."

The officer looked over the kids and seemed to come to a decision. Brian nodded to Robert and removed the badge from his chest. He placed the silver shield on the desk, his hand lingering on the badge for a moment, then he stepped out from behind the counter as he pulled his rifle from his Inventory.

"What about you?" Robert asked, looking at me.

"No, there's going to be fallout from this." I shook my head. "If questions start getting asked, far too many groups will be looking for me. It's best that I give them a second trail to follow. I'll play bait to draw attention away from wherever you're going."

Robert nodded in understanding. He opened his mouth, about to say something else, but I held up a hand to stop him.

"Don't tell me where," I said. "If the worst happens, it's best I don't know."

The old man looked at me seriously for a moment then held out his hand. "Thanks. For getting that damn collar off my neck and freeing all of us. "

I shook the man's gnarled hand and waved away the gratitude.

I was no hero to be lauded. Even now, people were likely dying in the city because of my actions. I'd had ulterior motives for almost everything I'd done. But I wouldn't say it. Not here, and not now with young men and women packing the courthouse lobby.

There was nothing left to say, so I turned away to open the front door. I held it to let Robert lead the first of the kids out of the building. They hurried after him without complaint and streamed out quietly, two or three at a time. Several whispered their thanks to me as they left.

When the first of the older teenagers filed past me, I stopped the blond girl with an upraised hand and held out one of the refurbished police rifles I had looted when I cleaned out the armory. Her expression of surprise shifted to one of determination before she grabbed the weapon and the matching box of ammunition, which disappeared into her Inventory.

The rest of the looted rifles, I handed out amongst the other upper-class high school students. The monsters of the dungeon world wouldn't care that they were kids. At least this way they might have a chance to defend themselves.

I just hoped Robert wouldn't be too upset if he realized where the rest of his armory had gone.

Gabrielle and Jordan Thomas nodded to me respectfully when they walked out of the building, clearly recognizing me from our previous encounter. I jerked my head to the side after I handed them weapons, and the two split off to stand beside me as more children streamed out of the building.

I kept one foot in front of the door to hold it open and turned toward the pair as I summoned Zeke's Warhammer from my Inventory. With one hand just below the massive head and the other at the base, I held the weapon toward the two youngsters.

"This was your father's," I said. "He would have wanted you to have it. With everything going on, I forgot to give it to you the last time we met."

The teenagers looked at each other, unable to speak, and Jordan nodded to his sister. Gabrielle stepped forward and lifted the weighty weapon from my palms. Though she struggled to lift the Warhammer, the determined look on her face made it clear she would do anything but let the weapon fall to the ground.

Even if she was nowhere near the Strength levels required to wield the hammer effectively.

Jordan brushed his hand over the weapon. The pair worked together to hold it up while they inspected it. After they struggled for a moment, the Warhammer disappeared into the girl's Inventory.

"Thank you," Gabrielle choked out. Emotion filled her voice, preventing the young woman from speaking further.

"This means so much to us," Jordan said. "We've lost everything, but now we have something of dad's." The young man breathed deeply, reining in his emotions. "Thank you."

I nodded, finally feeling my debt to Zeke fulfilled, despite completing the man's Quest long ago.

The Thomas kids thanked me again before they hurried off to catch up with the last of the children who had left the building. As Gabrielle and Jordan stepped beyond the gate surrounding the complex, a notification blinked for my attention, but I ignored it for now.

Brian brought up the rear of the group, and I let the doors close behind us as I walked with him to the gate.

"Good luck," Brian said over his shoulder as he continued to follow the group.

"You too," I replied.

The sharpshooter pulled a rifle from his Inventory before jogging to join the tail end of the straggling line of rescued youth. The disorganized troop snaked away through the parking lot. Those in the lead had already turned to follow Second Avenue and I lost sight of them soon after in the nighttime shadows that shrouded the city.

Once they were all gone, I summoned my bike from my Inventory and mounted it. Throttling up, I drove west to circle the block before I swung around onto the Boulevard of the Allies. The road climbed along the side of the incline here, and I slowed to a stop after the road leveled off.

Only a few lights glittered in the darkness through the Southside Flats on the far side of the Monongahela River, but the view remained scenic as the moon rose higher in the early evening sky.

With no one in view, I finally had the chance to acknowledge the blinking notifications in the corner of my vision that demanded my attention.

Quest Complete!
You have successfully located and freed the children kidnapped by the Krym'parke slavers.
25,000 Credits and 20,000 XP Awarded.
-800 reputation with Goldmiser Cartel*
-1000 reputation with Krym'parke affiliated factions*

The asterisk after the final lines caught my attention and a linked notification appeared when I examined those messages more closely.

* These reputation changes are held in abeyance for 347 Galactic Standard Days. Should a member of the noted faction report evidence of your involvement to their faction leadership within the abeyance period, the reputation loss with that faction will be fully applied.

Apparently, if I stayed under the radar for the better part of a year, and no other evidence came to light, I might not end up as hunted as I thought. Still, it would be best not to stick around to find out.

Level Up! * 2

You have reached Level 19 as a Relentless Huntsman. Stat Points automatically distributed. You have 4 Free Attributes and 1 Class Skill Point to distribute.

A successful quest completion and two levels. Not bad for an evening's work.

I decided to hold off on distributing the points for now. Unfortunately, my night was far from over. To put distance between the kids who would be going into hiding and me, I planned to drive well beyond the city limits along Interstate 376.

Fortunately, between my regular Inventory space and the specialized equipment storage of Right Tool for the Job, I had plenty of gear and supplies for a trip through the wilderness.

Maybe if I killed enough monsters and grew strong enough, someday I'd come back and see if any of the Krym'parke had survived the battle with the goblins.

I took one last look at the city, struck by the feeling that I wouldn't be back any time soon.

Less than two weeks ago, I'd been a simple bail bondsman with a damaged body and a broken mind. I pursued lawbreakers through the city to distract myself from the struggle my life had become.

The System changed everything.

The Mana that flowed through the world had restored my physique to prime condition and bestowed literal superpowers. The struggle for survival continued, but it was different now that I had superhuman abilities, laser pistols, and magic. And a railgun.

My nightmares had seemed diminished lately too. The fact that I could finally sleep through the night without waking up in a cold sweat, especially as little as I had been sleeping lately, was almost worth the cost of the worldwide calamity.

At least to me.

While not everyone would agree, the monsters spawned by the System were tangible foes I could fight, and I looked forward to growing stronger as I continued to face off against the challenges of this new Dungeon World.

I'd lingered here long enough. The time had come, and I needed to move on.

My bike roared back to life, and I leaned low over the handlebars as I throttled up.

Asphalt disappeared beneath my tires, and I shot down the street. The ramp for 376 East veered off to the right, and I swept down it onto the wider highway below.

I settled into the comfortable seat of the motorcycle, knowing it would be a long night of driving.

And there were miles to go before I could sleep.

Epilogue

An image wavered in the shimmering pool of crystal-clear water at the center of a raised and elegantly carved granite basin. Chiseled into the stonework were armored hunters mounted on horseback, armed with spears and bows, followed snarling hounds as they pursued dainty, humanoid figures through the sculpted trees.

An image hung suspended within the rippling liquid that filled the cauldron. First the brown-haired man with the scarred face slumbered in the reclined driver's seat of an ungainly rectangular vehicle, a four-wheeled contraption with a combustion engine. The scar tissue that marred him disappeared under the collar of the man's shirt, evidence that the damage continued farther down along that side of his body.

The image wavered and showed the man in a running gunfight with another human in white coveralls. A moment later, the liquid swirled to reveal that the man now fought a giant bear before flames filled the pool and the vision shifted to another scene.

The man stood behind the vehicle this time, and he quickly spun around with a weapon raised before the pool wavered again.

Each time the waters within the basin rippled, the man appeared, usually locked in combat against another foe.

Monsters, men, and even a jabberwock.

The viewers watched in silence until the vision faded. Their last glimpse of the human showed him astride a two-wheeled vehicle, looking out over a city as night fell upon it.

"This? This is to be the next member of the Hunt?" an imperious voice demanded of the swirling pool.

"Your Majesty, the Mana formations on the new Dungeon World are not yet stable," replied the Seer who tightly held the edges of the basin. Her hands still glowed from the powers she channeled through the stone and into the waters within.

A silvery crown set with deep blue sapphires reflected the pool's light from the brow of the authoritative ruler. She sniffed, her expression a haughty sneer, before turning away from the Seer and her vision.

"I am not impressed," the queen said as she walked away.

A cloaked figure stepped out of the shadowy recesses that edged the room and opened the heavy wooden door. Light streamed through the doorway into the darkened room, but distorted around the cloaked figure, leaving him shrouded in umbral gloom despite the open door's illumination.

Outside the door, guards in silvery plate armor waited stoically in formation.

"Shall I have the affront to our people removed, my queen?" said the cloaked figure.

The crowned figure sniffed again disgustedly then paused. "No. Let the System play its games. Not even the Questors dare thwart the System's will for long." She stepped into the doorway and looked back at the hidden figure. "If he proves unworthy, then you may release the hounds."

The woman stepped out of the room and into the center of the guards' formation. The troop immediately marched smartly down the hall, their crisp steps matched to the pace of their monarch.

The cloaked figure grinned after them, the whites of his sharply pointed teeth the only feature visible in his otherwise hooded face. He closed the door and turned back to the Seer.

"Show me this human again…"

The adventures of Hal will continue in

Dungeon World Drifters

In the meantime, keep reading for the short "Hunting Monsters,"

first published in

The System Apocalypse Short Story Anthology Volume 1

Glossary

Relentless Huntsman Skill Tree

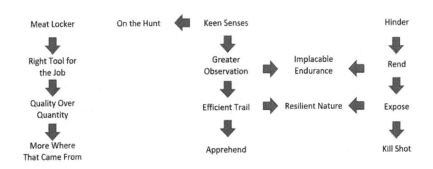

Meat Locker	On the Hunt ←	Keen Senses		Hinder
Right Tool for the Job		Greater Observation →	Implacable Endurance ←	Rend
Quality Over Quantity		Efficient Trail →	Resilient Nature ←	Expose
More Where That Came From		Apprehend		Kill Shot

Hal's Skills

Hinder (Level 2)

Effect: All physical movement by a designated target within 15 feet is significantly impaired for 1 minute.

Cost: 40 Stamina + 20 Mana.

Keen Senses (Level 1)

The user is more in tune with their body and more accurately interprets information gained from their surroundings. This manifests in the user as increases to vision, audition, gustation, olfaction, tactition, and proprioception. Mana regeneration reduced by 5 Mana per minute permanently.

On the Hunt (Level 3)

The Relentless Huntsman has a reduced System presence and increased ability to disguise their visible titles, class, level, and stats. Effectiveness is based on the user's Skill level and Charisma. Mana regeneration reduced by 15 Mana per minute permanently.

Meat Locker (Level 1)

Effect: The Relentless Huntsman now has access to an extra-dimensional storage location of 20 cubic feet. Only deceased bounty targets or slain creatures may be added to this location and must be touched to be willed inside. Mana regeneration reduced by 5 Mana per minute permanently.

The Right Tool for the Job (Level 1)

Effect: The Relentless Huntsman now has access to an extra-dimensional storage location of 5 cubic feet. Items stored must be touched to be willed in and may only include weapons, armor, equipment, or supplies owned by the Relentless Huntsman. Any qualifying System-recognized item can be placed or removed from this inventory location if space allows. Cost: 5 Mana per item.

Greater Observation (Level 1)

Effect: User may now detect System creatures up to 50 meters away and is provided an analysis of the subject upon detection. Increased Skill levels may reveal additional System information not normally available. Depending on comparative overall level and Skills in effect, the target of focused Observation may know that the user has gained some level of information. Mana regeneration reduced by 5 Mana per minute permanently.

Rend (Level 1)

Effect: Physical weapon attacks that cause health damage apply a bleed effect, causing the target to bleed for 15 damage over 15 seconds. This effect can be stacked if the health damage occurs at a different location on the target.

Cost: 10 Stamina.

Implacable Endurance (Level 1)

Effect: Reduces Stamina cost for physical exertion and activated physical abilities by 25%. Does not stack with other Stamina reduction skills. Mana regeneration reduced by 5 Mana per minute permanently.

Spells

Minor Healing (I)

Effect: Heals 20 Health per casting.

Target must be in contact during healing. Cooldown 60 seconds.

Cost: 20 Mana.

Frostbolt (II)

Effect: Creates a Frost bolt from the user's Mana, which can be directed to damage a target. The dart does 30 Ice damage and slows the target by 3%. Slow effect stacks up to three times (9%). Cooldown 10 seconds.

Cost: 25 Mana.

Frostnova (I)

Effect: Creates a ring of Frost from the user's Mana which blasts outward in a 3-meter radius centered on the user. The ring does 12 Ice damage and may affect enemies with a Freeze effect, rooting them in place for up to 8 seconds. Cooldown 30 seconds.

Cost: 50 Mana.

Equipment

Silversmith Mark II Beam Pistol (Upgradeable)

Base Damage: 18

Battery Capacity: 24/24

Recharge Rate: 2 per hour per GMU

Luxor Series III Projectile Pistol

Base Damage: N/A (Dependent Upon Ammunition)

Ammo Capacity: 12/12

Ammunition Types: Standard, Armor Piercing, High Explosive, Tracer, Hollow Point

Tier IV Knife

Base Damage: 11

Durability: 140/140

Special Abilities: None

Tier III Hand-axe

Base Damage: 25

Durability: 200/200

Special Abilities: None

Banshee III Hybrid Gauss Rifle

Base Damage: N/A (Dependent Upon Ammunition)

Ammo Capacity: 15/15

Battery Capacity: 30/30

Recharge Rate: 4 per hour per GMU

Cost: 5,400 Credits

Rudianos Class IV Outrider

Core: Class IV Hephaestus Mana Engine

CPU: Class E Xylik Core CPU

Armor Rating: Tier V

Hard Points: 2 (1 Used for Nano Garage Module)

Soft Points: 2 (1 Used for Neural Link)

Optional: Neural Link for Remote Activation

Battery Capacity: 60/60

Tier V Neural Link

Neural link may support up to 4 connections.

Current connections: Rudianos Class IV Outrider

Software Installed: Rich'lki Fire-wall Class IV, Rudianos Class V Controller

Hunting Monsters

By Craig Hamilton

(This short story first appeared in
The System Apocalypse Short Story Anthology Volume 1)

Only a monster could have left such carnage.

I stood in the doorway of a tiny apartment, the stench of decomposition wafting out to fill the dimly lit hallway. The deputy who had opened the door had already fled down the corridor before retching and emptying his stomach. I ignored the officer. Just as I ignored his partner, who glared at me as I took in the scene inside the room. His skepticism affected me as much as the smell—not at all.

The cops may not have known me, but death was no stranger. Nearly two-thirds of humanity had died ten months ago, the day the System came online and ended the world as we knew it. Monsters spawned everywhere and massacred mankind as our lives became governed by the System's video-game-like rules. Rules that allowed no replays or extra lives. Those of us remaining had seen plenty of death, but I may have seen more than most.

That fateful day began as I pursued a man who had skipped out on his bail. When the man unexpectedly opened fire and fled, I had refused to let the criminal get away, even as our world changed. The pursuit, and ensuing gunfight, led to my first experience gained under the System. Before I even had a chance to select a class, I had earned a level from killing another human. The System rewarded that achievement with an Advanced Class that matched my actions, and I had been hunting monsters ever since.

I stepped cautiously into the hotel room turned apartment. There was no avoiding the dried blood that stained the floor a rusty red, but I kept my feet away from the larger lumps. Crouched beside a pile of organic material, I let myself study the viscera that remained of a human torso. The edges of the gaping wounds were sharply cut. My eyes traced over the slashed flesh to the arcing spatters of dried blood, following the pattern backward and rebuilding the scene in my mind. I moved from one chunk of gore to another, careful to touch nothing. Slowly and deliberately, I lost all track of time as I pieced together the horrific puzzle.

Eventually, I stood and brushed aside a System notification for a skill increase in Forensics. As I turned toward the door, a glimmer of reflected light caught my eye. A framed holograph, splashed with blood, was centered on a bookshelf filled with knickknacks. I picked it up and wiped the glass covering. Crusted flakes fell free and revealed an image that made my breath catch in my throat. The six smiling faces in the image were a jarringly bright reflection of the agonizing jigsaw assembled in my mind. A family—as much as anyone had these days after the System Apocalypse—with parents caring for children not their own and children clinging lovingly to adults with no blood relation.

After replacing the holograph on the shelf, I absently pulled a flask from my inventory and took a long pull. I should have felt more for the family. Anger that their lives had been stolen. Rage at the potential snuffed out. A passion to bring their killer to justice. Instead, I felt nothing. Not even the burn of the whiskey pouring down my throat. My System-enhanced constitution easily resisted weaker poisons and dulled any sensation the alcohol may have once given me. Though I had no proof, I suspected the System similarly affected mental resilience, blunting the horrific impact of how many humans had died in the previous ten months. Despite the tragedy, people had simply moved on with their lives. Most even calmly accepted the arrival of the Galactics—aliens from throughout the wider System universe—as they settled in on Earth. In most places, these new arrivals promptly took over.

I was currently in one such location—a Truinnar-owned village in what used to be western Pennsylvania. When I'd crossed into the town limits, I had picked up a System-generated quest to track down a killer menacing the human population. The few local law enforcement officers left alive had apparently been unable to catch this killer. While the identity of any criminal could be purchased from the System, that criminal could also have Class Skills or spells that would assist in hiding them. The cost to purchase the identity from the Shop would increase with each obfuscating ability added, quickly making the price prohibitively high. It often worked out cheaper to hire or post a quest for someone to hunt down the criminals who took these precautions. Which led to Adventurers picking up side gigs as bounty hunters.

Turning my focus back to the room, I closed my eyes and cast a newly acquired Class Skill. The nauseating aroma of the room assaulted my nose as Blood Scent settled into place. Six distinct tangy bouquets hung heavily tangled in the air, and I spent several minutes locking each one into my memory. I wasted no time looking for the scent of the killer since no evidence had been found at any of the earlier crime scenes and I expected the same again here.

I cracked my eyes open and left the room but stopped where the two police officers waited. The younger man, sweating and pallid, stood behind his partner and looked anywhere but through the apartment door. Both noticed the flask still in my hand, neither able to hide their disdain.

Officer Robert Richardson (Guardian Level 36)
_HP: 960/960_

Officer Thomas Cook (Guardian Level 11)
HP: 280/280

"Six dead," I said, addressing the more experienced officer. "Three adults, two teenagers, and one toddler. Two days ago."

"That matches the apartment registration," Officer Richardson replied stoically. "And the last time anyone talked to the occupants."

"No one heard anything?" I asked.

"No," Richardson said, his eyes distant. "No one heard a thing."

"The killer disabled them all quickly," I said. "Then he took his time cutting them apart bit by bit. The others were forced to watch."

The rookie cop looked as if he was about to be sick again.

"The killer?" Richardson peered at me sharply. "Not a monster?"

"Oh, it was a monster," I replied. "Just not a System-spawned one. Your killer is human."

Leaving the two astounded cops, I headed down the hall toward the stairs. Maybe it was a leap to claim the culprit was human, but my gut was convinced. This building was a Safe Zone, so no System monster could have spawned inside the room. The Galactics who ruled this town had no issues striking down a human in cold blood, but none of them had any reason to hide it behind closed doors. Just the opposite, in fact. Any killings were usually public examples being made of criminals, troublemakers, or those who violently resisted Galactic rule. Most humans were second-class citizens, if they mattered at all, so no Galactic would go through the trouble to cover up a series of murders. On top of that, most Galactics now on Earth were so highly leveled that they would gain little, if any, experience from killing low-level humans.

Only a human would have felt the need to hide these massacres from their own kind. Especially murders performed in a place like this—an apartment building converted from a pre-System hotel—in the middle of a Safe Zone. A home where the most vulnerable, those without combat classes, were meant to be protected. Instead, the people here were terrified, knowing a killer lurked in the night and anyone could be next. I was certain the culprit fed on the desperate atmosphere, relishing the terror his work left behind.

More than the deaths of the family, this annoyed me. That a predator could feel superior in stalking the weak and the helpless left me feeling raw. Despite my antisocial tendencies, I still regarded humanity as my own. I felt a primal need to deal with that which threatened my people. The Galactics were outside of my capabilities for now, though that was an itch I looked forward to scratching.

Once outside on the sidewalk, I took a deep breath of the fresh evening air. Blood Scent remained active, slowly draining my Mana and allowing me to follow the faint coppery tang. The sun had dropped below the horizon, but enough light remained for me to get my bearings in this unfamiliar small town.

Other than pursuing System-generated quests or bounties for broken Galactic Contracts, I spent the majority of my time alone, grinding out levels in the wilderness and occasionally partying up with other Adventurers to clear the odd dungeon or two. I had passed through here before, but the few surviving rural burgs throughout this part of the country sort of blended together at this point.

"So, you're the latest to pick up the quest for our town's little murder mystery," said a voice from behind me.

I looked back at the man who leaned casually against the building, beside the door I had just exited. I raised an eyebrow in response, looking him over as he examined me. The man wore civilian clothes—a beige trench coat over a light-blue collared shirt and khaki pants. He was shorter than average and slightly balding, which told me the man was either too proud or too broke to purchase Genome Treatment from the Shop. An examination of his System status revealed his class and indicated the latter.

Scott Davis (Journalist Level 7)
HP: 140/140

"Latest?" I asked.

"Adventurers passing through, like you," Scott replied. "They all disappeared shortly after beginning their investigations though."

"Is that a threat?" I growled. My eyes narrowed as I turned to face the man completely.

"Not at all," the journalist replied hurriedly. "I just wanted to warn you that whatever is doing the killing doesn't seem to want anyone investigating too deeply."

"And a journalist doesn't investigate?" I asked.

"I report the facts," Scott said defensively. "It's common knowledge, once the police publish their reports. At least for the bodies found in town."

"So, there are also bodies found outside of town?"

The journalist looked around nervously then nodded. "Back when the System first came online, the town hunters would find convoys that had been slaughtered outside the town limits. People headed here for safety but never made it. Or roadways covered in blood with the area all torn up but no bodies. Everyone thought monsters did it, but then the killings started in town."

"This almost sounds like the work of a System-enhanced serial killer," I speculated. "What's the body count from in town?"

"Nobody is really sure," Scott replied with a shrug. "The numbers really climbed after families started showing up as victims, so at least fifty have been confirmed. But with the number of transients and Adventurers passing through, on top of the killings outside of town, it could easily be hundreds."

The ominous bits of news were troubling since the System quest had made no mention of anything outside the town or that the body count was so high. If the killer had been active since the System came online, the experience they'd accrued would be sizeable and would have led to the killer obtaining higher levels than normal.

"Why has no one bought the killer's identity from the Shop if things are this bad?" I asked.

"It's too expensive," Scott replied. "No one can afford it on their own, and every time people try to pool their resources to buy it, the price jumps."

That was really bad news. It meant the killer was inside the community and able to take precautions.

"That's really all the info I've got for you. I hope it helps." The journalist turned and walked away. After a few steps, he turned back toward me. "Good luck," he said with a solemn nod.

The journalist had given me plenty to think about. That the man had been waiting for me outside the latest crime scene meant that word was spreading that a new Adventurer was looking into the killings. As plugged-in to the community as the killer seemed, they would soon be aware that I was hunting.

I headed south, tracking the faint aroma of blood that the killer had left behind. With dusk setting in, most of the local businesses along Main Street were closing up as I passed. The shops sold locally made goods using resources looted from System-spawned monsters. The human craftsmen making those items were still fairly low-leveled, so the System Shops generally had higher-quality, and thus more expensive, goods. The likelihood of finding upgrades for my gear was slim though, so I passed the stores without a glance. Most of my attention remained focused on following the scent, but I was well aware of a few townsfolk eyeing me nervously and giving me a wide berth.

As I reached the southern edge of the business district, the storefronts of the downtown area gave way to residential homes. I also felt the onset of a headache caused by low Mana and quickly cut off Blood Scent before Mana fatigue could fully set in. The conversation with the journalist had taken longer than I would have liked and leaving the Class Skill active during that chat had drained my Mana. I would have to let my Mana regenerate before I could continue my hunt. A downside of the physical benefits of my class was that I tended to be far weaker on the spell-casting side of things.

No longer focused on my Class Skill and intently following my nose, I became aware of the music that emanated from a solid brick building ahead of me. Live music tended to be somewhat rare since musicians had generally fared poorly in surviving the apocalypse. The full sound of a stringed instrument pulled at me, and I found myself walking several steps toward the building. I forced myself to stop, disconcerted that the unexpected music had attracted me so strongly.

Mental Influence Resisted

468

The conscious mental effort and notification explained the powerful draw and aroused my curiosity. I had fairly significant mental resistances, so a musician who could challenge them with a compulsion certainly seemed worth checking out. Now that I was somewhat closer, I gave the building a more thorough examination. It looked like a pre-System dive bar, only somewhat cleaned up by new management. Galactic runes above the door proudly proclaimed Gimsar ownership and that Adventurers of all types were welcome.

Gimsar were like dwarves from fantasy legends, except that their craftsmen were no more talented than anyone else in the System universe. Hard drinking and hard fighting, they were often seen as honorable mercenaries. So long as one avoided insult to a Gimsar's clan, beard, or axe, they tended to be fairly good-natured.

I stepped into the building and found every eye in the place glancing in my direction as I eased the door closed. I was pretty confident of what they were seeing. Some used high Charisma to enhance their looks. I used my Charisma to ensure others saw exactly what I wanted them to see. A tall, brown-haired human man with a muscular build wearing a dark-gray combat jumpsuit. A sword sheathed across my back and holstered pistols on both hips. Standard Adventurer chic, nothing out of the ordinary.

Hal Mason (Hunter Level 29)
HP: 220/220

A granite-topped bar counter ran along one side of the room. Surprisingly, the bar top looked to be at a normal height for a bar despite the older, gray-bearded Gimsar tending bar from behind it. The bartender conversed with a group of Gimsar taking up about half the high stools at the closer end of the bar. Behind the bartender, above the racks of liquor, hung a massive double-headed battle-axe. From the notches and scrapes on the weapon, I could tell the axe had been well used.

Several tables of Hakarta mercenaries promptly ignored me, going back to a complicated series of card games. The green-skinned aliens were similar in appearance to fantasy orcs, but I preferred to think of them as high-tech supersoldiers. The Hakarta typically operated in well-disciplined squads, so if you saw one out in the wild, there were probably several others nearby keeping you in their sights.

A group of Yerrick took up a large table in the far back of the bar, out of the way. The nine-foot-tall minotaurs were thick with muscle and commonly employed as Adventurers. I recognized none from this particular group, but I had worked with Yerrick in the past and found them more than capable.

The rest of the clientele scattered throughout the bar was a mix of human and Truinnar. Nothing about the humans stood out—exactly the shady types of people I would expect to find in a seedy dive bar. The Truinnar, on the other hand, were eye-catching. Dark elves with lithe figures, midnight-black skin, and exotic hair colors, they moved with ethereal grace. Truinnar politics followed a labyrinthine feudal system I barely grasped enough of to know that Earth fell just inside their Galactic territory. Like this town, large portions of North America were now also under direct Truinnar control.

Across the room from the bar, an elevated platform served as the stage for a Truinnar woman vigorously playing a stringed instrument similar to violin. As captivating as the music had sounded outside, I found the instrumentalist dancing across the stage even more mesmerizing. A silver corseted dress hugged the woman's slender, athletic frame and sharply offset the onyx skin of her bare shoulders. Her shapely legs flashed through slits in the dress as she spun, kicked, and twisted around the platform. Platinum hair dyed in waves of cerulean and crimson streamed behind her as she danced with her eyes closed, lost in the enchantment of her own musical creation.

Pulling away from the enthralling vision on the stage, I headed to the empty end of the bar and perched on one of the high stools.

Walking along a ledge on the backside of the bar, which kept him at a normal height, the Gimsar headed toward me. "What'll it be, lad?"

"Whiskey," I replied. "Neat."

The dwarf grabbed an empty tumbler from a rack behind the bar and poured in a generous quantity of amber liquid from a recognizable green-tinted bottle. Sliding the glass toward me across the bar, he held up several fingers, and I transferred over the requested number of Credits as well as a small tip. The dwarf nodded in acknowledgement and headed back to the other end of the bar.

Glancing at my status, I saw that my nearly empty Mana pool had barely begun regenerating. Making a mental note to put more points into Willpower, I resigned myself to waiting until my Mana refilled.

"Well, well, you're certainly an interesting human, Harold Mason."

The sultry voice from behind tingled down my spine, and the use of my full name sent adrenaline rushing through my system. Twisting around on the barstool, I instinctively dropped my right hand to the pistol on my hip as I found myself facing the musician from the stage.

Dayena Baluisa, Sultana of the Whispering Strings, Mistress of Shadows (??? Level ???)

HP: ???

Up close, I found her even more stunning, and her loveliness momentarily arrested my panic at the realization that she had likely read my full System status. I'd barely glanced at her before luminous amethyst eyes captured my attention completely. Caught by surprise, I vaguely felt a sense of being analyzed and mentally stripped bare. I forced myself to blink rapidly and shifted my gaze away from her sharply angular face, breaking the spell.

Mental Influence Resisted

"That was rude," I growled, now on guard as I looked back at her.

"Oh, I'm sorry," Dayena replied, her skin flushed as she blinked innocently. "I forget how easily my influence overwhelms most humans."

Despite my initial reaction, her response struck me. Maybe her influence still affected me, but my intuition told me that her words sounded genuine. She appeared as ageless as most Truinnar, yet I got the sense that this woman was younger than I would have expected.

"May I join you?" she asked politely.

"Sure," I said as I released my right hand from the holstered pistol and waved at the barstool beside me.

Dayena gestured to the bartender, who brought over a recognizable cocktail as she gracefully slid onto the stool.

"You drink Manhattans?" I asked incredulously as I turned back to my drink.

"It's a recently acquired taste," she said defensively. "Pity about the city."

I snorted. "Pity about most of our cities."

She looked at me with her eyes narrowed. "You don't actually care, do you?"

No accusation tainted her tone. No judgment. Just observation. I sipped my drink while I considered my response.

"No. Not really. Nothing can change what happened, so there's no point in feeling upset. And yet I feel the need to do something about it. To protect what little is left." I knew she was getting me to open up more than I should, but I was always a sucker for a pretty face. "So, what's a high-class dame like you doing in a dive like this?"

Dayena's lips quirked into a slight smirk, acknowledgment that she was well aware of my attempt to change the subject away from myself. "Checking out all of the opportunities a new Dungeon World offers. There are plenty of possibilities in a place like this for those seeking fame and fortune."

"Sure, but you don't strike me as someone lacking in either," I said.

Dayena flinched and turned her head to look at me sharply. I had struck a nerve. "No, but sometimes accomplishments gained by others leave one wondering what can be achieved on their own without depending on others for protection."

I nodded in sympathy for the young Truinnar. Alone in the wilderness, reliant on only my own abilities to survive and eliminate System-spawned monsters, I felt invigorated. The chaos of combat banished the numbness and emotionlessness that had ruled me ever since the System initialized. Out in the untamed wilds, I fought to become stronger. If she desired to get out from under someone's thumb, building her strength on a Dungeon World was certainly one way to do it.

"Sometimes the most freedom comes when there are no strings to catch you if you fall," I replied.

"Exactly!" Dayena exclaimed, then sobered. "But my family doesn't see things that way."

The young woman stayed silent for a minute. I waited. She would either choose to continue and open up more or not.

"I'm just a pawn to marry off," Dayena said as she stirred her drink. "I won't be free to be my own person. Bundled off into an arranged marriage with another house, I'll be safely tied up in responsibilities and obligations."

"Maybe your family is right," I warned with a shrug. "On your own is a dangerous way to live."

"That's the only way to thrive under the System," she countered emphatically. "And so I ran away."

"It doesn't tend to work out for everyone though. What's stopping your family from tracking you down?"

"Nothing." Dayena sighed. "I'm sure they already know where I am. They just have to send someone to get me, and I'm not strong enough to stop them. Galactic society respects the strong." She turned half toward me, her look analytical. "The strong and the resourceful."

"I've been lucky." I shrugged. At this point, we both knew she could easily read my System status despite my pretended nonchalance.

"What if I said I'm interested in hiring you?"

"I'd be skeptical of what someone your level would need of someone as low-leveled as me," I replied. "Besides, I'm currently on a job."

Dayena looked away as she fidgeted with her drink. The sense of youth was back, along with a hint of vulnerability and a whiff of desperation. "That quest hasn't gone so well for anyone else."

"So I've heard. Fortunately, I'm not just anyone. But why do you care?"

"I'll tell you if you take the job," she shot back. "I guarantee that I can pay more than you'd make collecting on contract breakers or crime solving anywhere on this planet."

Clearly Dayena knew that bounty collection on individuals who broke their System-enforced Contracts was a lucrative business and my primary source of Credits. My current income was higher than average and one reason I still lived when so many others lay fallen. If she had access to the kind of resources necessary to research me with little more than a glance, her job offer would be interesting and likely worth my while. More Credits meant I could afford more, and better, skills and equipment from the Shop.

"Tell you what," I said. "Look me up after I finish up this quest. If you're really offering that many Credits, I'm interested."

"Good," Dayena said. "I'll be in touch."

With that, Dayena threw back the rest of her drink and returned her cocktail glass to the counter as she slipped off the barstool. She glided back to the stage and quickly returned to her melodic performance.

The position Dayena offered would likely involve me heavily in Truinnar politics. Once finished with this job, I needed to research Truinnar society. My lack of knowledge would be a significant handicap if I ended up working directly for a Truinnar noble. Especially with the cutthroat politics her family history implied. I had little doubt she was far more than a minstrel.

I shelved that train of thought and lost myself to the music flowing from the stage, helped along by a few more of the bartender's generously poured rounds. Eventually, I checked my status to find my Mana pool nearly full. I finished my last drink and nodded respectfully to the Gimsar bartender as I stood to leave. It was time to get back to work.

Back outside the dive bar, I reactivated Blood Scent and once again followed the faint trail south. Night had fallen completely, the darkness broken only by sparse streetlights and the occasional storefront sign. The streets were deserted, not a person to be seen. I followed the scent traces, the footsteps of my armored boots the only sound in the stillness.

The scent soon cut across the main thoroughfare, then turned back north, still following the sidewalk along Main Street. Before long, I passed back through the downtown area and found myself across the street from the hotel where I'd begun tracking the killer.

The trail continued north, and my gut told me the end of the trail was nearby. I followed the scent for another half block before the trail cut back across Main Street and west down an alley, between an old theater and a store built of weathered brick. At the end of the alley, I found a small parking lot bordering the backside of several buildings. The trail crossed the parking lot and led to the back door of a narrow two-story house.

I stood in the middle of the dark parking lot and stared at that door for several minutes. I then turned toward the back of another building that bordered this small parking lot. The beige brick building that had been my first stop in town after I'd accepted the quest to hunt down the killer. It was the old pre-System municipal building, which currently served as the police headquarters.

I was unsurprised when a shadow detached from the building and glided toward me. The figure stopped a dozen paces away. I knew who it was long before the figure came to a halt. Human, levels above average, and able to wander leisurely around town after making any kill.

"Officer Richardson," I said.

The police officer, still in his uniform, cocked his head and examined me. "How did you follow the trail? No one else has ever come anywhere close to figuring it out."

"Easy," I replied. "I just followed my nose."

"Impossible," Richardson said, his brow furrowed in confusion. "I cast the Cleanse spell. There was nothing of me to scent."

"Sure," I said with a triumphant smirk. "But you cast it while you were still in a small room reeking with the blood of your victims. I followed their scent, which clung to you as you left."

"Well," said Richardson, his eyes wide, "I'll have to remember that the next time."

"There won't be a next time," I growled.

"Sure," he replied as he gestured to cast a spell at the surrounding area.

Despite the spell not being cast directly at me, I identified it as some kind of area silencing ability. The spell prevented any noise from escaping the area—clearly how the killer had kept anyone from interrupting his killing sprees.

Long knives shimmered into existence in Richardson's hands. As the weapons appeared, I pulled a pistol from each of my thigh holsters. The comfortable weight of the System-upgraded Colt M1911, magazine loaded with hand-crafted ammunition in .45 caliber, filled my right hand. My left carried a sleek, lightweight beam pistol constructed of Galactic composite materials, the popular Silversmith Mark II.

Richardson charged toward me with a speed that defied belief. Just as quickly, I opened fire. The beam from my Silversmith hit a shield before reaching the advancing officer, and the rounds from my M1911 sparked off the same shield as they were deflected. The shield flickered as I fired my fourth round from the Colt, and it dropped completely on the fifth, but Richardson was now within arm's length.

I tried to step backward as he swung, but momentum was on his side, and I was forced to deflect his blades with the barrels of my pistols before I could get out of range. The upgraded metals in the Colt held up to the blow, but the other knife sheared completely through the Silversmith. I hurled the sparking mass of severed electronics at Richardson, but he ducked under the throw. The officer's dodge gave me time to fire several more shots from the Colt. Each round took small chunks from his health.

Then the slide locked back on the handgun, the magazine empty.

A downside of the physical ammunition fired by the high-powered weapon was the magazine only carried seven rounds with an additional one in the chamber. The advantage of handcrafted ammunition was that each round could be given bonuses by the crafter, which provided significantly higher damage than any mass-produced ammunition. In this case, my first magazine had been filled with rounds designed to break energy shields.

I summoned a full magazine from my inventory as I reversed direction and twisted in an attempt to get past the rushing cop. A line of fire ripped through the back of my left thigh as Richardson caught my leg with one of his knives.

Hamstrung!
You have received a debilitating blow to your left leg. You will not be able to run on your left leg until you are healed.

I managed to finish the reload on the Colt despite the crippling pain in my leg. With my mobility severely limited, Richardson was all over me within a moment, and his knives tore through my defenses. My status became a mess of debuffs and damage notifications.

Stunned!
You will not be able to move, use mana, or react in any way while stunned. You are stunned for 4.3 seconds.

Disarmed!
Your weapon has been removed from your grip. You will need to pick it up or equip a new weapon.

Bleeding!

You have received a bleeding debuff. You will lose health so long as the wounds are not treated.

-2 Health per second

Richardson swept a leg through mine, which collapsed me onto the pavement on my back. I lay unable to move as the stunned debuff ticked down ever so slowly. I looked at the killer above me as Richardson stared into empty space just above my head. I realized he watched my health bar as my nearly empty health pool drained from the bleeding effect.

"Why?" I asked. "Why did you kill all those people?"

"Because I could," Richardson sneered. "They were weak, and this is a world where only the strong survive."

"I don't believe that," I replied quietly. "You're a monster."

"You're a monster too," Richardson said gloatingly. "You care for nothing but the thrill of the hunt, and you're too weak to survive, just like everyone I've killed. That's why you're about to die."

Maybe he was right to call me a monster, but I felt almost disappointed by the trite explanation. I'd thought a killer with such a body count would have a better excuse, even if only a deluded one.

As the last of the health points disappeared from my visible health pool, I remained absolutely still and held my breath. This was my favorite part of the hunt. When the monster sensed victory and I got to snatch it from their grasp.

Richardson still stared above me, fixated on my empty health pool as he waited for his experience notifications.

Nothing appeared for him.

Richardson's gaze flicked to me, then back up at the empty health pool. Confusion crossed his face when he looked back down at me again. This time, I blinked.

"What?" The killer recoiled in surprise.

I pushed myself to my feet with no sign of my earlier injuries. I activated The Right Tool for the Job as I stood. The Class Skill instantly pulled weapons from a dedicated inventory space and filled both of my thigh holsters with new pistols, equipped a shoulder harness rig with a pistol under each armpit, and materialized a pair of MP5K machine pistols, one in each hand.

Confusion warred with surprise across Richardson's face as I kept my eyes locked on his. I relished his expression as I deactivated most components of my penultimate Class Skill, On the Hunt. With my true class and attributes no longer disguised by the System, my health bar snapped from empty to over three quarters full.

Harold "Hal" Mason (Relentless Huntsman Level 29)
HP: 710/930

Wide-eyed, Richardson stared at me as he gaped. He closed and opened his mouth several times as he attempted to say something. "How?"

"Maybe I am one"—I grinned savagely— "but I hunt monsters."

I raised the MP5Ks and squeezed the triggers of both automatics. Flame and thunder poured from each weapon. Normal recoil from fully automatic weapons would have been difficult to keep steady, but my System-enhanced strength was easily up to the challenge. Richardson attempted to dodge by diving to the side and rolling to escape the line of fire.

Despite his attempt, my rounds stayed on target. The fire from my guns robbed Richardson of his momentum and knocked him prone. He stopped moving as my weapons ran dry. After only seconds of automatic fire, the thirty-round magazines were empty. I stashed the weapons in my personal System armory provided by The Right Tool for the Job and strode over to the broken body of the killer I had tracked through town.

Richardson wore armor under his uniform, but the close-range fire of armor-piercing ammunition had left his torso a shredded, bloody mess, and air wheezed from a punctured lung. Even with those injuries, he would recover if given enough time. Time I would not allow him.

I summoned a Smith & Wesson Model 29, once claimed as the most powerful handgun in the world, from my inventory and pointed the massive revolver at Richardson's head. The hammer clicked back as I pulled the double-action trigger and continued to squeeze. The .44 Magnum round almost blew off the killer's head. I fired a second time, finishing the job. Notifications flooded my vision. I quickly flipped through them to confirm the quest completion for tracking down the town killer.

I touched the corpse and pulled it into another System inventory space with the Meat Locker Class Skill. Never knowing when the next conflict might come, I took the time to pull the spent weapons from my inventory, checked them for damage, and reloaded them. I then picked up the pieces of my Silversmith beam pistol, found my dropped Colt, and looted Richardson's daggers. With those items picked up, only the pooling blood splattered across the pavement remained as evidence of the fight that had taken place. I glanced around to ensure I'd left nothing behind, but I quickly noticed that I was no longer alone.

Surrounding the parking lot, Truinnar in the uniform of the town guard formed a perimeter that cut off any route out of the area. At the mouth of the alley waited a Truinnar more finely dressed than the uniformed guards who stood behind him.

The guards eyed me warily as I approached the finely dressed figure, which gave me time to examine the man. He had the typical tall, slender build of the Truinnar, though he somehow seemed softer than the guards and most other dark elves I had encountered. The elf also seemed younger even than Dayena. He carried no weapons, clearly trusting the escort behind him for protection.

Lord Aradin Daxily, Baron of the Argent Sea (??? Level ???)
HP: 790/790

The noble's level and class were hidden, likely by a Class Skill, but the meager health points hinted at his level being quite low. Especially low if he was the man who, I suspected, ruled this town.

"Adventurer Mason," greeted the young dark elf in a high, nasally voice.

"Lord Daxily," I replied politely.

"Thank you for ridding my village of that menace," said Daxily, which confirmed that he indeed owned the town. "He was a drain on resources and lowered my village's value."

"You knew he was the killer."

Daxily sniffed. "Of course. I know what goes on in my village."

"And you did nothing?" I asked, annoyed by his inaction in the face of lost human lives.

"It was a human problem." The dark elf waved dismissively. "I leave human problems to humans. But now you've become a problem for me by breaking the peace in my village."

I was seriously aggravated by his knowledge of the killer and his lack of action. That he now declared my action of taking out the killer as problematic made me debate whether to show this spoiled punk a real human problem. I kept my face blank, but something of my intent must have leaked out because two of the guards stepped up beside the noble, their weapons half-drawn.

I examined the guards critically. I figured I could take the ones in front of me, along with the noble, but at least another half dozen guards were somewhere behind me. They would call for assistance, and I would certainly not survive if the entire town guard were called in.

Before the situation could escalate further, a figure materialized out of the alley shadows. Hips swayed as the figure sauntered toward us, and I recognized the seductive silhouette of the musician from the bar. The sensuous dress from earlier had been exchanged for an armored jumpsuit, one of significantly higher quality than my own, but it still managed to give her slender figure mouth-watering appeal.

Mental Influence Resisted

"Take it easy, boys," said Dayena.

The sultry voice grabbed the attention of everyone in the alley.

As if hit between the eyes by a hammer, the wide-eyed Truinnar noble seemed stunned. "C-countess? I knew you were in town, but what are you doing here?"

Fantastic. The spoiled noble had revealed my potential employer as a ranked member of the Truinnar peerage. Her comments in the bar made more sense now. I needed to be wary, or else I'd quickly become buried in

Truinnar politics. Unfortunately, my gut had the sneaking suspicion my caution was entirely too late.

Dayena gestured toward me and looked pointedly into my eyes as a prompt appeared before me.

Contract Initiated between Dayena Baluisa and Harold Mason.
Do you accept? (Y/N)

"The huntsman works for me," Dayena stated confidently while she stared at me intently and ignored the other noble.

I got the hint. She'd just made me an offer I couldn't refuse. I accepted the prompt and resigned myself to working for the gorgeous elf in a deal that would clearly be in her favor.

Contract Agreed Upon by Dayena Baluisa and Harold Mason.
Further Details? (Y/N)

I ignored the prompt and hoped for a chance later to read through the fine print.

"What? Is this true?" the young noble demanded, finally recovering from being hit with the full force of Dayena's charms.

"Yes," I replied, though I found it safer to say as little as possible.

"Fine," Daxily huffed. "I want you both out of my village. I rescind my hospitality, Countess."

"We'll be gone before daylight." Dayena turned to leave the alley. "Come on, Adventurer Mason."

I followed the woman and nodded to the town guards as I passed. I ignored the spoiled noble. The guards tracked me warily, likely aware that any violence would end poorly for all involved.

Once we reached the main street at the end of the alley, Dayena turned back toward me. "Is there anything you need in town before we leave?"

"No. I only needed to finish the quest here, and that's done."

"That was an impressive fight," she said. "I enjoyed how you toyed with him. It almost reminded me of court politics back home."

"Speaking of politics," I said with an arched eyebrow. "Countess?"

Dayena shrugged dismissively. "It's just an honorific. My family is complicated, so I have no lands or responsibilities. I want to forge my own path and not have it dictated to me. And now I have you to help."

A moment later, the woman climbed onto a sleekly armored motorcycle that materialized on the empty street in front of us. I summoned my bike from my inventory and mounted it beside her.

"Help with what?" I asked.

"Hunting monsters, of course," Dayena replied with a wink. A helmet snapped up out of her collar and over her head. Tires squealed, her bike shot forward, and she quickly left me behind.

Resigned, I kicked my bike into gear and followed the Truinnar countess off into the night. Hunting monsters, indeed.

The End

Authors' Note

I want to thank you for taking the time to read this book and I really hope you enjoyed this new adventure within the System Apocalypse Universe. Ever since I wrote the short for the Anthology (also included here as a bonus!), ideas for Hal have been bouncing around in my head and I wanted to tell his origin story before I took his story further.

I really appreciate Tao providing the opportunity for some of those ideas to hit the pages here, and for allowing me to play in his playground.

If you enjoyed this book, please leave a review! Reviews are the lifeblood of indie authors and they encourage us to keep writing.

  - *Craig*

When I first created the anthology, one of its many goals was to find new authors, some of which might even work in my world. Some of those authors have gone on to write their own series – R.K. Billiau wrote his highly successful Primeverse series and others, have stopped writing for the time being (or changed their pen names!).

Craig's story about Hal always intrigued me and I've been curious to see what he finally chose to do with it. Of course, the pandemic and life got in the way so it took a little longer than normal to get it finished; but I'm excited to showcase Hal's debut into the System and his continuing adventures on Earth as well as expanding the universe.

In addition, I expect to release another adjacent series from *K.T. Hanna*, one of the most respected authors in the universe with her take on the System Apocalypse, family and Australia. Keep an eye out for it!

  - *Tao*

About the Authors

Craig Hamilton

Craig Hamilton is a technical sales engineer who spends most of his day translating tech speak to a non-technical crowd. While writing has been taking up most of his free time lately, Craig also appreciates playing tabletop RPGs or board games with friends. When his inner introvert demands a break from polite company, Craig can be found sprawled on a couch with a book or playing a video game with spaceships and entirely too many spreadsheets.

Follow what Craig is doing on his Author Page:

https://www.facebook.com/AuthorCraigHamilton

Tao Wong

Tao Wong is an avid fantasy and sci-fi reader who spends his time working and writing in the North of Canada. He's spent way too many years doing martial arts of many forms, and having broken himself too often, he now spends his time writing about fantasy worlds.

For updates on the series and other books written by Tao Wong (and special one-shot stories), please visit the author's website:

http://www.mylifemytao.com

Or visit his Facebook Page: https://www.facebook.com/taowongauthor/

Also, subscribers to Tao's mailing list will receive **exclusive access to short stories in the Thousand Li and System Apocalypse universes**.

About the Publisher

Starlit Publishing is wholly owned and operated by Tao Wong. It is a science fiction and fantasy publisher focused on the LitRPG & cultivation genres. Their focus is on promoting new, upcoming authors in the genre whose writing challenges the existing stereotypes while giving a rip-roaring good read.

For more information about latest releases and new, exciting authors from Starlit Publishing, visit our website or sign up to our newsletter list!

https://www.starlitpublishing.com/

For more great information about LitRPG series, check out these Facebook groups:

- GameLit Society

https://www.facebook.com/groups/LitRPGsociety/

- LitRPG Books

https://www.facebook.com/groups/LitRPG.books/

Preview my other series:

the System Apocalypse

Life in the North (System Apocalypse Book 1)

Chapter 1

Greetings citizen. As a peaceful and organised immersion into the Galactic Council has been declined (extensively and painfully we might add), your world has been declared a Dungeon World. Thank you. We were getting bored with the 12 that we had previously.

Please note that the process of developing a Dungeon World can be difficult for current inhabitants. We recommend leaving the planet till the process is completed in 373 days, 2 hours, 14 minutes and 12 seconds.

For those of you unable or unwilling to leave, do note that new Dungeons and wandering monsters will spawn intermittently throughout the integration process. All new Dungeons and zones will receive recommended minimum levels, however, during the transition period expect there to be significant volatility in the levels and types of monsters in each Dungeon and zone.

As a new Dungeon World, your planet has been designated a free-immigration location. Undeveloped worlds in the Galactic Council may take advantage of this new immigration policy. Please try not to greet all new visitors the same way as you did our Emissary, you humans could do with some friends.

As part of the transition, all sentient subjects will have access to new classes and skills as well as the traditional user interface adopted by the Galactic Council in 119 GC.

Thank you for your co-operation and good luck! We look forward to meeting you soon.

Time to System initiation: 59 minutes 23 seconds

I groan, freeing my hand enough to swipe at the blue box in front of my face as I crank my eyes open. Weird dream. It's not as if I had drunk that much either, just a few shots of whiskey before I went to bed. Almost as soon as the box disappears, another appears, obscuring the small 2-person tent that I'm sleeping in.

Congratulations! You have been spawned in the Kluane National Park (Level 110+) zone.
You have received 7,500 XP (Delayed)

As per Dungeon World Development Schedule 124.3.2.1, inhabitants assigned to a region with a recommended Level 25 or more above the inhabitants' current Level will receive one Small perk.

As per Dungeon World Development Schedule 124.3.2.2, inhabitants assigned to a region with a recommended Level 50 or more above the inhabitants' current Level will receive one Medium perk.

As per Dungeon World Development Schedule 124.3.2.3, inhabitants assigned to a region with a recommended Level 75 or more above the inhabitants' current Level will receive one Large perk.

As per Dungeon World Development Schedule 124.3.2.4, inhabitants assigned to a region with a recommended Level 100 or more above the inhabitants' current Level will receive one Greater perk

What the hell? I jerk forwards and almost fall immediately backwards, the sleeping bag tangling me up. I scramble out, pulling my 5' 8" frame into a sitting position as I swipe black hair out of my eyes to stare at the taunting blue message. Alright, I'm awake and this is not a dream.

This can't be happening, I mean, sure it's happening, but it can't be. It must be a dream, things like this didn't happen in real life. However, considering the rather realistic aches and pains that encompass my body from yesterday's hike, it's really not a dream. Still, this can't be happening.

When I reach out, attempting to touch the screen itself and for a moment, nothing happens until I move my hand when the screen seems to 'stick' to it, swinging with my hand. It's almost like a window in a touchscreen which makes no sense, since this is the real world and there's no tablet. Now that I'm concentrating, I can even feel how the screen has a slight tactile sensation to it, like touching plastic wrap stretched too tight except with the added tingle of static electricity. I stare at my hand and the window and then flick it away watching the window shrink. This makes no sense.

Just yesterday I had hiked up the King's Throne Peak with all my gear to overlook the lake. Early April in the Yukon means that the peak itself was still covered with snow but I'd packed for that, though the final couple of kilometers had been tougher than I had expected. Still, being out and about at least cleared my mind of the dismal state of my life after moving to Whitehorse. No job, barely enough money to pay next month's rent and having just broken up with my girlfriend, leaving on a Tuesday on my junker of a car was just what the doctor ordered. As bad as my life had been, I'm pretty sure I wasn't even close to breaking down, at least not enough to see things.

I shut my eyes, forcing them to stay shut for a count of three before I open them again. The blue box stays, taunting me with its reality. I can feel my breathing shorten, my thoughts splitting in a thousand different directions as I try to make sense of what's happening.

Stop.

I force my eyes close again and old training, old habits come into play. I bottle up the feelings of panic that encroach on my mind, force my scattered thoughts to stop swirling and compartmentalise my feelings. This is not the time or place for all this. I shove it all into a box and close the lid, pushing my emotions down until all there is a comforting, familiar, numbness.

A therapist once said my emotional detachment is a learned self-defence mechanism, one that was useful during my youth but somewhat unnecessary now that I'm an adult with more control over my surroundings. My girlfriend, my ex-girlfriend, just called me an emotionless dick. I've been taught better coping mechanisms but when push comes to shove, I go with what works. If there's an environment which I can't control, I'm going to call floating blue boxes in the real world one of them.

Calmer now, I open my eyes and re-read the information. First rule – what is, is. No more arguing or screaming or worrying about why or how or if I'm insane. What is, is. So. I have perks. And there's a system providing the perks and assigning levels. There's also going to be dungeons and monsters. I'm in a frigging MMO without a damn manual it looks like, which means that at least some of my misspent youth is going to be useful. I wonder what my dad would say. I push the familiar flash of anger down at the thought of him, focusing instead on my current problems.

My first requirement is information. Or better yet, a guide. I'm working on instinct here, going by what feels right rather than what I think is right since the thinking part of me is busy putting its fingers in its ears and going 'na-na-na-na-na'.

"Status?" I query and a new screen blooms.

Status Screen			
Name	John Lee	Class	None
Race	Human (Male)	Level	0
Titles			
None			
Health	100	Stamina	100
Mana	100		
Status			
Twisted ankle (-5% movement speed)			
Tendinitis (-10% Manual Agility)			
Attributes			
Strength	11	Agility	10
Constitution	11	Perception	14
Intelligence	16	Willpower	18
Charisma	8	Luck	7
Skills			
None			
Class Skills			
None			
Spells			
None			

Unassigned Attributes:

1 Small, 1 Medium, 1 Large, 1 Greater Perk

Would you like to assign these attributes? (Y/N)

The second window pop's up almost immediately on top of the first. I want more time to look over my Status but the information seems mostly self-explanatory and it's better to get this over with. It's not as if I have a lot of time. Almost as soon as I think that, the Y depresses and a giant list of Perks flashes up.

Oh, I do **not** have time for this. I definitely don't have time to get stuck in character creation. Being stuck in a zone that is way out of my Level when the System initializes is a one-way ticket to chowville. The giant list of perks before me is way too much to even begin sorting through, especially with names that don't necessarily make sense. What the hell does Adaptive Coloring actually mean? Right, this system seems to work via thought, reacting to what I think so, perhaps I can sort by perk type – narrow it down to small perks for a guide or companion of some form?

Almost as soon as I think of it, the system flashes out and only the word Companion appears. I nod slightly to myself and further details appear, providing two options.

AI *Spirit*

I select AI but a new notice flashes up

AI Selection unavailable. *Minimum requirements of:*

Mark IV Processing Unit not met

I grunt. Yeah, no shit. I don't have a computer on me. Or... in me? No cyberpunk world for me. Not yet at least, though how cool would that be with a computer for a brain and metallic arms that don't hurt from being on the computer too much. Not the time for this, so I pick Spirit next and I acknowledge the query.

System Companion Spirit gained

Congratulations! World Fourth. As the fourth individual to gain a Companion Spirit, your companion is now (Linked). Linked Companions will grow and develop with you.

As I dismiss the notifications, I can see a light begin to glow to my right. I twist around, wondering who or what my new companion is going to be.

***

"Run, hide or fight. Ain't hard to make a choice boy-o."

Look, I'm no pervert. I didn't need a cute, beautiful fairy as my System Companion Spirit. Sure, a part of me hoped for it, I'm a red-blooded male who wouldn't mind staring at something pretty. Still, practically speaking, I would have settled for a Genderless automaton that was efficient and answered my questions with a minimum of lip. Instead, I get... him.

I stare at my new Companion and sigh mentally. Barely a foot tall, he's built like a linebacker with a full, curly brown beard. Brown hair, brown eyes and olive skin in a body-hugging orange jumpsuit that's tight in all the wrong places completes the ensemble. Ali my new companion has been here for all of 10 minutes giving me the lowdown and I'm already partly regretting my choice.

Partly, because for all of his berating, he's actually quite useful.

"Run," I finally decide, pulling apart the chocolate bar and taking another bite. No use fighting, nothing in the store that could scratch a Level 110 monster is going to be usable by me according to Ali and while there's no guarantee one of them will spawn immediately, even the lower level monsters that will make up its dinner would be too tough for me.

Hiding just delays things, so I have to get the hell out of the park which really, shouldn't be that hard. It took me half-a-day of hard hiking to get up this far in the mountain from the parking lot and the parking lot is just inside the new zone. At a good pace, I should be down in a few hours which if I understand things properly means there aren't that many monsters. Once I'm out, it seems Whitehorse has a Safe Zone, which means I can hunker down and figure out what the hell is going on.

"About damn time," grouses Ali. A wave of his hands and a series of new windows appear in front of me. Shortly after appearing he demanded full access to my System which has allowed him to manipulate the information I can see and receive. It's going a lot faster this way since he just pushes the information to me, letting me read through things while he does the deeper search. The new blue windows - System messages according to him - are his picks for medium and large perks respectively.

Prodigy: Subterfuge

You're a natural born spy. Intrepid would hire you immediately.

Effect: All Subterfuge skills are gained 100% quicker. +50% Skill Level increase for all Subterfuge skills.

"Why this?" I frown, poking at the Subterfuge side. I'm not exactly the spying kind, more direct in most of my interactions. I've never really felt the need to lie too much and I certainly don't see myself creeping around breaking into buildings.

"Stealth skills. It gives a direct bonus to all of them which means you'll gain them faster. A small perk would allow us to directly affect the base Stealth skill but at this level, we've got to go up to its main category." Ali replies and continues, "If you manage to survive, it'll probably be useful in the future anyway."

Quantum Stealth Manipulator (QSM)

The QSM allows its bearer to phase-shift, placing himself adjacent to the current dimension

Effect: While active, user is rendered invisible and undetectable to normal and magical means as long as the QSM is active. Solid objects may be passed through but will drain charge at a higher rate. Charge lasts 5 minutes under normal conditions.

"The QSM – how do I recharge it?"

"It uses a Type III Crystal Manipulator. The Crystal draws upon ambient and line specific…" Ali stares at my face for a moment before waving his hand. "It recharges automatically. It'll be fully charged in a day under normal conditions."

"No Level requirements on these?"

"None."

I picked Ali because he knows the System better than I do, so I can either accept what he's saying or I can do it myself. Put that way, there's really not much of a choice. It's what we talked about, though that Perk Subterfuge isn't really going to be that useful for me. On the other hand, any bonuses to staying out of sight would be great and the QSM would let me run away if I was found out. Which just left my Greater Perk.

Advanced Class: Erethran Honor Guard

The Erethran Honor Guard are Elite Members of the Erethran Armed Forces.

Class Abilities: +2 Per Level in Strength. + 4 Per Level in Constitution and Agility. +3 Per Level in Intelligence and Willpower. Additional 3 Free Attributes per Level. +90% Mental Resistance. +40% Elemental Resistance

May designate a Personal Weapon. Personal Weapon is Soulbound and upgradeable. Honor Guard members may have up to 4 Hard Point Links before Essence Penalties apply.

Warning! Minimum Attribute Requirements for the Erethran Honor Guard Class not met. Class Skills Locked till minimum requirements met.

Advanced Class: Dragon Knight

Groomed before birth, Dragon Knights are the Elite Warriors of the Kingdom of Xylargh.

Class Abilities: +3 Per Level in Strength and Agility. + 4 Per Level in Constitution. +3 Per Level Intelligence and Willpower. + 1 in Charisma. Additional 2 Free Attributes per Level.

+80% Mental Resistance. +50% Elemental Resistance

Gain One Greater and One Lesser Elemental Affinity

Warning! Minimum Attribute Requirements for the Dragon Knight Class not met. Class Skills Locked till minimum requirements met.

"That's it?"

"No, you could get this too."

Class: Demi-God

You sexy looking human, you'll be a demi-god. Smart, strong, handsome. What more could you want?
Class Abilities: +100 to all Attributes
All Greater Affinities Gained
Super Sexiness Trait

"That's not a thing."

"It really ain't," smirking, Ali waves and the last screen dismisses. "You wanted a class that helps you survive? That means mental resistances. Otherwise, you'll be pissing those pretty little Pac-Man boxers the moment you see a Level 50 monster. You wanted an end-game? The Honor Guard are some mean motherfuckers. They combine magic and tech making them one of the most versatile groups around, and their Master class advancements are truly scary. The Dragon Knights fight Dragons. One on one and they sometimes even win. Oh, and neither, and I quote 'makes me into a monster'."

"If these are Advanced Classes, what other classes are there?" I prod at Ali, still hesitating. This seems like a big choice.

"Basic, Advance, Master, Grandmaster, Heroic, Legendary," lists Ali and he shrugs. "I could get you a Master Class with your perk, but you'd be locked out of your Class Skills forever. You'd also take forever to level because of the higher minimum experience level gains. Instead, I've got you a rare Advanced Class - it'll give you a better base stat gain per level and you won't have to wait forever to gain access to your Class Skills. Getting a Basic Class, even a rarer Basic Class would be a waste of the Greater Perk. So, what's it going to be?"

As cool as punching a dragon in the face would be, I know which way I'm going the moment he called it up. I mentally select the Guard and light fills me. At first, it just forces me to squint but it begins to dig in, pushing into my body and mind, sending electric, hot claws into my cells. The pain is worse than anything I've felt and I've broken bones, shattered ribs and even managed to electrocute myself before. I know I'm screaming but the pain keeps coming, swarming over me and tearing at my mind, my control. Luckily, darkness claims me before my mind shatters.

Read more about the Life in the North

https://readerlinks.com/l/1340826

To learn more about LitRPG, talk to authors including myself, and just have an awesome time, please join the LitRPG Group:

https://www.facebook.com/groups/LitRPGGroup/

Made in the USA
Middletown, DE
26 April 2022

64781614R00302